KILL

Simon Shaw trained at the Theatre School and became a professional actor in 1979. He has worked in rep, fringe, TV and in the West End. *Murder Out of Tune* was his first novel and was followed by *Killer Cinderella*, which won the Last Laugh Award. Simon Shaw has now written a sequel to *Murder Out of Tune*, *Bloody Instructions*.

KILLER CINDERELLA

by

Simon Shaw

GOLLANCZ CRIME

Gollancz Crime is an imprint of Victor Gollancz Ltd
14 Henrietta Street, London WC2E 8QJ

First published in Great Britain 1990
by Victor Gollancz Ltd

First Gollancz Crime edition 1991

A catalogue record for this book
is available from the British Library

ISBN 0-575-05034-9

Printed and bound in Great Britain
by Cox & Wyman Ltd, Reading

KILLER CINDERELLA

I

Mark turned off the engine at the top of the drive. In the beginning he had turned off the lights as well, but after cruising squarely into a cow a fortnight ago he had decided to forsake a little stealth for safety. Of course the cow shouldn't have been there in the first place, but with farmers as dozy as the Trumans there was no guarantee that it wouldn't happen again. The cow had cracked a headlamp. The car did not seem to have made any impression on the cow.

He put the engine into neutral, took his foot off the clutch and let the car glide down towards the house. There was a slight incline for the first fifty yards, during which he could rely upon picking up a little speed, before the drive bottomed out and the gravel changed gradually to grass, slowing him to a crawl (if he got it right) by the time he fetched up against the muddy bank which served as his parking lot. That was the plan anyway. As he approached the thick smudge of hedge that marked the field boundary his dimmed lights picked out a row of metallic shapes double- and triple-parked over his own private patch. At the same time he heard the party noises from next door.

He let out a strangled roar and thumped the steering wheel with the palms of his hands. Then he hunched his upper body into a tense muscular ball and shook his head from side to side like a demented terrier.

"Bloody trespassing bastards!"

He yelped as he hit his hand too hard against the dashboard.

The car, meanwhile, had veered seemingly of its own accord away from the drive into the field proper, where it bulldozed a pile of fresh cowpats before coming squelchily to rest amidst more of the same. Gingerly he opened the car door and contemplated the short distance back to the drive, like a bather on the edge of shark-infested water.

It had rained heavily all through the day; he could smell the wet in the cold night air. His first step out of the car sank him ankle-deep, his second drenched the other sock. By the time he reached the gravel both feet were evenly daubed with mud and cowshit. He cleaned his shoes as best he could with a tissue. He stood with clenched feet and gritted teeth staring at his neighbours' house.

His new neighbours, the Talbots. Reg and Sharon by name: you could tell a lot by people's names. The previous occupants had been the Dawsons, Major and Mrs. He had never known their Christian names. They had behaved exactly as polite neighbours ought, rarely seen, never heard. When they moved out it was as if they'd never been. Now, scarcely a month later, he wondered sometimes if they had actually been, or if they had only existed in his imagination. Whatever curious dream might have spawned them, it was nothing to the replacement nightmare: Reg, Sharon, two miniature Talbots, a large dog and five cars, one presumably for each of them. They had arrived with a vanload of builders and an excavating machine. The builders were still there. So, unfortunately, were the Talbots.

The day after their arrival he had come down to breakfast to find a cheap manilla envelope sitting on the mat. Inside was a business card:

> **REG TALBOT**
> Used car's bought and sold/all makes
> "You wannit? We goddit!"

Scrawled on the back was an invitation to drinks at six. Also an offer of £300 for "that rusty Wop heap out front". There was an illegible signature underneath.

His shout of indignation had brought Maddie running half-dressed out of the bedroom. For the first time in over a year they had actually found something to agree about: on no account would there be any social mixing with the Talbots. The offensive invitation had been ignored. So had all the others. The Talbots, it seemed, were inveterate party-givers.

Now, standing in the drive in sodden feet with the night wind whipping round his ankles he remembered vaguely that Maddie had muttered something about another invitation at breakfast yesterday. Naturally he hadn't been listening. Naturally she knew. Naturally neither of them gave a damn.

The party was not so noisy tonight, no doubt on account of the chill. On fine nights festivities spilled out into the garden, to the accompaniment of various musical cacophonies belted out at full volume on the kind of speakers that had made a whole generation of rock stars deaf. The loud music was almost certainly employed to drive the guests into a sexual frenzy. Twice Maddie had trawled used contraceptives from their fish pond.

"At least somebody's getting some fun round here," she had remarked archly, both times.

That reminded him. . . .

He turned his attention from the Talbots' house to his own. The light was on in Roger's attic, as usual, but the rest was in darkness. That didn't mean anything, of course. She had never liked doing it with the light on. Even at this moment she was probably entangled in a heap of limbs with her lover on the bean bag. It had taken some punishment recently, that bean bag. Mark had almost caught them on it three times in the last fortnight. The last time Roddy hadn't been able to get his trousers on again quickly enough and Maddie had made a grab for her workbox, muttering something about sewing a button back on.

"Button come off these too?" Mark had asked casually, holding up her knickers between fingers and thumb. It had been the high spot of his week. The question was, would tonight be a repeat?

He opened the gate. He was on the drawbridge now, he could hear the stream gushing away under his feet. He always referred to it as the drawbridge, and to the stream as the moat. It helped foster the illusion that one's home was one's castle, although in reality the moat could be easily stepped across without breaking stride and the rickety drawbridge was nothing more than a couple of old planks roughly nailed together.

He paused, one foot on the drawbridge, the other on the path. He held his breath. A sliver of light spilled out through a crack in the curtains of the living-room window. Was it his imagination, or had the curtain twitched?

He raced up the path, digging frantically in his pocket for his keys. He snatched at the front-door handle, fumbling for the keyhole in the dark. He found the lock and gave a half-twist to the right. The door didn't budge. He tried again. It seemed to be catching at the top. Of course! She'd bolted it!

He ran round the side of the house, clattering into a wheelbarrow and a collection of unidentified gardening tools. He skidded on the wet grass as he turned the corner, lost his balance and fell heavily against the back door. His fingers felt for the chunky key, the deadlock. She couldn't have bolted this one, it didn't have any bolts. He yanked it open and tore into the kitchen. Three strides and he was at the living-room door. He flung it open with a flourish.

"Good evening, darling!"

Maddie looked up from her book. She was sitting in the armchair by the fire dressed in her pink fluffy slippers and dressing-gown, Maud Gonne on her lap. She squinted at him critically. Her gaze came to rest on his feet.

"What have you been walking in?"

He didn't answer. His own attention was focused on the bean bag in the corner. The dent in the middle definitely looked fresh.

"Brass monkeys tonight!" he declared heartily, taking a step towards the fire and craning his neck to peer round the back of the sofa.

"Lost something?"

He stiffened. The mockery in her voice was unmistakable. He was close enough to get a good look at her now, even though the light was dim. Her hair was tousled, she definitely had a ruffled look. She was wearing her blond wig, her favourite, the one she said made her look like Marilyn Monroe. She only wore that for special occasions. A sudden thought struck him: if the light was that dim. . . .

He snatched the book out of her hands and held the spine towards the fire. He just had time to make out the gold lettering before she snatched it back again.

"Learnt anything useful?" he jeered as he sprang back towards the door. "Or do you know *Practical Aero Modelling* by heart?"

Much as he would have liked to stay and savour her response he realised that precious seconds were slipping by. So he allowed himself just one all-purpose sneer, then stepped smartly out of the living room, whipped the door shut behind him and froze instantly into a pose of feral watchfulness.

He stood in the kitchen darkness, listening. The only sound that came to him was distant Talbot party noise. The house was silent. Not a mouse, not even Roger, stirred. Where had she hidden her paramour? Had she hidden him at all, or had he made his escape? Mark doubted it. From the time of the curtain twitching to his bursting into the living room no more than thirty seconds could have elapsed. Even if he had been fully dressed he wouldn't have had time to make it out the back and out of sight that quickly. They must be operating on some kind of contingency plan. Mark turned the possibilities over in his mind, succulently.

He pulled open the kitchen drawer and took out his three-in-one torch. He turned on the main beam. He decided to check outside first, just in case.

He knelt down and studied the ground outside the back door. It was still wet, the grass glistened in the torchlight. He could see his own fresh footprints, but no sign of Injuns.

A noise made him turn. Somewhere a door had clicked. He scrambled back inside, vigorously waving his torch.

"Ah-ha! Gotcha!"

"Evening, Mark."

The challenge died on his lips. He coughed.

"Getting a cold?"

The kitchen light came on. Feeling rather foolish Mark turned off the torch and put it down on the table.

"Just a bit of a snuffle thanks, Roger."

Roger opened the fridge. He stuck in one of his bony hands and pulled out a large margarine container. He raised it to his nostrils and sniffed suspiciously. Mark wasn't surprised. Whatever was in the container it wasn't margarine. Some sort of brown organic sludge. Despite its scatological appearance it must have passed the sniff test. Roger dipped in a finger and licked it clean.

"Tasty?" Mark enquired.

"Alright," came the reply. It must have been good, Mark thought – "Alright" was Roger's equivalent of "Wildly fantastic".

Mark edged past Roger and the fridge towards the dining room. He noticed that the living-room door was still shut. Maddie was no doubt mugging up on balsa-wood glider construction.

"Been down much tonight?" he called back softly over his shoulder, although it was a long shot expecting Roger to have noticed anything.

"Not been down at all," muttered Roger, his head back in the fridge. "Been watching the telly all night. Terrible thing, the telly. Terrible rubbish, see."

The gloomier Roger's mood the more his Welshness surfaced. As he was always pretty gloomy he always sounded pretty Welsh.

"Jolly good!" murmured Mark, who tended to respond to any kind of regional accent by adopting a Blimpish tone. From where he stood he could just see into the hallway. The front door was still bolted.

"Excuse me a sec. . . ."

He marched smartly through the dining room into the hall. With Roger in the kitchen there was no way out through the back. He dashed up the stairs. The attic trapdoor at the top of Roger's ladder was open, light pouring through. The rest of the upstairs was in darkness. Quickly he pushed open all the doors, flicking on the switches. He went into all the rooms in turn, first the spare room, then his study, then the bedroom. In each he took one look under the bed and one into the cupboards. One look was enough: the cupboards were bare.

He turned off the lights and dashed back downstairs. The living room door was still firmly shut, Roger was messing about in the kitchen. The field was narrowing. He flung open the bathroom door: nothing. He stepped back into the hall. His eyes came to rest on the cellar door. He tried the key. It was unlocked. He pushed open the door and turned on the light.

The light was a single weak bulb. It didn't reach into the shadows, beyond the heaps of coal and the piles of rummage, and the great white oblong of the freezer. Mark shivered. The freezer had been another of Maddie's stupid ideas. It must have been the most understocked freezer in England. What was the point of having a freezer if all you ever put in it was a packet of frozen peas and a couple of Bird's Eye beefburgers? It had cost nearly three hundred quid, that freezer. You could buy a rusty Wop heap for that.

Roddy sneezed. At least Mark assumed it was Roddy. It was unlikely that Maddie had changed lovers since Monday. Mark stood rigidly at the head of the stairs, listening and watching. It had been a very slight sneeze, no doubt muffled into a hand, but a sneeze it had been. A minute passed. Mark smiled to himself. His eyes had adjusted to the light and he could make out a pair of feet protruding from beneath his plastic car cover. Did Roddy actually think he'd got away with it? He really was a prat. Perhaps he and Maddie deserved each other.

Mark smiled to himself as he stepped back into the hallway. He closed the cellar door and turned off the light. He locked the door and put the key into his pocket.

"Goodnight Roger!" he called out in the direction of the kitchen. "Goodnight darling!"

Neither of them responded. Mark whistled jauntily as he took the stairs two at a time. He went into his study.

It hadn't been such a bad evening after all, he thought to himself, as he slipped off his jacket and settled into his black and chrome swivel chair. He hadn't actually caught them at it, but he had certainly given them a fright. And he had locked Roddy in the cellar. He giggled to himself. After a few moments his giggle turned to a frown. The one disadvantage of his study was that it overlooked the Talbots' garden. As he watched, two women came running through the french windows and started screaming. Two shouting men followed and chased them across the patio. They disappeared amongst some shrubbery, re-emerged a few moments later and dissolved into a noisy heap of limbs somewhere in the middle of the lawn. Chez Talbot appeared to be only one step removed from Sodom and Gomorrah. And it was going to get worse. The giant yellow excavator had already ripped a great hole out of the lawn. For the first week Mark had been rather intrigued to watch its progress; for some curious reason he had decided that they must be building a nuclear shelter. Then one day the truth had dawned: it was going to be a swimming pool. Already his dreams had been plagued by images of second-hand car salesmen lining up to hurl their fat bellies at the water. The reality was bound to be much worse.

He closed the curtains and tried to ignore the racket outside. It was only just gone half past ten. There'd be hours of it yet. There was no point in even thinking about sleep. It was just as well he had plenty to be getting on with.

He was working on two models at the moment. One was a 54mm plastic 17th lancer in campaign dress (Crimean War), the other was a scratchbuilt wooden replica Luger pistol. The Luger was only half-finished but he suspected already that he was going to be as fond of it as he was of the Walther P38, which it so closely resembled. The Walther had been his first. It was James Bond's gun, that was the reason he'd modelled it. He had made a shoulder holster out of two belts and Maddie's old handbag. Sometimes he wore it under his jacket when he went to the modelling club. He couldn't wait to try the Luger for size and show it off to Martin Bird.

But tonight he was going to devote to the lancer, as he had devoted so many nights in the past few months. Time was running out: it was Wednesday already and he knew from experience that Saturday, the day of the Fareham Modellers Club Annual Show and the major event in his calendar, would be on him in a flash. If he was going to be in with a chance of the coveted trophy he would have to work with a vengeance.

The kit had been put together from amongst the heaps of plastic torsos, limbs, heads and the assorted weapons and accoutrements that filled his workbox. Much of the work had gone into the animation, the knifework necessary to convert mass-produced plastic into an individual creation. But the painstaking and eye-straining effort had been worth it: he had managed to breathe life into the plastic, creating a figure who, with his newly bandaged arm and freshly filled pipe could be seen to be meditating upon the very stuff of life and fate. He was going to call it "Reasoning Why".

The key was the face; it always was: no matter how good the rest, cross-eyes or a glassy expression would render it a waste of time. This one he'd got dead right. It was the face of a veteran, a no-nonsense old trooper with leathery tanned skin and steel-grey hair. He had a wonderful pair of mutton-chop whiskers and a moustache like a squirrel's tail. A thin scar above the eyebrows completed the details. He was a real original this chap, a character. More than that, he was a potential competition winner.

Mark reached for his mixing tray. It was time to give the boots and *czapska* (hat) a second coat. The first coat had been a little too glossy, too much varnish. He reached for his tube of Lamp Black.

The door was flung open and Maddie burst in. Mark bent over the desk and examined one of his brushes intently.

"Mark! Where's the key to the cellar?"

"Mm?"

He had noticed a few flecks of gold paint still lodged in the brush hairs.

"Mark! Will you stop playing with your toys and answer me?"

Mark frowned. She didn't usually come up with a variant on the "toys" jibe until at least five minutes into an argument. She wasn't playing by the rules. He put down the brush and swung round in his swivel chair to face her.

"I'm sorry, what did you say, sweetness and light?"

"You heard me!"

She was trembling so much she could hardly get the words out. He couldn't repress a smile: when she trembled her fat wobbly body put him in mind of a jelly. Marilyn Monroe indeed!

"What's so funny?" she demanded through gritted teeth.

You are, he thought. With your enormous bottom and double chin, and all those silly diets which you manage to stick for half an hour before stuffing your face with chocolate biscuits. And your ludicrous pink dressing-gown and lacy underwear. Who do you think you are? Brigitte Bardot? Or Mrs Babar?

He said: "Why do you want the key to the cellar, darling?"

This was not a question she had anticipated. He leaned back in his chair, folded his arms and adopted a casual pose. Maddie's jaw hung slackly down. He had her stumped alright.

"That's irrelevant!" she managed at length, huffily.

Mark shrugged. "I'm just interested, that's all. What could you possibly want in the cellar?"

"Fishfingers."

"What?"

"Fishfingers. I bought an economy size pack of 36. It's in the freezer."

Mark looked extravagantly at his watch.

"What do you want with fishfingers at half past ten?"

"I'm hungry."

"Why not have a biscuit?"

"I want fishfingers!"

She stamped her foot. Her voice sounded choked, her face was turning maroon. She'd better watch out, he thought, or she'd give herself a coronary: she ought to be careful carrying that much weight around.

"Mm, let me think," he said, scratching his head. "Where did I see that key?"

His voice trailed away as he saw a tear roll out of her eye and run down her cheek. He felt a guilty pang. It wasn't any fun if she didn't want to play by the rules.

"You bastard!" she said simply.

Now he felt embarrassed. Verbal fencing was one thing, but drawing blood overstepped the mark; the satisfaction lay in outwitting the opponent, in scoring points, not in a knockout.

"Mm, yes," he muttered into his chin, feeling in his jacket pocket.

He pulled out the big rusty key. "Ah! Here it is . . . I wonder how it got there!"

She snatched the key from him and stormed out, slamming the door behind her. His pistol collection rattled gently on its hooks.

"Hey! Steady on!" he muttered, pointlessly.

After a few moments' reflection he went back to his model. A minute later he heard the back door open. He turned off his desk light, peeped out of the curtains and was just in time to see a tell-tale white blur scurry away round the side of the house. Poor Roddy. Mark could almost have sworn he had heard his teeth chattering. He wondered where he had left his car. Probably in that lay-by the other side of the Trumans' farm. It was cold tonight. He'd be lucky to get away with double pneumonia. Mark reached for his tube of Lamp Black.

At half past eleven he cleaned his brushes and tidied up. The cottage was quiet: he had heard Maddie come up to bed half an hour ago, since when there had been silence. Of Roger he had heard nothing, but that was Roger's chief attraction, he was practically noiseless. There was still a faint murmur coming from the direction of the Talbots, but it was drizzling steadily outside and that, thankfully, had put an end to garden pranks. All in all it was remarkably peaceful. It would remain that way, if past form was anything to go by, until about one o'clock, when there would be a sudden eruption of car doors slamming, engines roaring and drunken farewelling. If he was lucky he might just manage to sleep through it, but it was hard to feel sanguine: somehow luck was not a commodity with which he freely associated himself.

He went down the creaky stairs in darkness and felt his way to the bathroom. Not simply the stairs, but the whole cottage creaked at night; beams and timbers moaned with old age. Mark always adopted a half-crouching position going through the house, a quite unnecessary precaution as he was too short even to be bothered by the lower beams. Roger was not so fortunate, his skull was usually festooned wih bumps and bruises. Mark found this both comforting and disquieting: he had never been able to come to terms with Roger's suicidal lack of physical coordination.

Roger had been with them for four years now. It had been Maddie's idea to take a lodger, although recently she had taken to pretending that it had been his. This infuriated Mark. He had argued with her for weeks at the time. It would ruin their life together, he said (at that stage they still had a life together), and, moreover, there was absolutely no reason for it; they didn't even need the money. Unfortunately this last assertion had not been borne out by events: Mark's promised promotion had failed to come through and his salary had remained more or less static: Roger's contribution to the housekeeping had proved significant. But Mark wasn't to have known that at the time. Maddie's behaviour had been wilful. She had decided she wanted a lodger and that was that. She felt lonely when Mark was out, it would be nice to have company until the baby came. Mention of the baby always shut Mark up; it was a really below-the-belt way to stop an argument. It was absolutely no earthly use trying to point out to Maddie that the only baby that was coming was strictly in her imagination. Her persistence amazed him. She had been "pregnant" once for eleven months before admitting that she might have made a mistake. He had lost count of the total number of phantom pregnancies, but he remembered the first one well enough. It had been seven years ago, just after they'd moved to Willow Cottage. He had come home from work and found a candlelit dinner waiting. At first he had assumed that there had been an electricity cut, but when Maddie entered in her best blue velvet evening dress (the one with a bunny bow at the back) he knew that something was up. Naturally he'd been delighted.

It had taken Mark six months to find out the truth. What a fool he'd felt then! His ears still burned at the recollection. But how could he have known? In those days Maddie had still had a good figure. Then month by month the belly had expanded, in no time at all she had outgrown her entire wardrobe. He had noticed vaguely her increased appetite, but he had put that down to her physical condition: "I'm eating for two now", she would say slyly, cramming in another cream cake. In bed at night she would take his hand and place it on her stomach. "Feel that!" she would say eagerly, and then "Ooh!" at the imagined kick. Mark had gone along with it. He hadn't felt anything at all, but as he had no idea what it was that he was supposed to be feeling, he put it down to his own ignorance. He only found out the truth by accident.

Dr Mitchell had come into the bank to order some escudos. They had chatted for a bit about the Algarve, then the doctor had asked if Maddie was managing to stick to her new diet. What diet would that be, Mark asked, something special for the baby? What baby would that be? the doctor had asked, puzzled. Really, doctors! thought Mark, and it's due in three months . . . why Maddie's of course, he said jocularly, and surely the doctor didn't mean to suggest that he had impregnated anyone else! Well he certainly hadn't impregnated Maddie, the doctor said very quietly. Could he spare a moment, perhaps he should step outside for a confidential word.

The scene that night had been catastrophic. Enough gnashing of teeth to keep the dental profession in business for years. It had been bad news for their crockery as well; the next morning he had found only one unbroken plate. She had entered defiantly, crunching her way across the wreckage-strewn floor.

"What makes you think the doctor knows better than me?" she demanded angrily. "A woman's body tells her things, you know. Just like a man not to want to believe her!"

He'd said the wrong thing of course, some waffly suggestion that she pull herself together in some undefined way. But whatever he'd said would have been the wrong thing. She wanted him to believe her, which of course was out of the question. It had ended with her flinging the last remaining plate against the wall. A succinct commentary on the state of their relationship.

That had been it really, as far as their relationship was concerned. They still slept together, for a time they had even continued to make love, but as each physical contact seemed to result in another phantom pregnancy Mark's sexual appetite had politely waned. On the rare occasions when he felt a stirring in his nether regions he would pop upstairs for an hour or so of serious modelling and it would pass.

Mark finished in the bathroom and checked that the house was all locked up. He climbed the creaky stairs. Maddie and Roger had both gone to bed.

He wasn't really called Roger at all. He was David, but he was the lodger, and therefore he couldn't be David, he had to be Roger. Roger had been meant as a private nickname, but they had both kept calling him Roger to his face and he hadn't objected, so it had stuck. Maddie had grown to loathe his gloomy complacency, she had recently taken to dropping hints that perhaps he'd be happier elsewhere but, perversely, Mark had become quite attached to him. Attached in an animalish rather than a human way: Roger had spaniel eyes. Of course, anyone whose favourite topic of conversation was suicide could tend towards the wearisome, but he was by nature a listener rather than a talker and he always seemed quite happy to sit in silence for half an hour (nodding occasionally) whenever Mark had anything to get off his chest. The really comforting thing about having Roger round the house was that he wasn't Maddie. If it had been just the two of them he'd have probably strangled her before now.

Mark pushed open the bedroom door quietly, expecting to find his wife asleep. Instead she was sitting up in bed, a magazine open on her lap. Maud Gonne stirred from her position at the foot of the duvet. Both cat and mistress stared at him coldly.

"Night, darling," he said meekly, feeling unaccountably guilty. Maddie folded her arms.

"I'd rather you didn't sleep here tonight, thank you."

"But that's not fair!" he blurted out, feebly.

"Not fair? Oh, so it's not fair, is it? And could you kindly tell me what is fair about your deliberate attempts to make my life hell, your merciless persecution of me and my friends?"

"Look, I said I was sorry about what I said to Lizzie Skinner – "

"I wasn't thinking about your rudeness to Lizzie, although don't think I've forgotten because I haven't." Her lip twitched: "I'm talking about Roddy."

He was unable to conceal his surprise. She noted it and smiled thinly.

"Yes. Roddy."

This was unheard of. She never mentioned Roddy. Apart from that time when he had caught him with his trousers down, and she hadn't had much option then. He knew that she was having an affair with him, she knew that he knew, and so did half of Fareham, but by tacit consent they had always treated Roddy as if he were the Invisible Man. It was part of the game, and she enjoyed the game as much as he did, he was sure of that. He knew her well enough to know that she had succumbed to the allure of the illicit tryst. It was difficult to think what else she could have succumbed to. Roddy's charms were conspicuous only by their absence. Mark grinned stupidly.

"Oh yes, Roddy, that chap who was at Martin's party. The Roundhead fellow."

"He's a Cavalier actually."

"Oh well, it's all the same to me, ha ha!"

Although he was making light of it this was one thing that really irked him about Roddy. After all those years of poking fun at his modelling, all those insults about childish behaviour, who should she go off with but a prize wally in fancy dress? Roddy was a halberdier in the Fareham muster of the English Civil War Re-enactment Society. It was his one ambition in life to be promoted to corporal.

"That's right, make snide remarks as usual. That's typical of you, stabbing someone in the back when he's not here to defend himself."

"How can I stab him in the back if he's not here?"

"Don't quibble with me! You're just jealous. He's twice the man you'll ever be, Mark Harvey!"

"You mean literally?"

"You wimp! Thank God I've found a real man at last!"

A real man! That blubber pudding! Mark stuttered incoherently.

"When I think of all those years I've wasted with you it makes me sick! The best years of my life! You used me and then discarded me, like an empty wrapper. You cruel man! I hate you!"

She hurled her magazine at him. He pushed it away and it landed on the bed an inch from Maud Gonne's tail. The cat regarded him with cynical indifference.

"You bastard!"

From somewhere she'd got hold of a book. He only noticed it when it was in mid-air. He just managed to duck in time; it shaved his hair.

"Not that!"

It was his transistor radio. Her arm was raised ready for throwing. His eyes pleaded with her. She hesitated.

"Please don't break anything else. I'll go away, I won't bother you, I'll sleep next door, promise! Please. . . ."

She lowered her arm slowly. When she spoke again the anger had ebbed out of her; her voice lacked any emotion.

"Get out."

"Yup. I'll just get these. . . . "

Fortunately the chest of drawers was within reach. He snatched out a fresh pair of pyjamas and backed away quickly, closing the bedroom door. He went back to his study.

The study contained a hard narrow bed which he kept made up for emergencies. He changed into his pyjamas and got in. He realised that he didn't have his clock. Should he go back in and get it? She might think he was breaking his word and throw the transistor at him. It was only a cheap little thing, but he'd had it for twenty years, he was fond of it. It had come from Bournemouth, and whenever he looked at it he thought of the seaside and his last holiday with his parents. That had been the year Dad died. He'd had his nineteenth birthday during the holiday. Where would he be for his fortieth, next month? He ought to do something special, it being such a landmark. He settled back in the bed, trying to make himself comfortable. He would just have to do without the clock and hope he'd wake up in time. He turned over on to his side.

He felt restless. He wanted to sleep and he couldn't, and that made him irritated which in turn rendered sleep even less likely. Inevitably the Talbot noises began to sound louder. He stuck his head under the pillow. That was no good, it made his head feel stuffy. The rest of him shivered. It was a chilly night, and the study was colder than the bedroom anyway. It was a bit much of her to keep the warm bed and the thick duvet all to herself. And the electric blanket. Who had paid for the bloody blanket? Silly question. And now he was being turfed out of his own bed just because she was in a bad mood with him. Anyone would think he had been having an affair. She was the adulterer, the sinner. Not that he was about to cast the first stone. He was one of the bloody meek, he was. Inherit the bloody earth, he would. Surely it wasn't too much to ask for a bit of respect. It was his house they were using for their illicit copulations. And his bean bag they were doing it on. It was disgusting what they'd done to it. It looked like the Grand Canyon now, with a great dent in the middle caused by their combined critical mass. Imagine if Isaac Newton had been hit by those two. He'd have discovered gravity and black holes at the same time. Not that he was jealous or anything like that. In fact if anything he was grateful to Roddy for taking on his marital chores. Thinking of Maddie he even doubted if he could have managed it himself any more. Lucky for Roddy he was so short-sighted.

The noise from the Talbots grew apace. They must have opened the french windows again. It was hopeless trying to sleep. What could he do about it? Maddie had said something about getting on to the Noise Prevention Society. Of course she wanted him to do it. He had hummed and haa'd. The truth was that he hated a fuss. It irked him when she called him a wimp. He didn't want any trouble, that was all. Just wanted to live his life in peace. He turned over, tried the other side.

He opened his eyes wide, stared into the darkness. He felt wide awake. A horrible thought nagged at him.

What if she wanted to leave him? What if she asked for a divorce? He hadn't worried about that for ages, although in the beginning it had consumed him. No, she wouldn't be so mad. He was hardly well off, but Roddy didn't have any money at all. He sold industrial vacuum-cleaners on commission, and as he never sold any cleaners he never got any commission. He lived practically rent free in a friend's house, otherwise he wouldn't have been able to survive at all. He couldn't afford to support a wife! But what if she tried to support him? She could make him sell the house and take half the money. And he'd have to pay alimony. Yes, they probably wouldn't marry for a while, they'd get him to support them. And what would become of him then? How much money would he be left with? About enough to buy a rabbit hutch in this area.

He lifted both arms out of the blankets. He no longer felt cold; he was sticky with sweat.

Things had got a bit out of hand recently. He really shouldn't have gone so far as he had. He'd been too harsh with Maddie after the trouser incident. He had enjoyed rubbing it in, but it had scared and upset her. He had overheard her whispering to someone on the phone that she was afraid he might turn violent. Probably to Lizzie Skinner, she always reserved a funny look and a sarcastic comment for him whenever he went into her shop. Now that really wasn't fair. She was the violent one, she seemed to love smashing things up. If she hit him he never hit back. Well, hardly ever, and only under extreme provocation. It was a travesty of the truth to accuse him of violence.

He turned on the bedside lamp and looked at his watch. A quarter past twelve. He hated not being able to sleep. He got out of bed and went over to his desk. He returned with a couple of magazines. One of them had a feature about the English Civil War Re-enactment Society. There was no sign of Roddy in any of the photographs; presumably the photographer had forgotten his wide-angle lens. The article said that members of the Society would be next appearing at the Fareham Modellers Club Annual Show in October. He turned the page quickly. He had been trying to forget that.

Half an hour later he turned off the light again and managed to doze off. He was woken almost immediately by the sounds of car doors slamming and engines revving, and the usual screechings and yellings that attended the closure of next door's Bacchanalian revels.

2

The Harveys had lived in Willow Cottage for the last eight years. They had moved to the Fareham area from Reading, where Mark had worked since leaving school. In those days Maddie had had a job as a receptionist for a large pharmaceutical company, but she hadn't worked since moving to the country. Neither of them had ever anticipated that she would have to.

They both thrived on country life. They loved the clean air, the long walks, above all the peace and silence. Besides Major and Mrs Dawson their nearest neighbours were the Trumans, whose farm was more than a mile down the road. At the same time they were just a ten-minute drive from Fareham, and although they could afford only the one car there had been a good bus service (at first) and Maddie enjoyed cycling. Nowadays the bus service was no more, and the thought of Maddie on a bicycle was simply inconceivable. If such an image did come into Mark's brain, which it did occasionally for a fleeting moment, the recollection would be as if sepia-toned: a thing historical, lacking immediacy, like an old print or a frame from a pre-war newsreel. All of his memories of that time had a kind of embalmed quality: it was curious, improbable even, to contemplate now their younger selves living in the same house, visiting the same people and places, but under utterly different circumstances. Why, once they had been happy in each other's company. Perhaps they had even been in love once. Not that he felt especially unhappy now. It was just that his life always seemed to be idling in neutral gear; his accustomed mood was one of resignation. He had been more optimistic, once.

The move to Fareham had involved promotion for him. It was small-town stuff (glorified village stuff even) but Mark got an office all to himself, with the words "Assistant Manager" on his door. A few of his friends had warned him about going out of town, they were worried about his being forgotten in the sticks, but the manager of the Fareham Branch was getting on and Mark's superiors in

Reading had implied that once he retired the top job would be his. As soon as he had made it to manager, of course, the world would be his oyster, he'd be able to pick and choose his next career step. Only it hadn't worked out like that. No doubt his Reading superiors had been in earnest, but by the time the Fareham managership became vacant they too had moved on. Even then all might have been well, had it not been for the television.

Television has a great many more serious charges to answer to than the mere propagation of mindless sex and violence. Perhaps the most serious of all is its pernicious tendency to put ideas into people's heads.

Walter Winston Vernon (b.1940, middle name a giveaway) was a middle-ranking, middle-aged executive with a bright future. He had been with the bank since coming down from Oxford and had watched his career and salary advance at a highly satisfactory and predictable rate. Then he had seen a television series called *Telford's Change*, in which a successful city banker, played by Peter Barkworth, gives up the rat-race to manage a humble branch in the provinces. At round about the same time Mrs Vernon (Vera, same vintage) became hooked on repeats of *The Good Life*, a comedy series in which Richard Briers and Felicity Kendal opt out of the twentieth century and grow their own vegetables. The combination proved irresistible; life needed no further invitation to imitate art: when Vernon applied for the vacant Fareham managership he rather expected to encounter at the very least heartfelt pleas not to throw away his glittering future, but in the event only a few eyebrows were raised politely. Evidently *Telford's Change* was exerting a considerable influence. Unless, of course, W.W.Vernon was a great deal less popular with his colleagues than he supposed.

There was, at any rate, no serious obstacle to his claiming the Fareham plum. Mark Harvey's application was sympathetically heard and all sorts of nice noises were made about faithful and devoted service (always a sure indication of a short straw being fixed), but it was ignored. Better luck next time, old boy, was the general message, and sorry about old Vernon, just a peculiar whim of his, but we have to indulge it because he went to the right school, oops! I mean he's jolly senior and all that, do you think we've still got time for a round of golf?

What could Mark do but accept his lot? Jobs were thin on the ground and he certainly couldn't afford to resign in protest. In any case he had to face up to the fact that he wasn't exactly the last word in executive dynamism. The chance did come up of a move to London, but property prices had become prohibitive. For all practical purposes he was stuck where he was. Occasionally he kicked his heels, but his will had been sapped. He had only one serious ambition left in life: he would like to murder Walter Winston Vernon.

Mark had overslept. He woke with the mental equivalent of a bad taste in his mouth – the residue of poor sleep and bad dreams – to discover that it was gone eight-thirty and he was in danger of being late for work. He threw on yesterday's clothes, raced through the bathroom and dashed out of the front door still pulling on his jacket and breathing through a mouthful of half-chewed bread and butter. He plunged across the soggy field and jumped into his car, noting with distaste that his shoes were now thick with mud again. He turned the ignition key and the engine started third time, which wasn't bad for a rusty Wop heap. He took his foot off the clutch and put the other down injudiciously hard on the accelerator. The engine moaned and the car slewed a few inches to the left. The wheels were spinning helplessly in the mud. He tried again, harder, his foot pressed almost to the floor. It was hopeless, the tyres refused to grip. He knew he was only making it worse, but still he persisted, cursing and shouting and smacking the steering wheel with his fist. He hated cars! Bloody stupid mechanical inventions, always choosing with sadistic relish the exact moment of maximum inconvenience at which to cease functioning. And with all the money it cost to run the bloody thing! The heater wasn't even working properly, the windows were misting up. He tried first gear but the car only jerked a few inches the other way. He felt like crying.

He jumped out of the car. Perhaps there was something he could put under the wheels, bits of wood or some such. Was there anything in the boot? He opened it and had a look. From nearby he heard the sound of another car. He glanced up and saw a black Jaguar drive out of the Talbots'. He stuck his head back in the boot and rummaged around. He tried to ignore the sounds of the Jaguar stopping and a door opening and shutting.

"Stuck, are you?"

Mark's first impulse was to climb into the boot and pull it shut after him. He realised, however, that this might look a little odd. Eventually, therefore, and with scarcely disguised reluctance, he lifted his head and turned to meet his fate.

"You're stuck then, eh?"

The first thing Mark noticed about Reg Talbot (or perhaps the second thing, the first being a capacity for stating, then repeating, the obvious) was his highly polished shoes, not simply because their condition was in stark contrast to his own footwear, but also because it wasn't quite what he would have expected of a second-hand car salesman (scuffed toecaps at the least, probably suede). The cut of his dark suit was equally fine, expensive, not even spivvy. Perhaps, then, he wore a medallion under his shirt, and chunky gold bracelets? Mark thought he detected a glint of metal at Talbot's cuff. He stared hard at his wrist.

"Something the matter?" Reg Talbot asked, sounding a little uncomfortable and sticking his hand in his pocket. Mark saw that the metal on his wrist was only his watch face.

"Oh no!" said Mark hastily, and then laughed. "I'm just a bit of a stick in the mud!"

He cringed at the feebleness of his own joke. Reg Talbot frowned. He looked as if he was the sort of man who frowned a lot, because his forehead was lined and his eyebrows were thick and Healeyish. There was in fact something rather emphatic and stubborn about all of his facial features. Mark stared at him curiously, trying to work out exactly what it was, then came to the conclusion that it was probably a question of everything being just a little too outsized. The nose, for example, was far too round and fleshy, like a fat old apple stuck as an afterthought on to the face of a snowman. He had a pronounced widow's peak where his dark hair was receding. He was probably about fifty.

Reg Talbot cleared his throat. Mark's stare, and his peculiar clipped laugh, were as disconcerting as they were unexpected. He frowned.

"Don't you work in the bank?"

It was a tentative question, delivered in such a tone as to suggest that the expected, or hoped for answer would be no. When Mark nodded Reg's frown deepened: odd sort of behaviour in bank officials was not something of which he could approve.

"I'm Reg Talbot," he announced belatedly, half-extending a hand.

Mark didn't reply. He had stuck his head back into the boot and was muttering something about three hundred pounds and a bloody insult. Reg stared blankly at his back.

"I've got a rope!" he announced brightly after a pause, and hurried away to fetch it from his boot. He tied one end to his tow bar and held out the other. Mark came squelching across the mud and took it from him. Cursing under his breath he ran it round his bumper and fixed it securely with a crude knot. Both men got behind their steering wheels. The rope tautened, the powerful Jaguar engine growled, and with one bound the rusty Wop heap was free. Mark hurried out and untied the rope.

"There now, that wasn't so bad, was it?" said Reg pleasantly.

Mark smiled back thinly. He handed Reg the end of the rope.

"Thanks," he muttered, as near inaudibly as possible.

"Anytime!" said Reg magnanimously.

"Let's hope there won't be another bloody anytime!" muttered Mark rather more audibly than before. "How do you think I got stuck in the first place? Don't you lot ever sleep?"

And with that Mark jumped back into his car, slammed the door shut and accelerated away, recklessly overtaking the Jaguar in the narrow drive. At the end of the drive, a hundred yards on, Mark got out of the car, opened the gate, went through and closed the gate again before driving off down towards Fareham. He did not glance back. Had he done so he would have seen Reg Talbot standing exactly as he had left him by the boot of his car, the end of the rope hanging limply in his grasp and an expression of mounting indignation blossoming all over his face.

The church clock was already striking nine when Mark drove into Fareham High Street. It took another five minutes to get to his usual parking place in Church Road. He was the last to arrive at the bank.

As bad luck would have it Vernon had been looking for him. Mark ran a comb briefly through his hair, wiped some of the mud off his trouser leg, then went and knocked on Vernon's door.

"Tut! Tut!" said Vernon affably, tapping his watch. "Bad mark eh, Harvey?"

Vernon snickered. Mark smiled thinly. For nearly five years now he had been listening to the same jokes. Five bloody years of banal banter and schoolboy innuendo. Vernon was supposed to have got a First at Oxford. What in, for God's sake?

"You wanted to see me, sir?"

"Yes, didn't I ask you to find the Waterstone's file?"

"Yes. It's on your desk."

Mark indicated the pink folder which was sitting, almost literally, under Vernon's nose. Vernon stared at it like a card-sharper's dupe.

There was a knock on the door and Miss Price entered. Miss Price was the Chief Cashier.

"Can you open the safe please, Mr Vernon?"

Vernon got up and went to the old black wall safe. He always insisted on opening it himself, despite the fact that Miss Price, along with Mark, was entrusted with the combination herself. It was his office, after all, so therefore it was his safe. Mark and Miss Price were careful never to go anywhere near it.

Vernon handed her the money for the tills, wads of new and used notes, neatly bagged heaps of coin. Mark held the door open for her as she left, laden with loot.

"Will that be all, sir?" Mark asked, hovering in the doorway.

"I have merely one small note to add in passing. It comprises a sartorial observation: do please try, old thing, to maintain a standard of personal cleanliness commensurate with your responsibilities, in short to endeavour to resemble a servant, however humble, of a great financial institution, in preference to an agricultural labourer. You must keep up to the mark, Harvey! *Pour encourager les autres*!"

Mark left Vernon happily snickering to himself and flicking ineffectually through the pink file. He knew perfectly well that the moment the door was closed Vernon would retrieve his putter from where he had leant it against the desk and recommence the important work of trying to sink golf balls in the waste-paper bin. Mark rarely left the manager's office without a feeling of bitterness. He couldn't help thinking of what might have been; what indeed, by the laws of natural justice, ought to have been.

The day did not get much better. Initially some mugs of instant coffee had a revitalising effect, but soon his want of a proper breakfast began to gnaw at his stomach and distract his attention. At half past ten he could bear it no longer. He checked that Vernon was still occupied (the clinking of the balls in the metal bin could be heard clearly through the door), then muttered to Miss Temple that he was just popping out for five minutes.

The bank lay at the bottom end of the High Street, opposite the

Fire Station and between two of the village pubs. The only shops at this end were hardware and electrical. He would have to go right up the High Street if he wanted to find anything to eat.

This operation was slightly more complicated than it need have been. To simplify matters Mark adopted two plans, which he christened mentally "Plan A" and "Plan B (Contingency)". Mental neatness always came naturally anytime he was in the vicinity of the bank. Putting "Plan A" into effect he crossed the High Street and marched up boldly past the video shop, the "other bank" (never referred to by name), and the toy shop. This brought him to the bakery, whereupon he stopped suddenly and glanced extravagantly at his watch, a gesture which enabled him to sneak a surreptitious sideways look through the bakery window. He did not linger on the tempting array of pies and tarts, but concentrated his attention on the shop assistants, two young girls in striped aprons and cardboard hats. He breathed a sigh of relief: "Plan B" was henceforth redundant, a pleasing development as it would have involved the purchase of something barely edible from the small supermarket across the street. With a song in his heart Mark stepped into the bakery.

As he approached the counter, debating inwardly the merits of custard tarts as against apple turnovers, the bead curtains at the back of the shop parted and Lizzie Skinner came out. The smile froze on Mark's lips.

"Oh well blow me down, look who it isn't!" declared Lizzie with a sneer, or at least with what was probably intended for a sneer: Lizzie's tone of voice was so nasal and twangy anyway that even her innocent remarks (which were few) sounded bitchy. She leant her bony elbows on the counter and stared at him with her basilisk eyes.

"Ah yes! It's me. Ha! ha! How are you? Mm. . . . "

Encounters with Lizzie always had an unfortunate effect on his ability to construct coherent sentences.

"Ooh! Look who's asking? How am I? he asks. Very nice of him, I'm sure, and never a word for his poor wife. You remember your wife, do you? She remembers you alright. . . . "

"I'd like two sausage rolls, please," said Mark to the nearest of the assistants. He didn't want a sausage roll at all, but the savoury tray was the nearest and it was imperative that he make his purchase and exit at speed. Lizzie continued to address him while the assistant transferred the rolls by tong into a paper bag.

"Yes, love and cherish and honour it says, doesn't it? Till death do us part. There's a thought, eh? Poison his coffee, I've said to her, on more than one occasion, nobody would blame you, even a male judge would be sympathetic, we'd all stand by you!"

"Fifty p. please."

Mark banged the sweaty coin down on the counter, snatched up his sausage rolls and lunged for the door.

"Going so soon, are we?"

"Yes! Must – ha! – dash! Bye!"

He rushed out of the shop and round the nearest corner, where he pressed his back against the wall and stood heaving for breath. He mopped his brow and his handkerchief was sopping wet.

That had been a mistake! It had been just a matter of greed – his eyes were bigger than his brain. Why take a risk like that? It was stupid! Lizzie was not simply Maddie's best friend, she was also Chair of the Fareham Feminist Discussion Group, an organisation which had adopted him, Mark Harvey, as official Chauvinist Hate Figure. Pat Truman, the Secretary, had even renamed one of her pigs after him. The discussions, as far as he could gather, consisted almost entirely of Maddie telling the rest of them what it was like to live with a heartless bastard, whereupon a Motion of Solidarity and a Declaration of Sisterhood would be passed, and they would all repair to the pub and stick pins in his wax effigy. It was humiliating, infuriating and utterly unfair. And there was nothing at all he could do about it.

He tramped morosely back down the High Street. Just as he reached the bank (chomping vigorously on the second sausage roll, flakes of pastry cascading down his shirt front), the door opened and out stepped Vernon.

"Heavens above, sneaking off to the tuck shop in office hours! Nought marks out of ten, Harvey!"

When Vernon had gone Mark kicked open the door and marched back inside angrily. The staff looked alarmed. Unbidden, Miss Temple went to make him a coffee. For the rest of the day he threw himself furiously into his work.

All in all it was not what he could have called a good day. Early that evening, as he arrived home, he did permit himself the faintest glimmer of what almost might have been a trace of satisfaction: leaving his car (in its customary place, not the middle of the field) he caught a glimpse of Reg Talbot through one of his upstairs windows. At least, Mark thought to himself as he opened his garden gate and stepped on to the drawbridge, at least I gave him a piece of my mind! He knows what's for, alright, and no mistake!

Mark strode proudly over the moat and into his domain, head held high and shoulders firmly set. He wished, for at least the ten-thousandth time, that the drawbridge could have really lived up to its name, that he might have raised it, lowered the portcullis, and shut out the whole troublesome world.

3

Only when Mark had disappeared from view did Reg Talbot turn away from his bedroom window. He had dashed upstairs on hearing the approach of the car and had framed himself behind the glass in the hope of eliciting a friendly wave or even a perfunctory nod. In this, as in so many things, he found himself disappointed.

He had been hoping for much, much more from his new neighbour. And his wife. He had heard about them the day after moving in, at the vet's, where he had taken old Boxer for another injection. Just as well he's getting on now, the vet had nodded in Boxer's direction, we don't want him giving poor Maud Gonne a hard time. Who? Reg had inquired, naturally enough. Maddie's cat was the answer, or hadn't he met his new neighbours yet, Mark and Maddie? No, he hadn't, but what was that name again, wasn't it a little peculiar for a cat? Well, it made a change from Kylie, said the vet, who went on to explain that Maud Gonne was the name of an Irish poet's bird.

Reg had been impressed. We're talking class here, he thought to himself excitedly, as the vet tried to coax Boxer into lying still. He knew he'd made the right decision in moving out to the country, leaving behind all the mod cons of life on a neo-Georgian estate. Sharon and the kids missed that life already, and he knew their moanings were going to get worse, but this was one time when he just felt it in his blood that he'd been right to put his foot down, and they were just going to have to lump it. You met a better class of person in the country, alright. Their last neighbour had had a mongrel Burmese called Kylie.

Unfortunately all of Reg's attempts to make contact with his superior new neighbours had been rebuffed. At first he had put it down to standoffishness or English reserve, but as the rebuttals mounted the suspicion dawned that the manner of his initial embassy might have been lacking in tact. Perhaps Billy had been an unfortunate choice for ambassador.

Billy Barker, Sharon's brother, no longer lived with them (another instance in which Reg had had to put his foot down very firmly), although he spent so much time hanging about the place that you could be forgiven for thinking otherwise. As it happened, the only time in the last seventeen years in which he had been of any use had been during the move a month ago, when it had been a question of all hands to the pump, regardless of their provenance. Reg had even been moved to admit, in a rash moment, that Billy was a "godsend", a remark which, naturally, Sharon had reported back to her brother at the earliest opportunity, and which had resulted in a look of permanent and unbearable smugness taking up residence on his gormless, moon-like face. Everyone has their cross to bear, Reg had been heard to mutter to himself at frequent intervals during the last seventeen years. It was merely bad luck that he should have the entire Barker family suspended from his.

That first evening in the new house it quickly became apparent to Reg that the earlier usefulness of said "godsend" had run its course. A number of spurious errands had been invented as means to remove his presence from the house, one of which had been his employment as a messenger to the new neighbours. If only Reg hadn't been so busy, if only he hadn't been in the middle of unpacking the best china, he would of course have gone himself, but the chance to get Billy out of the house was too tempting to be passed up. So Billy had gone, and he had returned, and only now was Reg beginning to suspect the worst, for at the time Billy had come back saying nothing more than that they wasn't in, a piece of news which had not disturbed Reg unduly, he thinking simply that there'd be plenty of time for getting to know each other once the dust had settled. That the invitations which had followed hot upon one another in the interim had remained unanswered touched a nerve.

But was there an explanation after all? Mark's reference to three hundred pounds in the field that morning had baffled him. In fact, Reg had found his whole manner baffling but then, as he was driving to work, a horrible thought had struck him. Once at the office he lost no time in taking Billy to one side (for an additional pound of nails in the cross he wore was the unemployable godsend's position as assistant sales rep at the showroom) and nudged him towards reconstructing the events of that evening a month ago. Fortunately Billy was not at that moment engaged in any serious undertaking: he was comparing the knockers on Misses January and February in one of the nude calendars that adorned his stretch of wall. This was an activity which swallowed a considerable number of hours in his average working day.

"Just try and think back for a moment will you, Billy," Reg began patiently. "When you said they weren't in, you didn't actually see them or anything, did you?"

No he hadn't, he replied, scratching his head and dusting his shoulders with dandruff.

"Not the second time either?" Reg pursued, for he had sent him back an hour later.

"The second time?" repeated Billy with a puzzled air, for his return trip had slipped, like so much else, from his memory. He tapped the side of his head with his knuckles, as if hoping to knock the particular recollection back into place. It seemed to work, for his round dull eyes glimmered: "Oh yeah, that wuz when I left the invite!"

And so it had come out, bit by painful bit. Billy had scrawled something on the back of a business card and shoved it through the door. Which card? Reg asked, the old or the new? for there was an important difference, the older, short-lived design being the vulgar product of his recently sacked marketing manager. How he hated those cards! They'd been printed and distributed during his summer break, entirely without his authority or approval. He had been furious on his return. How could he be expected to raise the tone of the business if it was being marketed under the illiterate slogan "You wannit? We goddit!"? Billy, needless to say, had approved wholeheartedly of this catchy little phrase and had clung on to a stock of the offending cards long after their official withdrawal from circulation. It seemed inevitable, therefore, that one of these ghastly objects had borne Billy's hastily scribbled invitation. But an invitation to what? This question taxed to the uttermost Billy's powers of recall; a Niagara of dandruff descended on his check jacket. At last he had to admit himself defeated and say that he just couldn't remember the model, although he was sure that he hadn't offered more than two hundred quid.

No wonder his neighbours had been behaving oddly! No wonder they had ignored him. Only the other day, on his last foray, he had seen the curtains twitching, and he had even glimpsed a pale face

34

framed with golden hair, undoubtedly the romantically inclined cat owner herself. He had felt her eyes bore into his back as he retraced his footsteps over the stream that divided their properties, and he had marched stiffly and proudly, conscious of his dignity. If they declined to answer their door to him, whatever their reasons, then so be it: a man could go so far and then no further. He would cease to issue party invitations.

What a fool he'd been! That stupid Billy! He'd give Sharon a piece of his mind about that moronic brother of hers, just see if he didn't! But even as the mental resolution was made Reg knew that he would never get round to saying anything at all. What was the point of saying anything to Sharon about anything, ever? The thought of his own wife, mentally superimposed on the image of that flaxen-haired creature next door, gave him a dreadful pang. How he longed more than anything to mingle with intelligent company, above all to talk to a sophisticated woman! He had never even seen Mrs Harvey except through glass, once through that window and two other times, in the distance, behind the wheel of her car, but he felt sure that she was a woman of refinement, of delicacy and taste. What a lucky man her husband must be. . . .

Reg walked slowly down the stairs. The din of the television blared out from the living room, through whose door he could just see the feet of his children, Danny (14) and Kelly (12). The noise was matched from the kitchen, where Sharon had the radio on at full volume and was singing along tunelessly to a Country and Western ballad. Cautiously Reg stuck his head round the kitchen door. His heart sank as he saw the table laid for five. Sharon turned round at that moment, looking for her lighter, and he smiled in a friendly fashion.

"What time's dinner, darling?"

"Soon as Billy gets here."

It was hard to hear her over the radio racket, but her speech sounded slurred. As if to confirm his suspicions she lit her cigarette from the wrong end. His eyes strayed to the sideboard, where a half-empty bottle of gin stood next to tonight's meal, an unappetising pile of frozen food waiting to be heaped into the microwave. Sharon, meanwhile, had thrown away the first cigarette and lit another. She let it dangle out of one corner of her mouth while she concentrated all her mental energies into picking up the beat from the radio. Was she really only thirty-six years old, he wondered, actually twelve years younger than him? Each year that passed she seemed to catch up, to lessen the gap. Even as he considered the actual physical impossibility of this time-bending he felt unable quite to discount it, for there was no point of contact in his memory between the Sharon who stood before him and the girl he had married seventeen years before. Whenever he looked at the wedding photograph by their bed he found it hard to repress a smile of pleasure at the thought of how little he had changed, but the smile dissolved and his habitual frown returned as soon as his eyes strayed to the bright-eyed elfin creature in white who stood blushing by his side on the church steps. How his friends had envied him, shacking up to such a tasty little number: what a lucky man, all that virgin innocence, how did he do it? Reg the Ram, they had called him, and he had to admit he'd smirked a bit and gone blasé, as if he were a regular Casanova. But it wasn't an accurate picture. For one thing he hadn't done anything, she had done it. And virgin innocence was stretching a point to say the least. Mind you, she had had to be good at something; she was the worst secretary he'd ever employed. He had actually been on the point of sacking her when she had seduced him in the storeroom. At the time he had put it down to his irresistible charms (though nowhere in prior evidence) but the truth had finally dawned at the wedding reception two months later when Uncle Charlie had publicly congratulated her on nabbing the boss and he had seen on the faces of her assembled relations that this had not been intended as a joke. Uncle Charlie had been only the first to have enjoyed a period of lucrative employment at the Talbot showroom. Reg himself was clearly a Barker family investment, a walking meal-ticket for life. It was a curious if unfortunate quirk of nature, a genetic malfunction of scientifically staggering proportions, that every single owner of the Barker surname should have turned out to be a cretin. Reg had a further horrible suspicion that it was a dominant gene. Whenever he looked at his children he was reinforced in this belief.

The doorbell rang. Reg was in the act of opening a bottle of wine, salvaged from amongst last night's party leftovers.

"Answer that, will you?" he called out through the kitchen door.

"Answer it yourself, Fatty!" yelled Danny.

Sharon guffawed as she lit another cigarette. She could have answered it, he thought bitterly. She could have supported him, dealt firmly with the children, backed him up. But no, she had never taken his side, she had always let them do whatever they pleased, and always opposed him as a matter of principle. Stiffly, in his own time, he put down the bottle of wine and trooped off to the door, briefly lightening his step as he entertained the improbable fantasy that it might be his next-door neighbour, or even his mysterious wife.

"Good evening, Billy," he said dully, when the truth was revealed in all its glory. Billy ignored him.

"Wotcha Shaz!" he bawled out, heading straight for the kitchen. "Wotcha kids!"

Reg closed the door and leant against it, taking the weight off his feet, conserving his strength. He was going to need it all for later. Sharon's incessant party nights were bad enough, but at least in the press of guests it was possible to lose oneself, even to lose sight from time to time of the ubiquitous Barkers. To be stuck over dinner with the worst of them, to be plagued through all the hours of consciousness, at work and at rest, with unremitting singularity by the egregious Billy was more than any mortal should be expected to bear. Reg's frown darkened. Oh for a life of peace and quiet, he thought, of gentle nourishment for the soul. He must, whatever the cost, break out of the stifling atmosphere at home. He must expand his circle of acquaintances, find people of culture and refinement with whom to share his aspirations. He must, in short (and he felt the urgency of it with such force that he gripped the door handle behind his back so tightly that it hurt), make friends with his neighbours.

Just as Mark came in from work the phone began to ring. He presumed that Maddie would answer it, but as he hung up his coat he saw a strip of light under the bathroom door and heard the faint hiss of the shower. He hurried into the kitchen and snatched up the receiver.

"Fareham 4113, hello?"

"Maddie?"

Instinctively Mark held his breath. He knew the voice at once: two syllables were quite enough to spot the ponderous poutiness of Roddy's tone.

"Maddie darling, are you there?"

Mark smiled. Roddy was endearingly thick sometimes (and unendearingly thick the rest of the time). Why did he always assume that it was Maddie who answered the phone? Or was it a question of him being partially deaf as well as short-sighted? All physical malfunctions seemed to be met in some degree in the person of Roddy. Mark contemplated stringing him along (he had overheard enough whispered conversations to be confident of remembering his lines) but the thought of addressing Roddy as "My little chubby knees", or "Roly panda" made him snicker.

"Who's that?" demanded Roddy, suddenly gruff. Mark literally tried to wipe away his grin.

"Just the butler," he said in his best Ealing comedy style. "I'll see if milady has finished with the gamekeeper."

Mark danced a little reel out into the hallway. He banged on the bathroom door.

"That gentleman with a hearing problem on the phone again, darling!" he called out gaily, and then dashed up the stairs two at a time, humming happily.

He went straight into his study, flung off his jacket and hurled himself into his chair. He took a moment or two to calm his boisterous spirits, then delicately took hold of the base of the lancer between finger and thumb and held it up to the light. There was a satisfying gleam on the black-coated boots. Time for some shading. He opened a pot of French Blue.

"Mark?"

He jumped, almost knocking over the paint.

"God almighty! Don't do that!"

Roger looked embarrassed. He took a step back towards the open door, his rubber soles brushing the carpet, while his whole body compressed itself downwards into a cringe. He mumbled an apology.

"I'm sorry, I didn't mean to disturb you. Very sorry, I'll go. . . . "

He continued exiting backwards, his head bobbing up and down ever so slightly in an attitude suggestive of Oriental submission. His quiet servility made Mark feel embarrassed. Roger was a kind of sympathetic Uriah Heep.

"It's alright Rog, I haven't started yet," Mark said, putting to one side his still clean brush. Roger hovered in the doorway.

"New model, is it?" he asked, in the tone of voice one might use in asking the doctor to confirm that one had less than a week to live.

"No, I've been working on it for quite a while," answered Mark, spotlighting it with his desk lamp and becoming animated. "It's a lancer from the Crimean War. I've got to get it ready for the show on Saturday."

"Crimean War, is it? Florence Nightingale and that?"

"Yes, that's the one."

"Very bloody war, that. Death and destruction and untold misery. . . ."

Roger seemed to cheer up at the prospect. He would have probably been quite at home in the hospital at Scutari: The Manic Depressive with the Lamp.

"No, it can't have been much fun," Mark agreed, "especially for this chap. He would have been one of the six hundred, one of the Light Brigade."

"Battle of Balaclava, is it?"

"Yup, that's the one. 'Cannon to left of them, cannon to right of them, volley'd and thunder'd!'"

Roger nodded his head slowly.

"Daft really, innit? Naming a battle after an hat. It'll be battle of trilby next, I suppose."

"Ha! ha!" said Mark, a little uneasily. Roger hardly ever made jokes. Whenever he did it was a sure sign of imminent major depression. Mind you, thought Mark, if his jokes were as bad as that he'd feel depressed too.

"Anything bothering you, Rog?"

"Mm," said Roger very deliberately, crossing his arms and leaning against the door. "I was wondering if you could spare a moment?"

"For what?"

"I need a witness."

"A witness?" Mark was puzzled. Was Roger planning to commit an offence, or thinking of entering into partnership with Jehovah?

"I've a document, see. Upstairs."

To emphasise the location he raised a bony finger. Mark rose from his chair.

"Let's go up then."

He followed Roger out and down to the end of the landing, where a ladder with padded rungs led up to a square opening in the ceiling. Roger went first, swinging his long hairy arms to get a high grip then stumbling up like an anorexic Johnny Weismuller. Mark followed cautiously, with due respect to gravity.

Roger's den was in its usual state of iniquity. He gave the impression of a man who collected empty cardboard containers without having any idea of what to do with them: old boxes, take-away coffee cups and fast-food packages lay piled up in various niches as if awaiting classification and storage. Discarded clothing added to the detritus, the unwashed items festering in piles, the washed (the term was relative) dotted over the rest like afterthought cake decorations. It was a Miss Havisham sort of cake at that: the dust was thick and settled and the cobwebs had preservation orders on them.

Roger banged his head three times on different beams before coming to rest at the little table and chair stuck under the nominal attic window. A while ago Mark had made Roger a present of a construction worker's hard hat, advising that he wear it when "at home", a not entirely frivolous suggestion given the scarred and cratered appearance of Roger's scalp. The household obstruction had not been invented which Roger was incapable of walking into. For him even to have contemplated taking an attic room with a low sloping ceiling was an act of suicidal imbecility.

Mark sat down on the edge of the bed, pushing to one side a leaning tower of books and magazines, which promptly toppled over.

"What's this document then, Rog?"

With an uncharacteristic flourish Roger whipped a sheet of paper out of his ancient portable typewriter. He handed it over without a word. Mark turned on the bedside lamp and read it:

> This is to ceRtify that I, Daffydd (David) TeRence Jones, being of sound mind and body, do, this __ day of NovembeR, 199_ (Anno Domino) make these pRovisions foR my last will and testament, viz: I leave all my woRldly goods to my sisteR MRs.Eluned Watkins of Swansea, with the exception of my moped which I leave to heR son (ie my nephew) BaRRy John Watkins and my collection of Judge DRedd comics which I leave to heR otheR son (ie also my nephew) Phil Bennett Watkins of the same fixed abode. I entRust to my executoR _____ the destRuction of all peRsonal papeRs Relating to me.
>
> SIGNED   WITNESSED:
>
> D.T. Jones

"I was wondering, you see," Roger began, the moment he saw that Mark had finished reading, "if you would do me the honour of agreeing to act as my executor as well as my witness. Only I don't know anyone else to ask, see, and I'm a bit stuck with not having an executor for my estate, because I know that's the law now, isn't it?"

Mark put down the paper, crossed his hands in his lap and stared at them pensively. He cleared his throat.

"Actually I'm not entirely sure that this is quite legal, Roger."

"Oh it's the right jargon alright, Mark, I read it out of a book."

"Er, yes. Still, I would think it more advisable to consult a solicitor, if I were you. You might get into a bit of a legal wrangle with a document of this sort. Um, it doesn't look terribly professional, if you'll forgive me for saying so."

"I'm afraid it only does a capital R, my machine."

"It's not just a question of that, Roger, although that doesn't help."

"Oh. And you think that might result in a delay in the settlement of my estate?"

Mark nodded. He wore a serious air, as befitted the subject under discussion, but it was difficult to see what it was in the 'estate' that was worth making any fuss over.

"Yes I do. This sort of thing is best dealt with by professionals."

Roger nodded gloomily.

"Cost a bit, I suppose," he murmured with masochistic relish. "I'll be needing it soon enough though, I expect."

"Ah yes." Mark looked at his watch.

"Got to be getting on, have you?" asked Roger, sadly.

Mark shrugged, as if to say "sorry, but . . ." which in fact was exactly what he felt: "sorry but I have no desire to sit here and listen to your morbid ramblings for a moment longer". Now was exactly the right time to go, before Roger got warmed up and on to his favourite subject, suicide. Mark was a little intrigued to know which method of self-dealt death he was interested in at the moment (it had been electrocution last time and poisoning the time before that) but not intrigued enough to risk upsetting the digestion of his evening meal: he still dreamt from time to time of Roger's alleged friend of a friend who had attempted to take his own head off with a Black and Decker circular saw. It was not a particularly pleasant dream.

"Thanks anyway Mark, you're a pal!"

There was so much sincerity in Roger's voice he nearly choked. Mark felt embarrassed. He muttered his farewells and disappeared hastily down the ladder.

As he set his feet back on the landing he became aware of a pleasant aroma diffidently teasing his nostrils. It was a warm, meaty, stewy smell and it made him feel hungry. It was only just gone half six, dinner wouldn't be for at least an hour, so he decided that a raid on the biscuit tin was called for. He headed downstairs, intent on the kitchen, but hardly had he set foot in the hall than the front doorbell rang. As he was only about eighteen inches away he didn't feel that he had much option but to open it, although as he wasn't expecting anyone he would much rather have left it to Maddie. An anonymous shape moved on the other side of the frosted glass. As his fingers closed on the handle Mark froze: it couldn't possibly be the wretched neighbour, could it, trying to make friends again on the basis of their introduction this morning? It was too late to run away now, he'd been seen through the frosted glass. He opened the door a couple of inches and peeped out through the crack.

The face on the other side was also pressed close to the crack; their noses almost touched. Both of them started. Mark gazed in some amazement at the chubby white head confronting him.

"Good evening, Roddy," he said at length, when he had recovered his tongue.

4

"Well, aren't you going to invite me in then?" said Roddy sniffily, taking off his glasses and putting them in his breast pocket. He was always taking off his glasses, for it was a matter of faith with him that he was not chronically short-sighted. Even that description veered towards the euphemistic.

Mark considered his request. The only invitation he had ever considered extending to Roddy was a heartfelt imprecation to get stuffed. It had never occurred to him that he might be required to ask him into his own home. He stared at the interloper coldly. The question had been put with bluff jocularity, but it was apparent that Roddy's casual tone was an act. He was nervous: he shifted uneasily from foot to foot and kept putting his hands in and out of his pockets; the muscles around his flabby mouth twitched; a bead of sweat clung to the tip of his nose, glistening in the porch light. Mark relaxed. Obviously Roddy knew that he wasn't playing the game.

"Of course! Do come in, old chap. What a pleasant surprise!"

He even slapped him on the shoulder as he came past, a thoughtless exaggeration which Roddy interpreted as a hostile act.

"Watch it!" he hissed, backing into the umbrella stand and half-raising his bunched paws. Mark decided to ignore him.

"Maddie!" he called, leaving Roddy and going into the dining room. "Someone to see you!"

He stopped in his tracks as Maddie came out of the kitchen, drying her hands on her apron. It was not the sight of her in domestic armour that arrested him, rather the look in her eyes, which was of a steeliness he had never encountered before. He was momentarily nonplussed.

"It's old Roddy Whatsisname to see you, darling," he managed at last.

"I know," she said, very calmly. She took off her apron as Roddy came into the room.

"The name's Maclean actually," he said impatiently, rising to the bait. "It's Roddy Maclean."

Maddie all but ignored him. She too took off her glasses, perhaps in a gesture of solidarity. Love really was blind with these two. She said:

"Would you mind coming into the living room for a moment with us please, Mark? We need to talk."

He knew, then, what was coming.

He took the chair by the fire. She sat on the sofa opposite. After a moment's hesitation Roddy sat beside her.

"Roddy's got something to say to you," said Maddie.

Roddy looked at her in some surprise, as if to say "Have I?" Maddie continued to stare at Mark. He looked away, at Roddy. As Maddie said nothing more Roddy was forced to turn to Mark, whom he attempted to fix with a penetrating glare, although as he actually couldn't see his eyes, what he fixed was a spot on the back of the chair about an inch from Mark's ear. Mark found this disconcerting.

"It's like this, Mark," he squeaked, and then stopped. He cleared his throat. He hadn't meant to squeak, but his voice was naturally rather high-pitched and in moments of tension it had a tendency to go Disneyish. He dipped his chin, as if trying to summon up a baritone. "It's like this, Mark. Things have gone far enough."

Having made this pronouncement, he sat back in the sofa, folded his arms over his spherical belly and gave the spot an inch from Mark's ear the full benefit of his most withering look. Silence ensued.

"Was it raining when you came out?" Mark asked at length. His eyes had strayed to the window, on which he could see little bubbles of moisture materialising. It had looked rather overcast earlier; he shouldn't be at all surprised if they were in for a wet spell.

"I don't think you realise the gravity of the situation," said Maddie icily.

"That's right!" added Roddy with an emphatic nod. "This is no time to be flippant."

Mark sighed. Suddenly he felt overwhelmingly tired. His life seemed to be a merry-go-round of trivial confrontations, a pygmy struggle devoid of dignity. His only real contentment lay in solitude. Why were people always intruding? And why were they always so unpleasant?

"Who's being bloody flippant?" he snapped. Roddy twitched. "It was a perfectly sensible question. Just an innocent little enquiry about the state of the weather. A damned sight more useful than anything you've said so far. All you've managed to come up with is some drivel about things having got worse. What am I expected to do in response to that? Assume the lotus position and contemplate my navel for a fortnight? You ought to write a bloody book. The Roddy Whatsisname bloody book of homebrew philosophy for morons. Bertrand Russell eat your heart out."

Roddy and Maddie were both on their feet, shouting and waving their podgy limbs about wildly in all directions. They looked like a bad variety act: The Michelin Twins. Mark couldn't conceal a smile. That made matters worse.

"And you can wipe that smirk off your face too, Mark Harvey!" screamed Maddie.

"That's right!" Roddy roared, stamping his foot. "This is no laughing matter!"

Both of them were maroon in the face. It was quite a change in Roddy, whose complexion was naturally pasty-white. Maddie merely looked as if she'd stuffed a couple of extra apples into her cheeks. The veins on her forehead stood out like a relief map. She was gasping for breath.

"You'd better watch it," Mark warned. "You'll burst a blood vessel."

He was on his feet as well, there was nothing else for it. Roddy had backed off a little but Maddie was pressing close, waving a threatening fist under his nose. She really ought to be more careful, he thought to himself.

"You're far too overweight for this, dear, you'll give yourself a coron-"

She slapped him hard across the face, burst into tears and ran out of the room. Mark fell back into his chair holding his cheek, which stung for a moment then went numb.

"You lay a finger on her again and I'll kill you!" said Roddy, without, however, a great deal of conviction.

"It was actually she who laid a finger on me, mate," said Mark bitterly.

Roddy looked surprised. He hadn't noticed Mark sit down again. He had been addressing the wall.

"That's as may be!" he exclaimed huffily. "But don't quibble with me, mister!"

Mark laid his head back against the chair rest and closed his eyes. It was hardly surprising that he felt tired, he hadn't slept well the previous night. He really couldn't be bothered with all this, now. The whole little scene was bad enough, but Roddy's spineless evasions made it unbearable. By what thin threads did a man's life hang (that was another chapter heading for Roddy's book). Martin had only invited Roddy to his Christmas party by mistake. He had thought he was somebody else. An easy enough mistake to make at one of those Civil War re-enactments, with everyone wandering around in silly hats and fancy dress. Mark had always considered Martin's involvement with the Society an eccentric whim. Given the fatal consequences it was an opinion that demanded revision.

"What does she see in you?" Mark murmured aloud.

"What was that?" demanded Roddy with a bark, and then, when he didn't answer, "are you talking to me, mister?"

Where had he got this "mister" thing from? Some old gangster movie? Or was he a fan of the Mr Men? Now that he thought about it, Mark did detect a certain physical resemblance.

"No, I wasn't particularly talking to you, although seeing as you're still here perhaps I should take the opportunity of saying a few words man to man, if that isn't too much of an exaggeration. You see, although I put up with a great deal, there are limits. Not many, but a few. I don't actually mind you bonking my wife. I don't even mind you doing it here, in this room, although that is my bean bag, you know, and I don't see why you couldn't at least bring your own. No, no, steady on, don't interrupt! I'm not going to make an issue of the bean bag, it's alright, sit down and relax. It's just the principle of the thing in passing, that's all. My point is this – do please sit down and stop spluttering; there's dribble on your chin by the way. What I'm saying is that this particular Englishman's home may not amount to much as a castle, it may even have sunk to the status of casual knocking shop, but he would still like to be able to reserve for himself the liberty of claiming that however modest a thing it may be, it is his own. In short, if I may sum up in a few words, I would like to be allowed to relax in my own home without you stomping around threatening me. And if you do have to dribble so much try not to get it on the carpet."

It was a moot point as to which of them was the more surprised, Roddy by Mark's speech, or Mark by his own eloquence. Certainly Roddy appeared to be too flabbergasted to speak, and Mark was in no hurry for his answer. He enjoyed the silence that followed, reflecting on his hitherto unguessed-at rhetorical skills, his pithy phrases and his cool, deadly delivery. So preoccupied was he that he hardly noticed Maddie come back in.

"Well?" she demanded of Roddy with a sniff, for she had only just stopped crying. "Did you tell him?"

She took one of his hands between hers and squeezed it imploringly. Roddy looked uncomfortable.

"Er, not in so many words."

Mark laughed. Maddie turned on him ferociously.

"Shut up, you! You evil, wicked, cruel man! I must have been mad to have married you! You've destroyed my life, you've utterly – "

"Yes, yes!" said Mark short-temperedly. "I have heard all this, I've got the original cast recording upstairs."

"Don't talk to me like that!"

"That's right, don't talk to her like that, mister!"

"Put a sock in it, Whatsyername!"

"The name's Maclean actually, Roddy Mac- "

"Shut up the both of you!"

They both shut up. Maddie's voice was hoarse from crying and shouting. She took hold of Roddy's arm and pressed herself up close to him. She stared at Mark defiantly.

"Roddy has got something to say to you. Please say it, Roddy."

Might as well, thought Mark as he sat down on the arm of his chair. Get it over with.

"I love your wife!" declared Roddy, flinging his arm round her suddenly. The tears gathered in her eyes again. Mark said nothing. He didn't really want to get involved in a discussion now. He wanted to have his dinner and get an early night. He wanted to spend an hour on his lancer, watch the news, have a bath. He didn't want to face up to the end of his marriage.

"I want a divorce."

He stared at her blankly for a moment then looked out of the window. It was definitely going to be heavy rain tonight.

47

"Roddy and I want to get married. I'm expecting Roddy's baby."

"You what?"

"Yes, that's right, I'm pregnant! I only discovered yesterday, you can't say I've kept it from you. I realise that you'll probably feel a little jealous, Mark, and I understand, it's only natural, but the simple fact is that Roddy has given me what you were never able to give me, through no fault of your own, I know, it was just your physiological condition, but he happens to be, in more ways than one it would seem, a better man than you, and I hope you won't hold it against him but accept it as Mother Nature's course. Though I have cuckolded you, Mark, I am not ashamed. I bear his child, and there can be no shame in that. Now I would like us all to have dinner together and talk about the future like three adult people. I should like – "

"You should what?"

"I should like us to be friends, I was about to say."

"You're mad!"

"Don't be bitter, Mark!"

"Watch it, mister!"

"Oh shut up, Bunter! Listen Maddie, we've had all this nonsense before. You're not pregnant, you're just fat. Face up to reality!"

Maddie's lips quivered. She raised a hand to her mouth and gulped back a sob. Roddy advanced angrily, waving his finger like a demented metronome.

"Don't you talk to my . . ." he began, and then petered out, unsure quite how to describe his relationship with Maddie. He coughed. "My fiancée!" he concluded defiantly.

"How can she be your fiancée, thicky, she's still my wife?"

"Well she's going to be mine!"

"And you're bloody welcome to her!"

"Stop it!"

Maddie clapped both hands over her ears and screamed. Roddy tried to say something but Maddie only screamed the louder. She ran out of the room and into the kitchen, slamming the door behind her. The screams continued for a few moments, to be followed by the familiar sound of a plate being smashed against the wall.

"If you want my advice," said Mark, "I'd invest in a stainless steel dinner service."

"I don't want any advice from you mister – "

"Oh shut up!"

Roddy jumped.

"Just shut up you!" Mark repeated angrily. "I've had enough of this. Get out of my house!"

He pushed Roddy away. Roddy stumbled backwards and fell into the sofa. Mark stood over him and glared down scornfully.

The doorbell rang.

"Who's that?" demanded Roddy shrilly, in the tone of a beleaguered settler praying for the cavalry.

"Probably just another one of her lovers," answered Mark acidly.

Roddy trembled. No doubt he would have liked to make a cutting response, but his helpless position on the sofa, in combination with his professional cowardice, had a debilitating effect on his powers of speech. He did manage a slight whimper.

"I'm going to go and answer the front door now," said Mark calmly, "and then I'm going to go upstairs. I shall give you ten minutes to sort out what you have to sort out with Maddie, and then I shall come down again and have my say with her. I do not expect to find you here. In fact, if I ever see you in my house again I shall probably kick your teeth out. I am not naturally a violent man but I'm prepared to make an exception in your case. In future you'll have to conduct your meetings somewhere else. And buy your own bean bag."

The spectacle of himself as decisive man of action, as, say, Fareham's answer to Clint Eastwood, did much for Mark's battered self-esteem. The voice he heard so eloquently phrasing and delivering mortal threats did not seem to belong to him; it was as alien as the physical aggressiveness which accompanied it. Yet it seemed to be called for: it is not every day that a man's wife declares that she is leaving him for another man, and parades the man for his consideration in his own living room. It is surely irrelevant that the marriage itself should be barren and loveless, and that the man paraded cut a preposterous figure. A question of dignity is involved, and the fewer the scraps of pride left to a man, the more will he cling on to them. So thought Mark, anyway, as he drew himself up to his full height (somewhat short of Mr Eastwood's) and gave Roddy one last scornful ultimatum with his eyes before turning his back on the scene of domestic degeneracy and going out to answer the door.

The bell rang again as Mark walked through the dining room. As he opened the door he was just in time to see a dimly outlined back disappearing down the path.

"Hello?"

The back stopped and turned round. The blur of a face emerged out of the darkness.

"Oh, hello there!" said Reg Talbot, with a nervous little laugh. Mark said nothing. He had had his share of surprises for one night. Reg shuffled back cautiously towards the door. "Just a neighbourly visit!" he said, laughing again. "I trust I find you and your wife well!"

Mark made a braying noise through his nose.

"Fine!" said Reg, clapping his hands together and stamping a foot against the cold. "We're well too!"

From somewhere within the house came a muffled noise, halfway between a scream and a sob. Mark stiffened.

"What was that?" asked Reg. Instinctively he tried to peer around Mark's body into the hallway. Equally, Mark half-closed the door behind him to block off the view. Mark rubbed his hands together.

"Brass monkeys, eh?" he laughed. "Still spitting a bit, isn't it?"

"Er yes, I just wondered, that is, my wife and I, now that we've settled in you see, and, er, all that, the community, you know, neighbourhood spirit, I suppose, well I was just saying to her only the other day – "

He stopped in mid-sentence, cut off by a shrieking female voice and the crash of breaking glass. Mark continued to grin fixedly at him.

"Er yes, so er, as I was saying I thought, or we thought, it was perhaps time we got better acquainted, and I wondered if you might like to come over for a drink some time – "

"How about now?"

"Sorry?"

"What a good idea! Let's go now!"

"Now?"

"Yes, no time like the present!"

"What about your wife, would she – "

But Mark had already gone, slamming the door behind him, brushing past Reg and tearing up the path towards the drawbridge.

"No, my wife wouldn't, she's not feeling very well. Come along then!"

Reg followed, feeling strangely reluctant. Yes, this was certainly what he had wanted for a long time, but it was only a part of it, and to tell the truth his neighbour, with his impetuous and unpredictable behaviour, cut a rather alarming figure. It was the wife he really wanted to meet, but then again, if that had been her voice coming from inside the house, what was the explanation for her evident distress? Was there marital strife in his home too? Suddenly Reg thought of Sharon. And of Billy. His mouth went dry. He couldn't see his neighbour in the darkness, but he could hear his footsteps ahead. He hurried to catch up.

"Actually, I've just had a thought. . . . "

He touched Mark's sleeve. Both of them stopped.

"Sharon — that's my wife — she's not feeling too well either. Would you mind if we went out and had a drink somewhere else?"

Mark hesitated.

"We could go down to the pub," Reg suggested. "It's alright, I'll drive!"

Mark gave a bitter little laugh.

"Worried we wouldn't make it in my Wop heap, are you?" He jingled his keys. "My car's perfectly safe, you know, and it's parked just here."

Reg felt himself blush. This wouldn't do at all.

"Ah, yes I've got a little confession to make, if you'll allow me to explain — "

"Ssh!"

Behind them a door had slammed.

"Look!" said Mark hoarsely. "There he goes, sneaking away with his tail between his legs!"

Reg blinked. He couldn't be sure whether he had just seen something, a white blur at hedge height on the edge of the next field, but his neighbour had dashed off in that direction and was busy picking handfuls of gravel off the drive and hurling them at the hedge, while bellowing incomprehensibly at the top of his voice. Feeling rather alarmed, Reg backed away.

"Forget about the drink then, shall we?" he called out half-heartedly over his shoulder, but his neighbour couldn't possibly have heard: he had run some considerable distance along the hedge and was still screaming and throwing gravel.

"Some other time then," murmured Reg, casting a wistful glance in the direction of his neighbour's house. He would still like to meet her, the famous cat owner, Maddie. If her husband's behaviour tonight was anything to go by she must have a lot to put up with. Was he perhaps mad? It must be a strain on a lady of refinement. He could sympathise. He had strains of his own.

A little while later, when he looked again out of his bedroom window, he was not surprised to see the figure of his neighbour still running up and down alongside the hedge, baying.

5

Mark woke very early on Saturday morning. Although he hadn't got to sleep till late the previous night he didn't feel tired; he was much too excited. No doubt it would all catch up with him, but for today he would be sustained by pure child-like energy. This was his favourite day of the year.

He went out at nine o'clock, clutching his carefully packaged lancer under his arm. Nobody was stirring, the house was quiet. He had moved all his things into his study now and saw very little of Maddie anyway. They had had one brief acrimonious dispute late on Thursday night in the wake of Roddy's ignominious flight across the fields, but since then she had refused to talk to him or even, except in exceptional cases, to acknowledge his existence. Yesterday evening, for example, they had both been in the kitchen at the same time, she wolfing down an enormous plate of stew (eating for two, he'd presumed) while he wrestled with a packet of frozen beefburgers. To his inquiring after the location of the salt she had responded with stony silence. Eventually he had gone over to the table and waved his hands in front of her eyes. Anybody in? he had asked. Evidently not, he had concluded. Would she mind if he consulted her solicitor concerning the whereabouts of the salt? Could he take her silence for assent? She had talked about her solicitor a great deal on Thursday night, although as far as he was aware she didn't have one. From an overheard telephone conversation he deduced that she was going out to look for one at the beginning of next week. Apparently she was planning to file for divorce on the grounds of mental cruelty.

But he wasn't going to think about that today. The disruption of his life, the inevitable sale of his home and the division of chattels, all oppressive thoughts would be swept aside for twenty-four hours. Today was the day of the Fareham and District Annual Modellers' Show.

He arrived at Martin Bird's house at a quarter past nine. He saw Jean's head through the kitchen window and she nodded to him to go round the back. As he unlatched the garden gate he heard a loud report, like an engine backfiring. He also heard laughter. Martin was not alone.

He was at the end of the garden in company with two other members of the Civil War Re-enactment Society. The sight of the familiar scarlet coats of the Fareham Regiment of Foote made his heart stop for a moment, but he quickly perceived, even at a distance, that the two visitors were quite the wrong shape to be mistaken for his least favourite halberdier. They were in fact musketeers and their names were Paul and Ted.

"Or Aramis and Brut to their friends!" added Martin jokily. He held in his hands a long-barrelled seventeenth-century-style pistol. He passed it over for Mark's inspection. "Just showing off my little toy," he announced modestly.

"Beautiful!" declared Mark, when he had given the pistol a thorough examination. It was very heavy, solidly constructed and with an elaborately detailed mechanism. He returned it to its owner, who carefully pulled back the cock.

"Ready?"

They all nodded. Martin raised the pistol and aimed it at a metal bucket sitting in the grass only a few feet away. He pulled the trigger and after a split-second pause there was a flash, a puff and a loud bang. It was the same backfiring noise that Mark had heard a few minutes before.

"Got quite a kick!" Martin exclaimed, tucking the pistol under his arm and rubbing his right wrist with his left hand.

"Phew!" said either Paul or Ted (Mark had forgotten which was which). "Look at that!"

He was pointing to the bucket, which had a big round hole in the bottom. Martin picked up the bucket and held the hole to his eye, peering at the others as if through a telescope.

"Kiss me Hardy!" he said, and they laughed.

"There's a hole in your bucket, dear Liza!" said Ted or Paul, and they laughed again.

"What the hell did you do that with?" asked Mark.

Martin put down the bucket and stuck a hand in one of his deep coat pockets. He pulled out a fistful of metal balls and offered them to Mark. He took one and examined it critically. It was heavy and solid and perfectly round.

"Soft lead. Made with my own fair hand," Martin said.

"You'd certainly know about it if you got hit by one of these!" said Mark, and Ted/Paul agreed. They all looked at the bucket for confirmation. The hole in the bottom had been punched out cleanly and the missing ball was too deeply embedded in the lawn for them to be able to get it out with their fingers.

"It's like I've always said," Martin continued, "despite all the inaccuracy and inefficiency of your old muzzle-loaders, once you get down to the nitty-gritty, at point-blank range they're every bit as deadly as your modern handgun. I have to admit to one small cheat — I've used firing caps instead of flints, but apart from that this is in every respect your one hundred per cent genuine reproduction article."

They all made admiring noises. They agreed that this time Martin had excelled even by his own standards. His skills as a metalworker and amateur gunsmith were legendary, and he supplied not only his own Civil War Society but others as well, not to mention a couple of American Civil War groups, the Buckinghamshire Jousters and the ever popular Berkshire Housecarles. And nor was he cheap: muskets and arquebuses started at over a hundred pounds, and a full set of medieval armour could cost anything up to a grand. Most re-enactors had, perforce, to settle for something less than the full rig. Roddy, for instance, had made do with a breastplate (£65) and halberd (£27.50, all prices inclusive of VAT).

After the demonstration the two musketeers went off to practise their drill in preparation for the afternoon's regimental muster. Martin took Mark into his workshop, where Jean brought them coffee. Mark was glad of the chance for a chat. He told his friend about recent developments.

"I never liked that prat Roddy!" declared Martin roundly. "Would you like me to put my boot in at the muster?"

Mark laughed.

"I'm serious!" said Martin, pointing a finger for emphasis. "I'll have a word with some of the lads. He deserves punishment, you know. That kind of behaviour isn't allowed in the King's army. Roundheads do that sort of thing."

"You don't have a ducking stool, do you?"

It did Mark good to laugh. Martin told him about seventeenth-century methods of torture and Mark had to draw up a list of the order in which he would like them inflicted on Roddy. Mark's only worry was that Roddy might be too big to fit the various apparatus. Martin promised that he would cut him down to size.

"If it all gets too much for you at home," said Martin seriously, "you know that you're more than welcome to come and stay here. Remember, we're going away next Friday, and we'll be gone for a fortnight. You could have the place to yourself."

"Thanks Mart, you're a pal," said Mark with genuine feeling. "I may have to take you up on that. Things have been getting a bit on top of me recently."

Martin patted him on the shoulder.

"In a way I feel it's all my fault. If I hadn't invited him to my Christmas party Maddie would never even have met him."

"Don't be silly. Let's not talk about him any more. I want to enjoy myself today."

They set off for the show just before ten. The doors weren't due to open until half past, but they noticed on their arrival that quite a large crowd was forming already.

As usual, the show was being held in the Fareham community centre. This was a large, modern building situated over the road from the bottom of the High Street on the outskirts of Fareham park. There was a large car park, room inside the extensive main hall for all the trade stands and display tables, and loads of space outside where the various re-enactors could do their stuff. Re-enactments were increasingly a feature of all the modelling shows. They weren't Mark's cup of tea, but there was no denying that they were crowd-pullers.

Mark registered his model at the competition table. It was nearly 10.30 and the stallholders were making their last-minute preparations. As the doors were about to open Mark retreated into a corner and consulted his programme, planning how best to spend the action-packed day.

The various types of events were neatly cordoned off by area. The left-hand side of the hall was devoted to trade stands. This was the part Mark always enjoyed most: he relished the opportunity of speaking with the manufacturers, examining the year's new offerings at first hand and giving his suggestions for new lines. The right-hand side was given over to the war gamers, who were putting on demonstration games covering all periods from Ancient to Modern with a couple of SciFi/Fantasy scenarios for good measure (Mark had already been asked if he fancied being an Orc Commander in a Participation Game, to which he had happily replied in the negative). He liked looking at the games, admiring the well-painted little figures and the cleverly constructed terrain, but he had never enjoyed playing them. It had been the same at school: team games had never appealed to him; he had always been a bit of a loner. He couldn't conceive of a more suitable hobby than the solitary pursuit of model-making.

The small stage at the back had been designated a Refreshment Area, and there was a makeshift Bar and Cafeteria. Doors on either side of the stage led off to the Competition Room, where all the models, including Mark's, were displayed, and the Demonstration Room, where two Famous Modellers were giving examples of their Painting Techniques. Mark looked forward to meeting them, and to an exchange of views on the merits of commercially produced Weathering Powders. The other Demonstration Area was outside, where the acre or so of grass in front of the community centre provided ample room for the manoeuvres of the various re-enactors. There was quite a mixed bag this year, Napoleonic and World War II groups as well as Martin's Civil War lot. The Changing Area was in the Long Annexe. It was quite a relief after reading through the programme to turn to the Club President's Note of Welcome and read through two whole paragraphs devoid of all but strictly necessary capital letters.

Mark enjoyed the next few hours immensely, circulating, observing, purchasing, gossiping. It was particularly satisfying to meet up with old friends and exchange news and views. By lunchtime the hall was filled to capacity; it was scarcely possible to move. The show was becoming more and more popular with each passing year. Unfortunately, a disproportionately large number of people appeared to suffer from a serious B.O. problem. It was quite a relief to get outside again, where, at two o'clock, the English Civil War was due for re-enactment.

Not the whole Civil War, of course, but as much as could be reasonably represented by twenty-five participants. Martin was at their head, swaggering about in his enormous boots and breeches and black laminated armour. He wore an immense floppy hat with a plume like a feather boa. He was every inch a Cavalier and a gentleman. Ted/Paul and a few other musketeers were lining up behind him, and behind them came the pikemen and halberdiers. There was in addition a miniature cannon, which was hauled into place by a reluctant donkey and pointed menacingly at the crowd. A couple of halberdiers helped position it. One of them was Roddy.

It was definitely Roddy, even in the big helmet with the ear flaps tied down ("the moron in the morion" Martin had christened him). There was no one else who filled out his costume quite so extravagantly, and certainly no one who moved anything like as ponderously. If he hadn't helped position the cannon it would have taken half the time. His short-sightedness was so bad that when he rejoined the line of halberdiers he stood for half a minute facing the wrong way. Mark wasn't the only member of the audience to laugh, although he was certainly the noisiest.

"Enjoying ourselves, are we?"

Mark froze. The sarcastic nasal whinge was as unmistakable as it was unexpected. He turned slowly towards the voice, a stupid half-grin fixing itself on his features.

"Hello Lizzie. . . . "

He heard his own voice trailing away, the last syllable of her name dropping into silence and becoming one with those four dots that hung in the air like smoke signals. He mouthed another, dumb hello.

The words his lips framed were "Hello Maddie".

Maddie turned away dramatically. She had been crying and she was literally clinging with both hands to Lizzie Skinner's arms. She took away one of the hands long enough to dab at her cheek with a tissue, which she waved briefly and uselessly in the direction of the myopic halberdier.

"Yes, that's right, Mark," drawled Lizzie, "It's your wife. Or should I perhaps say your doormat?"

Maddie clung more tightly to her and sobbed. Mark's grin had extended to his ears. Lizzie's was one of those voices that always automatically evoked the analogy of a knife cutting through butter, although an entire dairy wouldn't have lasted five minutes. Already several heads had turned in their direction.

"Ha! Ha! Ha!" he laughed nervously. Perhaps he could pretend that it was all just joky banter; then perhaps the several heads would turn away. "What a pleasant surprise! Didn't expect to see you here!"

"It's a free country, isn't it?"

"Oh yes! that's not what I – "

"Just because you act the little fascist dictator at home doesn't mean you can get away with lording it over other people in public!"

"Oh no, I really didn't – "

"Everyone seems to be wearing fancy dress here. Why don't you go and dress up in your Hitler suit?"

"Ha! Ha! Ha! Ha!"

His laughter was worse than nervous now, it was frankly hysterical. A fair number of heads turned in his direction, drawn by Lizzie's fairground barking. He pulled up his collar and tried to retract his head. He prayed for an act of Divine Intervention and, curiously enough, God may have been listening. At any rate there was a loud bang and a great deal of commotion, and when all the heads turned round again to see if the interesting diversion would be resumed, Mark had sneaked away.

The loud bang was caused by the discharge of the cannon, which Martin always used as an attention-grabber. It was invariably a successful ploy, because the gun, although tiny, made an enormous amount of noise and produced clouds of thick white smoke. As Martin never announced the first firing of the gun it had the effect of a tremendous *coup de théâtre*. There was a ripple of spontaneous applause.

Mark shuffled along to the far end of the crowd, managing to blush and seethe at the same time. He heard Martin's voice, muffled by the bodies between them, introducing himself and his merry band.

This was unbearable! What was Maddie doing following him here? Was nowhere safe? It might be a free country, but what about his freedom to live in a bit of peace? And just like her to bring a minder, all to see her precious Roddy! There he was now, earnestly shouldering his halberd and stiffening to attention while Martin gave a quick resumé of seventeenth-century infantry tactics. The musketeers came forward and levelled their weapons.

"Oh God! I hope they're not going to fire those things over here!"

Mark pulled his collar up even higher and thrust his head down behind the nearest body.

"Oh dear, I hate guns!"

In its own way the voice was every bit as distinctive as Lizzie Skinner's.

"Darling, do you have any cotton wool on you, I think I should plug my ears. . . . "

He saw her as she stepped back out of the crowd, fiddling in her handbag: tall and rangy and red of face, looking as if she should have had 'Organically Grown' stamped across her forehead. And 'Bank Manager's Wife' sewn into her knickers.

"Oh Vera, do hurry, I can't stand loud bangs!"

The crowd jostled and parted and he caught a glimpse of him, standing with a face as white as his wife's was red, and both hands pressed to his ears: what would be sewn into his underwear? 'W.W.Vernon – Wimp'.

Was there no wretched corner of this allegedly free world where he could be left in peace? What in heaven's name were the Vernons doing here? Trouble to the left of him, trouble to the right of him. . . . He slunk towards some median point in the crowd and wove himself anonymously between the bodies, half-expecting them to reveal themselves as the Talbot family, Fareham's answer to the Munsters.

The muskets popped, quite loudly but hardly enough to engender panic. Some members of the audience emitted relieved laughter. Mark caught a glimpse of Vernon, still holding his hands up to his head, no doubt suspecting that this was only a prelude to more aural horror.

"Ladies and gentlemen, the Fareham Regiment of Foote bid you welcome."

There was polite applause, which Martin acknowledged with a cavalier bow.

"You have just witnessed a demonstration of musketry drill, one half of the components of seventeenth-century warfare. The other half being, of course, the pikemen or, less commonly, the halberdiers. Gentlemen of the Foote, present your pikes!"

Roddy and friends swung into action, thrusting their best feet forward belligerently and inclining the tips of their weapons towards the onlookers. Martin explained to the crowd that during their "battles" they always took care to keep their weapons pointed upwards; "Safety First!" was their unofficial motto.

"And now we will demonstrate the Push of Pike!"

The re-enactors split into two groups, dutifully keeping their weapons up. They lined up behind each other, like two tug-of-war teams. Roddy was near the front of his group. Ted and Paul, the musketeers, tacked themselves on to the back of the other group to provide greater depth. Martin drew his new pistol from its holster and aimed skywards.

"Pikemen at the ready!"

He cocked the pistol.

"And Push!"

He fired and the two lines clattered into each other, grunting and heaving. For a moment it looked as though Roddy's line had got the upper hand, but then the others managed to muster themselves for one decisive effort and they rallied back victoriously, knocking their front three opponents, Roddy included, to the ground, and scattering the rest. As the line rolled over the three "corpses" on the grass, Ted and Paul slightly detached themselves. While the others stopped to throw their caps and helmets into the air in victory celebration, Ted and Paul kept on running, towards where Roddy had fallen on his back after an elaborately cinematic death, arms and legs splayed like a starfish. Ted and Paul bunched up, dropped their heads and readjusted their pace.

Mark's mouth was dry. He could hardly bear to watch. The scene unfolded itself in slow motion.

The first boot swung up parallel to Roddy's legs and caught him full in the balls. Roddy's body jerked electrically and he tried to sit up, his cheeks inflating like a bellows. Almost at the same moment the second foot caught him squarely in the face and the cheeks deflated like a pricked balloon, sending the large white head cracking back against the ground. The two musketeers ran on and joined the cheering pikemen. Roddy lay completely still.

Mark held his breath. Despite his own impression he knew that the act of grievous bodily harm which he had just witnessed had been the work of moments, and well-concealed among the forest of legs and flying feet. At the same time it had been so blatant an act of aggression that it was hard to imagine it slipping by unnoticed. The men were lining up again now, reforming their ranks, and the "corpses" were getting up to join them. One of them shook Roddy's shoulder. There was no response. He knelt down and lifted up the head in his hands. As he did so the inert head rolled towards the crowd and the squashed and bloody pulp of his nose became visible. Maddie screamed and help came running.

Mark found himself jostled to one side as stretcher-bearers pushed through the crowd. Even with help they couldn't lift the lifeless body. They fumbled with straps and removed his breastplate and accoutrements.

"Isn't that Mark Harvey's wife, darling?"

"Where, Vera?"

Mark dived back into the crowd. Roddy's accident had really woken people up, and they were pressing in on the stretcher party from all sides; no one wanted to miss the sight of real blood. In the confusion Mark found himself thrown almost bodily against Lizzie Skinner.

"Hi there!" He beamed at her stupidly.

"I bet you had something to do with this, you nasty piece of work!"

"Ha! Ha! Must dash!"

Dash his brains out against the nearest wall, he thought to himself, as he slunk away back to the hall. Why was everyone so intent on ruining his favourite day of the year? What were they all doing here? Couldn't he get any peace anywhere? He ran off into the sanctuary of the members' room to ponder these and other related questions. The afternoon passed miserably.

About five o'clock Martin appeared in the doorway, grinning all over his face. No, Roddy was perfectly alright, he said in answer to Mark's question, although that certainly had been something worth laughing about! No, he hadn't come to bury Roddy, but to praise Mark.

"What do you mean?"

"You've won, lad, you're a star!"

"Won what?"

"What do you think? An Oscar? The Iron Cross, First Class?"

"You don't mean. . . ."

"Oh yes I do! You have won not only the Single Model Class First Prize but also the Best of Show Award, viz. the coveted H.G.Wells Cut Glass Bowl and inscribed silver-plated cup! What do you say to that, sunshine!"

There wasn't a lot he could say to that. He just sat down and stared at his friend, and enjoyed the sensation of baffled contentment. Martin grinned at him.

"Can't have you sitting here and moping all day," he said warmly. "I'll get some drinks in. Life's not all bad news, you know. And remember, we did stitch up that Roddy a treat!"

Mark laughed.

"You wouldn't like to do the same for her, would you?"

6

A warm glow was spreading through Mark's body. In part it had something to do with the considerable quantity of whisky and champagne which he had consumed earlier in the evening, but its true fount lay in the trinity of precious objects which he had lined up carefully on the sideboard: the cup, the bowl and, between them, *primus inter pares*, the triumph of his art, "Reasoning Why", in all its varnished glory.

He must make a special display cabinet for it, that was certain. The cup and the bowl would have to be returned next year, but he would commission replicas for permanent commemoration. A wall cabinet would be best, with three compartments side by side like a triptych, glass-fronted to keep the dreaded dust away. It should hang on the wall close to a window, where the light was good, perhaps with its own little spotlight for night-time illumination.

He refilled his glass and settled back comfortably in the armchair. The fire was blazing, it was cosy. Cosy and comfortable, being at home on his own (Roger was upstairs somewhere but he didn't count), sitting peacefully in his favourite chair and recalling the proudest moment of his life. It had certainly been that; nothing else came close: the memory of his standing there on the stage at the community centre, cup and bowl in arms, flanked by Famous Modellers, all beams for the local newspaper's photographer and for the applauding members and visitors massed below. . . . All he had lacked was a laurel wreath. And perhaps a slave to stand at his elbow and whisper from time to time intimations of mortality.

It was the first time in seven years that one of the Society's own members had won the coveted Best of Show award. One of the Famous Modellers remarked that he shouldn't be surprised if "Reasoning Why" made the front cover of *Military Modelling*. Mark's head swam with the thought of it. Or was it the whisky? Perhaps he should have another one, just in case. . . . He giggled to himself and lingered fondly at the sideboard with the bottle in hand, drinking in with his eyes the Configurations of Victory.

He sank back happily into his chair and turned his face towards the fire. Lazily he bathed in the warmth. It was cold out tonight, winter was drawing in. There would be a frost. There would be all manner of discomfort and unpleasantness in the coming times, but for the present he would forget about all that. He would sit before the fire, and doze and dream of his triumphs, and when he woke he would see the blessed trinity standing before him on the sideboard, and he would be the happiest man in the Kingdom. He would.

He woke with a start. There had been a loud noise, he had heard it even in his sleep. Was it a noise like gunfire, or had that been a dream? The fire was a little lower, but it was still bright. He looked at his watch: it was just after ten, he could only have been asleep a matter of minutes.

Someone was in the kitchen. He heard crockery being lifted out of the sink. It must be Roger. He yawned and rubbed his eyes. He had a bit of a headache. Not surprising, considering how much he'd drunk. His throat was dry. He could do with some coffee.

He walked out into the kitchen.

"Hi!" he said amiably, without looking.

It was Maddie.

He remained in the doorway, hovering uncertainly. After a moment she turned away from him and back to the sink. She lifted the last of the plates out and reached for the kettle.

"Fill it for two, will you?"

She didn't acknowledge him. She put the kettle on. She pulled one mug down from the rack. She lit a cigarette.

"You don't smoke!"

She walked away with the cigarette and stood staring out of the window into the darkness. Her eyes were red and swollen, but there was no expression in them. Her silence was impressive, but there was an underlying tension that belied her seeming calm.

"I think it'll rain."

She didn't answer. The smoke she blew out through her lips wreathed her hair, changing prettily from grey to blue in the uncertain light. That was nice, Mark thought. It would have made an arty photograph.

He turned away almost guiltily, treading lightly on the

floorboards, afraid of impinging on the quietness. He returned to the fire in the living room and warmed his hands for a minute.

Maddie came in, holding a cup of coffee. He edged away discreetly and she sat in the armchair. She turned on the reading lamp and opened a magazine. He went out into the kitchen.

The kettle was almost empty. He muttered irritably under his breath as he refilled it. He reached for the coffee jar and found it empty. He opened the cupboard and couldn't find any more. He went back into the living room.

"Look," he said, trying to sound calm and reasonable. "We may have had our differences, but let's at least try to live in a civilised fashion. You could have put enough in the kettle for me, you know, I did ask you. The coffee's finished. Is there any more?"

She shook her head, once. He shrugged and made an exasperated noise.

"Well, you could have bought some more. It's not much to ask."

He went back out to the kitchen and found an Earl Grey tea bag, which he dunked unenthusiastically in a cup of hot water. He added Long Life milk and a spoonful of castor sugar. It tasted like sweet milky water.

He returned to the living room. Maddie had turned off the main light, leaving only her table lamp to read by. That was thoughtless of her. Or had it been deliberate? The knot of irritation tightened in his stomach. He turned the main light back on again.

"Do you mind?"

The first words she had spoken to him in days evoked no response. He was staring at the sideboard.

"Why have you moved my things?"

His voice was a hoarse whisper. She tutted and muttered under her breath before returning to her magazine. He advanced on the sideboard in an agitated state and angrily pushed to one side the vase of flowers which she must have just replaced there. The bowl was behind it, and he saw that she had put the model on a chair.

"What have you done with my cup?"

She didn't answer. She turned the page.

"What the. . . . "

He had seen it now, or at least the bottom of it, the baize base of the black plinth. The cup was upside down in the waste-paper basket. His prize-winning cup.

"What did you. . . . ?"

He could hardly speak. The cup had become detached from the plinth, to which it had been firmly glued. She must have thrown it into the basket with considerable force to have done that. One of the handles bore a slight scratch. He put the plinth back down on the sideboard and the cup on top of it. It would be alright. He could fix it, but —

"How dare you!"

It was a scream of rage. At least he had found his voice. She couldn't ignore it.

"I could say the same!" she shouted back, throwing the magazine down and rising.

"How dare you damage my things!"

"How dare you destroy my life!"

"You stupid bitch!"

"Don't talk to me like that!"

"I'll talk to you how I want! It's my home, isn't it?"

"We'll see what my solicitor's got to say about that!"

"Stop going on about your bloody solicitor!"

"Don't swear at me!"

"Fuck off!"

"Fuck off yourself! I know damn well what you've been up to, you and your sick friends! Lizzie saw the look Martin gave you after they'd beaten up poor Roddy. You were all in it together, you're all in a conspiracy against me, against us, against the only man I've ever loved, who's worth more than the lot of you put together and all your stupid little cups and bowls and toy soldiers, you vindictive, spiteful, vicious man!"

"They're not toy soldiers."

"Don't interrupt me! I haven't finished!"

"Well I have! I've had enough of listening to this crap!"

"You're a disgusting coward! You can't even face up to Roddy man to man, you've got to get your friends to do your dirty work for you!"

"Face up to Roddy! It would be like throwing a cripple in the river!"

"How dare you talk like that about the man I love!"

"He's a wimp, Maddie! A pathetic, fat dumb no-hoper with MORON stamped all over his forehead in indelible ink!"

"I hate you!"

"You deserve each other! Good bloody riddance and the best of luck to him. If you need anyone to give you away at the marriage, give me a call, I'd be delighted, although none of us can pretend you're the bargain of the century!"

"You Nazi!"

"Oh, that stung! I thought you'd never get around to that one. Excuse me a moment, I've just got to pop out and annexe Poland."

"Don't be cheap! Thank God I'm going to have Roddy to protect me in future!"

"I'd rather have a brown shirt than a brown tongue."

"Don't be disgusting. I'm glad our child won't be raised in this atmosphere."

"Oh not that again! You're about as pregnant as this carpet, darling!"

She hit him. She was a big woman, there was a lot behind her slap. He staggered backwards, slipped and fell, clutching his jaw. He tasted blood. She was standing over him, shaking with indignation.

"I'm going to speak to my solicitor first thing Monday morning. I'm going to get a court order on you, get you out of my home and away from me as soon as possible."

"Your home!"

"Yes, I'm the one who slaves and cleans and makes it a home. You can get out, and take all your stupid things with you!"

"Maddie, no! — "

It was a piercing scream, enough to shatter glass.

"No!"

A crystal shower glittered in the air. Fragments caught the light, like tiny shooting stars that fell and gleamed as moondust on the carpet. The noise of breaking glass was loud and sharp. The wall behind him hummed; the plaster was dented where the crystal bowl had disintegrated against it.

She was speaking. He didn't hear it. She had turned, she was walking away, past the fire, towards the door. She had knocked over the cup in passing; it was rolling gently on the carpet from side to side.

He was screaming at her. He didn't know what he was saying. She stopped, she was shouting back. They were in front of the fire. She was red in the face, she was shaking her fist. His hands were round her throat. He shook her.

What was she saying? He couldn't understand it. There was a roar in his head, like the tide going out, the shooshing of sea over the pebbles. She was kicking him, his shins ached. He couldn't hear her now, although he could see her mouth opening and shutting. Her face was even redder. The thick veins stood out on her forehead. Her eyes bulged, like ping-pong balls. Her hands were vices on his wrists. She fell back. He had to let her go.

"You stupid bitch!"

She didn't answer. She had sunk back into the armchair. She was clutching at her throat, making a curious rattling noise. She looked almost comical. He would have laughed but he was still too angry.

"It's not even my bowl! I've only got it on loan for the year!"

His cheeks were hot. He brushed them with the back of his hand and found them wet with tears. He slumped on to the sofa and covered his face with his palms. Maddie gasped weakly.

"And the cup! You'd better not have damaged the model!"

He jumped up and ran back to the sideboard. He picked the diorama off the chair and examined it anxiously. It seemed to be alright. Maddie groaned.

"Oh shut up! Don't expect any sympathy from me!"

He put down the diorama and picked up the cup and loose base. It was definitely scratched.

"There's no need to behave like this, you know, there's no need. I didn't have anything to do with hurting Roddy, really I didn't, and I've never meant to hurt you either. We've had our differences, that's all, and you're always overreacting, you're always damaging things. Like that time you threw the teapot at me. That was my mother's teapot, I was very attached to that. You never think about the hurt you cause, do you? I've got feelings too, you know, you and your precious Roddy don't have a monopoly. How do you think I feel in all this? Pretty miserable, I'll tell you. Pretty miserable and lonely. I haven't got loads of friends to turn to like you have. If you kick me out of my own home where am I to go? I'm not trying to deny you your share, but you seem pretty keen on depriving me of mine. It's the injustice, Maddie, I resent. Let's at least behave decently towards each other and not break each other's things up. You've got less to be bitter about than I have, you know. At least you've got someone to look after you. . . . "

Suddenly it became unbearable. He sobbed. A tidal wave of self-pity swept over him.

68

"Excuse me. . . . "

He ran out of the room. In the hallway he almost knocked over Roger, who had just come downstairs.

"Is things alright, Mark, I've been hearing the most terrible racket. . . . "

He didn't reply. He didn't even hear the end of the sentence. He had run into the bathroom and locked the door behind him. He closed the toilet seat, sat down on it and burst into tears. There was a pain in his chest. There were aching twinges in other parts of his body, especially his fingers. He cried his eyes out, ripping great chunks of toilet paper off the holder on the wall. Eventually his sobs became dry. He washed his face and bathed his eyes with Optrex. He blew his nose one last time, thoroughly, and unlocked the bathroom.

"I'm sorry Rog, I'm a bit. . . . "

He didn't know what to say. He stood in the kitchen doorway, staring at the floor. Roger was making a cup of tea. He seemed to have found a fresh pack of tea bags from somewhere.

"S'alright Mark. No business of mine. Fancy a cuppa?"

He sounded quite bright and friendly. At least, he sounded considerably less gloomy than usual. In anyone else his tone would have probably passed for indifferent.

"I've had a good thought, you know," he said, tapping his nose meaningfully.

"Oh yes?" said Mark, sounding interested, which he wasn't, knowing perfectly well what species this "thought" must belong to.

"New technique I've worked out," Roger explained, fractionally lowering his voice. "Quick and painless. One hundred per cent success rate. No mess. Do you think Maddie would like a cup of tea?"

"I'll ask her."

He knew that she wouldn't, but he needed an excuse to get out of the kitchen. Anything was preferable to a conversation with Roger about suicide. Even Maddie.

He went back into the living room. She was still sitting on the armchair. The magazine she had been reading was on the floor, where she had thrown it earlier. He picked it up and turned to the back, where he found the Problem Page, his favourite.

"Roger says do you fancy a cup of tea?"

She didn't answer. He pursed his lips and carried on reading.

"I thought you wouldn't. I only asked. She doesn't want one, Roger!"

He read in silence for half a minute. He laughed softly to himself. A woman had written in to ask if her husband was a pervert because he kept wanting to do it in different places all round the house and not in the bed. She was worried about the postman peeking through the window and she didn't like it because it was uncomfortable on the floor. She wanted to know what she should do. It seemed obvious to Mark. Get a bean bag. He could sell her one cheap, secondhand.

"Amazing things they write in these magazines," he said, only half aloud. He didn't expect a response from Maddie. She had obviously decided to return to her old taciturn ways and wasn't going to talk to him again. No doubt he'd be having to write to her wretched solicitor for an update on the tea-bag situation.

"Shall I bring it in, Mark?" Roger called from the kitchen.

"Thanks Rog, that's good of you!"

He put down the magazine.

"Maddie, don't stare at me like – "

His hands fell limply to his sides. The blood drained from his head. He gaped at her with wide-open lifeless eyes. Eyes as lifeless as her own.

"Put it here Mark, okay?"

He didn't answer. He didn't even nod. He couldn't have done. There was no motion in his body, save the shallowest of breathing. Roger didn't seem to notice. He put the tea mug down on the small table.

"Night, Mark. Night, Maddie."

He didn't look at either of them. His eyes were on the floor, as usual. He sloped out of the room. Thoughtfully, he closed the door after him.

Mark heard him go up the stairs. He heard the scraping of his feet on the ladder to the attic. He could hear all the tiny sounds of the house, the faint creakings and the groanings, and outside the wind.

He knew what had happened. He had known it at once, in the same split second he had set eyes on her. It hadn't even occurred to him that it might be a trick of the light, a vision, a dream. And yet those would have been quite natural responses, if only for that fraction of a second. No, he knew what had happened.

He got up from the sofa. Strength came to him from somewhere, he did not feel it within him. There was nothing within him but a soggy pulp. He moved ethereally, but at the same time clumsily, as if finding himself in possession of an alien body and operating it by remote control. During an eternity he stepped across the carpet. He stood in front of the armchair.

He touched her face. It was warm, but a cold shock ran through him. He realised that the whole of that side of her body was warm, but it was the fire. There was no warmth in her blood. No life in her veins. Her ping-pong eyes seemed to be staring across the room, at the place where he had been sitting, but they saw nothing. They had not even seen him when he had sat there, a minute ago, reading her magazine. The soggy pulp inside him ran nauseous. He tried to keep the thought down, the thought which was trying to rise like bad oysters, the thought which ran:

I sat here and read the magazine and laughed in my head at her, while she sat opposite, dead.

Probably she had been dead for ten minutes before that. Probably, while he had sat weeping in the toilet, she had been gasping her last, dying on her own, in the armchair. While he had been feeling sorry for himself. Perhaps she had called out for help. And the one time he might have been any use to her he was sitting there pathetically in the bathroom, pitying himself.

He was sitting again on the sofa. He couldn't remember sitting down, but he was glad that he had done so: there was no feeling at all in his legs; not much strength in any part of him. What had happened? He had heard her making funny noises. She must have had a heart attack. He'd seen it coming for years. He'd warned her often enough. You just couldn't afford to behave like that, stuffing your face all day and never taking any exercise. There must have been so much cholesterol in her blood it was amazing that it could circulate at all. Why had she never taken proper care of herself? Fancy letting your arteries clog up with fat before even turning forty! She had only herself to blame.

"And you! You bloody strangled her!"

He jumped at the sound of his own voice. The sense of remote control was magnified a thousandfold; he didn't even retain the use of his own vocal chords. He hadn't meant to speak out loud. He hadn't meant to accuse himself. He hadn't done anything. They had had a fight, that was all. She had started it, she had smashed up his crystal bowl, and she'd kicked him, he had the bruises on his shins. He had only retaliated. He hadn't meant to choke her. He hadn't meant to press so hard on her throat. He hadn't meant to kill her.

He had killed her. He could see the red marks on her throat in the pattern of his finger spread. Perhaps the marks would go, but the pathologist would find the bruises underneath when he opened her up. There was no hiding that kind of thing from the eyes of the forensic scientist. There was no point in him trying to conceal anything, it would all come out at the inquest anyway. They would find out about the rows and the fights, piece it all together from the witnesses. Tonight even Roger had heard something, and he never noticed anything. He hadn't even noticed that she was dead, when he had brought the tea in! The tea must be getting cold now. He'd better have a sip before it was too late. No, it was too late. It was lukewarm, he only liked it piping hot. He staggered to his feet again. Everything was a bit of a blur. At least there was water in the kettle. He went next door into the kitchen and turned it on. What should he do? Call the police. He must do that, and right away, because they could tell what time someone had died, and if he left it too long they would think he was trying to cover it up. He couldn't have them think that, it was going to be bad enough for him already. No, he ought to face it squarely, conceal nothing, get it over with. He ought to be able to find character witnesses in his defence. Martin would say something good about him. The blame hadn't been just on his side, the rows had been going on for years, he'd just lost his temper for a moment and gone a bit berserk, and because she was so overweight she had had a coronary. That was it. A normal, healthy woman wouldn't have been affected by a bit of mild strangling. It happened in most marriages, after all. They couldn't even prove that that had been the cause of death. Even if they could it would only be manslaughter. He might not even have to go to prison.

A noise penetrated his thoughts. He thought it was a familiar noise but he couldn't recognise it, though it was very insistent. It was coming from the other side of the room. He walked over towards it, and when he saw the phone on the wall he realised what it was. Perhaps it was the police phoning him up, saving him the trouble of having to contact them. That was very thoughtful of them. They were very efficient, the police, and very clever. They had probably had some psychic intuition that there was going to be trouble at his place tonight. He lifted the receiver.

"Hello?" he whispered.

"Darling?"

The phone began to slip through his fingers. He caught it instinctively with his other hand. The rest of him was paralysed.

"Darling, are you there?"

He sounded anxious. No wonder he sounded anxious, with poor dead Maddie lying in the armchair next door.

"Roddy – "

"Oh darling, it's good to hear your voice!"

Mark stared blankly at the phone. He wanted to say something more, but he couldn't think what.

"Darling can you talk? Is he there?"

Of course he was there, Mark thought. He knew who "he" was, there wasn't much doubt about that, the poor simple little pronoun was parenthesised in venom. He was him, and him was on the phone. Him was talking to Roddy right now, or trying to, if only he could get his mind and body to coordinate properly.

"He is there, isn't he? Look, don't say anything, I just wanted to check you'd got home safely. I'll ring you in the morning. Sleep tight darling, and goodnight!"

"Roddy, there's something I should tell you."

"Tell me in the morning. I can tell by your whispering he must be close by. Goodnight my angel!"

The receiver clicked off. Mark heard the dialling tone. He uttered an expletive.

"I wasn't whispering! What are you talking about, you deaf old goat? Goodnight my angel! She is your bloody angel now! I'd like to see her dancing on a bloody pinhead. . . . "

His burst of eloquence dried up as suddenly as it had begun to flow. He was left staring at the silent receiver, aghast at his own tastelessness. Was it really he who had said that? Were there no depths to which he could not sink? As if committing a murder wasn't enough! Why did he have to crack jokes about it afterwards? No, that hadn't been his intention. He hadn't meant to murder her, and it was manslaughter anyway, not murder. Nor had he meant to be sarcastic afterwards. What if he said something like that to the police? Not deliberately, but what if it slipped out? It could, just like that. It wasn't at all far-fetched, it was just the sort of thing that might innocently come out; the sort of thing that when read aloud dispassionately in court sounded ten times worse than it really was.

He blinked sweat out of his eyes. He could feel it trickling down his collar. The back of his shirt was soaking. He was in such a state he could hardly stand. He sat down on the kitchen stool. Only then did he notice how much his legs were shaking; they were knocking together so much the kitchen table vibrated. He moved them away from the table legs. He crossed his arms on the table top and rested his head on them. He just didn't know what to do. He didn't know what to say, how to explain himself. He was frightened.

Even if he only got a few years how would he be able to cope? A prison was a prison, the term itself was secondary, it was the fact of the place itself that counted. They'd probably put him in with the other killers, hardened criminals, not his own, merely occasional type. Who might he find himself in a cell with? Some multiple axe murderer with incurable psychopathic tendencies, not to mention insatiable and perverse sexual desires? Nothing in Mark's life had ever prepared him for the idea of prison. He had no real experience of collective discipline, of arbitrary, tyrannical regimes. He hadn't even been to public school. He was far too young to have known National Service. And thank God for that! he'd always thought. He had found even the Boy Scouts too rough; he had handed in his toggle after only a fortnight. Life behind bars would be unbearable. Even six months would kill him. And what would he do when he got out? They wouldn't re-employ a criminal at the bank. Not at less than board-room level anyway. What then would become of him? Would he still get a pension? He'd have nothing else to live on. He would be forced to begin a life of crime in earnest, to survive. This was ridiculous!

He banged his fists so hard against the table that they stung. He saw his reflection dimly in the window pane and grimaced at it.

"This is ridiculous!" he groaned out loud. "Here am I with the dead body of my wife in the living room and I'm worrying about my career prospects. What's the matter with me? Have I lost all sense of perspective? I've got to face the consequences of what I've done! Face up to them like a man! Ring the police!"

He snatched up the phone and dialled 999 as quickly as possible, not giving himself any time to think. The ringing tone came on at once, but no one answered. He counted the rings. Twenty-one, twenty-two, twenty-three. . . . He would give it to thirty and then stop. It was answered on twenty-eight.

"Police!" he barked back at the operator, hardly giving her time to finish. This was it. He had to go through with it now.

There was a pause while he was connected. He counted away the seconds, the seconds of his freedom. How long would it take for them to get here? Perhaps only a few minutes. They would take him into custody tonight. He would have to sleep in a cell. With other criminals. Did they take the handcuffs off? What other criminals?

"Hello? Is there anybody there?"

The voice was not unpleasant. In fact it was rather gentle, with a trace of country burr. Surely the owner of this kind voice wouldn't leave him to the tender mercies of whatever violent offenders they were already entertaining for the night.

"Hello," he answered. He thought for a moment. What should he say first and why hadn't he worked it out before.

"Who is that speaking?"

"I'm a member of the public. I may have something to report. Can you tell me who else you've got in your cells tonight?"

There was no answer at the other end. Mark blushed.

"I realise this may seem rather a peculiar question, but you don't have any violent sex offenders in at the moment, do you?"

"Who the hell are you?"

"I'm just interested in who your other guests are, as it were, only it may have a bearing on the case at issue – "

"Look, mate!" the policeman cut back in tersely. The voice didn't sound at all soft and kind now. "It's arseholes like you who really piss me off. While you're blocking this line someone with a real emergency may be trying to get through, so why don't you – "

Mark slammed the phone down and jumped back a step, as if afraid it would bite. Perhaps prompted by that thought, he began to chew the back of his hand. His own cowardice amazed and disheartened him. What could he do? Take a leaf out of Roger's book and top himself? Why didn't he at least have a word with Roger? – talk with another human being before he went completely mad.

He walked out of the kitchen into the dining room. He hesitated outside the living room door. He could see the reflection from the fire on the far wall. Could he burn the house down, pretend that she'd gone up inside it? No, knowing his luck the Fire Brigade would burst in and drag out her smouldering corpse, forensic evidence intact. Or Roger would dash in to rescue her before the flames even had a chance to spread. Unless he didn't tell Roger. In which case he'd be charged with two murders. Then they'd lock him away in a cell with two sexual weirdos as punishment.

He walked slowly into the living room. He didn't mean to, he didn't even think about it, it just happened. He stood in front of the fire, not even looking at the body in the armchair. He spoke softly into the flames:

"Roger, it's like this, I've just murdered Maddie. No, that's not what I meant to say. I mean we had a row, and there was an accident, that is I accidentally strangled her, and then she died. But it was really the fault of her diet. All those sticky buns, you know, and clotted cream and all that, it's very bad for the heart, so it wasn't my fault really, you see, she was going to have a heart attack anyway, she just happened to have it after I'd been strangling her. Oh God. Oh God. Oh. . . . "

He looked at the body. The eyes were still staring at the sofa, still locked in redundant argument. In films people always closed the eyes, but he didn't want to touch. He shivered at the thought. He would never have made a Bluebeard.

Talk to Roger then, he thought. Get it over with, go up now.

He walked out of the living room door. He took the first step towards the stairs, and then a second. The phone rang. He raced to answer it almost happily, feeling reprieved.

"I want to talk to Maddie."

He froze. What could he say? What he did say was "Hello Lizzie."

"I don't want to talk to you, thank you," she answered crisply. "Get me Maddie, please."

"She's gone to bed."

"It's a bit early for her, isn't it?"

"She wasn't feeling very well."

"I'm not surprised with you around."

"Ha! Ha!"

"Don't snicker like that, Mark! You are infuriating! While I've got you on the phone, let me give you a piece of good advice. Not that I give a damn about you, you can go to hell for all I care, but keep well out of Maddie's way, that's all. You've caused her enough mental anguish as it is, and just as soon as she's seen her solicitor on Monday we'll put a stop to it, just see if we don't, so no more funny business from you, or else you'll only be playing right into our hands in court, and it's bad enough for you as it is already. That's my piece of advice to you, and if you've got any sense you'll take it, because one whisper of aggro and I'll have the full weight of the law down on you like a ton of bricks. Do I make myself clear? Good, I'll take your silence for a yes. Good night and good riddance."

He walked away miserably, the image of Lizzie's furious face terrorising his thoughts. He walked upstairs slowly, imagining her in the witness box, feeling the accusing finger search him out, like a heat-seeking missile. He went into his study and turned back the sheets. He got into his pyjamas. After Lizzie would come the rest of her friends, the Fareham Harpies, queueing up to damn his reputation and stick their hatpins in him. He got into bed and pulled the covers over his head. He knew that he shouldn't be doing this, but he didn't dare to do anything else. It would be best for him if he didn't wake up in the morning.

He threw back the covers and leapt out of bed. He grabbed for his dressing-gown and without waiting to pull it on dashed downstairs, almost tripping over his own feet in his eagerness. He raced manically into the living room and crouched with his hands on his knees for a few moments, regaining his breath.

Not wake up in the morning! Of course! His way out was clear – neon lights and flashing "Go!" signs exploded in his brain. The elements of the scenario fitted together like Giant Lego: Died in the night – Found in bed – Bringing in the morning tea – Shock Horror! – Call Roger, phone an ambulance. Of course! That was it! Of course, of course, of course!

Of course there would still be questions asked, but Roger would testify that she had still been alive when he came in with Mark's cup of tea, why else would he have said goodnight to her?! He couldn't disguise the marks on her throat, but no way would they be able to prove the connection. The point was that Roger had thought she was alive. The worst he would have to face was conjecture. All he had to do was get the body upstairs.

He hesitated. He hadn't even felt like touching the eyes, he certainly didn't want to pick it up. It wasn't as if it was just anybody, after all, it was his wife. Gingerly he reached out a hand and touched her. She was cold, almost clammy to the touch. He shivered. This wasn't going to be pleasant. But what was the alternative? He clenched his fists and teeth and steeled himself.

He ran out to the dining room and snatched a spare tablecloth out of the chest of drawers. Next door he draped it over Maddie's body. At least now he wouldn't see her face. He couldn't do it if there were anything personal. He pushed to the back of his mind for now the thought of having to undress and get her into bed.

He crouched down, grabbed the body under the arms and pulled it towards him. He dug his shoulder into her stomach, grasped her back with his hands and heaved. She hardly budged. He staggered back, gasping for breath and feeling more than a little nauseous.

She was so heavy! Of course, but what had he expected? It was not as if he'd been married to Twiggy. He realised for the first time what was meant by the expression "dead weight". If he strained any harder he'd put his back out. But what choice had he? He had to strain harder. He bent to it again and lifted with all his strength.

He groaned and heaved until his eyes stung and he ached like a victim of the rack. When his last ounce of strength was exhausted he trembled on the point of surrender for moments agonisingly stretched, until the image of Lizzie's hate-filled face appeared in his mind's eye with sudden stunning clarity and he heard at the same moment the cell key turn. He mouthed a silent scream and went beyond the limits of his strength. Defying gravity, he swung Maddie up over his shoulder in a monumental fireman's lift.

He stood like Atlas on the hearthrug, grunting and sweating with the weight of the world thrusting down on him. Who would fardels bear, when he might carry his own wife? Out she had to go, up the stairs and into bed, before the plot should have a chance to cool — the hot blood was all his; there was only Arctic in her veins.

He saw everything now through a veil of tears. There was no sense left in his arms and shoulders, only merciful numbness after the tearing pain. He moved like a wound-down clockwork thing, jerking out first one foot, then dragging the other along the floor behind it. He made his way at snail's pace across the dining room then squeezed out through the door into the hallway. At least there was only the door into the bedroom left. If he could make it up the stairs. He stretched out a tentative foot.

A familiar sound came to him, a grating of wood on wood. A light came on upstairs. He glanced up, bewildered, and saw Roger's legs swing down into view.

He backed off down the hallway. He couldn't return the way he'd come, Roger would overtake him on the way to the kitchen. He stumbled off towards the bathroom. He could hear Roger's heavy tread on the landing, even above the cacophony of his own breathing.

He pulled up short even as his fingers brushed the door handle. What if Roger wanted to use the bathroom? It was just as likely as the kitchen. What was he going to do?

The second stair down creaked, as it always creaked. He heard Roger cough.

Without thinking he pulled open the cellar door and scrambled inside. He made a lunge for the light switch with his free hand, missed and it was too late to try again: he had lost his balance and was falling forward, in the darkness. There were six steps down and his feet touched one, either the first or the second. With his spare hand he grabbed for the rickety banister, which made a cracking noise as his thigh slammed heavily into it. He tottered crazily, fell down another step and then down all the rest, somehow keeping upright even as the weight of his burden dragged him down. He hit the floor of the cellar at the run and shot across it like a bullet, only coming to a shuddering halt when he embedded himself into something hard and solid. He grabbed at the metal object for support and managed to steady himself. He felt along the smooth cold surface until he found a catch. It was the freezer.

"Who's that?"

His heart missed a beat, or would have done if it had been able to stop pounding for long enough. The voice had come from very close, it had sounded in the tiny cellar like an echo. Roger must be standing directly outside the door, which must have fallen shut again on its springs.

He could see nothing in the pitch dark. What could he do? He felt again for the catch and heaved open the freezer lid. The light inside came on, giving him something at least to see by. What could he do with the body? There was nothing big enough for him to hide it behind, not even the freezer, which was tight to the wall. He didn't have time to remove the bicycle and stick her where Roddy had concealed himself the other night.

"Who is there? I warn you, I'm armed!"

He didn't think. He just turned, and tensed, and heaved the body off his shoulders. It fell with a thump into the bottom of the freezer. He slammed down the lid, then jumped up and sat on it as the cellar door opened and the light came on.

"Hi Rog! It's only me!"

Roger looked relieved and, as he lowered the offensive umbrella he had been waving aggressively a moment before, a little embarrassed.

"What the hell are you doing here, Mark, in the dark?"

"Couldn't find the light switch, glad you came when you did."

"Oh. Looking for some food, is it? You won't find much in there, you know!"

Mark laughed carelessly and drummed with his fingers on the side of the freezer.

"No, no, I just heard a noise, like you. I was investigating. Mice, I shouldn't be surprised!"

"Mice eh? Tricky little devils, mice are. I've got some poison upstairs I was keeping for myself, but you can borrow some if you like."

"That's very generous of you! Are you sure you've got enough?"

"Oh, plenty! It never does to do things by halves, you know!"

"No, of course not! Well, I think it's too late to be catching any nocturnal prowlers now. It's off to bed with me, then!"

"And with me. Goodnight, Mark."

Roger went out. Mark heard him walking along the corridor and going into the bathroom. He shuddered at the thought that he had almost gone in there himself. It was cold in the cellar. He came out, went upstairs and got into bed, where he pulled the covers up right over his head again and concentrated on warming himself up. A few minutes later he heard Roger climbing up his ladder and that familiar sound he'd heard before – the wooden board sliding into place across the attic entrance. Mark lay in the darkness, listening. He gave it fifteen minutes, which was as long as his nerves would stand, then went back down to the cellar, this time putting a sweater on over his pyjamas. He opened the freezer lid and took a fresh grip on his wife's corpse.

Twenty minutes later he came up out of the cellar again, feeling exhausted. He went into the kitchen and made himself a cup of tea. After he had drunk it he returned to the cellar.

He came up again another quarter of an hour later, gasping for breath and clutching at his back with both hands. He lurched into the bathroom and leant heavily against the basin. He lifted his head slightly and grimaced at himself in the mirror. His back remained bent. It was too painful to straighten it.

"Put a disc out if you carry on like that, you silly bugger!" He muttered to himself half despairingly. Only half; he was too tired to feel anything in its entirety, even dejection.

"She won't budge!" he murmured miserably to himself, as he snatched a piece of paper off the toilet roll and wiped the tears of frustration from his cheeks.

"What an idiot! What a bloody, bloody fool! If I could only just get her out of the armchair, how the hell am I going to get her out of the bottom of the freezer?"

It was a rhetorical question, which was just as well. Had he presented it to himself in the form of a genuine problem, of the sort given to analysis and reduction, he might have felt bound to stay there all night until he had worked it out, no doubt putting each and all of his discs out, one by one. Thankfully he was spared; he was just too weary to think. He trudged out of the bathroom and slowly, painfully, climbed the stairs, pulling faces at each twinge of his ruined back. He got into bed, rolled over on to his side, his most comfortable position, and stared blankly at the wall, resolving to come up with some solution before morning. He cursed Roger, and he cursed himself, but he was only paying lip-service with his curses, there was no emotion in him. His mind was featureless, blank. He yawned. And upon reflecting that the best-laid schemes of even non-existent mice in the cellar may go astray, he closed his eyes and, against all odds, fell into a deep and dreamless sleep.

7

"Well, that seems to be that then! If you could just sign at the bottom, Mr Talbot, I'll have these faxed to head office and the money will be available as and when you need it."

Reg Talbot took his gold fountain-pen from his inside pocket and signed his name neatly. He chuckled to himself as he passed over the completed form.

"It's a wonder I didn't do this years ago. It would have been cheaper."

"Oh I don't know, probably not in real terms. And these things have some sort of internal logic of their own in my experience. Just now is a very good time for expansion. Small businesses have had a hard time the last few years, I'm sure you don't need me to tell you, but you're not that small any more. People need transport, Mr Talbot, especially in a rural area. You have a captive market. I may be a part of it myself in the not too distant future."

"Really? With a G reg XJ 6 parked in the forecourt. That is yours, isn't it?"

"You are observant! No, you're quite right, it's not for myself. I'm after a replacement for my wife's little runaround, a sturdy if unspectacular Renault of maturing vintage."

"Something in the same line?"

"Or whatever. I'm prepared to take good advice."

"Well, I couldn't begrudge you that, I've certainly taken enough of yours!"

"Ha! Ha! Do you think you might have something then?"

"Just the thing. Nice little D reg Polo. Lovely runner. One lady owner, less than fifteen thou on the clock. Sunroof, stereo cassette, covered seats, host of little extras. Took it as a trade-in last Saturday, it's being serviced and cleaned up even as we speak. Seeing as it's not yet been on the forecourt I don't see why I couldn't let it go at trade price, to the right buyer, as a favour."

"You're a very convincing salesman, Mr Talbot, I understand the secret of your success."

"Give us a bell this afternoon and I'll arrange a test drive."

"Splendid! Are you a golfer by any chance?"

"No, never got round to it, I'm afraid."

"You should, really you should. I'm a member of the Oaks Club, excellent links and, what's just as relevant, tophole clubhouse and recreational facilities. If you like I'll put your name forward for membership. It's not inexpensive, of course, but then it is somewhat exclusive. I'm sure a man of your stamp would appreciate that!"

"Very kind of you to say so, Mr Vernon."

"Not at all. We want to encourage only the right kind of chap to join, you know. Excuse me a moment." He pressed the buzzer on his desk. "Mrs Stephenson, I've a document needs faxing. And could you send in Mr Harvey?"

"Mr Harvey?"

"My assistant manager. Sound fellow. Pay you to know him, just in case you should want anything and I'm not around."

There was a knock on the door. Mrs Stephenson came in and took the completed loan application form. As she left Mark appeared.

"Ah, Harvey. I'd like you to meet Mr Talbot. We've just been arranging a capital loan. He's planning to buy Waterstone's garage in the High Street and convert it into a car showroom. He'll be our new neighbour." With a wave of his hand Vernon indicated the window, through which could be seen the bank's parking lot and, beyond, the offices at the rear of Waterstone's garage. "Splendid, what?"

Reg had risen from his chair. Rather sheepishly he extended a hand.

"Actually we've met, Mr Vernon. As a matter of fact we're neighbours."

"Good God! I thought you lived in the middle of a field, Harvey!"

"Oh no, Mr Vernon, Mr Harvey lives in a very pretty little cottage, and we have the house next door. It is a little isolated, though, I have to admit."

"Couldn't stand it myself. Nothing wrong with country living, don't get me wrong, all that fresh air, splendid! But I do like to be within hailing distance of civilisation. Live on the edge of the village myself. Stone's throw from the pub, jolly convenient, what?"

"As long as they don't start throwing stones, after closing time!"

"God no! Ha! Ha! Jolly good. Literally chucking stones, eh, better watch what I say. Perhaps you're better off in the middle of a field, after all, it certainly does get a bit rowdy here on a Saturday night. What do you say, Harvey? You're being jolly quiet!"

Mark looked round slowly. His eyes connected with Vernon's, but they didn't seem to meet. He seemed distracted. Vernon tapped the desk with a pencil.

"Wakey, wakey, no daydreaming! Up to the mark with you, Harvey!"

Reg smiled affably at Mark.

"Feel like that myself often enough on a Monday morning. I trust your wife is feeling better now, Mr Harvey?"

"Feeling better?" boomed Vernon. "Has she been ill or something? I didn't know!"

"When I last saw Mr Harvey – Thursday night wasn't it? – she was apparently a little under the weather, which was a bit of a coincidence because my wife was too."

"Well, that's women for you!" Vernon chuckled. He gave Mark a sharp glance. "You look a bit under the weather yourself, old chap," he said, without evident sympathy. "Probably caught something from Mrs Harvey, I expect."

Reg nodded wisely. Both men stared expectantly at Mark, awaiting confirmation of the proffered diagnosis. Mark stared back at them vaguely, but didn't speak. Vernon banged irritably on the table with his pencil and turned back to Reg.

"Well, Mr Talbot, as soon as those papers – "

"My wife's never felt better, thank you!" blurted out Mark suddenly. "Hundred per cent, tiptop condition, made a full recovery. I hope your wife is as well as mine is, Mr Talbot!"

"Pull yourself together, Harvey," murmured Vernon cautioningly.

Mark was sitting forward on the edge of his chair, fists clenched under his legs, staring at Reg with bulging eyes. Thick veins stood out on his forehead, which glistened with sweat; his face and body trembled. Reg sat back awkwardly in his seat, feeling alarmed: he remembered his neighbour's peculiar baying at the moon and had a foreboding that some other manifestation of eccentricity might be imminent.

"My wife has also made a complete recovery, thank you for asking," he said pre-emptively. "Perhaps, if you are both fit, you would like to pop round for a drink tonight? Say at half past six?"

The ensuing silence was profound. The only intrusion upon it was the leathery squeaking of Reg's readjustment of his bottom on the chair.

"Harvey!" hissed Vernon angrily.

"Is six thirty too early?" said Reg cheerfully. "How about seven then?"

"Seven?" repeated Mark faintly.

"Yes? Is that alright then, seven o'clock? My wife will be delighted. I shall look forward to making Mrs Harvey's acquaintance. And now, I think – look, is that the time! – I really must be getting my nose back to the grindstone. No rest for the wicked, eh Mr Vernon?"

"Ha! No, none at all I'm afraid. Pleasure to meet you, Mr Talbot. I'll give you a call this afternoon as soon as I've heard from head office, although as I said I'm not anticipating any hitches."

"Thanks very much. I'll get you all the info on that car."

"Splendid! And look forward to seeing you on the links!"

"I'll be needing some tuition first. Goodbye Mr Harvey, until this evening, that is."

"Mrs Stephenson?" Vernon called from the door. "Show Mr Talbot out will you?"

The door clicked shut. Vernon sat down again. He beat out a rapid drumbeat with his pencil.

"Whatever is the matter with you, Harvey?"

Mark jumped guiltily. Vernon was looking stern and headmasterly, one of his more natural poses.

"I'm sorry, sir."

"It won't do, Harvey, it really won't do. He's a very important client, Mr Talbot, at the very least I should expect you to treat him with civility. Why, he was good enough to enquire after the health of your wife. At the very least you could have returned the compliment."

"I'm sorry sir, I'm not feeling very well."

"Then you shouldn't be at work. It really won't do, Harvey. A sick employee is no earthly use to me, it would be much better for both of us if you looked after yourself in a responsible manner. Are you infectious? I don't want you spreading disease throughout the bank."

"I'm just a little run down sir, that's all."

"Then kindly take better care of yourself. You're not paid a generous salary to let yourself get run down. This bank did not achieve its position in the financial sector today through the efforts of an unhealthy workforce. Get yourself fit again before resuming your duties. Now the most useful thing you can do at the moment is behave graciously towards Mr Talbot. Why don't you go home, take the afternoon off and rest yourself in bed, and be in a position to give one hundred per cent tonight at our new client's little soirée? Just chat him up and listen politely and get in lots of little nudges about what jolly good chaps we all are here at the bank, you know the sort of thing I mean. Your wife will like that, chance to put on a new frock, you know the score. Will you do that for me, Harvey? Do you think you're up to the mark?"

"Yes sir. Thank you sir."

"Good, and someday soon we must have you all over to dinner, you, your wife and the Talbots. I'll have a word with Mrs Vernon. Off the top of my head, would next Tuesday suit you, a week tomorrow?"

"I think so, sir."

"Good. Jolly important this socialising, you know. Best place to do business, butter up the clients over a glass of vino. You'd better go now, Harvey, go home and get your head down for a bit."

"Thank you sir."

"Oh and one more thing. Just a little friendly word of advice, apropos of what I was saying: if you ever want to make manager, and you're still young enough, take a tip from me. Join a decent golf club. That'll be all, Harvey. I'll let you know about next Tuesday."

Reg Talbot was feeling excited and pleased with himself as he got out of his car and walked up to his house. He had spent all day looking forward to the evening and had done everything he could to stack the deck in his favour. The big break was that both the kids would be out. They had gone on to a birthday tea party straight from school and weren't due to be picked up till half past seven. Sharon, naturally, had delegated him for chauffeur duties, which had provided him with the opportunity for a masterstroke.

"Doing anything tonight, Billy?" he had asked casually, as the egregious brother-in-law had helped himself to another coffee during one of his extensive breaks.

"Shaz said to come by for grub 'bout seven, s'all," he replied, jamming his paw into the biscuit tin.

"You couldn't do me a favour, could you? Sharon asked me to pick the kids up from the Warrens' place at half past seven, but I've got a hell of a lot of paperwork to do tonight, what with all the takeover business. You couldn't be an angel, could you, and pick the kids up for me on your way out? It'll make you a bit late, but we'll save your supper for you, we're saving some for the kids anyway."

"Dunno Reg, Shaz gets dead pissed off with me if I muck her around."

"I'll square it with Sharon, just you leave it to me. And I'll make it worth your while."

The slow withdrawal of the wallet from the inside pocket had an hypnotic effect on Billy. His pupils dilated to pin size.

"Well worth your while," Reg repeated slowly, drawing out a crisp brown tenner, which he slipped between the first and second fingers of his left hand. Billy stared at it in silence. Reg folded the note into the palm of his hand and dipped his fingers back into the wallet. Another tenner appeared miraculously and the wallet was closed. The second note was folded about the first and both were pressed into Billy's breast pocket. Billy licked his lips.

"You'll have a natter with your missus, then?"

"I'll call her now."

Which he had done. She had reacted predictably:

"Why don't you pick them up yourself, you lazy bastard? Fancy conning poor Billy into doing your legwork for you!"

"Billy's very kindly doing it for me as a favour, darling. I need to be home early tonight, because I've invited our next-door neighbours round for a drink. They'll be coming at seven. I'm sure you'll enjoy meeting them."

"Why should I? Pair of stuck up lah-de-dahs. Never even turned up for one of my parties."

"Well, you'll be able to invite them personally to the next one. It'll be nice for you to meet some new people. You're always complaining about being stuck out in the middle of nowhere."

"What do you mean I'm always complaining? And don't tell me what's nice for me. I'm old enough to make my own mind up about things, thank you very much!"

"Yes darling," he had answered, and no darling, three bags full darling. Despite her protests he knew that she wasn't seriously riled. She just enjoyed the sound of her own voice.

"I'm home darling!" he called out cheerfully as he stepped through the front door.

"Why aren't you picking up the kids?" she demanded thickly from the kitchen.

Reg frowned. He closed the front door with rather less cheer than he had opened it. He didn't like the sound of her voice.

"Billy's going darling, remember? They're not due to be picked up for another half hour anyway, it's only half past."

He peeked quickly into the living room. It was far from immaculate, but reasonably tidy. He permitted himself a small sigh of relief before moving on to the kitchen.

"Hello darling," he murmured, at the door.

"Whassat?" She demanded shrewishly, pointing a finger at the bottle he held in his hand.

"Champagne. To celebrate."

"Whasser to sleberate?"

"The takeover. I told you over the phone. Remember."

"Well whaddya waiting for? Open it up for Chrissakes!"

"I think it needs cooling first. I'm planning to open it when our neighbours come round. You do remember that our neighbours are coming round, don't you?"

"Whaffor?"

"A drink. You remember what that is, I suppose."

"What?"

"Nothing."

"What are you doing here anyway? You're supposed to pick up the kids."

Reg didn't answer. He went to the fridge, moved some milk to make a space and deposited the bottle of champagne. There didn't seem to be much in the fridge besides the milk and a dozen or so small bottles of tonic water, several of which had been opened and replaced in a half-empty state. It was not difficult to guess where the missing halves were now. The only minor cause for wonder was the unprecedented amount of dilution that would appear to have taken place.

"Well?"

He turned back irritably from the fridge.

"Well what?"

"Dontcha snappa me like that!"

He sighed. "Look at you!" he said, quite audibly, but she didn't hear. Her back was to him, she was mixing another drink at the table, heaping ice into a glass and emptying the last of a litre bottle of Gordon's into the bottom. The bottle had been full yesterday, Reg was sure of that. What time had she had her first today, then? About five minutes after breakfast, by the look of her. She was still wearing her pyjamas and dressing-gown. Of course it was possible she'd just changed back into them, preparatory to having a shower or a lie-down, but it didn't appear that way: they had a crumpled look, as indeed did she: her hair was lank and greasy, her face blotchy and devoid of all but the remnants of yesterday's make-up; a bare trace of lipstick on her thin pale lips. She hadn't bothered to dress then, all day. She had probably not moved from the kitchen. She had spent the day with her best friend, and what was one green bottle more or less between friends?

The bottle lay on its side on the table where she had discarded it. Empty now, of no further use. She was a fairweather friend, loyal only to the dregs.

"Wheresa vodka got to?"

"I've no idea. Why don't you have some coffee?"

"You tryina tell me I'm nossober or summin?"

"I think you've had enough to drink."

"Whaddya mean? I'm sober's a judge!"

Only a violent fit of coughing cut short her laughter. She responded by lighting a cigarette. Reg looked distastefully at the overflowing ashtray.

"This place stinks."

"Wassalright till you came in."

She giggled. She hiccupped. He glared at her.

"I think you'd better get cleaned up. Take a shower. Get dressed. Our guests will be arriving soon."

"Guests can get stuffed. Hey!"

Her cry was in response to his taking the vodka bottle off her. He had seen it long before her, sitting on top of the fridge. He had ignored it, hoped that she wouldn't see it, which of course was far too much to ask — she had a homing instinct where alcohol was concerned.

"Gimme't back, you bastard!"

Drunk she may have been but she was no slouch: Reg saw only the blur of her hand as it snaked out for the draining board. The next moment she was waving a carving knife at him.

"Put that down!"

"Gimme't back!"

"I said put that down!"

"I'll slittyaup!"

It was not easy to disbelieve her. She took a swipe at his face and missed by millimetres. He jumped back, got tangled up in a chair and almost fell. She howled triumphantly as she ran round the kitchen table to have another go at him. He scrambled round to the other side, keeping the table between them.

"Don't be ridiculous. Put that down!"

"Gimme't!"

She took another swipe at him. It was wild and missed by a yard this time, but there was sufficient venom in it to give Reg pause. He slammed the vodka bottle down on the table.

"Here!"

She eyed him suspiciously. She advanced on the table but didn't lower the knife.

"Back off!" she scowled.

He edged away. She kept her gimlet eye upon him until he was pressed up against the wall, then refocused on the full bottle of Smirnoff. She licked her lips. She picked up the bottle with her left hand. She tried to unscrew the top with her other hand, but the seal was secure and she didn't have enough spare fingers. She put down the carving knife. Reg clenched his fist.

"Hey!"

Her scream was atavistic, the roar of an unreconstructed primitive defending her kill. As Reg lunged she spun half around and dropped into a crouch, enfolding and shielding the precious bottle in her bosom. Reg's fingers closed on empty air as he fell bodily across the table. She jeered at him and started to run for the door, but he grabbed at her dressing-gown belt and held her. She took one hand off the bottle and punched him in the eye. He bit her hand. She squealed and grabbed for the carving knife. Both of them touched the handle at the same time and it skidded away, falling from the table to the floor. Reg was still lying across the table, she had the advantage now. She bent down to pick up the knife and he saw her face at the level of the table, a foot from his own. As it came up again, the eyes flaring with bloodlust, he drove his fist into it.

He caught her jaw full on. He must have hit her hard, his knuckles stung like crazy. He must certainly have hit her hard: she went down like a sack of lead.

Fumes filled his nostrils – the vodka bottle had shattered, a pool of colourless liquid was spreading over the floor, eddying round the cataracts of broken glass. Sharon lay flat on her back in the middle of it, soaking it up. Perhaps she should bathe in it regularly, save herself the trouble of having to guzzle it down. Or he could buy her an intravenous drip for Christmas.

He picked her up under the arms and dragged her to a dry spot. He dried her hair, which was drenched, with a kitchen towel. He fanned her face, then slapped her none too lightly on the cheeks. She didn't respond, she was out cold.

He looked at his watch. The Harveys would be here in a minute. What would he say then, when he opened the front door?

"Actually my wife's lying in the kitchen in a drunken stupor at the moment. Why don't you pop into the living room for a moment while I empty a bucket of cold water over her?"

He grabbed her under the arms again and dragged her into the hall. He started backing up the stairs, this time holding her by the wrists, but at the fourth step an agonising pain streaked along his back and instinctively he let her go. She slid down to the bottom again, bumping her head on each step. He grimaced and massaged his back as best he could.

"You stupid bitch!" he growled, and poked her in the ribs with his toes. She didn't react. He doubted if even the bucket of water would get a reaction out of her.

He hobbled into the kitchen, still clutching his back. He got the dustpan and brush out from under the sink and swept up the broken glass. The vodka proved too much for a roll of paper towels. He went back into the hall and opened the broom cupboard. He pulled out the mop.

"Stupid bitch!" he repeated, with feeling, jabbing at her with the mop on the way back to the kitchen. He took his anger out on the floor, thumping the wet patch with the mop. A spasm of pain shot up his back. He howled and slumped miserably into a chair. The carving knife was on the table, where he had replaced it. He picked it up and stabbed the table top with premeditated viciousness. He left the knife standing, the tip buried in the wood.

"I've had it up to here!"

"Here" was a point two feet above his head, indicated by his stretching out an arm, the effort of which cost him another spinal twinge. He slammed his fist down on the table. His eyes felt watery, an equal collaboration of anger and frustration. His hand hurt from hitting the table too hard. His knuckles were still throbbing too.

"Stupid, slovenly bitch! Why can't she behave decently just once in her life? Why's she always having to show me up, drag me down, ruin everything? I've had it! I can't take any more! I've really had it!"

The water in the eyes was overflowing. He could taste his tears, running on to his lips. He snatched at a dry corner of a vodka-soaked paper towel and made its sogginess uniform. He blew his nose on another piece.

He hobbled out into the hall. Sharon was lying exactly where he had left her, her head propped up slightly against the bottom stair. He stroked his chin, wondering where to put her. There were bristles on his chin, he really ought to have a shave.

He popped into the downstairs bathroom and splashed some water on to his face while he had a think. The water didn't really help. He took his comb from his inside pocket and neatly parted his hair. After that he retied his tie. He looked at himself critically in the bathroom mirror. Things still didn't appear any clearer.

He went back into the hall and frowned at Sharon's inert body. Each step he took sent a warning hint to his back. He obviously couldn't get her upstairs. He obviously couldn't get her far. Could he manage to drag her through the living room into the sun room? Probably, but what if the Harveys asked to see the house? He had been looking forward to showing them the house. He couldn't hide her in the loo, someone would be bound to want to use it. Perhaps he could prop her up behind the kitchen door? No, Mrs Harvey might want to see the kitchen. No room in the house was safe, unless he invented a pack of lies, and he wasn't very good at lying. He laughed bitterly to himself.

What would Mark Harvey say, if he only knew the truth? The possibility of a drunken embarrassment of a wife probably wouldn't have occurred to him in a million years. After all, he was married to a lady, a creature of refinement, not a gin-swilling, vodka-guzzling slut. Perhaps it was just as well that Sharon was out for the count. What would she have found to say to Mrs Harvey? Sharon was out of her depth. But he was damned if he was going to be pulled down with her.

He looked at his watch. Good God! he thought, it's seven already. And at that precise moment the doorbell rang.

He didn't think twice. He didn't have time. He just grabbed Sharon.

"Coming!" he called out gaily. "Won't be a sec!"

He had Sharon by the feet this time. She was just as heavy, and his back was just as painful, but he wasn't dragging her far, and it was only over bare, smooth floorboards. The broom cupboard was large enough for him to back in quite a way. He was able to get her half in before having to step out and push. Pushing was harder than pulling, but he was able to wedge her up between the Hoover and the garden hose without too much trouble. By the time he had finished he was panting heavily. And his back ached like crazy.

He lumbered across to the front door, took a deep breath and pulled it open. Mark Harvey was standing on the doorstep. He was alone. He was holding a potted plant. A torrent of words fell from his lips:

"Good evening Mr Talbot. I'm afraid my wife's suddenly been taken ill, a relapse, very unexpected as I've said already, but there you are, these things happen you know! She sends her apologies and wonders if your wife would care to accept this small gift as her way of apologising. Sorry! I should add that it's terribly infectious, I may have it as well, you'd better keep your distance!"

His face had actually disappeared behind the pot plant, which he was holding up with both hands at arm's length. The hands were far from steady; the leaves of the plant shook violently.

"Yes, you're not looking too well yourself," said Reg, trying to hide his disappointment, which was acute. "You'd better come on in out of the cold."

He stood aside and Mark entered the house.

"Where shall I put this?"

Reg stared blankly at the pot plant. He really didn't have the faintest idea.

"Oh, anywhere. . . . "

Mark put the plant down on a chair.

"Perhaps I should give it to your wife?" he said awkwardly.

Reg cleared his throat. "Funnily enough she's not feeling too well herself. She's, er, had to go for a lie-down. Perhaps she's got the same thing as Mrs Harvey?"

"I doubt it."

There was a pause. Mark thrust both hands into his pocket and stared hard at the carpet.

"So!" Reg announced heartily, clapping his hands. "It's just the two of us, then."

"Looks like it," Mark murmured in reply. There was another pause.

"Nice pot plant."

"Thanks." Mark transferred his weight from one foot to another. "I don't know much about plants myself. My wife chose it. She bought it herself."

"So she was up and about earlier was she?"

"Oh yes. She only had her relapse just now."

"Let's go into the living room and get a drink. What precisely is wrong with your wife?"

"Why? What's wrong with yours?"

"Er, she's got a fever." Reg hurried over to the drinks cabinet. Once again, he found his neighbour's manner disconcerting: he sounded surly and antagonistic and there was an aggressive look in his eye. Reg couldn't help wondering if perhaps Mark's own health problems had been mental.

"What'll it be then?" Reg asked, surveying the interior of the drinks cabinet. The choice appeared to be limited. Sharon had been doing the limiting.

"Oh, anything."

"I've got some champagne in the fridge. Shall we open that?"

"I'm not bothered."

"Oh. How about a Scotch?"

"Fine."

That was just as well, Sharon didn't care for Scotch. Mark took his with ginger ale. Both men sat down.

"Have you lived here long?" Reg asked after a half-minute's silence.

"Mm."

A series of further questions was required to elicit more detailed information. The conversation was carried on in this desultory manner for the next ten minutes. A pattern was quickly established: Reg would ask a perfectly ordinary question, on the subject of work, home, leisure etc. and would receive a monosyllabic reply. Follow-up questions would result in more monosyllables and very little else. Eventually the effort proved too great: Reg's stream of trivial enquiry dried up and both men sat in silence, staring glumly out of the window.

"Would you like to see the garden?" asked Reg forlornly, when the silence became too oppressive.

"Alright."

Reg rose reluctantly. He didn't really want to show Mark the garden, there wasn't much to see, and in any case Mark must have seen it already from the other side of the fence. But it was better than sitting in gloomy silence. He found the key to the french windows and they stepped out on to the patio. It was dark and cold. Reg pressed a switch and floodlights illuminated the patio.

"Very useful for parties," said Reg, indicating the lights. "Of course it'll be much nicer in the summer, and we'll have the swimming pool by then. We're having a party on Saturday, as it happens. I hope your wife's better by then, it would be lovely if you could both come. Sharon would love to meet her. Sharon adores parties!"

"I've noticed."

"Yes, I suppose we do make a fair amount of noise!" said Reg, laughing.

Mark smiled back thinly. A paved path led from the patio to the rear of the garden. Reg stepped on to it and Mark followed, both of them taking care to keep clear of the damp, spongy grass.

"Look at this!" said Reg, stopping on the edge of the gaping hole that was going to be the swimming pool. The great yellow hulk of the excavator loomed out of the darkness on the far side. "You wouldn't think it could possibly take anyone this long to dig a bloody hole, would you? It's not as if they're short-staffed, I've had half the population of Dublin running round here in the last month! You know what they did? They were supposed to dig out one shallow end and one deep end, the shallow bit here, nearest the house. So what did they do? Only dig out two deep ends! They've spent the last week piling back the loose earth. They swear they're going to lay the concrete down by the end of this week. They'd damned well better, that's all I can say!"

Mark peered into the black hole.

"There's not a lot to see really, is there?" he said morosely. He shivered.

"Yes, it is a bit nippy, isn't it? Shall we go inside?"

Back in the living room they resumed their former places and finished their drinks. Mark declined a refill.

"I'd better be getting back actually. Maddie may want something."

Reg couldn't repress a smile of relief.

"Of course! I understand! I hope she's better for Saturday."

"Yes," said Mark hurriedly, rising.

They went out into the hall. Mark had been wearing a windcheater, which he had left on the back of the chair with the pot plant. Reg held it for him as he slipped his arms in.

"What was that noise?"

Reg didn't answer. He held his breath.

"Nothing. Mice, I expect."

The noise was repeated, only more distinctly. It sounded like a moan, or a sigh.

"Funny mouse," said Mark suspiciously.

"Wind, I expect."

"A mouse with wind?"

"No, no, I mean the wind, very noisy, old house creaks a lot, you know."

Reg puffed his cheeks and made a half-whistling, blowing noise to pantomime the wind. He laughed and made his way to the door.

"Thanks for the drink, then," said Mark, zipping up his windcheater.

Reg did not get the chance to reply. He had opened his mouth to do so, but before he could utter a sound a muffled female shriek froze him into silence.

"Good God!" exclaimed Mark, considerably alarmed. "Where did that come from?"

Reg grinned at him blankly. Slowly Mark raised a hand and pointed.

"It seemed to come from . . . in there."

There was not much doubt really. Even as Mark spoke a woman's voice, blossoming with panic, cried out distinctly from the direction in which Mark's finger was pointing.

"Looks like a broom cupboard to me. . . . "

As if to confirm his supposition the narrow wooden door was pushed open violently from the inside and a broom tumbled out. A moment later it was followed by Sharon.

"Ah! Hello there!" said Reg jocularly. "I was wondering where you'd got to! This is my wife. Sharon, I'd like you to meet - "

"Help!" yelled Sharon, who had continued crawling towards Mark on her hands and knees. She sat back awkwardly on her heels and fixed him with bloodshot, crazy eyes. Her speech was slurred, no doubt due to the massive bruise on the side of her face, which must have made any movement of the jaw painful. "Help me please! My husband's tried to murder me!"

"Come, come darling, don't exaggerate!" admonished Reg quietly.

Mark ignored him. His face was colourless. His arms hung leadenly at his sides. He walked backwards, slowly, his eyes fixed hypnotically on Sharon. When the back of his legs came into contact with the chair he sat down, on the pot plant.

"Ah! That'll be the kids," said Reg hopefully, in response to the sounds outside of car doors slamming and whining teenage voices. He opened the front door.

"Who was that?" demanded Danny, when he and Kelly had barged their way inside past Reg. Kelly remained standing on the doorstep, gazing interestedly at the blur in a windcheater rapidly disappearing down the drive.

"Our new neighbour," answered Reg. "He had to dash."

A moment later, when Danny and Kelly had seen their mother crawling over the floor, Reg rather wished that he had made a dash for it too. Sharon began to scream incoherently, just as Billy came in.

"Who was that?" he asked, without evident interest, waving a thumb in the direction of Mark's retreat.

"That was our new neighbour," Kelly answered, sounding excited. "I think Mum's saying that he locked her in the cupboard and tried to murder her."

"Really?" Billy looked bemused. "Didn't look that sort of bloke to me. What's it all about then, Reg? Reg?"

But Reg was nowhere to be found.

8

Mark lay very still under his blankets. The blankets were pulled up over his head. Each breath brought the sheet brushing against his lips. The air he breathed was hot and damp. The sounds he made were loud in his ears. He wheezed like a hundred-a-day man.

He could feel the clamminess in his palms, which were pressed down against the sheet on either side of him. All of him felt uncomfortably damp. He was fully clothed. He was even wearing his windcheater, though mercifully unzipped. He would feel so much better if only he took it off . . . but the paralysis which gripped him was largely an act of will. Discomfort was his medicine. He had better take it, lying down.

What day was it? Monday. Whatever had happened to Sunday? He couldn't remember . . . what time was it? He didn't know. The watch on his wrist might have been on the moon. He sensed darkness outside his blanketed world, but that didn't mean anything. It had been dark at five o'clock. The winter dark was full of chill and foreboding, best to be snug in bed. He breathed the fetid air, content with the sense of timelessness, conspiring, indeed, to deprive himself of all sense. There was such a clutter in his head. Even in the silence and the stillness, the linen prison in which he had immolated himself, it would not go away.

He had problems. And problems never went away. He had learnt that years ago, but his instinct had always been to brush things under the carpet, to forget about them and hope they'd go away. Why do today what you can put off till tomorrow? That had always been his motto. He had bought time with delay, one of the most potent of all illusions, but illusion feeds on illusion and reality, held at bay, has a habit of winding itself up like a spring, then unwinding violently in your face . . . problems only breed more problems. To force them underground creates the worst illusion, that they've gone. But they've not: they're just whizzing around in ever decreasing circles, within the Chinese boxes of the mind.

He was aware that his breathing was faster now, and increasingly irregular. His lungs yearned for fresh air. It was all staleness in his brain; no oxygen. He was afraid to sleep, to let his subconscious loose. Even when he could not recall his dreams they left behind unpleasant sensations. The dregs of his images; images in the first place corked.

He had problems. What were his problems? It might do him good to think them through, to try to approach things rationally. If he dealt with his problems out in the open, calmly, sensibly, then perhaps they wouldn't leap up and engulf him at unexpected moments. Relax, he thought to himself, as he had thought a thousand times, without conviction. If he could relax, then his brain would clear and he could think. Think of what? Solve his problems, some of them at least; he couldn't solve them all. One in particular — no! he mustn't think of that . . . thinking of that destroyed all hope of relaxation. It brought the blood pounding through his ears, it woke the dormant Kraken in his head. So, think of other things, and let the tension pass . . . let it seep out of those stiff clenched muscles. Now the knot in the stomach dissolves, but slowly, like an unstirred sugar cube. Let the soothing images play across the darkened screen. Memories can be pleasurable, here's one: a fresh print, full Technicolor picture: standing on stage with the Famous Modellers, the Distinguished Judges. Enthusiastic applause from friends and strangers. Holding the cup aloft, with shy pride, while the local photographer clicks away. He's promised to send on a contact sheet. Holding the cup and the bowl.

The bowl. He had tried to keep the bowl out of his mind but it had a habit of appearing there, just like that. Only this very morning he had been in the middle of dictating a sentence to Miss Temple when, suddenly, there it was! He had had to ask her to repeat the half-sentence three times before recovering the gist of it. The bowl seemed to have come to some sort of tenancy agreement with his sub-conscious; eviction orders had gone unheeded. He had, however, been working on a plan concerning the bowl, although he had a nagging suspicion that it wouldn't hold water. The plan, that was. The bowl would hold about a pint and a half. His mind was wandering again. . . . The bowl had come from a firm in Worcester. If he could get hold of an exact copy, and have the names of the previous winners engraved on it, then he would be able to pass it off as the original. Only he kept remembering (however hard he tried not to) that Martin had said that it was just as well that they'd bought the bowl when they had because the line had been discontinued. Perhaps he could get one from somewhere else? It shouldn't be utterly impossible to get hold of a replacement bowl. Unlike a replacement wife.

He kicked and punched out violently, gasping for air. The sheets and blankets flew intermingled across the floor, leaving him flailing emptily on the mattress. He fanned his face with his hands. The air was sharp and sweet. He gulped down lungfuls. Then he began to shiver. The heating was off and the night time cold was in the room. He drew his knees up to his chin and embraced his legs. He listened to his breathing. The house was full of other noises, creaks and groans. Downstairs the phone was ringing.

There was that problem above all. The big one. The one that if he tried to shove it under the carpet it would pop straight out again. Out of the freezer. This room was a freezer. He couldn't stop shivering. But he didn't want to get the blankets. He didn't want to move at all, but stay in the dark security of his lair. That was the biggest illusion of all! There was no security in pretence. He hardly dared any more to leave his room. He couldn't bear to be with other people, he knew that they could see the guilt in his eyes, that they were just tormenting him by keeping quiet. Work today had been a nightmare, what followed worse. What had that woman been doing in the broom cupboard? What was it she had said about murder? Had it all been some elaborate ploy, some test of his conscience, a trap to spring a confession? Of course not, of course not, how could they know, but still . . . he had a feeling of subtle and inexorable forces working against him. Ignorance magnified his fears, ignorance and guilt. What in heaven's name had been the meaning of that little scene next door? What sort of a household did they run, chez Talbot?

"Mark? Are you there, Mark?"

He didn't breathe. He seemed to have stopped breathing a long time ago. If only he could bring himself to stop altogether then the problems would dissolve. That would be the easy way, Roger's way, the big sleep.

"It's the phone, Mark," Roger was saying, outside the door. "It's for Maddie. I haven't seen her. Is she out?"

"Out for dinner."

"What?"

He blinked. He was surprised. He hadn't meant to say that. He was breathing again. He hadn't meant to breathe either. He was full of involuntary responses. He stood up. He wasn't sure if he had meant to do that or not.

"She's not in," he said, opening the door an inch. He could see Roger's dog-face hanging in the crack. There was no gleam in the sad brown eyes; they were matt with their own dullness.

"Out is it, then? I'll tell the chap that. He rang before."

And he'll ring again, thought Mark, as he watched the drooping shoulders sink away down the stairs. He closed the door. He sat on the edge of the bed and stared. It was not quite pitch black in the room: a sliver of light crept in under the door from the landing. He could see the shapes of his pistols on the wall. He listened to the murmur of Roger's voice below. He heard him come up the stairs again, and up his ladder. The trapdoor squeaked shut.

When he went out on to the landing he had to shield his eyes from the dim light. He had grown used to darkness, and in any case he knew by heart the simple geometry of the house. He hardly needed light. He didn't touch any switches coming down the stairs into the hall. He fumbled at the cellar door for a few moments, but that was because the key was rusty. He went down the six rickety stairs without hesitating. The blackness down below was impenetrable, but he knew his way.

The light that came on when he opened the freezer lid blinded him. For half a minute all he could see was spots in front of his eyes, and when the spots cleared there was the mist, the semi-opaque freezer air. Perhaps it was on too cold. It needed defrosting. He was careless about maintenance, Maddie was always complaining. She had a lot to complain about, really.

"Is that you?"

He whispered his question. His breath became mist; he could feel the cold in his teeth. He stared into the bottom of the freezer. The old tablecloth had a frost on it now. He could just make out the pattern. It was supposed to be an Indian design. They had bought it in Poole, years ago. It was stained and frayed now. He'd never much liked it anyway. Curious, though, how it should have ended up, as a shroud. There was no suggestion of shape underneath. It just lay there, a featureless old tablecloth, covering the corpse of his wife. There was something sitting on it at the bottom, by her feet. At least he thought that was where her feet were, though he couldn't be a hundred per cent sure which end was which. What he could be sure of, however, after a closer inspection, was that the something in question was a box of fish fingers, which was a bit mysterious. He couldn't remember seeing them before, yet they must have been there, for only he had been down in the cellar, only he had a key. Perhaps they had been in one of the wire-mesh trays above and had been dislodged when he'd thrown her in. That was possible. It was the only thing in the freezer. Apart from you-know-who. He picked out the box and examined it with interest. It was unopened. The wording on the packet led him to believe that it contained thirty-six fish fingers. It was a bit of a stroke of luck really. He tucked the box under his arm and closed the freezer. Once again, he climbed the rickety stairs in darkness.

He turned on all the lights in the kitchen. Kitchens were dangerous places, he didn't want to burn himself on the gas ring. He turned on the grill. How many should he have? He wanted to have six, but that would be greedy. On the other hand, he hadn't eaten anything all day, and who would be there to witness his greed? He opened the packet and tipped out six fish fingers. He put them under a medium heat. He found a tin of curried baked beans in the cupboard, emptied them into a saucepan and put them on. His stomach juices began to flow.

The phone rang. He tried to ignore it, but the bell on the kitchen extension was loud and tinny. He snatched it up, to stop the sound.

"Hello?"

"Maddie?"

Oh not again! What was the matter with him? It couldn't be a bad line every time!

"Maddie's gone out!" he barked gruffly. There was hesitation at the other end.

"When are you expecting her back?" said Roddy at length.

"No idea. Goodnight!"

He put the phone down decisively. He couldn't help but feel a little satisfied. Still, dealing with Roddy was easy. The problem was Lizzie. He had been expecting Lizzie to ring. Today was the day Maddie had been threatening to find a solicitor. Lizzie would be sure to want a report.

He grabbed the grill in the nick of time. The golden breadcrumbs were just beginning to speckle black. He turned the fish fingers over and gave the beans a stir. Some were stuck to the bottom of the pan. It was not going to be a gourmet feast.

Something brushed against his leg. He was surprised to see Maud Gonne rubbing herself against his ankle. The cat never came near him, he was quite sure she hated him; a true familiar. Yet here she was, staring up at him with almost a plaintive look in her dark imperious eyes, and even making little noises in her throat. There was a clean cat bowl on the draining board. He filled it from a handy packet of Meow-Mix. When the fish fingers were done he put one into the bowl and cut it up. They both set to their meals vigorously.

His hardly satisfied him. He hadn't realised how hungry he was. While he waited for the kettle to boil he finished off a packet of digestives. When he had made his cup of tea he did his usual security check, then went upstairs to bed.

It was only just after nine. He went into his study and lay on the bed in the darkness, sipping his tea. Now and again he heard Roger shuffling about in the attic. Lucky for him that Roger was such an oddball. Fancy not even noticing that Maddie was dead! It was quite funny really, in a tasteless sort of way. Like Roddy never recognising his voice on the phone. Sometimes it seemed that everyone around him was either mad or stupid. Look at the neighbours. What about the woman in the broom cupboard? That was quite funny too. Had old Talbot really tried to do her in? Perhaps they had something in common after all.

He smiled. He put down his empty cup and lay back on the bed. He still felt light-headed, it would take time for the nourishment and energy to circulate. Should he have eaten those fish fingers, after all? They had been lying on top of you-know-who for two days. That couldn't have been good for hygiene. Still, the box had been unopened. Still, she had been his wife.

He rolled over on to his side. He felt restless and uncomfortable. And nauseous in his stomach. It probably hadn't been such a good idea after all. What condition would she be in after two days in the freezer? Blue with cold, stiff with ice and rigor mortis. Not corrupt, but not pleasant. There was no dignity in that death. Packaged with the processed remains of anonymous cod.

He swung his feet on to the floor and sat up. He no longer felt like lying down. He knew that he must do something, occupy his mind. He stood up and walked unsteadily to his desk. He did not turn on the lamp but focused on the window, concentrating on the thick darkness beyond. Twin headlamps swung into view. A car was coming up the drive. Its lights were dimmed, it came on slowly. He found it oddly comforting, this evidence of human life. He watched it till it was out of sight. Then he turned away suddenly and walked out to the landing.

He went into the bedroom furtively, as if into a forbidden place, which in a sense it was: even after Maddie's death her interdiction lingered. He kept his gaze fixed rigidly ahead, metaphysically blinkered. He couldn't find his way round in the dark here, he had to turn on the light. He tried not to look at Maddie's things laid out in front of the mirror, the items of make-up, the towel, the tissue box, the favourite blonde wig and the second favourite chestnut on their blocks. Of course, he couldn't help but notice: he had pushed so much to the back of his mind that there just wasn't any more room there. He whistled to himself. Whistling while he worked, distracting his thoughts. He opened the bottom drawer first, scooped out clean underpants and socks. Then the top drawer, a couple of shirts. There wasn't much left in the drawers, he would have to do some laundry soon. He wasn't sure if he could remember how to operate the washing machine. As for ironing –

He stopped in the act of closing the drawer. It squeaked as he shut it, but it hadn't been that noise which had made him pause. No, it had been the creak of a hinge, and it had come from outside. He heard a footstep on the wooden drawbridge. It was very quiet and the window was open. He could hear everything.

"Maddie!"

The drawer remained half-shut. He turned away silently and sat down on the bed, not pressing down too hard on the creaky mattress. Everything in the house creaked and groaned.

A handful of dirt and small stones pattered against the window. It sounded like a hailstorm in the tomb-like silence of the bedroom.

"Maddie, it's me! Where are you?"

The voice was hoarse but loud, an exaggerated stage whisper. Mark stared blankly at the floor. He didn't know what to do. That wretched dressing-table light was the problem. With a beacon like that to guide him, even the half-blind lovesick swain on the path outside couldn't go amiss.

"Maddie, is he there? Is it safe for you to talk?"

Mark rolled over on the bed. One complete turn brought him to the far edge. He swung over his feet and sat up, keeping his head down and leaning in towards the window.

"No, it's not safe!" he hissed.

He held his breath. There was an unbearable pause. He heard the sound of gravel crunching under feet.

"Oh my darling!" Roddy cooed. "What has he been doing to you?"

"Nothing!"

"But why don't you ever answer the phone? Why didn't you call me back? I've been going frantic!"

"He's keeping an eye on me."

"What?"

"I said he's watching me. Not safe. My solicitor said to keep a low profile. We don't want him to get nasty in court."

"Has he been threatening you? I'll kill him!"

"No, no!"

Mark coughed. Maintaining his whispered falsetto was a strain. He felt dry.

"Are you alright, darling?"

"Yes. Bit of a sore throat."

"Oh Rapunzel, Rapunzel, let down your hair. . . . "

"Ssh! Keep your voice down!"

"Sorry!"

Roddy must have backed away; again Mark heard the scraping of gravel underfoot.

"Oh darling, why don't you come down and give me a kiss!"

Mark frowned. Deaf and short-sighted Roddy may have been, but at point-blank range even he might have been able to spot the difference. Mark had to throw him off the scent. What was it Maddie had called him?

"Roly-panda!"

"Puffball cup-cake!"

"What?"

In his surprise his falsetto completely deserted him. He broke into a strategic coughing fit.

"What is it, my little strawberry mousse?"

Mark took a few moments to digest this latest endearment. It was easy to see why neither of them had ever succeeded in dieting. Mark felt an hysterical twitch beginning somewhere in his diaphragm. He bit his lip.

"Oh Roly-panda, I can't come down and kiss you. You know who might see us."

"Then at least come to the window and show me your sweet face!"

"Er. . . . "

He was almost on the point of laughter. He bit his other lip and screwed up his face.

"Roly-panda isn't going until his Puffball cup-cake blows him a kiss!"

"Ah."

He had a suspicion that his impersonation had about reached the limits of possibility.

On the other hand . . . crazy as it might be, it did appear that not so much as a glimmer of the truth had penetrated Roddy's fevered mind. Mark heard him clearing his throat and then crooning in a clear, rather girlish voice:

"Moonlight becomes you, it goes with your hair. . . . "

There was a thumping noise from out on the landing. Roger was coming down his ladder.

"Quiet!" Mark hissed.

But Roddy was too far gone to heed caution.

"Let him come!" he declared dramatically. "I don't care who sees or hears me!"

Mark scurried across the floor to the dressing table. He snatched the blonde wig off its block and pulled it over his ears. It was a good fit. Maddie's spare glasses were next to the block. He brushed hair out of his eyes, put the glasses on and stumbled back to the window, barely able to see through the thick lenses. He dragged back the edge of the curtain and thrust out his chin boldly.

"Here I am! Now for heaven's sake shut up and go away!"

"How can you talk to your chubby knees like that?"

"Very easily. Go on, get away with you!"

A long drawn-out squelchy sound from below indicated that Roddy was blowing him a kiss. Mark pouted and reciprocated.

"I can see your lovely face so clearly, darling!" Roddy billed.

"And I yours, Roly-panda!" whispered Mark romantically.

"Will you miss me?"

"Puffball cup-cake always misses her spotted dick!"

"Naughty cup-cake! Are you alright? What's the matter, are you crying?"

"No, no! Bye! I must go!"

Mark pulled his head back in and slammed the window shut. He took off the glasses and flung himself face down on the bed, burying himself in the duvet. He had realised as soon as he made that remark about spotted dick that it had been a mistake. Not that Roddy had seemed to mind; indeed, he'd lapped it up, but for Mark it had opened the floodgates of hysteria. He lay on the bed shaking with dry laughter. He felt weak and empty-headed. He lay there for a long time, long after he had heard the sounds of Roddy's car starting and heading off away down the drive. When he finally emerged from the bedroom (remembering at the last moment to remove the wig) the phone was ringing downstairs. He had decided to ignore it, but Roger answered.

"Is Maddie back yet?" he called up the stairs.

"No. Who is it?"

"Lizzie Skinner. She rang earlier. She says will Maddie ring her back."

"I'll give her the message."

A few minutes later Roger clambered back up the stairs again and into his attic. He had turned off all the lights, there was no need for Mark to go out again. He undressed and lay in bed, staring into the darkness and listening to the house groan and the owls cry.

Out in the fields a lone figure tramped along the hedgerows. Reg Talbot had already done two complete circuits of the Trumans' farm in the last hour, covering himself to the knees in mud and muck, but although he was tired and it was late he prepared to embark on a third. He didn't really want to continue walking, but he certainly didn't want to return home. However miserable he felt alone out in the fields, it would be much more miserable there. Only once in the course of his walk had there been a moment of cheer: it had been at the beginning of the second circuit, just as he had crossed the drive into the long field that ran parallel. His eyes had strayed to the one lighted window in the Harveys' house, and in that moment he had seen the blonde head of Mrs Harvey, framed like a pre-Raphaelite goddess by the golden light behind. For a minute she had lingered in his view, like a vision glowing in the night, feeding the barren places of his heart. Then she had gone. And he had walked on, into the fields, listening to the owls, and the long-withdrawing engine of a single car.

9

Mark woke early, almost with the dawn, as he had done on the two previous days. For an hour he lay watching the grey light spread, listening to the redundant ticking of his alarm clock. When at last it rang, he didn't respond but lay apathetically staring at the ceiling while the bell rang itself out. A quarter of an hour later he rose, put on his dressing-gown and slippers and went downstairs. There was a letter on the doormat. He picked it up and went into the kitchen.

Roger came in just as the kettle boiled.

"You're late today," he said, rummaging in the fridge for something organically sound. He sounded surprised: Mark was usually gone by the time he came down: he wasn't used to seeing him in his dressing-gown.

"I'm not well," Mark explained.

"Taking the day off then, is it?"

Mark nodded. Roger perked up.

"Serious disease, do you think?"

"Just a touch of 'flu, I think."

"Can be nasty, 'flu, you know, killed millions in its time. . . . "

For the next five minutes Roger talked happily about death.

"Did you know there was a plague pit in Fareham?"

"No."

"Oh aye, down by the churchyard where the fire station is now. Full of corpses buried in quicklime!"

"It's a quarter past nine, Roger."

Roger gulped down a last mouthful of some bilious liquid.

"Hope you get better soon, then," he said without apparent conviction. "I'll be back late tonight. See you then, perhaps. . . . "

His unspoken thought seemed to be " . . . if you're still alive".

Mark watched him through the window, dashing across the drawbridge and clambering on to his moped. "Late" meant that Roger wouldn't be back until at least 11 p.m.; tonight he must have

108

earmarked for one of his rare social excursions, a trip to the Red Lion for a pint of mild and a round of darts with Mr Singh, who occupied the next counter to his in the Post Office. At least Mark would have the house to himself. He listened gratefully to the tinny roar of Roger's moped, echoing away down the quiet country lanes.

He picked up the phone and called the bank. Miss Temple answered. Vernon wasn't in yet, she would pass the message on when he arrived. No, there was nothing urgent to be dealt with. He should take as much time off as he required, and not come back till he was a hundred per cent again, that was her advice. He was wrapping up warm, she hoped.

"Is Mrs Harvey there to look after you?"

"She's in the house, yes."

It took him five minutes to get rid of her. In the end he had to say that he was feeling ill and must run to the bathroom. She was still talking when he put down the phone.

He examined the envelope which he had picked off the mat. It was addressed to him and had 'By Hand' printed neatly in the top corner. He opened it and saw Reg Talbot's letter-heading.

Dear Mr Harvey

I would like to apologise most sincerely about what happened last night. As I explained, my wife has not been feeling quite herself recently, in fact she has been a bit "under the weather". I believe that one of the conditions from which she suffers is called agrophobia. As a result she has a tendency to hanker after confined spaces, hence her unfortunately rather embarrassing visit to the broom cupboard, a habit which she seems to have got into recently. This is a very depressing condition from which to suffer, and I hope you will understand why she has had on occasion a tendency to overcompensate with the odd extra dose of "mother's little helper"!

I do hope that Mrs Harvey is feeling better and that you will both be able to attend our little soiree on Saturday. The "fun" begins at eight. It should be a terrific evening!

Yours very sincerely,

Reginald R. Talbot

Ps. My wife is in a somewhat delicate situation from the medical point of view and I would be most grateful for your discretion in this matter!

Mark dropped the letter into the bin. He could be discreet alright. He would discreetly ignore the Talbots and their wretched party. He would wear ear muffs on Saturday night.

The phone rang. He hesitated before picking it up, but then thought that he'd better, just in case it was Vernon checking up on him. But it wasn't Vernon. It was Lizzie.

"No, she's not up yet," he said in answer to her question.

"Please ask her to ring me when she is up," said Lizzie coolly. "You are passing on my messages, I hope."

"Of course!" said Mark indignantly.

He slammed the phone down. He was annoyed. He went out into the hall and banged on the cellar door. He couldn't open it, the key was upstairs in his jacket pocket.

"Maddie!" he shouted through the keyhole. "Lizzie says to ring her back!"

He nodded decisively to himself, as if to say "There!" Then he went back up to bed.

He spent the rest of the day under his blankets, getting up only to use the bathroom and make some buttered toast for lunch. He lost count of how many times the phone rang. It woke him whenever he dozed off. Nothing frightened him so much as the telephone. His waking moments became an agony of suspense. The first ring made his heart cold. He was being slowly crucified by British Telecom. He wondered about leaving it off the hook, but that might arouse suspicion. Roddy would be sure to come round again. For how much longer could he fool him? How much longer could he postpone his fate? He wasn't even sure why he wanted to postpone it. All he needed was a little courage and it would be all over. What was so precious about his freedom that he should wish to preserve it? What was so wonderful about his life?

He drew the sheets back over his head, closing in the boundaries of his world. There was nothing in his life worth fighting for. Nothing had ever happened to him; nothing ever would. He was nearly forty years old. They would put him away for twenty years. Perhaps he'd get out after fifteen. He would be a fifty-five-year-old dependent of the state, an ex-con, an ex-respectable person; a non-person. The story of his life. From non-entity to non-person in one consistent downward curve. He would have no job, no friends, no means or reason for existence. Probably he would not live long. He would never be able to show his face in Fareham again. Perhaps he would end his days as an off-season lodger in a seaside boarding house. He could see himself, hunched and grey, shivering under the thin blanket. He didn't deserve that. He had done nothing wrong in his entire life. Except murder his wife.

He reached out a hand and fumbled for the radio. It was just five o'clock, he heard the pips and then the news. The winter's day was almost over, the room was dark again. Soon it would be time to sleep, and then to wake again, to face another day. How many more would there be? How long before Roger or Roddy finally noticed? Or Lizzie. Lizzie was the real danger, she was the clever one, the true enemy. Probably her suspicions were aroused already. The Fareham Feminists met every other Wednesday. Not the one coming, thank God, but soon enough. They would come looking. Even if he did manage to fob off Lizzie, it could only be in the short term. Unless he could think of something. . . .

He got up, pulled on a sweater over his pyjamas, and then his dressing-gown. Did anyone have reason to doubt that Maddie was alive? Roger didn't, and he lived in the same house. He hadn't even noticed that she was dead. Roddy had "seen" her last night, two whole days after her death. Lizzie was the problem, Lizzie hadn't seen her since Saturday and there was no way that he could fool her over the phone. Would Roddy come back tonight? He had better be prepared.

He went into the bedroom and sat down at Maddie's dressing table. He put on the wig and stared at himself in the mirror. He didn't look remotely like Maddie, but he didn't look bad. He had a soft, round face, rather feminine in fact. There was just a trace of shadow on his chin, but nothing that a quick shave wouldn't remove; he wasn't naturally hairy. He had never noticed what long eyelashes he had. He fluttered them at the mirror. Quite the little coquette, he thought. The eyebrows were a shade too thick, but nothing that a little adroit plucking couldn't put right. He picked up a tube of lipstick. He couldn't resist it; he felt intrigued. It felt funny, greasy on his lips, but he liked the bright red look of it. He rubbed his lips together, as he had seen countless women do, and pouted at his own reflection. It was amazing what a difference just a smear of lipstick made: he quite fancied himself. . . .

He sorted through all the little bottles and flasks, sniffing and admiring. He applied mascara to his eyelashes. The first time he didn't do it very well, so he wiped it off and tried again. It gave his eyes a luscious, exotic look. A light brown pencil made his eyebrows look more refined. Rouge put some colour in his cheeks. He overdid that the first time too. Nothing too whorish, he thought, toning himself down; he didn't want to give Roddy the wrong idea. He highlighted his cheekbones and the bridge of his nose. He knew about shading a face, he had painted so many models. It was nice to see a practical skill coming in useful. He powdered his face, delicately covering the thin lines. He had a long, smooth neck, he looked younger than his years. Make-up suited him. Perhaps being a woman suited him. He rummaged through Maddie's jewellery box and came up with a pair of clip-on jade earrings and a necklace of oriental design. He stood up and admired himself in the full-length mirror by the bed. He looked even better from a distance – from the adam's apple up.

He opened Maddie's wardrobe. The interior bulged with clothes. He took a few dresses out and held them against him. They were like tents. He saw a plain black suit wrapped in dry cleaner's polythene. He hadn't seen that suit for years, and no wonder! he thought as he took it out: Maddie wouldn't even have been able to get it over her head these days. He took off the polythene bag and laid the suit out on the bed. It was made of plain black wool, good quality, with large glossy black buttons. He threw off his dressing-gown and tried on the skirt. There was a little too much room round his hips, but he found an adjustable tag and tightened it up. It was a good length, coming almost exactly down to his knees. He had the opposite problem with the jacket, which was slightly too tight. Still, it wasn't an impossible fit. Perhaps his pyjamas constricted him unnecessarily. He took them off and tried on the jacket again. There was a distinct improvement.

He opened the bedroom door and walked down to the end of the landing. He turned back at the top of the stairs, from where he could see himself fully in the bedside mirror. He didn't recognise himself at all. With Maddie's glasses on, not even his own mother would have recognised him. From a distance, if only from the neck up, he might even have been mistaken for Maddie.

He went back to the bedroom. He sat down on the bed. He could see himself in the dressing-table mirror. It was more than enough to fool Roddy, who would see only the shock of blond hair and perhaps the glint of the glasses. But Roddy was half blind, not to mention half deaf and at least three-quarters stupid. Would it fool anybody else?

Why ever not? If someone was expecting to see Maddie, then what reason would they have for suspecting that what they were actually seeing was a female impersonator? No one besides himself knew what had actually become of her. No one had any reason to suppose that anything untoward had happened at all.

He stripped off. He was only faintly aware of the cold. He was excited and intent on what he was doing. He found a pair of black tights in the cupboard and pulled them on. If he looked closely he could see the hairs on his legs through the mesh, but no one was going to look closely. He selected a bra and filled out the cups with some more tights. He was careful not to overdo it, remembering the tight fit of the jacket. For the same reason he chose a blouse of thin material. It was almost a see-through effect. He buttoned up the jacket all the way, for modesty's sake.

He walked slowly to the door. He wasn't used to taking such small steps, walking came awkwardly. His bra pinched. His legs had an unfamiliar, nylon feel. He felt not only a different person, but a different animal: his first experiences as a woman were utterly alien. He marched up and down the landing a dozen times. It was like learning a new dance step. He stood in front of the long mirror, turning from left to right, examining himself critically from every angle. He had never thought of himself as tall before, but he was tall now; tall for a woman. He was tall and graceful, rather refined. He had a good figure, narrow at the waist and perhaps too straight in the hips, but quite eyecatching. His legs were amazing. He lifted the hem of his skirt a little, flirted with the mirror. The only item he lacked was shoes. His own feet weren't large, but Maddie's were dispropor- tionately small, and he knew that she had nothing he could have squeezed into. In any case she had seemed to spend most of her time in ghastly old sandals, hardly his style. He went through his own cupboard and selected a pair of plain black slip-ons. They did look like men's shoes, but they weren't bad from a distance. Distance was all that mattered.

He looked at his watch. It was twenty to six. Ten minutes to Fareham if the traffic held. As long as he made it by six he would be alright.

He descended the stairs awkwardly, unused to the tightness of the skirt. He took Maddie's gaberdine from its peg in the hall and slipped it on. Room for one more inside. Her red silk scarf hung on the next peg. He hung it loosely about his shoulders, as he had seen her do so often. He took her umbrella, not that it looked like rain, but just in case: he didn't want to ruin his wig.

He closed the front door with exaggerated care and tiptoed up the garden path. It was dark, there was no movement at the Talbots', but he proceeded nonetheless with caution, barely brushing his feet over the wooden boards of the drawbridge, and hugging the hedge on the other side. He pulled the car door only half-shut after him, not wanting to make any noise. He started the engine, and when he was sure that it was running smoothly, turned on the lights.

He went too fast up the driveway. Over the years he had learnt to take it slowly, to nurse his suspension over the uneven surface, but tonight he drove like a boy racer. Or a lady rally driver. He opened, drove through, then shut the gate at the top behind him in record time, despite wanting to take much bigger steps than his skirt would allow. He took the road to Fareham.

There wasn't any traffic until the main road, and then it was only two cars cruising behind an elderly truck; or what passed for rush-hour congestion in Fareham. As he drove into the High Street he tried instinctively to retract his neck, but as far as he could see none of the pedestrians even glanced at him. At this time of the evening people were hurrying everywhere, hurrying to get home, or to catch the shops before closing. Many of the shops were shut already, but a few remained open till six, among them Lizzie Skinner's bakery.

He pulled over on the other side of the road, stopping almost directly outside the garage which Reg Talbot had just added to his empire. The bakery was brightly lit. There were half a dozen customers inside. The two usual girls were serving as rapidly as they could, but even as Mark watched three secretary types came in together and topped up the queue. Lizzie Skinner's bread and cakes were popular. She did a special afternoon bake to net the homegoing trade. One of the assistants looked up as the secretary types came in. She spoke to the other, who flicked back the bead curtains and called into the back room. A moment later Lizzie Skinner came out, wiping her floury palms on her apron.

Instinctively Mark wiped his own palms, on his skirt. The engine was still running, he pressed his foot down on the clutch and put the car into gear. His other foot twitched on the accelerator. He watched Lizzie serve the next customer. She took some money and went to the till. He pulled Maddie's glasses out of his pocket and put them on, instantly blurring his vision. He could just see normally over the top of the lenses. He sounded his horn.

Lizzie looked round. So did everyone else in the shop, but Mark paid them no attention. He saw Lizzie look at him, a blank expression in her eye. It must have been hard for her, staring out of the lighted shop into the darkness. He raised a hand and waved. After a moment she smiled and waved back. She beckoned to him, to come inside. He shook his head and pointed at his watch. She nodded, and mimed speaking into a phone. He nodded back, waved again, and took his foot off the clutch.

He had driven nearly fifty yards, almost to the bottom of the High Street before he realised that the reason why he couldn't see anything was that he was still wearing Maddie's glasses. He snatched them off and was just in time to avoid an ambling pedestrian. He felt exhilarated. It had gone brilliantly. There hadn't been even a flicker of suspicion. He put his foot down heavily on the brake, tried to concentrate on driving sensibly. His tyres squealed as he raced out of the High Street. He just couldn't get over his own boldness, not to mention his cleverness. He had bought himself a breathing space. Quite what he was going to do with it was a question that would have to be deferred for the time being.

There was almost no traffic coming home. He drove with care, keeping within the speed limits and signalling and using his mirrors punctiliously. Bold calculation had carried him successfully thus far; he didn't want to throw it all away by some rash and entirely avoidable act.

He stopped at the entrance to the drive and got out of the car to open the gate. It was a tedious procedure which he still resented after seven years. But it was the unavoidable price of living next to a field of cows. He got back into the car and drove it through, stopped on the other side and got out again. He had pushed the gate right back on its hinges to an angle of ninety degrees, where it held fast against the overgrown grass. He grabbed the topmost bar and pulled.

A car appeared from round the next bend. It was a big car, but its engine was smooth and low. Mark only heard it at the last moment. He looked up and the headlamps blinded him. He heard the decelerating moan of the engine. The car turned off the road and stopped a few feet away. When the spots had cleared from before his eyes he saw that it was a black Jaguar.

Mark stood like a rabbit in the headlamps. He could still hardly see, but he heard the door open and feet scuff the gravel drive. He heard a voice he knew.

"Are you alright?" asked Reg Talbot.

Mark had buried his face in his hands. Fingers and fear muffled his voice.

"Yes, It's just the lights. . . ."

"Oh, I'm sorry," said Reg, reaching back into his car to turn them off. Mark snatched Maddie's glasses from his gaberdine pocket and put them on. Now he could see even less than before.

"You must be Mrs Harvey. I'm Reg Talbot, your neighbour. Perhaps your husband has mentioned me? I'm delighted to meet you."

The voice had been getting nearer and nearer. Mark started as a clammy hand took hold of his own. He laughed nervously. Reg could be no more than a couple of feet away; it was a good thing he had turned off those lights.

"Yes, Mr Talbot, I've heard all about you," said Mark softly. He had decided that by speaking softly, rather than trying to raise his pitch, he sounded more natural, more feminine. It also put less strain on his voice.

"Nothing too bad, I hope!" declared Reg loudly, sounding rather pleased with himself. "I'm glad to see you up and about again, Mrs Harvey. You're feeling better, I trust. My wife and I both hope that you'll be able to come to our party on Saturday."

"We'll do our best, Mr Talbot. Lovely to have met you, excuse me – I must be getting along now. . . ."

Mark backed away towards his car, guided by the sound of the still running engine. He tilted his head just enough to be able to see under the glasses and find the car door.

"Lovely to meet you too, Mrs Harvey," said Reg, who now sounded rather disappointed. "It's alright, you can leave the gate to me. . . ."

But Mark had already left the gate. He scrambled into the car, grabbed the steering wheel, found first gear and let off the handbrake in one continuous action. He thrust his foot down hard on the accelerator and the car jerked away, the exhaust rattling over the potholed surface. He knew that he was driving too fast, but he couldn't stop. He didn't know what he was doing. Blind panic had gripped him. Literally, he couldn't see a thing. The car was hurtling along, and the faster he went, the less he saw; it was mad, it made no sense.

That's silly of me, he thought, I should take off Maddie's glasses.

He slammed on the brakes, but it was too late. The car hit something. The impact flung him forward, throwing off the offending glasses. He hit his head on the steering wheel. The car slewed round in the mud and slithered off the drive into the parallel hedge. From somewhere close by a cow gave an injured moo.

Mark threw open the car door and staggered out. Hands gripped him, helped him along. He felt a burly arm round his shoulder, supporting him. Reg Talbot's breath was hot on his cheek. Mark smelt whisky.

"Are you alright? Good God, you're bleeding!"

Mark touched his face. There was a cut on his forehead, he blinked blood out of his eye. Reg dabbed at it with a handkerchief. Mark took the hankie from him and held it to his face, covering his features.

"You were lucky!" said Reg, who sounded as shocked as Mark. "You could have got glass in your eye."

Reg held Maddie's glasses in his hand. Both lenses were cracked.

"Shall I call an ambulance?"

"No, no! I'll be alright, it's nothing!"

"I wouldn't call it nothing! Those bloody cows, they shouldn't be here at night in the first place. I'll give those bloody dozy Trumans a rocketing, I will!"

Reg had gone round to the other side of the car to inspect the damage. Mark took a quick look at himself in the wing mirror: the cut looked much worse than it really was. More importantly, it hadn't affected his disguise. Nervously he patted his wig back into shape.

"We'll have to pull it out in the morning," said Reg, wrestling with a growth of hedge. "I'll give it a tow out, it won't be the first time!"

He came back round to Mark and looked at him anxiously. Mark lowered his face into the hankie.

"Are you sure you don't want me to call you an ambulance, or a doctor?"

"Quite sure thanks. I've never felt better."

"That's the spirit. Come on, I'll drive you up to your house."

"No, I don't want to be any trouble – "

"It's no trouble at all. Come on, I insist."

117

Reg took him firmly by the arm and led him to the Jaguar. He opened the door for him and, when Mark was inside, carefully tucked in the hem of his coat before closing it.

He certainly knows how to treat a lady, Mark thought.

"Is your husband in?" Reg asked, as he got back into the car after closing the gate.

"He's out for the evening," Mark answered hastily.

"Oh, that's a pity," said Reg, sounding as if he meant the opposite. Mark glanced at him suspiciously, but could see nothing except the outline of his face in the darkened interior. For the first time he realised that Reg was a little nervous of him, perhaps even disliked him.

Him, that was. Not her, as he was at the moment.

"Thanks for the pot plant," said Reg.

"Oh yes. I chose it myself."

"Your husband said. Very kind of you."

Reg stopped the car at the end of the drive, next to the drawbridge. He insisted that Mark stay put while he came round and opened the passenger door.

"Very gallant, Mr Talbot," said Mark, who was doing his best to behave in a ladylike manner, whatever that might be: it wasn't as if his own particular role-model had ever been much of an inspiration.

"Allow me to escort you to your door, Mrs Harvey."

"No, no Mr Talbot, you've been too, too kind already."

"On the contrary, Mrs Talbot, I feel it is my duty to aid a lady in distress. It's what good neighbours are all about."

Mark felt Reg take his arm again and lead him towards the drawbridge. He sneaked a quick look at his watch (hidden under his cuff) and saw by the luminous dial that it was twenty past six. The house was dark. He usually left the hall light on when he went out; he couldn't think why he hadn't this time. He fumbled in the darkness for the front-door lock. He realised that he didn't have a handbag, and he felt awkward taking the key out of his pocket. Reg was standing very close behind him, almost breathing down his neck, and that made him feel even more awkward. At last he got the key in the lock and turned it, once only. He must have forgotten to double-lock it, his usual practice. No doubt it had slipped his mind in all the excitement.

He pushed open the front door and stepped inside. He felt for the light switches, taking care to pass over the hall light, which was bright, and selecting instead the dim imitation candles on the stairs.

"Well, thank you very much, Mr Talbot, it's been more than kind of you."

He began to close the door. Reg made no move to go.

"Not at all, Mrs Harvey," he said, putting a hand against the door frame. "Are you sure you're going to be alright now?"

"Yes thank you. A nice cup of tea will do me the world of good!"

"Sure you wouldn't like anything stronger? I must say, I wouldn't say no to a drop myself!"

Mark stared at him blankly. There was no doubt about it, he really was inviting himself in. What a cheek! Mark thought. He wouldn't behave like this if he thought my husband was about.

"If you don't mind Mr Talbot, I think I'll – "

He stopped dead in mid-sentence. From behind his shoulder, from up the stairs, came a long drawn-out creaking noise, a noise as unmistakable as it was familiar – the unoiled protest of the trapdoor hinges.

"Mark?"

Roger's voice echoed cavernously from within his attic lair. Mark froze, not daring to look behind him, not daring even to breathe.

What the hell was Roger doing at home? Why hadn't he seen his moped? What had happened to his darts evening?

"Do you have someone staying with you?" asked Reg nosily.

"The lodger," whispered Mark. Reg seemed pleased.

"That you, Maddie?" called Roger from on high.

Mark coughed into Reg's hankie.

"Yes," he squeaked faintly.

"Oh good!" said Roger. "Lizzie Skinner just phoned, asked if you'd call her back. And that Roddy fellow left a message, I wrote it on the pad by the phone, he said you'd understand."

"Thanks!" said Mark, and coughed again.

There was a moment's silence. Mark waited for the sound of the trapdoor closing again. Instead he heard the clump of Roger's feet on the top step of the ladder.

Mark wheeled round. Roger's legs had swung into view, he was on his way down. Mark turned round again. Reg was still standing on the doorstep, grinning pleasantly. Caught between the devil and the deep blue sea.

"Why don't you come in and have that drink, Mr Talbot?" said Mark, and didn't wait for his reply. He grabbed Reg by the sleeve, pulled him in and slapped shut the door. Reg looked faintly surprised, but not displeased.

"This way," said Mark, pulling him over to the dining room door. He stole a quick glance up the stairs and saw Roger's shoulders appearing through the attic hole.

He flicked on the dining room light and walked on through into the living room, which he traversed in darkness. He turned on the reading lamp above the armchair and retreated immediately to the comforting shadows by the drinks table.

"Quite dark in here," observed Reg, truthfully enough.

"My eyes are sensitive," Mark answered.

"Of course. Don't you think you should see about that cut?"

"It's not bleeding. I'll see to it later. Would you close the door please."

Reg closed it. Mark indicated the armchair and he sat down, blinking at Mark, for the light was in his eyes. Mark remained where he was, listening out for Roger. A crashing sound from the kitchen confirmed his proximity.

"A little water in mine, please," said Reg, hinting.

Mark poured two whiskies into tumblers. There was a little water left in the jug.

"Do you have any ice?" Reg asked.

"No," answered Mark quickly. "The freezer's on the blink."

"Not to worry."

Mark handed him his whisky, then retreated to the far end of the sofa, where he sat down and took care to keep his hands out of sight. His hands were the least convincing part of his disguise: he hadn't got round to painting his nails, which were in any case overdue a manicure; more seriously, he realised that he wasn't wearing any rings.

Something stirred at the other end of the sofa. Mark gave a little gasp, but it was only the cat.

"You go to Dr Spicer too, don't you?" said Reg.

Mark nodded. Dr Spicer was the vet. Reg droned on about his dog, Boxer, who was very old and might have to be put down soon, which would break his heart, not to mention the kids'. Mark scarcely even feigned to listen. Roger was still clomping about in the kitchen.

"Of course I do love Yeats," said Reg, after a pause and a throat-clear. "He's one of my favourites. Must be one of yours too."

"Yes," said Mark distractedly. He had just heard the kettle boil. With any luck Roger would be gone in a minute, unless he broke something.

"It's a lovely name for a cat, Maud Gonne," said Reg.

Mark looked at the flea-bitten tabby sitting next to him. Bloody silly name, he'd always thought. Maddie had agreed with him. They had inherited the cat from her mother, the most pretentious woman he had ever met.

"I think it's so sad and romantic," said Reg wistfully, "to have loved a beautiful woman from afar without ever attaining the object of desire, if you'll forgive my use of language."

There was the sound of smashing crockery from out in the kitchen. Roger had broken something.

"Mm, yes," murmured Mark, taking a sip of whisky. He would have liked to have knocked it back in one, only he guessed that that sort of thing might have appeared unladylike.

"Do you mind if I have another?" asked Reg boldly, not suffering under the same impediment.

"Help yourself."

He did so. Mark leaned along the sofa, cocking his ear towards the door. He thought he might have heard the kitchen light being switched off. Maud Gonne stared at him suspiciously.

"My wife doesn't care for poetry," said Reg softly.

Mark jumped. Reg had crept up right behind him and was leaning one hand on the back of the sofa. Mark felt his fingers brush against his shoulder. He felt the whisper of his breath against his neck. The breath was even more whisky-soaked now.

"Will your husband be out late?"

Reg's voice sounded low, husky with drink. He was very close.

"I shouldn't think so," said Mark smartly, and got up and went to the drinks table. He moved to the far side, where he could keep an eye on Reg, and poured himself another drink. He took a deeper draught than before, not caring what Reg thought. Reg was beginning to annoy him. There was an air of brashness about him which he had not noticed before. Perhaps he had been drinking heavily earlier in the evening.

"I think he's mad," said Reg cryptically.

The front door slammed. For a moment Mark refused to believe it, but then he heard Roger's step on the path outside and heard his tuneless whistling. Mark pressed his back against the wall, keeping away from the window. He heard the drawbridge shake under Roger's heavy boot, and a moment later the feeble popping of the moped. Instinctively Mark pressed his free hand to his heart. With the other he raised the whisky tumbler to his lips. His hand was trembling.

"I will arise and go now, and go to Innisfree – "

"You'll what?"

Mark didn't mean to snap, but his nerves were stretched. He had had enough of his unnatural act, the exhilaration of deception had been replaced by the terror of detection. Roger was gone, the way out was clear. He had only to get rid of this idiot – half-drunk and red in the face, swaying limply from foot to foot like a sock in the breeze – and he could get these stupid clothes off and be himself again. The look of relaxed contentment on Reg's face only made his irritation worse.

"I said I'll go to Innisfree – "

"I think that would be a very good idea!"

"But I haven't finished my drink – "

Nor did he have time to finish his sentence: Mark whipped the glass out of his hand and propelled him with a most unladylike shove towards the door.

"But we were having such a nice little talk!" Reg protested, sounding mortified.

"I'm sorry, but I'm not feeling well, Mr Talbot. I want to get cleaned up and have a lie-down. Here." He shoved the bloody hankie into Reg's hands. Reg protested.

"Please keep it!"

"No thank you. . . . "

They were in the hall. Mark pulled open the front door with one hand and bundled Reg out with the other.

"I'm sorry Mrs Harvey, have I offended you?"

"No, no."

Mark tried to close the door. Reg put his foot in it.

"What about the car?"

"I'll do it in the morning."

"You'll need a tow. Here's my telephone number. Please call."

He pressed a card into Mark's hand, squeezing his palm unnecessarily. He made no move to disengage his hand. He leaned into the door, pushing it back a little and relocating his foot further in.

"You're a very beautiful woman, Mrs Harvey. . . . "

Mark felt his jaw drop. It was a very peculiar sensation, and not one he had ever experienced before. It was something one read about in books, an exaggeration, not an accurate description, for nobody's jaw actually dropped . . . his did: he heard it go, clunk. His mouth hung hugely open, like a slack-jawed whale's.

Reg's hand was now on his shoulder. He felt the fingers playing with his bra strap. Total paralysis threatened. His eyes were out of focus; a vague shape loomed in front of him. Suddenly the hand was round his neck and pulling him with force. Reg's wet and squashy lips were pecking at his own.

"Mr Talbot!"

Strength returned to him just in time. He managed to raise his forearm and wedge it in under Reg's chin, levering him away. He only just held him at bay; the pressure was maintained.

"Whatever would Mrs Talbot say!"

"My wife doesn't understand me. Our marriage is dead and barren. . . . "

His voice cracked. He sniffed.

"Please forgive me, Mrs Harvey. I shouldn't have tried to take advantage of you like that. . . . "

He released Mark and stepped back, his arms falling limply to his side. He sniffed again, and smothered a little whimpering noise in his throat. Suddenly he seized Mark's hand again:

"Please say you'll forgive me, Mrs Harvey!"

He sobbed. Mark had to look down at his feet. It was rather embarrassing, really.

"Of course, Mr Talbot. Think nothing of it."

"Thank you!" said Reg, squeezing his hand so hard he almost yelped. "Oh thank you, thank you!"

And with that, Reg turned abruptly on his heels and ran away into the darkness.

Mark slammed the door and fell against it, gasping for breath. His knees were literally knocking together, behaving in much the same exaggerated manner earlier adopted by his jaw. For a minute he remained clinging to the door for support, waiting for his pulse to settle. He noticed the message pad by the phone, on which Roger had written the message to Maddie. He looked at it, but it was too dark to read in the hall. He put it in his pocket and went upstairs.

Wearily Mark slumped down at the dressing table. He stared at himself in the mirror. There was a smear of dried blood above his eyebrow, but it looked worse than it was, the cut was little more than a scratch. He was relieved. He didn't want to start losing his looks when he'd only just discovered that he had any.

He pushed back the stool to gain a little distance and examined himself thoughtfully. He was surprised at what he saw; he hadn't realised he looked that good. Rather reluctantly, he had to admit to himself that his features were decidedly feminine. He had never noticed what fine, delicate bones he had. Perhaps he even understood what Reg saw in him. As a man he had always been nondescript. Of course, the blond wig suited him, much more than it had ever suited the real Maddie. That was a strange thought – that the neighbour should think of him as both Mark and Maddie; stranger still that he should be at best neutral about the one and have quite a crush on the other. Mark giggled to himself in the mirror. He brushed his fingers through his hair and smiled coyly. Blondes definitely had more fun.

He remembered the piece of paper, Roger's message. Roger's handwriting was terrible, and he had to study it hard. Eventually the disjointed schoolboy letters took the form of words:

Let down your hair tonite, Rapunzel! – Roddy

A sound made him jump. He couldn't think what it was, but it was loud and familiar. He turned towards it, towards the window, and a moment later knew it for what it was, the rattling of small stones on the glass pane.

"Cup-cake! It's Roly-panda!"

Oh my God! thought Mark. Not again. . . .

10

The next morning Mark spent much longer than usual in the bathroom. Only in the cold light of day did he notice how many smudges of make-up remained on his face. With cleansing cream and soap and water he set about removing them. He was able to take his time, because he had waited for Roger to leave the house before coming down. He wasn't planning to go to work today. He had sounded genuinely rough on the phone yesterday and he doubted if they would even expect him in.

When he came out he noticed a white envelope lying on the mat. He recognised Reg's handwriting. It was addressed to Mrs Harvey. He put it into his dressing-gown pocket. Then he went upstairs and leaned as far as he could out of the bedroom window, from where he could just see over the hedge beyond the moat into Reg's forecourt. There was no sign of the black Jaguar. To his surprise he noticed that his own car was parked in its usual place. He dressed hurriedly and ran outside. The front headlamp was cracked and the wing slightly dented, but that was all. He went round to the driver's door and saw another white envelope, this one unaddressed, lying on the seat. Inside was a brief note, unsigned, saying that apart from the slight visible damage the car seemed to be okay. The keys were in the ignition.

Mark wandered over thoughtfully to the Talbots' house. There were only two cars parked in the forecourt. The house looked empty. Oddly enough, he couldn't recall quite as much neighbourly noise as usual during the last twenty-four hours. He stuck his head round the gatepost and saw a man in a donkey jacket smoking a cigarette. The man eyed him suspiciously.

"Anyone about?" Mark asked.

The man didn't answer. He continued to look at him suspiciously.

"The name's Harvey. I live just there," Mark explained.

The man looked relieved. It occurred to Mark that he might have thought he was a Talbot employee, checking up on him.

"No one about at all," the man replied in an Irish accent. "Er, I'm Murphy."

"Jolly good," said Mark, putting on his Colonel Blimp voice.

They exchanged a few words about the weather, then Mark walked back towards Willow Cottage, somewhat light of step: workmen he could cope with; he felt somehow safer if there were no Talbots in the vicinity. Back home he made some breakfast. As he took his first bite of toast the phone rang.

"Hello?" he answered in the feeble tone of a terminal patient, in case it was the bank.

"Darling?"

"Go away, Roddy!" he shouted in his gruffest, most masculine voice, and slammed the phone down. He chomped angrily on his toast. It really annoyed him that Roddy had rung. He had thought that he'd got rid of him for a bit last night.

He had had to employ somewhat drastic measures:

Hardly had he positioned himself by the window in wig and broken glasses, than something heavy had crashed against the windowsill and he had realised, to his horror, that it was the top of a ladder. A moment later and the windowsill began to vibrate: Roddy was coming, like King Kong for his Fay Wray. He had reacted fast. He had had no choice.

"Get back, Roddy! Mark's here, he's got a gun!"

The vibrating had stopped. Roddy's moon-like face hung whitely in the air, like a Duke of York's man, neither up nor down.

"That's right, whatsyername!" Mark boomed in his best *basso profundo*, throwing down the glasses and tearing off the wig in one movement. "If I ever see you round this house again I'll give you both barrels!"

And with that he seized the top of the ladder and pushed it away violently. Roddy squeaked as he fell into the rose bushes. Mark put on his falsetto and screamed:

"Run away Roddy! He's coming downstairs, he's got the gun!"

"That's right!" he thundered, continuing the monologue in his alternative manifestation. "I'm coming to get you now!"

Actually it had taken him ten minutes to get out of Maddie's clothes and make-up, to clamber into his pyjamas and dressing-gown, snatch an imitation Colt off the wall of his study and rush out into the garden, trying to look like a scene from *Miami Vice*. But of

Roddy there had been no sign, although there was evidence of his precipitate departure: the ladder still lay across the rose bed. Mark had hidden it round the side of the house.

He laughed out loud as he finished off his toast. It was quite funny really, Roddy must be terrified of him. If only he would stop phoning. Why couldn't they all stop phoning?

The phone was ringing again. Two calls in the course of one piece of toast. He wanted to ignore it, but what if it were Vernon? The thought of Lizzie made him hesitate, but then he picked it up.

"Hello?" he inquired, even more feebly than before.

"Could I speak to Mrs Harvey, please?" asked Reg Talbot in a muffled voice.

"She's not in," said Mark aggressively, and then, suspiciously: "Who's this speaking?"

"No one. Just a friend."

The line went dead. Mark replaced the handset, even more annoyed than after Roddy's call. Perhaps he should disconnect the phone. If every successive call was to irritate him more, then soon he would have no option. He had known that it was Reg Talbot's voice instantly, despite the pathetically attempted disguise. It was as unmistakable as his handwriting. That reminded him, he still had Reg's letter in his dressing-gown, upstairs. He started on his second piece of toast.

The phone rang again.

"Yes!" he barked into it angrily.

"I'm sorry, is Mark there?"

"Yes, yes, it's me. I'm sorry, I'm not feeling too well. . . . "

It was Martin Bird.

"I'm sorry to hear that," Martin said. Mark said that it was nothing really. "I'm pleased to hear that," Martin continued. "Look, it's about the house. We're going away either Friday or Saturday. I've no idea how things are with you and Maddie at the moment, but if you need a break from it all the house is all yours."

"That's very kind of you."

"Not at all, anything to help out an old friend. Actually, it's a shame we're not going to be here the Saturday after next. There's going to be a big muster over in Langley. Would be a good opportunity to put the boot in on your friend in the Halberdier Corps!"

They discussed Roddy for a minute. Mark said that things were okay with Maddie, but they weren't on speaking terms, which was at least half true. He thanked Martin again and said that he'd let him know.

He put down the phone, picked it up again and dialled the bank to let them know that he wouldn't be in. Miss Temple was solicitous. Vernon didn't want to talk to him. Everyone wished that he would get well soon.

He replaced the receiver and went upstairs. He wondered how long it would be before it rang again. Who would it be next time? Lizzie? Roddy? Reg? To hell with it! Let them . . . his free time was his own: it might not be free for very much longer, he wasn't going to let unpleasant thoughts get him down. He would push the world and all its encroachments to one side. He had thought that he might get on with his models, put the finishing touches to his Luger. But when he sat down and took up his brushes no feeling of enthusiasm came. He stirred a paint pot limply for half a minute, then replaced the lid. He just wasn't in the mood. He knew what he would like to do, but he couldn't. Or he shouldn't. Or he oughtn't. He wasn't quite sure why, but he knew it would be wrong. Then again, it wouldn't really be doing any harm, would it?

Go on, he thought to himself, be a devil!

He took off his shirt and sweater and got back into his dressing-gown. He went next door to the bedroom. He sat down at the dressing table.

With a rush of excitement he ran the tips of his fingers over the rows of jars and tubes and tins. There were enough of them: Maddie had never stinted. He squeezed Elizabeth Arden foundation cream on to his hand and smoothed a lovely, even colour over his entire face. He brushed lightly across the lines around his eyes and made them disappear. He disposed in similar fashion of the tiny scar that marked his accident of the night before. He felt his chin critically and gave it a mental pass: his shave had been close enough. No stubble, but still he frowned at his reflection in the mirror. Those eyebrows . . . he took her tweezers and began to pluck. It was nasty work, he hated it and his eyes stung, but he knew what a difference it would make, so he gritted his teeth and persevered. Now he applied eyeliner and mascara. He liked this best, working the eyes. He liked it all, it was such fun: dressing up, disguise, deception . . . he put blusher on his cheeks; powder. With trembling hand he pulled on his wig. Now he was almost complete. He noticed a stray chest hair just above his collar bone, frowned and plucked it out. He frowned again when he examined his nails. They were far too short, and painting would only draw attention to the fact. He would just have to wait for them to grow, and meantime keep them clean and neat. His hands annoyed him. Without his hands he would be perfect.

The phone was ringing downstairs. The phone was always, always ringing. He didn't want to speak to anybody. Neither of them did. He let it ring. Eventually it stopped. Afterwards he wondered who it could have been, Lizzie, Roddy, Reg, but it was too late now. He remembered Reg's letter, sitting in his dressing-gown pocket next door. He went and got it. Back at the dressing table he opened it. There was one sheet of paper inside, filled with neat lines of what looked like poetry. Mark scanned it through quickly, frowned, then read it again, with mounting surprise.

A fourteen line poem, or: A Sonnet.

Your face, I have no doubt, could launch a thousand ships.
Your eyes are full and beautiful, and so are your lips.
Your hair is soft as silk and your voice is as the lark
When I see you driving by, I have to pull over and park.
I stare at you from afar, my love dares not speak its name
But love it is, it burns within me, it is a pain.
But I would not stop it, no! not for a million pounds.
Although it is forbidden, lo! such love is out of bounds.
Why should this be? Wherefore? It is not fair,
My feelings are passionate and if not unique, quite rare.
I have tried to keep them to myself, but it's impossible,
And the thought of being without you is really horrible.
It is my inmost hope that you my love someday will return,
Till then I'll keep my passion secret, although I yearn!

SIGNED: An anonymous admirer

Further re-readings did nothing to lesson his astonishment. He put the paper down and stared at himself in the mirror. His lips were very bright today, he noticed. There was a darker red, a more subtle shade that might suit him better. He should try it. It was a revelation, what cosmetics could do for him.

There was a mischievous gleam in his eye. It quite took him by surprise, he wasn't used to seeing so much animation in his own reflection. A smile spread across his ruby lips. He lifted the poetic paper to his mouth and, just beneath the anonymous "signature", planted a moist lip-print. His own vermilion "signature" was full and fluttering, like a butterfly's wing.

"Quite a little stunner aren't we, Maddie?" he said into the mirror.

Maddie fluttered her eyelashes back at him. She pouted her lips and blew a delicate kiss.

Reg Talbot sat at his desk with his hands clasped in front of him over the book he had been reading. He was wearing his glasses and his most headmasterly air. Billy stood opposite him, hands in pockets, uneasily transferring his weight from foot to foot. Reg did not look at his face. He examined instead his stained tie, his unironed shirt and dirty shoes. He made a mental note – Must Try Harder.

"What is it, Billy?" he asked curtly, when he had grown tired of the silence. Although, of course, he knew perfectly well what it was.

Billy cleared his throat uncertainly. He stuck his tongue into his cheek and rolled it around, desperate for inspiration. Reg felt quite sorry for him: appointing Billy to the role of emissary was a bit like putting the Pope in charge of family planning.

"Shaz says she'll be back this afternoon to get her things, and she doesn't want you there. She says you're not to try to ring her 'cos she won't talk to you. She says her lawyers'll do the talking. . . . "

Billy's words came out in a low monotonous rush. A look of some relief crossed his face when he had finished, like that of a constipative happily surprised by the efficacy of a new brand of laxative.

"Is that all?" said Reg coolly. This time he looked Billy squarely in the face. Billy could not meet his eyes.

"Yeh, that's all," he answered uncomfortably, and then, with pathetic simplicity: "I'm really sorry about all this, Reg, from a personal point of view, you know. . . . "

Reg said nothing to that. It would be too hypocritical, he thought. After all, it was precisely from this particular personal point of view that one of the most attractive by-products of his estrangement from

Sharon had emerged, namely the removal of one Billy Barker from his domestic orbit.

"Well, Billy," Reg began magisterially, opening then reclasping his hands in a gesture suggestive of the immense impenetrability of the mysteries of life, "what can I say? You're not married yourself, and you can't be expected to appreciate all the little ups and downs and ins and outs of the married state. These things just happen, that's all. I know that Sharon is your sister, and blood is thicker than water, but I'm sure you understand that there are two sides to any coin. So let's just try to go about our daily business with as much dignity as possible, okay?"

This little speech affected Billy: he bowed his head and pressed his hands to his breast in an uncharacteristically devotional attitude. His lips quivered.

"Alright Billy," said Reg quickly. "You'd better get back to work now."

He had no wish to witness his brother-in-law burst into tears in front of him, an event which in the circumstances he deemed a fair possibility. The Barkers were a sentimental lot. Billy shuffled away miserably, like a man condemned. Reg was stony-faced. There was more to Billy's attitude than fraternal devotion, the shared experience of a family trauma. Something deeper was at work within him: a glimmer of light had pierced his antediluvian brain: the merest hint of a notion that perhaps the gravy train was shunting up a one-way siding.

Had it yet penetrated to Sharon? wondered Reg, when he was alone again. So little penetrated through the alcoholic haze she wore, like a deflective aura. Perhaps she had had a point, screaming at him the other night – shoving her into the broom cupboard had not been entirely in the spirit of the marriage vows. On the other hand, what had she ever contributed to their marriage? At first he had been shocked by her declaration that she wasn't going to spend one more night under the same roof with him, nor the children either. The children, of course, were completely disinterested. They just sat watching the television, as usual, and, when Sharon and Billy came downstairs with some hastily packed suitcases, refused to leave until they had watched George Michael on *Wogan*. After that there was something else on, so they watched that too. When, finally, they did go, Reg had felt only relief.

He missed none of them, except perhaps the dog. Boxer was the only one who had ever shown him any affection. For a while after they were gone he found the silence disconcerting, but it had grown on him. No more blaring radio or tv vibrating through the house: no more of Danny's nuclear-driven ghetto-blaster, diluting pure noise into the fractured air. And more blissful still, as he quickly came to appreciate, no more human voices.

She was going to divorce him, she said, in their one telephone conversation, the following morning. Her mind was made up, there was no point his trying to talk her out of it. She was going to stay at her mother's until she found a house, somewhere nice on a proper estate like they'd lived on before, not some dump in the middle of nowhere. If they hadn't moved in the first place none of this would have happened, he did know that didn't he? He'd better be prepared to cough up for a new pad, or else, and on the alimony front too, she didn't care how he paid for it. She said she'd already spoken to her solicitor.

"We're gonna skin you!" she had declared smugly, and slammed down the phone.

Actually he rather doubted it. He was not stupid about financial matters. She'd do alright out of him, but no better than that, and frankly, if it would get rid of her, he wouldn't begrudge a single penny. In fact, it was a bargain. The price was right. Meantime, she would have a few unpleasant surprises in store. He smiled to himself. It would have been worth quite a lot just to see her face the moment she discovered that he'd cancelled all her charge cards.

He rested his chin contentedly on his hand and turned the page of his book, his now familiar and well-thumbed anthology of English verse. He felt so relaxed, now. Never in a million years would he have left Sharon, but now that she had left him he felt ten years younger. Youthful passions, rekindled on the altar of hope, gambolled through his veins. He tried to read 'Byzantium', for the twentieth time. He knew it must be good, because he didn't understand a word. He read it very slowly, half aloud, thoroughly impressed by the extent of his own incomprehension. This was the real stuff alright.

At last, and with a sigh, like a good boy who has made a stab at his difficult homework and at least gone through the motions, he flicked the pages back to where they fell open naturally on some shorter poems of Tennyson. Reg smiled happily to himself. This was his treat, this was what he liked best, even if he did understand it so it couldn't be much good. He cleared his throat, stood up and clasped the anthology firmly in both hands. As he strode about, his *piano* gradually became *fortissimo* until, a minute later, a casual passer-by might well have been surprised (and was, it was Mr Thomson from Spares) to hear a full-throated, no holds barred rendition of 'The Charge of the Light Brigade' coming through the boss's door.

11

Dear Roddy

I do hope that nasty husband of mine didn't give you too much of a fright last night! I'm afraid he meant it, he's very violent. Besides the shotgun he has a whole arsenal of lethal firearms, not to mention a machete and a hatchet which he keeps at all times by his bedside. Incidentally, I have seen him practise with them on a pumpkin, and I'd advise keeping well out of his way when he's in a bad mood, which I'm afraid seems to be whenever he thinks of you. I know it's just jealousy, and who wouldn't be jealous of a real he-man like you, but for heaven's sake keep out of the way for a bit. I told you what my solicitor said about stirring him up. Your showing your face round here is like waving a red rag at a bull! I think it's a bad idea even to use the phone. Just hearing your voice puts him into a violent sulk. So write if you want to, but that's all! I ABSOLUTELY FORBID you to come round visiting again. I know it's hard for you, Roly-panda, and believe me, it's not easy at this end either. How your little gooey cream-cake misses your scrummy wobbly body! We'll be together again soon enough, my man-size slice of passion cake, but in the meantime you'll just have to be patient and keep away for the sake of our future together. Mum's the word!

I'm sorry to use a typewriter. It's not very intimate or romantic, I know, but I'm trying to improve my wpm, just in case I need to go back to work to contribute a few feathers to our little love nest!

Love and hugs and kisses from your favourite sweet trolley,

Maddie (XXX)

Dear Mr Harvey

I'm very sorry but something has come up rather suddenly and my wife's had to go away for a while. Therefore, it is with regret that I have decided to postpone our party next Saturday, due to "unforeseen events". I do hope that this has not caused you too much inconvenience.

I look forward to seeing you and your charming wife at the Vernons' next Tuesday.

Yours sincerely (or perhaps "neighbourly"!)

Reginald R. Talbot

Dear Mads,

I keep ringing but all I get is your husband or that wretched half-wit lodger. It really was unforgivable of M-k (I can't bear to write his name) to inflict Roger on you in the first place. It always smacked of a male conspiracy to me. Are they passing on my messages?

I wish you'd been able to drop in for a chat yesterday. We're always pretty busy at that time of night (as you must have seen) but I would have loved the chance of a few words. I've been out quite a bit recently, so perhaps you have tried to ring and not been able to get through, but I'll be furious if those wretched men haven't passed on my messages. The thing is, I'm going away on Thursday evening for a few days and I won't be back till Sunday. I shall be in Oxford with poor Clare Ogden again. That awful man she was living with has been crawling round begging her to take him back and I detect alarming signs of weakening resolve. A couple of days of sisterly bucking up should do the trick. These really are exciting times we live in – Clare and you in one week! They may be small steps for woman, but they're giant leaps for womankind!

I'll try and drop in on Sunday on my way back. Till then, courage and resolution.

Yours on the barricades.

Lizzie

My dearest cup-cake

It's so horible to think of you living in the same house as that gastly, evil man. He's so sick I'm really worried. I can't help worrying, because are you safe? He is obviously got violent tendencies, as you say, with all those guns and things lying about, are they legal, that's what I want to know? You have to get certificates for guns, I think it's a disgrace they give them to people like that. There are enough weirdos and nutters around without encouraging them, I say. They ought to bring back capital punishment for people like that. I think I could sue him for causing me bodily harm. It can't be legal to go about pointing guns at people and threatening them. Do you suppose he is a homicidal maniac? If he is, you ought to be careful living with him. I wasn't frightened myself of him the other night, he doesn't scare me, and he knows that, which is why he keeps threatening me with guns. If he had any guts he'd come and sort it out with me man to man, but of course he hasn't, people with guts don't go around waving them at people. That's guns I mean. I know you want to make sure you get your share of the house and he doesn't muck your things up, but don't you think you could get a court order or something on him, tell him to go away and leave you in peace. I wish you could come and live with me. I know it's only one room and a bit poky, but there's a nice big bed for us to cuddle up in and we could have lots of fun, naughty but nice! I do miss you and I am passionate to think you miss me too. Roly-panda desperately wants to get his paws on his furry honey bear! I know you've got Roger in the house so he won't dare to do anything, but if he gets nasty again I really think you should call the police. If you bring this up in court you can really stitch him up. I'll be a witness about his violent behaviour. He deserves it. I've got a tooth loose, that's from when I got kicked at the muster. I'm really looking forward to the next muster, which is the weekend after next at Langley. I've got a new hat with a green plume, more comfy than a helmet. I would like you to see me in it very much. I'll try to be a good boy and not phone but it's very hard to live without your sweet singsong voice, my little blue tit. (That was naughty, I'm your blushing little robin redbreast!) Why don't you phone me when you know he's not around. Who is your solicitor, you haven't told me? I hope you got Mr Murray like you said, he's very good. You don't say if you've had the tests back from the clinic yet. I'm keeping my fingers crossed, but don't get too excited yet, remember when you thought you were pregnant six months ago, and you weren't really, although I'm sure you are this time, if you say you are. Write to me soon and let me know what's going on. Tell me a time when we can meet, then if you can get away from him you can come round here for the evening. He does still let you use the car I hope.

I sleep with your last letter under my pillow. It would like another to keep it company.

With millions of hugs and kisses and delicious naughty thoughts.

Your panting panda,

Roddy XXXXXXXXXXXXXXXXXXXXXXXXX!!!!

Mr Harvey

Just a little "Get Well" card from all of us here at the bank! Hope to see you on the feet again soon. Hope too you like the card — we think it's rather sweet!

With best wishes for a speedy recovery,

Alice, Flora, Eleanor,
Janet, Bob, Jamie, W.W.Vernon (See enclosed)

My dear chap,

This is just to confirm that we are expecting you and Mrs Harvey for dinner next Tuesday. Nothing too dressy, but presentable please. 7.30 for 8. Might be forward policy to offer Talbot a lift. Please be punctual.

W.W.V.

Dear Creamy Sponge Slice,

I'm still waiting for a reply from my last letter. How can you be so cruel as to deprive me of your tender thoughts, so full of love and naughtiness! When I get into bed all alone at night, with just my hotty botty and Brian Bear for company, I feel all sad and want to sigh! My life is very boring without you. I want to hear your sweet lovely voice again and cover your bright red cheeks with squashy kisses. If you don't speak to me soon I'll have to phone you up or even come and see you. If I am shot it will be a small price to pay for bliss. Yummy, yummy, I've got love in my tummy! Let me know how things are going with the divorce. We shall have our own little bear cave soon, and who knows, perhaps the sound of baby paws running around too. Please, please write back, toot sweet!

Zillions of love,

Roly-panda

DeaR MaRk,

Could you please sign the enclosed wheRe it says "witness" and just leave it on my laddeR. It's my Revised last will and testament.

CheeRs

RogeR

Dear Maddie,

I hope you don't mind me addressing you by your Christian name. "Mrs Harvey" sounds so formal, and although we have met on only the one occasion, I feel that I know you very well already. Incidentally, of what is your name an abbreviation? I hope it is Madeleine, which is a beautiful name. I wanted to call my daughter Madeleine, but my wife chose Kelly. I do not think this is so distinguished as Madeleine.

Anyway, the reason why I am writing personally to you is to say that I am very sorry we have had to "postpone" our party this weekend, which is on account of my wife's indisposition. I have already written to your husband, but I wanted to let you know personally how very sorry I am that I will not have the honour of your presence in my abode on Saturday night, although of course the pleasure does await at Mr Vernon's on Tuesday.

I have just been reading "Byzantium", which is a most interesting poem, although I have to confess there are one or two bits I don't understand. Perhaps you would be willing to elucidate me over a glass of sherry. If you are free anytime over the weekend maybe you would like to pop over. I would enjoy very much a serious discussion on poetry with you. Poetry, as you have probably guessed already, is a very great interest of mine. In fact, as you may have realised, I have even had a "go" from time to time myself. . . .

It is a delight to have made the acquaintance of so charming and erudite a lady.

With sincerest regards,

Reginald R.Talbot

P.S. I happened to be in the library today renewing my books and I was conversing with Miss Blunkett, the assistant librarian, who said she knew you, although she seemed surprised to hear that you were so interested in poetry. Perhaps she doesn't know you as well as she thinks! Anyway, in the course of our conversation I learnt that there used to be a Fareham literary discussion group, run by a friend of yours, Miss Lizzie Skinner, although it had not met for several years. She gave me Miss Skinner's phone number, so how about if I give her a ring and invite her around as well so the three of us could discuss revitalising this important institution. I would be only too pleased to host any cultural evenings in my own home.

I hope that this idea excites me as much as it does you!

Dear Mark,

I keep trying to get you on the phone but there's never any answer. Has everyone gone deaf, or what? I still don't know if you'll want the house while we're away, but if you do need a break it's all yours. The spare room's a bit of a mess, so use our bedroom. We'll leave some fresh sheets out. Spare keys will be hidden in the usual place in the shed. Talk to you when we get back if not before.

Yours aye,

Martin

Dear Mr Harvey,

Please find enclosed one plastic pig (Britain's farmyard animals range). The award is made for the second consecutive year after a unanimous vote. We trust that you will display it in a prominent place and will experience a profound sense of shame and guilt whenever you look at it.

Yours,

Elspeth Truman (Chair) on behalf of the Committee of the Fareham Feminist Discussion Group.

Dear Mr Harvey,

Thank you for your letter. With regards to your enquiry, I am afraid that the "Presidential" range of cut-glass bowls was discontinued in 1986. I enclose a copy of our current catalogue. The nearest equivalent is the "Heirloom" range, made from the highest quality lead crystal, not simply an ornament but an investment which your family will wish to keep and treasure for generations to come.

Yours faithfully,

B.J.Pinkerton
(Asst. Chief Marketing Executive Consultant)

Dear Mr HARDY

READ THIS CAREFULLY!

You have been PERSONALLY SELECTED to take part in our amazing BARGAIN OF THE DECADE! Luxury Holiday Villa Scheme. In addition to the fantastic cut-rate special price which we are offering (see below) your name has been entered, FREE, in our LUCKY DIP SUPER PRIZE DRAW, 1st Prize £10,000 CASH. Just rub away using the edge of a coin the window below to reveal your UNIQUE PERSONAL COMPUTERISED NUMBER! No obligation, just tear off the coupon and POST TODAY! All you have to do to collect one of our fabulous selection of prizes (see below*) is to turn up in person at any one of the following venues on these dates when you will be asked to take part in a brief video demonstration, complete with free buffet

*subject to availability (Contd.Over)

Does the crash write-off Lancia in front of your house belong to you? If you are selling for scrap please contact me. I am working next door at Mr Talbot's.

Jerry Murphy

BY PERSONAL DELIVERY:

A sonnet entitled:

"Oh Madeleine, Madeleine, wherefore art though Madeleine?"

If thou were Sharon it would be alright,
I bet you anything we'd never fight.
Thou by the river Amazon couldst repine,
While I'd be by the Thames, come back about nine
And spend eternity gazing into your eyes,
And if you got bored with listening to my sighs
I'd take you for a spin in my new Jaguar,
Out to the country, though not too far,
Just till we got to some nice lover's lane,
Where I could hold your hand and kiss your lips again.
And we could be so happy just gazing at the moon,
How I hope to see you again, very, very soon.
Although my love is secret, for now it's anonymous,
I think you'll guess I live close by, in a very near house. . . .

Dear dear Scrummy Sponge Cake,
    Where are you? As you can see because I've delivered this by hand I
have been round to see you. I had to. I couldn't help it. No phone
calls and no letters. Where are you? The house seems empty. I know
he might shoot me, but I'm worried he might do something to you
too. He's so violent and I can't sleep at night worrying about my
tender precious darling under the same roof as a raving madman.
Please, please please call me soon!

                         Roly-P XXX

PS. I bought a new pair of floppy boots to go with my Halberdier
uniform. They look terrific!
PPS. I'll be around again tomorrow night if I don't hear from you. I
have to!!
PPPS. I saw Mr Murray in the High St yesterday and he told me you
hadn't got in touch with him. Have you got another solicitor then?
Please let me know!!!

DeaR MaRk,

Just a note to say could you RetuRn my will as soon as poss. I may be needing it soon. I wRote down some messages foR you and Maddie by the phone.

CheeRs

RogeR

"Oh, I was just going to leave this for you, outside your door. Only I'm off, see. . . . "

Roger's thin voice, hesitant at the best of times, trailed away into a black hole of indecisiveness. A hint of red touched his pale concave cheeks. He wouldn't meet Mark's eye. Instead he looked down at the floor, to the bedroom threshold on which Mark's feet were daintily planted. Mark looked down too. He frowned. The shoes really didn't look right, too flat, too dull. They didn't go with the black fishnet tights at all.

"Thank you, Roger."

He took the thin sheet of cheap paper with its few typewritten lines. His nails still didn't look right either, even with the glossy varnish. It would take weeks for them to grow.

"It's about my will, see," explained Roger in a very faint voice, his chin compressing his adam's apple.

"You want me to leave it on the ladder? Of course I will, Roger. I'll sign it today."

The thought briefly crossed his mind – sign it as what?

"Thanks very much," mumbled Roger, whose cheeks were now nearly as scarlet as Mark's lips. He began to back away.

"Oh, Roger?"

He stopped. He even dared to look up briefly, to catch Mark's eye. His expression was embarrassed, furtive.

"What day is it, please?"

For a moment Roger looked surprised, but it was only fleeting: too many surprises had just been queueing up to assault his senses for him to feel put out by a question that could not have been described as anything more than mildly disconcerting.

"Er, Saturday. I've got to go out now. Be back late."

"Saturday, eh. The weekend already. Who'd have thought it?"

Mark laughed softly to express his amazement at the flight of time. Roger laughed along with him, a touch hysterically. He stopped abruptly, and recommenced backing away.

"Better be off now. . . . "

"Roger!"

He stopped immediately, like an obedient dog. Not a muscle twitched. His eyes were once more firmly on the floor, his attitude submissive.

"Roger, it's not what you think. Don't get the wrong idea, please. I wouldn't say you're the sort to jump to conclusions, would you?"

"No," whispered Roger, almost inaudibly.

"Good. Thank you Roger, that's all."

Mark didn't wait for him to resume his backwards shuffling act. He stepped back inside the bedroom, closed the door firmly and locked it. For three days now he'd kept it almost permanently locked. Three days and three nights. He wouldn't have thought it had been that long. Was it really Saturday? For the first time he noticed just how stale the air was in the room. Hardly surprising, after three days with the windows shut and the curtains drawn. Stale and dark, a fetid atmosphere, his own recycled breath polluting his lungs. That was how it was: nothing could intrude on his narrow enclosed world, not even oxygen.

He sat down at the dressing table and turned on the light. He stared aghast at himself in the mirror: he really did look terrible; no wonder Roger had been evasive! He reached for the tissues, dipped his fingers in the cold cream, and began to rub the caked muck off his face. His wig was all over the place. It hadn't been designed to be slept in, he should have taken much better care of it. When he had wiped the cream from his fingers he took off the wig, replaced it on its block, and brushed out the tangles. He sprinkled on some water to flatten it a little, then doused it liberally with hairspray, reinvesting the tired tresses with a bouncy wave. Inside it was damp with sweat and distinctly unpleasant. He opened the window and put the wig next to it, to air.

He stripped off. Peeling away the layers of crumpled, dirty clothes he began to get quite cross with himself: he couldn't think how he had become so slovenly; he felt like a right slut. Of course, he hadn't realised just how long he'd been in isolation, but that wasn't the point. Nice girls took proper care of themselves. This was letting down the team.

He kicked his dirty underclothes under the bed and put on Maddie's voluminous dressing-gown. Her pink fluffy slippers were of course far too small, but for some reason she had cut the toes out, so he was able to squeeze into them all the same, stretching the flimsy fabric to tearing point. Then he snatched Maddie's towel from the radiator and went downstairs.

He quickened his pace when he reached the hall. He kept his eyes straight ahead, locked in imaginary blinkers. His sleeve may have brushed the cellar door, but he affected not to notice. He didn't like nasty things. Unpleasantnesses had to be ignored. He entered the bathroom almost at the run and hurled himself into the shower. He stood dripping blissfully under the stream for a good ten minutes.

Upstairs again. He laid fresh clothes out ready on the bed before removing his dressing-gown. He couldn't help but be aware of his body in the shower, but in the bedroom he wished only to minimise his nakedness. He threw off the dressing-gown and pulled on the clean underwear as quickly as possible, trying to ignore the inconvenient reminders of his own gender. Only when he had zipped up the skirt and was buttoning his blouse did he allow himself to relax a little. He sat down at the dressing table and prepared to reapply his make-up. He was dimly aware of a paradox: to the casual eye it might have appeared that he was putting on a mask, when in fact the opposite was the case: he was not putting on, he was putting off: in covering the surface he was shedding himself, from the outside.

"Madeleine is a lovely name. Nicer than Maddie. Mads is terrible. I hate abbreviations. Length in a name is elegant."

He took care with his make-up. His face was a fresh canvas, scrubbed clean only to be retouched again. Restored to its greater glory. With every stroke his confidence grew. Mark was fading, and Madeleine was coming into focus. Madeleine had so much more to offer.

He looked at his hands with irritation. There was just nothing he could do about those stubby nails. It was a pity Roger had seen them. Who had Roger seen? Not Madeleine, that beautiful glamorous creature. It had been Mark.

"Silly Mark!"

Silly indeed, to let himself be caught out like that. Who did he think he was, a female impersonator?

"Ha! Ha!"

He'd been careless. Stupid to open the bedroom door like that without looking through the keyhole first. Of course he'd been unlucky, it hadn't been his fault that Roger had just happened to be standing there, but in some situations you had to make your own luck. He couldn't afford to be careless, not with all that unpleasantness about that he'd been trying so hard to avoid. People might gossip. Roger might tell. Whom might he tell? It probably didn't matter. Who would believe someone like Roger? Roger didn't have friends to tell anyway.

Madeleine had friends, friends and admirers. Gentleman callers, even. She had inspired poetry, she easily outshone her only rival, the other Maddie, the abbreviation. They had quite a history, those two, they went back a long way together. Of course, Maddie had always been jealous of Madeleine, although Madeleine hadn't always realised. No, she hadn't known at all, not until very recently. It was funny how suddenly things had swum into focus in the last few days. Sometimes all it needed was a little quiet time in which to think, to shape one's thoughts and let the obvious present itself. Poor Maddie, one had to feel sorry for her! Trying so hard to keep up with her glamorous sister, and never getting close. Madeleine was the one who turned heads. Poor Maddie was fat and plain. That was a euphemism. She had always tried to pretend that it didn't matter, but in retrospect her resentment was obvious. And she had never lost an opportunity for stabbing her supposed friend in the back, as Madeleine now sadly realised. It was hard not to feel bitter. Impossible not to feel disillusioned.

Madeleine smiled softly at the reflection in the mirror. There was compassion and understanding in that smile; Madeleine was at heart a good sort. One had to rise above the vicissitudes of friendship and fortune . . . Madeleine blinked. There was something out of place at the bottom of the reflection: amongst the cosmetics a sheaf of papers obtruded. On top was Roger's note, the latest addition to the week's correspondence. The letters had not been answered, there was discomfort here, potential unpleasantness. But what the eye didn't see . . . the eyes were bright and round, fixed on their own image in the glass. They did not blink again, though they may have seen, out of the corners, the hand that neatly scooped the papers into the bin. Now the dressing table was cleared of all but the essential accessories of beauty, which was how a dressing table should be. Madeleine had always had very clear principles in life, and was determined to adhere to them. Most people just had too many things on their minds, they couldn't see the wood for the trees. But if one concentrated rigidly on the way ahead, and ignored the little by-ways and deviations that cropped up on the straight and narrow, then one could just proceed at a steady, regular pace and be sure of getting there in the end. Of course, it was difficult for the modern woman, she had acquired so many new roles, not instead of but in addition to the old ones. One had only to glance through the women's magazines to see just how much more demanding life had become.

Madeleine sat down in the armchair by the window and opened a copy of *Cosmopolitan*. It was well-thumbed already, but that was the thing about glossy magazines, it didn't matter how many times you looked at them, there was always something new to see. The advertisements alone were an Aladdin's cave of riches. So many things to buy! So many styles and fashions, and products and fabrics. So many and such little time. It was a private, woman's world, with its own rules and codes. It was comforting to scan through the offerings, to enjoy the stimulation of the new, and the reassurance of the familiar.

The pile of magazines shrank, the hours passed. At about half past two Madeleine noted the time and instantly felt peckish. Amongst Maddie's store in the kitchen were some packets of diet soup. It was important to watch one's figure, although in Maddie's case one couldn't help but wonder if it was worth the effort. How it must have disconcerted her, seeing Madeleine's trim, calorie-controlled waist-line. No wonder she hadn't been able to do any better than Roddy, hardly a knight in shining armour to set a damsel's heart a-flutter.

The water boiled, the soup was sipped, thin but tasty. Some toast would have been nice, but temptation was there to be resisted. Madeleine had always had much greater self-control than Maddie. The phone rang. Madeleine answered it.

"Who's that?"

Madeleine took an instant dislike to the voice. It was not so much the rather common nasal twang (Madeleine was not a snob) but the aggressive tone that made her hackles rise. This was a woman who thought rather too much of herself.

"It's Madeleine."

"Madeleine? Madeleine who?"

"I could say the same myself. Who might you be?"

There was a pause at the other end. Madeleine examined her nails.

"I don't know why you're pissing me about, Mark, but you can stop right now."

Madeleine froze. Something unpleasant was humming down the phone lines.

"Just get Maddie for me, Mark. I've had enough of your sick —"

Madeleine put down the phone. Her hand trembled. Her legs were shaking too, she had to sit down. She reached for a piece of kitchen towel and mopped her brow. The piece of towel became brown with foundation. She was peeling.

The phone rang again. It was very loud. Ring-ring, it went, she counted ten times. She thought it might stop then, but no, on it went, eleven, twelve, thirteen, fourteen —

"Hello?" said Madeleine, her voice a mixture of despair and defiance.

"Madeleine? Is that you?"

Oh yes, yes, yes! Madeleine's heart sang.

"Er, it's me. It's Reg."

Of course it was Reg, the voice was unmistakable. Awkward, bumbling Reg from next door. He knew who Madeleine was alright.

"Er, I wondered if you'd got my letter. . . . "

Perhaps he caught the ecstasy in Madeleine's voice. At any rate he grew in confidence, and soon he was bubbling away. Of course she'd received the letter, it was so nice of him to write, she told him so. No, she didn't think it "forward" at all, she laughed at him, gently of course, he was such a silly! Then he said something about Mark, and for a moment everything was spoiled. He must have known he'd said something wrong, for he apologised, though it was obvious he didn't know what he was saying sorry for.

"He's not here," said Madeleine curtly. "He's gone away."

"You mean . . . you mean you're all on your own?"

Something very strange had happened to Reg's voice. It sounded as if he was being strangled.

All on her own? Yes, in a manner of speaking. Roger didn't count, and as for the abbreviation. . . .

"Yes! Yes!" said Madeleine suddenly, not even waiting for the end of Reg's next question. The knot round Reg's throat was loosened: elation flooded down the phone:

"You mean . . . you mean you will have dinner with me tonight?"

Madeleine did not withdraw her acceptance.

"That's, that's . . . " but his vocabulary was inadequate. "Shall we go out, or, or perhaps you'd like to come here?"

Madeleine thought it over for a moment.

"Here. I mean there. Your place."

"That's . . . eight o'clock?"

"Fine."

Madeleine put down the phone.

"There!" she exclaimed aloud, and paused, as if daring the world to contradict her. But the world didn't dare. She went out into the hall. She banged on the cellar door.

"There!" Again she paused, leaving time for a response. There was none. "See! Somebody wants me!"

Satisfied by the silence she turned away, and went upstairs, and rummaged in Maddie's wardrobe.

She found what she was looking for at the back, the dark-blue velvet party dress with a bow at the back. Maddie hadn't worn it in years. She couldn't have done. Anybody else would have thrown it out, but not Maddie. She had probably gone on believing that she would slim back into it until the very end; until her dying day. Poor Maddie, poor self-deluding Mads.

"Your loss, my gain," said Madeleine, trying on the dress in front of the mirror. It was no use getting sentimental about Maddie. "You've only yourself to blame."

The dress looked perfect. The style may have been a little old-fashioned, but that was Madeleine for you, by instinct conservative. The material was in excellent condition, it could hardly have been worn. Dark blue was probably her best colour. She stood back, admired herself full-length. That spoiled the effect – it was those wretched man's shoes! She had another look through Maddie's shoes, though of course that was a waste of time: not only were they all too small, they were plain inappropriate; all she seemed to have were flat-heeled sandals.

Madeleine sat down at her dressing table and had a think. Maddie's handbag was on the floor, where it had been for a week. There were twenty pounds in the purse, and some loose change. She went next door, to the study, and emptied Mark's wallet and trouser pockets. Mark wouldn't mind, he'd do anything for Madeleine. That yielded another thirty pounds. So she had more than fifty. That ought to be enough. She changed back into her day clothes. She put all of the money back into Maddie's purse, along with the car keys, and went downstairs.

She hadn't used the car since the night of meeting Reg. It had a habit of behaving temperamentally when it had been ignored for a few days, and she put in the ignition key with trepidation. But she needn't have worried, it started first time. The collision with the cow didn't seem to have caused any real damage. Perhaps the car just responded better to a careful lady driver. She drove to the end of the drive, went through the familiar routine of opening and closing the gate, then took the road to Fareham.

It was a busy Saturday afternoon. The car park off the High Street was almost full, she got one of the last places, thanks to the chivalry of a gentleman in a Mercedes who let her take the one they had both aimed for. The car park was at the bottom end of the High Street and she wanted the top end. She walked up past the bank where Mark worked, past the other bank, the nasal woman's bakery, Reg's recently acquired garage. She felt a strange thrill seeing all these familiar places, almost as if it were for the first time. When she entered Footloose, the shoe shop, it really was for the first time. Madeleine had never before darkened its portals.

There were four other ladies already in the shop, quite enough to occupy the two assistants. Madeleine sat down in one of the chairs provided and waited patiently to be served. She knew precisely what she wanted, she had already spotted it in the window.

"So sorry to keep you waiting, madam," said the elder of the two assistants, probably the manageress, when at last she was free.

"That's alright," said Madeleine generously. "Saturday must be your busiest day."

"It certainly is," agreed the manageress, with a rueful chuckle.

"I don't know," said Madeleine, "the weekend! Supposed to be a time when you can put your feet up, and all that. Alright for the men, I expect. They would put their feet up, wouldn't they!"

They certainly would, agreed the manageress. She told Madeleine about her sixteen-year-old son, about what a mess he always made and how she had given him an ultimatum: if his room wasn't cleared up by the time she got home tonight, there'd be no supper for him!

"That's a jolly good idea," said one of the other customers, a red-cheeked, rather overweight lady dressed in a sensible tweed suit. She laughed throatily: "Jolly well got to hit 'em where it hurts, that's what I say!"

Madeleine smiled rather graciously. It was so nice and relaxing being in a proper women's shop: no hurry, always time to stop for a chat.

"How can we help you, madam?" asked the manageress.

Madeleine pointed out the shoe she wanted in the window. She gave the manageress her size. Then she took her seat again while the manageress went to see if they had it in stock. She returned a minute later, carrying a shoe box.

Madeleine hardly breathed as she watched the lid come off, and heard the tissue paper rustle. One gleaming black leather shoe was withdrawn and held up for her inspection. She nodded and the manageress bent down to help her put it on. She had already kicked off her own shoes. She buckled on the new one, stood up, flexed her toes. It was a perfect fit.

"Would madam care to try on the other?"

Madeleine nodded. The manageress buckled it up. She indicated the full-length mirror on the far wall.

Slowly, like a trick walker on stilts, Madeleine approached the mirror. It took an age to cross the parquet floor. She felt impossibly tall in her new high heels, and very unsteady. But she had fallen in love with them already, and she knew that they were just the thing. How delicate and dainty they were! How thin the narrow strap that bound them to her ankle, how tiny the glistening silver buckle.

"Does madam find them comfortable?"

Madeleine's smile lit up her face. The manageress responded in kind, sharing her evident pleasure. They were more than comfortable. They were divine. The manageress replaced them in their box and put the box into a smart green carrier bag. Madeleine opened her purse and counted out four ten pound notes. She had never in her life parted with money so gladly.

"Wait a minute!" said the manageress sharply.

Madeleine turned back from the door. The manageress's tone of voice alarmed her. What was the matter? What had she done? The manageress must have noticed the worried look in her eyes. She smiled reassuringly.

"Here." She held out a hand. "You forgot your change."

Later, at home, Madeleine learnt to walk again. It had been easier in the shop, on an even surface. The cottage floors were worn and oddly angled. Crevasses yawned between the floorboards on the landing, traps to catch a heel. The stairs, of course, were the worst, and going down much more difficult than coming up. She had to take it slowly. One false step and she'd be sure to twist her ankle.

The shadows were lengthening by the time she felt sufficiently confident to traverse the house without keeping her eyes glued to her feet. She needed to feel that confidence. She needed to know that she would look her best tonight.

13

It was unseasonally warm for October; a mellow evening and still, the sky threaded with bright stars. The silence of the country was profound; nothing disturbed its intimacy. Romance was in the air.

Reg looked at his watch, again. He had been looking at it so much that there probably wasn't a lot of point in his taking his eyes off it between checks: he might just as well have sat there with his eyes glued to the face, watching the hands crawl round.

What is the matter with me? he thought to himself. It's only ten past, it's a woman's prerogative to be late, and what's ten minutes anyway? If she were a client I wouldn't be worried. But to how many clients do I give a candlelit dinner?

He had lit the candles already. The warm light glowed off the polished silver candlesticks, the best cutlery, the best glasses. The tablecloth was white and spotless. A single rose was laid out by her place. The table stood in front of the open french windows, giving a view of the floodlit patio beneath the canopy of stars. It was perfect. And the food? The prawn cocktails were laid out on their little beds of lettuce, just like in the picture on the packet. The Marks and Spencer salmon en croute were sitting ready in the microwave next door. Not much left to chance there. He touched the lip of the wine bottle, sitting in its icy bucket, and found it reassuringly cool.

He shivered. On account of nerves, not temperature. He walked around the table, checking for the umpteenth time. He stopped. That frisson again: he felt a gelid tingle on his neck.

What exactly did he think he was doing?

Here he was, a respectable married man, father of two, pillar of the business community, a man proposed for membership of the golf club, and how was he spending his Saturday night? In planning the seduction of his neighbour's wife. It was scarcely credible. It was so completely out of character. What had Mark Harvey ever done to him, that he should use him thus? And what had given him the idea that a woman like that could ever be interested in a wretch like him?

Quite right that he should shiver and shake; it was the proddings of conscience. But when he considered the object of his desire it was time for conscience to take a back seat.

He knew exactly what he was doing.

And why not? She said yes, didn't she? He thought he'd blown it, that time he tried to kiss her and she pushed him off, but he couldn't blame her for that, he had been the worse for drink! The significant thing was that she hadn't shut the door on him. No doubt she had a conscience of her own, but that very morning, when he'd asked her, she had been delighted, she had sung her pleased acceptance down the phone. And not a word to her absent husband, he'd bet his bottom dollar on that. She wasn't naive, she wasn't a fool. And he had some indemnity against his bet.

That girl in the library, Miss Blunkett, the one he'd spoken to about the literary society, she told him that Mark and Maddie were barely on speaking terms. Their marriage was a disaster, he treated her badly, the whole village knew that. Reg had been furious. Mark had no right to treat her like that. A woman of her charms and accomplishments. She was worth ten of him. Why should she continue to throw herself away on a worthless husband? Why should she be denied forever the chance of true love? Good questions with which to knock the stirrings of conscience on the head.

Questions to which Reg Talbot thought he had the answer; he had heard the housewife's prayer.

Only one thing was bothering him; one little thing Miss Blunkett said . . . but he wasn't going to worry about that now. What she said was ambiguous anyway.

The adhesive properties of his watch reasserted themselves. Where was she? Had she forgotten? Steady on Reg, he told himself, stop acting like a teenager! Be patient, mate. Be confident. And think positive: don't underestimate yourself, Reggie my boy, you've got a lot going for you. You're no mug!

He adjusted his sleeves, showing a glimpse of cuff. It was his best shirt, ironed by his own fair hand. He checked the knot of his tie. It was still there. He looked around the room, again. He had spent the afternoon dusting, hoovering, cleaning. The house had never looked better. He hoped she'd want to see it. There were clean sheets on the bed upstairs. Would the evening end there? He blushed at the thought. That's not what he was about. He was annoyed with himself, even for thinking it. His motives were pure, and besides, she was a lady. Mere sex was not his aim; he desired the poetic fusion of souls. Should he read to her beneath the stars? A book of verse, an M&S baguette . . . and then would he touch her hand, and then? He had to get annoyed with himself again: somehow his thoughts kept directing themselves to the bedroom.

The doorbell rang at last. It was time to banish smutty thoughts. It was time. . . . He went out into the hall to meet his destiny. He paused a moment, noticed that his hand was steady. He felt relaxed. He felt good. He opened the door.

It was a vision.

She stood ethereally in the lambent porch-light. She gave a little laugh, and her laughter was like the tinkling of the Trevi fountain in the spring. She was saying something, though he could hardly make sense of it in the rush of blood to his head. He realised she was apologising; she was saying that she hoped she wasn't too late.

"Oh no, no! not at all!" He shared her laughter.

He took her coat. Funny, he thought, he hadn't noticed how tall she was until tonight; a tiny bit taller than him, perhaps. Some men might let that worry them, but not him. She was very elegant in her sophisticated evening wear. She looked fantastic. Her blond hair fell lusciously to her shoulders; her eyes were melting sapphires. He breathed deeply and took the scent of her deep into his lungs. He had to resist the impulse to seize and kiss her passionately.

Instead he said, "Would you like to come out on to the verandah?"

She said she would. They went out through the french windows and sat side by side on the garden chairs. He gave her a vodka and tonic. They talked.

"It's a beautiful evening," he said. "I'm so pleased you were able to come!"

Yes, she agreed, it was nice.

"Did you say Mark's gone away?" he asked as casually as possible.

She hesitated before answering. She seemed uncomfortable. Yes, she said, he's gone away, he's staying with a friend.

"Does he know you're having dinner with me tonight?"

No, she said. She sounded faintly surprised at the question.

"Is he the jealous sort then?"

Again she hesitated. Let's not talk about Mark, she said.

He was happy to oblige. It was a good sign. She asked about his wife. That was a good sign too, he thought. Both clearing the decks for action. Should he reach out a hand, and take hers, gently? No, he decided reluctantly. Mark time, play cool. . . .

"I'm afraid that Sharon and I have reached the point of no return. Well, I'm not afraid, exactly . . . " (Little laugh) " . . . these things happen, we've grown apart. Or at least, I think I've grown away from her. That's not to knock her, it's not her fault, she's a smashing girl, but . . . it's odd, isn't it, how long it can take for two people to discover they don't belong together. How long have you and Mark been married?"

She shifted uncomfortably. Twelve years, she murmured.

"It's taken us sixteen. Sixteen years, two children, and what? My wife doesn't understand me. To be fair, I don't understand her either. I mean, how can you understand someone like that? No interests in life. No conversation. No ambitions. Just a question of getting from one drink to the next. I hope I don't sound bitter, it isn't Sharon's fault, that's just the way she is, but she's got no soul. No soul, no poetry. I can't see a man offering up a sonnet to her. . . . "

He paused, leaving the naked implication, the admission of what she must know already, hanging in the air. Their eyes met. Madeleine smiled. Her eyes had a dreamy, far-away look. They did not spurn him.

"Of course, some people might not think that my line of business and poetry can go together. They'd be wrong. There is poetry in all things, wouldn't you say?"

Madeleine smiled again. She nodded happily.

"Mark doesn't strike me as the sort of chap who'd be interested in poetry."

Her smile disappeared. She looked melancholy. She said, "I said let's not talk about Mark, please", and at that "please", to emphasise the point, she reached out a hand, and gently squeezed his.

She had touched him. Even though she took away her hand immediately his skin tingled deliciously. His throat was dry.

"Shall we go and eat?" he asked hoarsely.

They went into the sunroom, where the table was laid out. He closed the french windows, for the sake of intimacy, and against the cooling of the evening: it would be a bad omen if a sudden draught should blow out the candles.

They ate the prawn cocktail. She commended it. He was proud that he'd got it right, it looked so professional, just like in a Berni Inn. She liked the wine too. It was chilled to perfection. He refilled her glass then went into the kitchen to microwave the main course.

They ate the salmon with mangetout, very elegant on best china. He hadn't bothered with potatoes. She was probably much too refined ever to bother with potatoes. And as for him, he was too starry-eyed to have much of an appetite. She had, though. It all went. And so, a little later, did the chocolate mousse he'd bought for dessert. In fact, she liked it so much she asked for more. And she played her part in finishing the wine. She seemed very merry. She said, you're a wonderful cook, much better than me! He laughed. He let her have her little joke. He went to make the coffee.

When he returned, bearing the tray, she was standing by the french windows looking out at the garden. Under the patio floodlights the garden looked like a fairy grotto. He put down the tray and waited for her to sit, hoping she'd choose the sofa, but she took the armchair instead. Disappointed, he sat alone on the end of the sofa, as close to the armchair as possible.

He didn't know what to do next. The preliminaries had gone well, but that's as far as he'd planned. He just wasn't practised in this sort of thing, he hadn't chased women since those far-off bachelor days. And he'd never been any good at it then.

"Would you like to see the house?" he asked, thinking, despite himself, that if he took her upstairs, and into the bedroom, then. . . .

No thanks, she said, she was quite happy where she was. She sipped her coffee.

"I've just bought a new property in the village," he said. He told her about the garage, trying to impress her. She didn't look impressed.

"I might give your friend Lizzie Skinner another call tomorrow. Try and get the both of you round here some time."

"She's no friend of mine!"

It was a voice to splinter glass.

He froze in the act of raising his coffee to his lips, stunned by her venomous expression. She was sitting on the edge of her chair, clasping the arms with her fists, glaring at him.

"Who told you she was a friend of mine?"

"Annie Blunkett, the librarian – "

"And she's an interfering bitch too!"

She slammed down her cup on the glass coffee table.

Something was wrong. She was rising to her feet. Reg rose with her.

"Are you alright?"

He was desperate, and he sounded it. She seemed so angry and hurt. He couldn't understand what he'd done to offend her. He had a brainwave:

"Would you like a turn round the garden? A breath of air. . . . "

She hesitated. He ran to the french windows and flung them open.

"Come on! Just the thing, after a meal!"

He offered her his arm. After a moment she came and took it. He was acutely aware of the pressure of her hand as he led her out on to the patio, and up the garden path.

"I'm sorry I brought that up," he said gently. "I must have misunderstood."

"I think you did," she answered evenly. The grip on his arm tightened ever so slightly, but she seemed calmer now. "She's trouble, that woman. I'd keep away from her if I was you."

And off the subject altogether, he thought to himself, as they stopped by the edge of the swimming pool. He cursed himself for bringing it up, but how was he to have known? Annie had spoken of Lizzie and Maddie as bosom pals. He'd mentioned Lizzie casually enough in his letter, talking about the literary society, but of course Madeleine hadn't replied. Perhaps that was why she hadn't replied. He experienced a sensation of nervous chill: all this time he'd been treading on the thinnest of thin ice, and hadn't known it.

"Look at that, will you!" he said with excessive heartiness, pointing at the swimming pool and hoping she wouldn't notice the abrupt change of subject. "Swore blind they'd do it by Friday. Like hell!"

She seemed not to mind the change of subject. She stared into the black hole at their feet and appeared mildly interested.

"Do what?"

"The bottom of the pool. And the sides. Surface it."

"You mean concrete?"

"That sort of thing. I mean, you couldn't pour any water into it now, it'd just drain away!" He chuckled to himself at the idea. "I got really tough with them this morning, and not before time. I said that if they hadn't done the first stage by lunchtime tomorrow they wouldn't be getting a penny out of me, not a penny. You should have seen the look on Murphy's face! You mean get the boys to turn out on a Sunday? he asks. Get himself to turn out's more the problem if you ask me. He's done it though, sworn by all the saints and whatnot he'll be here first thing, and. . . . "

He didn't finish his story. Madeleine had disengaged her arm and turned away. He couldn't see her face in the darkness, but he sensed that she was preoccupied. He gave himself a mental ticking off: what did he think he was doing, boring her with the details? A woman like that wasn't going to be interested in the finer points of swimming-pool construction.

"Excuse me," she muttered suddenly, and walked away, back up towards the house.

"Want to go inside, do you?" He said, running to catch up. He had to keep running, she was walking very fast. He said something else, about the weather, the mild night. She didn't answer.

"Shit!" she said.

Her heel had caught between two of the patio flagstones. He bent down and helped her lift out her foot. The heel had broken. She unbuckled the shoe and took it off.

"Bit of a nuisance, that," he said as they went inside, cross with himself for not having made more of the opportunity to caress her ankles. It had been her aggressively unladylike use of language that had put him off. It had seemed so out of character but then, he realised, of course he knew so little about her character. He walked over to the drinks cabinet, ready to offer her a brandy. He wondered how he could manoeuvre her over to the sofa. He wondered if now was the time to kiss her.

"I'm sorry," she said quickly, "but I've got to go."

His hand froze on the decanter. He stared at her blankly.

"It's been a lovely evening, but really I must get home. . . . "

She seemed ill at ease. Or perhaps it was only the effect of hobbling on one and a half feet that made her seem that way. She had already hobbled as far as the door.

"But – but I wanted to show you my poetry!"

"Some other time."

He ran after her into the hall, still clutching the decanter.

"What's the matter? What have I done?"

She was already pulling on her coat. She must have heard the despair in his voice, she couldn't have failed to notice it written in his face. She hesitated.

"Nothing, nothing at all," she said matter of factly. "It's been a lovely evening, but now I have to go."

She laid a hand on the door. Reg stumbled towards her.

"But when will I see you again?"

"I don't know."

She started to go out. Desperately he grabbed her sleeve.

"Don't just walk out on me!"

She tried to brush him off, but he wouldn't let go.

"At least say when I can see you again!"

"I don't know. . . ."

"Tomorrow?"

He still hadn't let go. She gave up trying to wriggle free. Instead she looked at him with innocent trusting eyes:

"Please believe me, it's been a wonderful evening, I can't say how much it's meant to me. But I can't see you tomorrow. Maybe not for a while. You see, I'm going to have to go away for a bit, disappear as it were."

"It's your husband, isn't it? I know he mistreats you!"

"No, no, it's not Mark — "

"Someone else? Don't tell me there's someone else!"

She looked surprised.

"Of course not."

He still didn't look happy. There was something in his eyes, a struggle.

"What have you heard?" she asked sharply.

The struggle intensified.

"The librarian . . . she mentioned someone else. . . . "

It was out, the one thing that had been bothering him. She laughed.

"Not Roddy, by any chance?"

He nodded. Yes, that was the name. . . .

"He's just a joke!" she laughed again, scornfully. "Been after me for years; not a hope! There's no one else, I promise. Now please let go of me. And please don't try and contact me. I'm sorry to sound so mysterious, but I'll explain everything to you some other time. Just trust me, and don't ask any questions."

He opened his mouth, he wanted to protest, but she placed a finger on his lips. Her eyes implored him. He had to respond. He relaxed his grip and she slipped out like an eel. He thought of kissing her, but it was too late: she was disappearing from view already, hobbling away down the drive.

"Thanks for coming. . . . "

The night had swallowed her. She probably hadn't even heard. He stood staring at shadows, his mind numb with confusion.

He closed the door and walked back slowly into the living room. The delicious possibilities of the evening, so intricately imagined during the course of the day, had vanished on the instant; a heavy grille had slammed down before the portals of fancy. His emotions were a chameleon whirl: surprise, anger, humiliation, devastation, all played on him in turn, moment to moment. He didn't know what to think or do, he didn't know which way to turn. He found himself standing by the french windows.

He stared over the garden fence, at the Harveys' house. A light came on downstairs, Madeleine coming home, but there were lights on already, lights on upstairs. He was puzzled, he hadn't seen them before, when they were out in the garden. . . .

The penny dropped. He hadn't seen them because they weren't there. Perhaps Madeleine had noticed them come on. . . . She had seen that someone else was in the house; Mark must have returned unexpectedly. Naturally, she would have been embarrassed, too embarrassed even to explain to him the cause of her embarrassment. She didn't want Mark to know where she'd been, and if she didn't want him to know . . . it must be because she had something to hide. That was it, it had to be!

Hope reborn.

Trust her, she had said. There had been trust in her eyes. Something was bothering her, something she didn't want to talk about. He would give her his support, he would do as she asked, however painful it might be. He had to. He would not give up. A prize such as Madeleine Harvey was not to be won by a faintheart. From now on, single-mindedness and dedication to the cause must be his watchwords. It was up to him, he held his own fate in his hands: she was there alright, ripe for the picking, perhaps desperate for him to rescue her from her unhappy marriage. The only thing was that perhaps she didn't yet know it. It would be up to him to enlighten her. He would have to be patient, that was all.

With another song from the late subdued chorus in his heart, he began to clear away the dinner things.

He stopped in the hall, on his way to the kitchen. Something black on the floor had caught his eye, by the door. It was her broken shoe, she must have dropped it on the way out. It lent credence to his theory about Mark's unexpected return: she must have been truly startled to have hobbled away on her stockinged foot.

He put down the tray and picked up the dainty shoe tenderly, clasping it to his bosom. He smiled to himself, fancy's gate unlocked once more. No longer earthbound, the fairy tale had resumed, and he knew which foot fitted the shoe; he didn't have to look far:

His Cinderella was the girl next door.

14

"Mark? Is that you?"

The voice was tentative, as ever. It came from the other side of the cellar door. Mark stopped what he was doing and went to the foot of the stairs.

"Yes, it's me. You couldn't give me a hand for a moment, could you?"

There was a pause, then the door was pushed open a little, enough for Roger to be able to stick his head round. His lugubrious eyes expanded like rippling pools, straining to take in all that could be seen under the single dusty bulb. They flickered with momentary agitation as they came to rest on Mark. The agitation subsided: Mark appeared to be wearing trousers.

"Give a hand, is it?" he said, almost chirpily, beginning to come down the stairs. His relief was obvious.

Mark watched him closely. He watched where he looked. He saw his eyes linger for a moment on the freezer, now lying strangely on its side, the lid propped open by the shovel with which it had been levered over a short time before. Roger's eyes came to rest on Maddie's corpse, which was on the floor beside the freezer.

"It's a dummy," Mark explained, "you know, for making dresses. It's a surprise Christmas present, for Maddie. That's why I hid it in the freezer, because it's a surprise. A bit silly, eh?"

Roger made a little amused noise in his throat. They both stared at Maddie's body, now wrapped in a sheet secured with string, in addition to the frozen tablecloth.

"It's nice, that is," observed Roger. "Surprises. . . . "

"Yes. The only thing is, it weighs a ton. I've got to get it upstairs though, because I don't want anyone to see it. I'm going to hide it in the shed."

"Good thing to get the Christmas shopping out the way early."

"Yes. Now why don't you take that end – go up first. That's right. I'll take the weight."

"Ooh! That is heavy. I see what you mean!"

"Yes. Just back up slowly, easy does it. Do you know what the time is?"

"Can't really look at my watch now. After midnight though. I've been back at least an hour."

"Yes, I saw the lights on. Did you find your will?"

"Oh, yes thanks. Very kind of you to sign it."

"Don't mention it. It's good policy to have a will, you never know when you might need it."

"Mm. Where now?"

"Right. Out the front door."

They were at the top of the stairs. They paused for a moment, getting back their breaths. They shivered.

"Cold, eh?" said Roger, readjusting his grip on the frozen corpse.

"Yes. Shouldn't have left it in the freezer so long. Nearly there now."

They had done the hard work, not that it was that hard with two. Roger led the way through the hall and out of the door. They laid Maddie's body in the wheelbarrow, which Mark had parked earlier under the porch light.

"Great! I can manage on my own now, thanks. Very decent of you to help, Rog."

"Don't mention it. Anytime. Goodnight."

Mark watched him going up the stairs. He didn't look back. He had no natural curiosity. He had very little of anything. His legs disappeared up the ladder and the trapdoor was banged shut. Mark counted a minute, then pushed open the door softly and went back inside. He went first to the kitchen, and took his torch from the drawer under the sink. Then he crept back down to the cellar and eased the shovel from under the freezer lid. Outside again, he laid the torch and shovel next to Maddie. He picked up the wheelbarrow handles and wheeled his wife away.

It was harder than he had anticipated. Balancing the heavy weight on the one wheel required all his strength. Crossing the drawbridge he almost lost her; another inch and she'd have slipped into the moat. He gritted his teeth and strained to hold her. On the other side the wheel sank into mud, almost sticking. The going became firmer when he reached Reg Talbot's driveway, but the crunch of the gravel sounded unnervingly loud. He held his breath and aimed for the shadows, skirting the hedge. After a few yards the wheel ran off the gravel and on to the lawn. It sped silently across the grass.

The house was in darkness. The night was still mild, but there was a slight breeze, a little noise at least to muffle the sound of his passing. He would be cautious, he would go on tiptoe. Somewhere upstairs in the silent house Reg would be lying asleep, dreaming perhaps of Madeleine. He would be careful, he would not disturb him. He stopped the wheelbarrow at the end of the swimming pool.

He had to feel for the edge carefully, it was so dark. He took out the torch and shovel and laid them on the grass. He pushed the wheelbarrow as near as he dared, then lifted it up. He tipped the body into the pool. He heard the thump as it hit the bottom. He wheeled away the empty barrow and parked it next to a flowerbed. He returned to the pool, patted the grass until he found the torch and shovel, then jumped down into the hole at his feet.

It was about five feet deep at the shallow end. When filled, the water would come up to about half that. In the angle of the shallow end wall, the closest to the house, he placed his torch. It was a three-in-one torch, featuring in addition to the standard feature a flashing amber lens at one end and a narrow strip light along the side. He turned on the strip light. It cast a bluish glow, just powerful enough to see by, but invisible beneath eye-level, as it would be from the house. He started digging.

The ground was soft and easy to shift, and not just on the surface. He knew why. Reg had told him. It was those damned builders, excavating the wrong end, mechanically scooping out all that hard earth then having to replace it, loosely. It was time consuming to dig the hole, because he had to be careful, but it didn't tax him. He wondered if he had found his métier. All manner of criminals, it seemed, were met in him. First Fareham's answer to Dr Crippen, now Mr Burke and Mr Hare combined. Though he was not body-snatching, but body-planting. Would she grow? Could corpses sprout? He had a vision of her, emerging from the bottom of the pool, bursting through the crust of blue concrete and erupting out of the water like a vengeful Esther Williams. It was not a vision over which he wished to linger. He dug faster.

The hole was about four feet deep. That was as deep as the loose earth went. He found, when he rolled in Maddie's body, that it wasn't quite long enough, but by standing on her feet he was able to squeeze her in. He hoped it was her feet. Under the thick wrapping it was hard to distinguish which end was which, and he wasn't about to have a close look. His was a squeamish nature.

He piled the earth back on top of the body. There was too much now. The excess he heaped on the shovel and sprinkled round as evenly as possible. It took time. His arms ached. When he had finished he picked up the torch and examined the ground closely. There didn't seem to be too much of a bump; at least, the new bump was no worse than any of the others: the builders had left a far from smooth surface; the ridged prints of their feet all around. He patted down the freshly disturbed earth with the back of the shovel, as he reversed slowly to the edge. He climbed out of the pool, retrieved the wheelbarrow and laid the torch and shovel in it. He checked his watch. It was a quarter past one. An hour to bury his wife. A great deal quicker than a divorce.

He pushed the wheelbarrow home. He went as he had come, stealthily, on tiptoe. The night was still. The world was asleep.

Though not Roger.

Roger must have heard the stair's familiar creak as he came up on to the landing. He opened the trapdoor and stuck out his head:

"Fancy a drink?"

"Bit late, isn't it?"

"Not for some it isn't!"

Roger laughed. He didn't laugh very often, and the sound was unnatural. His voice sounded slurred. Mark was surprised. Roger wasn't a drinker. He was a depressive alright, but not an alcoholic depressive. It may have been his one redeeming feature.

Mark shook his head. He was going to say that it was too late for him, but Roger got in first before he could speak:

"Did you see that fellow round here again tonight?"

"Which fellow?" Mark asked, though of course he knew.

"You know, Maddie's friend, the shortsighted one. On the large side."

"What did he want?"

"Maddie."

Mark's foot was on the bottom rung. Roger looked at him hopefully.

"Fancy that drink after all, then?"

Mark nodded. He climbed the ladder. He stopped on the top rung, and stared at something that was tied round the rafter above his head. Roger laughed again, a sinister cackle.

"That's my latest idea!" he announced proudly.

It was a noose, fashioned of thick coarse rope and tied with a lumpy slip knot. Roger poked his head into it. He flicked the slack.

"Clever, eh! Just jump through the trapdoor and whoosh! Broken neck! Instantaneous fatality!"

Mark smiled thinly. He had never known how to deal with Roger's morbidity. He had never met anyone else whose hobby was death.

"When was Roddy round?"

"Just now. Half an hour ago. Don't you think it's neat?"

"Very. Did you speak to him?"

"Oh yes. Seemed quite irate, he did. I don't know why I didn't think of this before, it's so simple. The best ideas always are."

"What do you mean, irate? Hey, watch out!"

His warning came too late. He winced as Roger lifted his head too sharply and cracked it against the rafter. Another bump to add to the cratered dome that was his skull. It didn't seem to have affected him: he was bobbing up and down, skipping almost, from foot to foot, making a comical little gargling noise every time the rope round his neck went taut. He was in a very odd mood.

"You'd better take that off, Roger."

"Ha! Ha! Might do myself an injury!"

He appeared to relish the prospect. Nonetheless, after a moment he took his head out of the noose and draped it over its beam. He went over to the washbasin, where he rinsed out a glass and poured Mark a small measure of whisky. He topped up his own empty glass, rather more generously. They both sat down, Roger on the bed, Mark on the chair in front of the little table.

"Windy tonight, eh?" Roger observed.

It was beginning to blow. Not much, but sounds were exaggerated in the attic room. It was here that the groans and creaks were loudest. The one window pane, set at an angle above Mark's head, rattled and thumped.

"What did Roddy want?" Mark asked, patiently.

"Maddie. Fearful racket it was. Hollering, throwing stones and that at the window. Didn't wake me up because I wasn't asleep. Just as well, eh? Couldn't have slept through that. Had to come down and see what was the matter."

"You spoke to him?"

"Oh yes. Seemed to think I was you. It was dark, I know, but it's not as if I even sound much like you. A bit deaf I think he is. He wanted to know what I'd done with Maddie. What you'd done with Maddie."

The window pane shook with a sudden gust. Mark felt the draught tickling his neck.

"And what did you say that I had done with Maddie?"

"Well, to tell truth I was pretty pissed off. All that racket at half past midnight. And I'd had a few already, I have to confess. Made a joke of it, I did. You want to know what I said to him? What I said I'd done with Maddie?"

There must have been cracks in the window fitment. Cowboy builders had done that job. The wind had come up suddenly, from nowhere. It whistled persistently through the cracks, like a slow exhalation through teeth.

"Yes, please."

"I said . . . I said I'd bonked her over the head and dumped her body in the river!"

The wind died away suddenly. There was utter silence. Then Roger began to laugh, that strange sound again, like a smoker's wheeze. Mark said:

"That's very funny."

Roger nodded. He had finished laughing, as suddenly as he had started. He now wore his more customary gloomy expression. He drained his glass and reached for the whisky bottle.

"Want another?"

Mark held out his glass. Roger poured. Mark said:

"Roddy did realise it wasn't me, I hope?"

"Oh aye. When he found out it wasn't you he got even crosser. Wanted me to let him into the house. Said he wanted to talk to you, or see Maddie, or something. I said you must have gone out. He was pretty persistent. That's probably him now. . . . "

The phone was ringing downstairs. They both looked at their watches.

"Bloody silly time to ring," muttered Roger. "Inconsiderate."

"It is late. Why are you still up?"

"Could say the same to you. Insomnia, see. It's terrible."

Downstairs the phone stopped ringing. Roger drained his glass. Mark asked:

"Does that help?"

"No, but it makes me feel better. . . . "

He gave Mark the opposite impression. It was as if, having for a few idle moments abandoned himself to wild and alien glee, he was now making up for it by sinking into an extra deep depression. Paying the price for laughter.

"Thanks for the will," he murmured, his thoughts returning naturally to his favourite subject.

"That's alright."

Mark still didn't reckon it much as a legal document, but he didn't think that now was the time to voice his doubts. Roger seemed to be looking for something: he was riffling through a pile of papers on his bedside table. He pulled out a typewritten sheet, scanned it quickly, then passed it over.

"Here. What do you think?"

The paper contained a single paragraph:

> I apologise foR any inconvenience. I have decided to end my life because I do not think that it is woRth living. It is not a veRy inteResting life. It might have been diffeRent if a ceRtain lady was moRe inteRested in me, but she wasn't, and that's that, it's no use cRying oveR spilt milk. That's life, and that's death too. Please find attached my will, pRopeRly made out and signed and witnessed. I would like to be cRemated and have my ashes scatteRed oveR PoRthcawl funfaiR, which was the last place I RemembeR having a good time at, when I was 14. I have no RegRets, apaRt fRom M-. I apologize especially to MaRk. I have not Repaid him veRy well for his kindness. Once again I apologize foR the inconvenience.

"I wrote it yesterday," said Roger, staring at his empty glass. "I was going to hang myself last night, see, have done with it. But I didn't."

"Who's M-?"

"Myfanwy Roberts. I haven't seen her in fifteen years. That was when I left Wales, see. She married Ieuan Davies. My best friend."

He held the empty glass to his lips and tipped up the bottom. A single drop of whisky trickled slowly into his mouth.

"Roger –"

"Don't try and talk me out of it!"

Roger slammed his glass down on the bedside table. Mark froze.

The fury and despair in Roger's voice alarmed him: he was depending on Roger, he needed him: without his testimony that Maddie had been alive during the past week then the story that he'd been planning to tell, that she'd just walked out on him without saying a word and disappeared into thin air, would be useless. He would have to handle Roger carefully, humour him. Try and get him off the subject of suicide, unless . . . he had cried wolf so many times, surely he didn't have the nerve. Perhaps he could be frightened out of his mood. . . .

"So you've decided on hanging, have you?"

"What's it to you?"

Somehow Roger managed to sound both belligerent and self-pitying at the same time. It must have been the whisky, revealing new sides to his character. Mark had never thought of him as self-pitying. Gloomy, yes, but he so manifestly derived satisfaction from morbidity. Mark had never known him be aggressive in any circumstances. So he said, warily:

"Nothing. I'm just taking a friendly interest."

"Don't try and stop me!"

"Alright."

Roger lurched to his feet and snatched up the whisky bottle, glaring at Mark as if daring him to interfere. Mark said nothing. Roger returned to his spot on the bed and stared grimly at his refilled glass.

"I'm going to do it!"

"Alright," said Mark coolly. "In that case I should say hanging's as good a way as any."

Roger's eyes softened. His lip and chin quivered. Quite suddenly, tears were running down his cheeks.

"I'm sorry. . . . " He had slumped physically. His voice caught in his throat. "I'm sorry, it must be terrible for you. . . . "

"Why should it be terrible for me?" Mark asked, feeling rather puzzled. After all, he wasn't the one who was planning to hang himself.

"Terrible!" Roger sobbed. "All me thinking about is hanging myself, and there's you having to find the body, and call the police and deal with my will. Thinking only of myself, as usual. Selfish. I'm sorry, Mark. Please forgive me!"

"Oh do stop crying!" Mark snapped, in spite of himself: he was getting distinctly irritated by Roger's mawkishness.

"I'm sorry!"

"Stop it!"

But even as he spoke Roger fell forward, slipping off the edge of the bed on to his knees. He scurried across the floor like a clockwork Toulouse-Lautrec, grabbed Mark round the legs and thrust his head down somewhere between his shins. He heaved and shook. Mark heard a noise like a terminal rattle emanating from below his knees. Rather awkwardly, he patted Roger's head.

"There, there!" he said, trying to sound as solicitous as possible.

Roger withdrew his head enough to get a grubby handkerchief up to his nose. He blew noisily and at length. He tried again to apologise, but he was trembling so much that he couldn't speak.

"It's alright," said Mark reassuringly, this time patting him on the shoulder. The head was rather greasy and not entirely dandruff free. "Have another drink."

He took Roger by the arms and helped him to sit up in the chair. He topped up Roger's glass and gave it to him, but this time Roger didn't drink. He put the glass down on the table, next to where Mark had left the suicide note.

"What do you think?" Roger asked, tapping the sheet of paper.

"Oh, very good," Mark replied, sitting himself down on the bed. "Very good indeed. Neat and to the point. I like your style."

"I'm serious, you know!" Roger declared, with just a trace of the old belligerency.

"Oh I do know. By the way, you haven't signed it."

Roger looked surprised. He picked up the paper and examined it sceptically.

"I don't have a pen."

"I do."

Mark took a pen out of his inside pocket and handed it over. Roger stared at it, and at the suicide note. For a moment he looked as though he was going to sign, then he put them both down, the pen on top of the paper.

"Perhaps I'd better not," he mumbled. "I may think of some improvements."

"You can always add a p.s." Mark suggested, helpfully.

"Have you got any suggestions?"

"Maybe."

Roger turned round in his chair to face the table, on which, amongst various piles of junk, there stood his typewriter in all its antique glory. He fitted his suicide note into the roller. From one of the piles of junk he extracted a sheaf of papers, which he chucked over towards Mark.

"Here. May give you some ideas."

Mark picked the papers up off the floor. Some appeared to be quite old; some, indeed, even dated from a time when the lower case "r" on the typewriter had worked. Mark counted sixteen separate sheets. They were all suicide notes.

Roger typed in "p.s." at the foot of his latest.

"What's there worth living for, that's what I'd like to know?" he demanded rhetorically.

"Have you ever thought of sticking your head in the gas oven?"

"Can't stand the smell of gas. Makes me sick."

"What about an overdose? Pills?"

"I don't want to start taking drugs. What shall I write?"

"How about something poetic? Farewell, vain world!, that sort of thing."

"Mm." Roger didn't seem too impressed. He indicated his suicide note collection: "Anything catch your eye there?"

"This Myfanwy girl. Seems to crop up a lot. Why do you just refer to her as M-?"

"Don't want her to get to hear about it. Feel guilty."

"That's very decent of you."

"She's bound to hear anyway. My sister'll tell her. Then she'll be sorry. . . ."

He leaned back in his chair, savouring the prospect. After a few moments of morbid relish he turned back to the typewriter, and frowned.

"I don't seem to be getting very far."

He got up. He walked over to the rafter and unhitched the noose. He slipped it over his head.

"What are you doing?" Mark demanded.

"It might inspire me," Roger answered, tightening the knot. He attempted to return to the chair, but the rope wasn't long enough. He tried to ignore it and sit anyway. He got cross when he couldn't. His reactions were slow, his manner made stubborn by alcohol. He kicked the chair.

"You do it!"

"Sorry?"

"You do it. You write it for me. Fresh approach, that's what's needed."

His voice sounded strangulated, which was not surprising, as he was leaning forward on tiptoe and straining against the tautened rope. He was making little gurgling noises in his throat, and swaying gently from side to side. He seemed to be enjoying himself.

Mark sat down at the table in front of the typewriter. Roger remained where he was, from which position he could just about stare over Mark's shoulder. They both looked at the suicide note.

"It's more difficult than it looks," Mark admitted.

"I know, and I've had a lot of practice. There's a lot to say and not much space to say it in."

"Yes, you've got to be pithy."

"Oh I'm pithy alright. I'm pithed as a fart!"

Roger guffawed and belched at the same time. His bad breath fanned Mark's ear.

"Don't crowd me, Roger. I can't concentrate with you standing so close."

Roger skipped away, still laughing. He started to sing:

"Hang out your bodies on the Siegfried line. . . . "

He was tugging on the rope, bringing himself up with an exaggerated twitch each time it went tight. He sang:

"Pack up your bodies in your old kit bag. . . . "

He repeated this line several times, obviously he couldn't think of another. His singing grew more and more ragged; he was laughing too much to be able to stay in key. He had probably never laughed so much in his life. He started to move towards the bed, but the rope pulled him up sharp. He pointed at it, quivering tautly, and laughed more than ever.

"Do shut up, Roger!"

Mark swung round in his chair. He gestured helplessly.

"How can I be expected to concentrate with you giggling like a madman? You'll have to write your own suicide note. I'm off to bed now."

Roger stopped laughing. He ran round to the trapdoor and stood in front of it, cutting Mark off.

"Don't go!" he pleaded, suddenly serious. "Stay with me a little longer!"

"It's the middle of the night, Roger."

"I know, I know. Just have one more drink with me. One more!"

It was almost a cry of fear. Mark saw in his eyes the true desperate look of the drunkard. Getting away would not be easy.

"Alright," said Mark reluctantly. "One more."

Roger looked relieved. He indicated the bottle.

"Have a drink."

There was still some left in Mark's glass. He topped it up fractionally. Mark indicated Roger's empty glass, but Roger shook his head.

"Just chuck over the bottle. . . . "

There wasn't much left. Most of it was already inside Roger. Mark screwed on the cap and tossed it over, gently. Roger still fumbled it.

"Watch out!" cried Mark.

Roger had stumbled backwards in trying to gather the bottle. His heel was on the edge of the trapdoor. He looked down vaguely at the landing below and shrugged.

"Going to do it anyway. . . . "

Roger tilted back his head, put the bottle to his lips and emptied it. The adam's apple moved up and down in exaggerated fashion. When he had finished he screwed up his face and gasped for breath.

"Ay, that's hard stuff. . . . "

His face was still contorted in an attitude of pain. He stared at the floor as he talked.

"Had a letter this morning. . . . "

Mark raised an eyebrow. Roger almost never received mail.

"From my sister. It's there." He waved vaguely at the table. Mark looked. The envelope stuck out amongst the old papers. Mark pulled it out.

"Open it," Roger murmured.

There was one sheet of paper inside.

"Read it. . . . "

It wasn't a very interesting letter. It was mostly about his sister's husband's back. One of the boys had done well in a rugby match.

"Read it, please. Aloud. . . . "

Mark read the last paragraph, aloud.

"I bumped into Myfanwy Davies last week, you know. Myfanwy Roberts as was. . . . "

Roger dropped the empty whisky bottle. It bounced against the edge of the trapdoor and fell through. Mark heard it smash on the landing.

"Sorry about the mess . . . " Roger muttered, almost inaudibly. His features still looked as if they had been frozen in mid-spasm.

Mark returned to the letter.

"I thought she was pregnant again, she's got six you know, but she's just put on weight. You can't help feeling sorry for her, when you remember what a lovely girl she used to be. . . . "

Roger sniffed. His nostrils and lips quivered, and his eyes sprang liquid. Mark could hardly bear to look at him. He turned half away in his chair.

"That friend of yours, Ieuan, treats her bad, I hear. Drinks, I hear. Shame, I think."

Mark watched him out of the corner of his eye. He stood loosely, his body slumped, half held up by the noose around his neck. He extended a hand, limply.

"Give me . . . please."

His voice was very faint. Mark offered him the letter.

"No. The other."

He indicated the typewriter. Mark extracted the suicide note and stretched out with it. Roger took it with his fingertips and read it through. He chuckled mysteriously.

"S'pose I'd better sign it," he said in a tone of almost humorous resignation. "Chuck over the pen, will you?"

Mark tossed his pen over, carelessly. Roger had to stretch for it.

He fumbled.

The pen was spinning like a drum-major's stick. It had bounced off Roger's hand, he had pushed it up, it was flying away from him, he grabbed at it.

The long central beam in the ceiling shuddered. Mark heard the crack of Roger's head and winced. Roger staggered.

The pen clipped the edge of the trapdoor, and dropped through. Roger was dazed, he groaned, he stumbled backwards, clutching his scalp.

"Roger – "

His heels touched space. For a second he balanced in purgatory, and then he shot through the hole in the floor like the demon king.

There was silence, utter silence, apart from the creaking of the attic beam, the creaking of the rope at the end of which Roger dangled.

The body was turning, slowly, a matter of inches, a little to the left, a little to the right. Only the top of the head was visible above the trapdoor. It was bent at an angle. The rest of him was hanging out of sight, below.

"Roger. . . . "

He mouthed his name. He was too shocked to speak it. Was it a joke? Was he standing on the ladder, pretending?

He got up. He walked over. He was frightened. More even than he'd been with Maddie. He didn't know why. After all, it wasn't as if he'd done anything. Except mis-throw the pen. But Roger was butterfingers. . . . His knees were knocking together so violently he could hardly stand. He steadied himself against the sloping roof.

He was on the edge of the trapdoor, looking down. There was glass all over the landing carpet. He wondered if there would be a stain. It was a light grey carpet, it marked easily. Silly choice of a colour really, he'd told Maddie so at the time. Too late now. He saw Roger's feet, pointing down. They weren't resting on a rung. Roger wasn't pretending. He dared to look at the head. The face was turned the other way, but he could see the hangman's knot, tied under the ear, and the swollen flesh beneath. Death must have been instantaneous.

He went back to the table and sat down. He didn't know where else to go, he knew that he couldn't have faced climbing down the ladder, past the body. He drank the whisky left in his glass. It made him feel nauseous, but he felt a need for more. There was a bottle of Haig in his study, but for that he would have to go downstairs. He glanced over again at the hanging body. He glanced down at the floor. He blinked and looked up again. It was still there. He couldn't believe it. He looked away once more. He saw the letter on the table. He picked it up. He read it again. Something to do.

His hands were shaking, the letter wouldn't stay still. The words just jumbled up and all swam together in front of him. He saw the girl's name. M-. His mind became a blur. Who was M-? He was confused. Why was Roger's sister writing to him about Maddie?

She was dead. Her body was hidden. Where? He had done it. In the river.

He had bonked her over the head and dumped her body in the river. No. What was he thinking of?

"Oh my God. . . . "

He couldn't think straight. It was all coming apart at the seams. Why tonight? Why after all the years of fruitless suicidal talk did Roger have to go and finish himself off now? What was he going to do?

The nausea he had felt in his stomach returned. He swallowed and kept it down; kept at bay the horrors.

The letter slipped through nerveless fingers. He watched it fall and settle. There was another piece of paper already there, on the floor by the trapdoor. Roger must have released the suicide note even as he fell, his last conscious act. Mark picked it up.

'P.S.' it said, at the bottom. That was all. There was plenty of empty space.

His head was aching. He had drunk too much. He didn't feel in control. His limbs were not quite a part of him. He sensed a general numbness, but it was not absolute: there was an elusive half-glimpsed something in his brain. What thing? What was it he was groping towards? Whose voice was that? He had heard a voice, someone speaking in the room. It had been his. He had been talking to himself, saying his thoughts, aloud. It didn't sound like his voice. Was he mad? It didn't feel like his body. These hands he raised, the thumbs and fingers loading the paper into the typewriter, were they his? His senses were dead, he felt nothing. The rush of blood in his head was a waterfall. Or a whiskyfall; his brain was soused. There was a voice back there, over the rapids, trying to tell him something, nudging, nagging him. Slowly the voice became almost clear. The whiskyfall receded; a distant tide went out.

He was aware of sound, and silence. The silence was thick, the quiet of a country night, in which such tiny sounds as there were became on the moment huge. He heard the gentle rattle of the window pane and the creak of the rafters. The creaks were rhythmical, tick, tock, the body a pendulum, engaged in the most imperceptible of motions. He could hear his watch, tick, tock. Time passed. It ticked away, much faster than the rhythm of the swinging body, which now was outside time. He could hear his breathing, loud in the silence, but calmer now, deeper, more relaxed. It had a steady rhythm of its own, like regulated time.

His thoughts crystallised. The soft-focusing effects of whisky and fatigue dissolved and became part of some scarcely to be imagined time before. The voice at the back of his mind was near and sharp.

Then it came to him, what he must do. All he wanted was resolution. He steeled himself accordingly: he couldn't afford to be squeamish or muddle-headed; he had to be bold. An unexpected opportunity had dropped into his lap. Dropped through the trapdoor.

There was plenty of empty space, an expanse of virgin white. 'P.S.' was all it said. The gap invited.

He typed. He had to press down hard on the old heavy keys. He watched the letters coming up, the worn edges, the damaged R's.

Tick, tock, he heard between the words. Time passed.

He didn't hurry. He took advantage of his clear-headedness to think things through. He needed to be thorough, it wasn't as if he had planned it this way. But he was getting used to playing the opportunist. He took his time, as much as he needed, as much as he could think to make use of. He did what he had to do.

In the end it wasn't so bad, going down the ladder. He kept close to one side, and only brushed lightly against the stiff cold body. He was getting used to dealing with bodies. He left this one where he had found it. It hung there through the night.

They didn't cut it down till half-way through the next morning. They had been all around it by then, examining it *in situ*. The police photographer took some time over his job, covering all the angles. He said to the sergeant afterwards that he was glad that that was over, he hadn't been able to hear himself think straight with all that racket from outside.

The racket came from next door, where an enormous machine was mixing cement, and workmen were entombing Maddie.

15

"Seen these?"

Sergeant Buck was carrying an armload of newspapers. He thumped them down on the scratched formica-topped table, generating a whoosh of air that sent some odd sheets of paper into aerodynamically foredoomed flight. He muttered an apology as he bent down to pick them back up again.

Inspector Morris didn't say anything. He watched patiently while his overweight colleague retrieved the scattered papers, grunting and groaning as he stretched for them. The Inspector didn't especially want the papers back. The table was filled with papers. He certainly didn't want the bundle of newsprint which the Sergeant had just thrown at him. He required very little from the Sergeant, he thought, as he watched him tucking his shirt back in again and pulling up his trousers, except his immediate exit from the office. The Sergeant did not oblige.

"Look at this one!" The Sergeant chuckled, pulling a tabloid off the top of the pile and holding up the front page. The Inspector didn't look. The Sergeant read it to him anyway:

" 'New Clues In Love Triangle Murder Horror!' "

Another paper was held up to view. Out of the corner of his eye the Inspector saw a photograph of David Jones, the lodger.

" 'The Killer In The Attic!' " the Sergeant read out melodramatically. "Here's a good one – 'The Face of Evil!' "

It was another picture, in another paper. Still the Inspector didn't look, though he did wonder which paper it was. It sounded like *The Sun*. Mind you, he thought, they all sound like *The Sun*.

"Ha! Ha!" the Sergeant guffawed excitedly. "Here's the best – 'Twisted Taffy's Killer Terror – Dai the Death!' "

The Inspector turned his head round slowly and fixed the Sergeant with his most pitiless stare. It took a moment for the Sergeant to notice. When he did so he stopped laughing instantly.

"That'll be all, thank you, Sergeant Buck," the Inspector said, in his best Welsh accent.

It had been fifteen years since the Inspector had transferred from Abergavenny. Fifteen years among the southern English, Offa's barbarians, had left their mark on his once fruity vowels, but the old intonations were only thinly submerged and could rise again at any time, though usually in connection with an oval-shaped ball. Then his wife (his English wife) and children would mock, fastening on key words and repeating *ad nauseam* his idiosyncratic pronunciation. The favourite word was "situation". He had never pronounced the t's, and never thought about it, because where he came from no one else did either. They said "sidduasian", a word like an immigrant neologism. Which was another thing his kids mocked him for. When they took him off they made him sound like Peter Sellers; they called him Inspector Vindaloo, to his face. He gave an inward sigh: why had he never managed to inspire any respect in his own family, when it came so naturally to all the criminals he collared? Criminals feared him. His own family laughed at him. Strange, really, when you considered how much his family had in common with the criminals.

Sergeant Buck slammed the door on his way out. The Sergeant always slammed the door. The Inspector was always annoyed. Sometimes he said something about it, and then the Sergeant would apologise, and even sound as if he meant it, but he would go on slamming the door just the same. The Inspector couldn't really blame him. It was his office after all, in normal times. Years of habitual slamming could not be exorcised in one week. Both men were in unfamiliar waters. Probably it had never occurred to the Sergeant that one day he might have to give over his working space to a major criminal investigation. Why should it have done? Major criminal investigations did not occur in Fareham. An increase in the crime figures in Fareham meant the issue of a couple of extra speeding tickets, or the non-return of wire trolleys to the supermarket. About a year ago there had been a spate of Saturday night fighting in the High Street after closing time, and a flasher had been reported in the park, but a spell of cold weather had driven off the flasher and the drunks had been deterred by an intensive high-profile operation, i.e. Sergeant Buck and a wpc sitting outside the pub in a panda. The Fareham crime wave had receded. Nothing had prepared them for the case of the Twisted Taffy Killer Terror. And nor did the

Inspector, despite a working lifetime's experience of violent death, feel much the wiser.

His eye strayed to the pile of newspapers the Sergeant had brought in. It was quite a collection. The ones on top were today's, the bottom ones went back as far as Monday. He pulled a few out at random. He had looked at these already; he grimaced to see them again. Normally he didn't mind the publicity. He and his colleagues would joke about it, try to make light of bearing the burden of the press, but it was usually a pleasure to read your own name in a national newspaper, as long as they didn't misquote you too wildly. Only this sidduasian wasn't normal. In fact, "normal" was the last word he would have applied to anything to do with this case.

LOONEY LODGER IN KILLER FRENZY

Last Sunday had begun ordinarily enough. He had been out walking the dog when the Superintendent rang. He hadn't even known where Fareham was. He knew now alright. He could drive there in his sleep.

SUICIDAL MANIAC MURDERS BLONDE

He had had a feeling the moment he pulled up at the house. "Willow Cottage". The little stream and the bridge into the garden; the ivy-covered walls; the pretty little low-beamed house with its quasi-rustic charm and sense of unimpeachable middle-class respectability – in short, the perfect setting for the perfect English murder.

And there was the murderer himself, the killer overcome with remorse, hanging from the attic with suicide note and confession to hand. The dramatic potential was undeniable. There was only one problem. Where was the victim?

MYSTERY OF MISSING MADDIE — POLICE BAFFLED

The Inspector's eye strayed from the pile of tabloids to the sheaves of papers with which the rest of the desk was covered. Conspicuous amongst these was a Xerox of the chief piece of evidence. He knew it practically by heart, especially the last bit, which ran

"P.S. I didn't mean to do it. I don't know what came oveR me. I dumped M-'s body in the RiveR. I am soRRY foR the inconvenience. I couldn't face going to pRison."

"Prison?" the Inspector had thought grimly to himself on first reading the letter. "It'd be the looney bin for you, boyo."

So an open and shut case, everyone assumed: the lonely and deranged lodger, his advances to his landlady rejected, murders her in a fit of passion, disposes of the body and then, overwhelmed by remorse, tops himself, leaving behind a typed confession. Very neat, only. . . .

"I dumped M-'s body in the RiveR."

What river? There weren't any rivers near Fareham. There was the little stream by the cottage, which was the tributary of a slightly larger stream that sprang from some hills not worthy of the name a few miles away, and trickled reluctantly into a little pool on the edge of the Trumans' estate. Police frogmen had spent all of Sunday and Monday dredging that stream, and very foolish they'd looked too, kitted out in all that gear to tramp through water that hardly came up to their knees.

So, what river? Someone suggested the Thames. Reasonable enough. The Thames was at least a river, not a stream, or a brook, or a pond, or a canal. Sergeant Buck had suggested that the note might have meant a canal. Alright, the Inspector had said, and which canal would that be? Sergeant Buck had looked blank. After a minute's humming and ha'ing he had had to confess that there weren't actually any canals anywhere near Fareham. They had pored over Ordnance Survey maps, measured distances to anything dignified with the title "river", even to reservoirs and lakes. A clutch of theories was put forward, not all far-fetched. The only problem was that none of them fitted the facts.

MY BEANO WITH BLONDE BOMBSHELL

Mrs Harvey had left Mr Talbot's house, in an agitated state, at a quarter to eleven. He was sure about that, because he had checked the *TV Times* and flicked through the channels to see if there was anything on. Moreover, he had checked his watch against the speaking clock on going to bed twenty minutes later. He remembered that clearly, because the watch had been a minute fast.

ROMEO RODDY'S HEARTBREAK HORROR

Mr Maclean was equally precise about the time. He had arrived at the cottage at midnight. He had heard the local church clock striking the hour. The Inspector had heard that church clock for himself: although it was some distance away the chimes could be heard clearly over the fields. It was at midnight, then, that Mr Maclean had had his confrontation with the lodger, Jones. Jones had said:

"I bonked her over the head and dumped her body in the river."

Mr Maclean had assumed that he was joking. A reasonable assumption, the Inspector had agreed, for what kind of an idiot would make a confession like that? Not having known Mr Jones personally he did not feel equipped, as yet, to judge exactly what kind of an idiot he might have been. About Mr Maclean, on the other hand, he felt much more sure. Mr Maclean was a complete idiot. Probably a moron.

MY MARVELLOUS MADDIE! TORMENTED ROMEO TELLS ALL

Nonetheless, Maclean had seen Jones alive at midnight, and Jones had said that he had bonked Mrs Harvey on the head and dumped her body in the river. Bonked? A curious choice of word. Were the old ugly twins of sex and murder rearing their double head? The press hadn't doubted it for a moment.

SPURNED SEX SAVAGE SLAYS BLONDE SIZZLER, 38

So, sometime between ten-forty-five and midnight, David Jones (whom Mr Harvey referred to as Roger, confusing everyone) murdered, possibly raped, and disposed of Mrs Harvey. In a river.

How?

She was a big woman, Mr Harvey had said, which Mr Maclean had confirmed, although he had insisted that she had lost weight through dieting. Although Mr Talbot had seemed quite annoyed when the Inspector described Madeleine Harvey as "fat", clearly he had been so besotted with the woman that allowances had to be made. The consensus of opinion was that Mrs Harvey had weighed in the region of 180lbs or rather more than Jones himself.

How had he got her body to the "river"?

Slung her across the handlebars of his moped and hoped for the best? It was a noisy little machine. Mr Talbot hadn't heard anything, and he had been awake until at least a quarter past eleven. The moped scenario was hardly likely anyway. Had Jones got hold of a car, borrowed or stolen? None of Talbot's cars had been used, he was sure of that. The lab boys had been able to identify all the tyre tracks outside the cottages, considerably aided by the isolated location of the scene of the crime. On the other hand, that very fact of isolation served to emphasise the recurring problem:

Seeing as they were dealing with the middle of nowhere, where the hell was the body?

Without a car, transportation to a "river", wherever that might be, would have been out of the question. Even with a car, the return journey to any of the nearest identified bodies of water, within the known time scale, would have been equally out of the question.

Without a body, there was only circumstantial evidence to go on, and the more closely it was examined the more ambiguous it became. David "Roger" Jones had not actually written "I killed Maddie Harvey". He had said that he had dumped M-'s body in the river. The river that didn't exist. He hadn't written anything about "bonking" her on the head. Roddy Maclean had used that word. Had Jones really said that? Roddy Maclean was a near moron, and in the Inspector's experience near morons made poor witnesses. Who was M- anyway?

"Myfanwy Roberts," Jones's sister had insisted. The Inspector had liked Eluned Watkins. She was his idea of a reliable witness. Furthermore, corroboration had come from a Mr Singh, a workmate of Roger's, who said that he had heard him speak about this Myfanwy on the very day of his death. Mr Singh had seen Eluned's letter, which Roger must have received that morning. They hadn't found the letter, but that didn't mean much. It had been a miracle that they'd found anything at all in Roger's attic.

LAIR OF THE LOONEY — IN THE DEN OF DAI THE DERANGED — EXCLUSIVE!

This Roger had certainly been an oddball, but nothing that the Inspector had heard about him suggested the make-up of a killer. A police psychologist had been anxious to get in on the act, and although he'd been happy enough to diagnose him as a suicidal depressive, he had failed to find evidence of violent tendencies. As a rule the Inspector was wary of psycho-speak, preferring to rely on his own instincts, but his instincts had been screaming at him that something was wrong almost since the off. The forensic evidence had reinforced his suspicions, and for a very good reason:

There wasn't any.

Not only wasn't there a body, there was neither a murder weapon nor any sign of a struggle. But if he really had "bonked" her over the head there had to be something, a blunt instrument, a blood stain, a hair, a fibre . . . but there was nothing anywhere to connect Roger with Maddie Harvey. Certainly no evidence of any sexual contact. In any case, he would have been too drunk for that.

According to the autopsy he had had nearly as much whisky as blood in his veins. If a murder had been committed, then it had been covered up with meticulous care. It had not, therefore, been committed by a drunk. Would a sober man have written that suicide note? Was it a kind of terrible fantasy, a nightmarish vision, spawned by a fevered imagination in a state of acute intoxication? Or was it, perhaps, the suicidal depressive's idea of a grim joke? It sounded bizarre, but the alternative, that Roger had somehow murdered Maddie Harvey and disposed of the body in any manner at all, let alone the one indicated, was more than bizarre. It was actually out of the question.

Whatever else Roger may or may not have done, the Inspector was now convinced of one thing: he hadn't murdered anyone.

What, then, was it all about?

BLONDE MADDIE WAS MINE, SAYS NEIGHBOUR

Maddie Harvey was alleged to have been involved simultaneously in two extramarital relationships. According to Roddy Maclean she had been about to end her marriage and go off with him, a claim supported by Ms Skinner, an acerbic but seemingly intelligent witness. Mark Harvey's evidence on this point had been ambiguous (as elsewhere; the Inspector thought him a confused witness, perhaps

184

not surprisingly). He had admitted that the marriage was in a rocky state, but claimed to know nothing about her alleged intention to divorce him. Maclean had counter-claimed that he was lying, and that Maddie had consulted a solicitor on the subject, but enquiries had failed to unearth any solicitor. The Inspector was inclined to believe Harvey on this point. He was strengthened in this belief by Maclean's insistence that Maddie had been pregnant by him, a claim which Mark Harvey had dismissed as a physiological impossibility. This had been confirmed by Maddie's doctor. Enter Reg Talbot. He was actually in the process of getting divorced and there were solicitors to prove it. As a result of Talbot's statement to the press, his wife had cited Maddie as co-respondent. Maclean had been speechless, Ms Skinner indignant. Mark Harvey had nodded wisely to himself and said that he'd suspected as much for a couple of weeks. Maclean had claimed not to have known anything about Talbot, but Talbot claimed that Maddie had told him that there was nothing between her and Maclean. He also claimed that she had said that Ms Skinner was poison and not to be trusted, which had stirred up a hornets' nest, some local women's group turning out with placards and banners to picket Talbot's house. There had been a breach of the peace and two arrests. All this had happened on Tuesday. The next day Sharon Talbot had given an interview to the press in which she claimed that her husband was a psychopath who had tried to murder her in a broom cupboard. She had cited Mark Harvey and her brother as witnesses. The brother, who was quite possibly even more stupid than Maclean, had confirmed this. Harvey had hedged, saying he couldn't remember exactly what had happened, though he admitted to being present. He did remember that Maddie had given him a pot-plant to give to Mrs Talbot, a baffling detail which the papers had latched on to and invested with mysterious significances – their letter columns were filled with strange missives from opinionated horticulturalists on the subject of plant symbolism. Talbot was denying everything and threatening writs. The Inspector was confused, which was hardly surprising, as the two conflicting versions of events appeared to be mutually exclusive. Only one person could solve the mystery.

HUSH-HUSH HOUSEWIFE IN LOVER DOUBLE TROUBLE

Unless the whole lot of them were liars then something very peculiar had been going on. And if they weren't lying, then it was logical to assume that they had been lied to, and had swallowed it all hook, line and sinker. Talbot certainly thought that Maclean was lying, and vice-versa, and charge and counter-charge were hurled about with passionate conviction. According to Maclean, Talbot had never even met Maddie and had made the whole thing up. He claimed that Maddie had actually gone out of her way to have nothing at all to do with her new neighbours, going so far as to draw the curtains and hide whenever they had been spotted coming anywhere near the house. Ms Skinner agreed, but this was all hearsay. Facts were what was needed, and there was only one person who could provide them.

MADDIE MAE — COME UP AND SEE ME SOMETIME

The Inspector lifted the pile of tabloids from the table and dropped them on to the floor. For once, he thought, their exaggerations might even have been pardonable: to them Maddie Harvey was the "Blonde Bombshell", the "Sexpot Sizzler". They hadn't actually said she was a tart, but they hadn't needed to, really. Outrage had been expressed in liberal quarters. "Who committed the crime?" a letter to *The Guardian* had screamed.

And yet, the Inspector mused, and yet . . . putting to one side that there was something decidedly odd about her taste in men, she must have been quite a lady: the men in her life twisted round her little finger, the husband impotent, the accredited lovers ignorant of each other's existence. It was hardly surprising that the press should have concluded that the desperate lodger was another on the list. She must have controlled them all with the adroitness of a puppeteer. She must have had a genius for deception. She must have been the greatest undiscovered acting talent of the age.

Must have been? the Inspector thought. No, must be. . . .

There was no evidence of murder. There was only a trail of deception. But there were so many little mendacious cul-de-sacs it was difficult to tell where the main trail ran.

Wearily, the Inspector pushed back his chair and stood up, stretching his legs. He had spent too much of the week cramped under his desk, sifting through the piles of unhelpful paper, information that had left him completely uninformed. There was nothing to be learnt from desk drudgery. He walked over to the window and stared out of the single pane of dirty glass.

He heard the Fareham church clock strike midday, the same clock which Roddy Maclean had heard strike midnight not so many days before. Was it only days? It was hard to believe. It felt like years.

There was a knock on the door and Sergeant Buck stuck his head round without waiting for an answer.

"Press are here, sir."

"Thank you, Sergeant."

The Sergeant nodded and went out again. He slammed the door. The Inspector swore at him under his breath. He returned to his desk and searched among the papers for the statement which he had prepared earlier.

The statement was bland, non-committal. It had to be. Although the Inspector had voiced his doubts to his superiors he had not leaked a word to the press. He would have to soon enough, and he would have to be very careful how he did it, but he wasn't going to risk putting his neck on the block until he was absolutely sure. After all, the press weren't going to like it. They wanted a dead body, and he wanted a live one. And if he did manage to produce Maddie Harvey, like a rabbit out of a hat, it would be scant compensation for a no-holds-barred all-in rape and murder. And it would make them look pretty foolish into the bargain.

The Inspector scanned his statement, then fitted it into his clipboard. It was time to go into the lions' den. He was glad that there weren't going to be any tv cameras; he hated the lights.

He glanced out of the window. It was going to be a nice afternoon, a good time to get away from his desk. He could see the backs of some houses, and, above the roofs, the trees of Fareham park. He paused. He was aware of a slight twinge in his stomach. He was acutely sensitive to gut feelings. Was his stomach trying to tell him something? Or had he just eaten his breakfast too quickly? His instincts were certainly playing up something peculiar. He turned away from the window, thoughtfully.

Somewhere out there was the missing clue. Somewhere out there was Maddie Harvey. Wherever she was, he had to find her.

16

The press conference was over in a couple of minutes. The Inspector read his bland statement, a few questions were lobbed up casually and neatly fielded; that was all. The half-dozen assembled journalists scrawled in their pads unenthusiastically, for form's sake. No cameras or photographers were present. There was no news. Which was bad news for Harry Craven.

The Inspector noticed Harry the moment he came in, partly because he was sitting apart from the others, partly because he was the sort of person it was hard not to notice. Harry seemed not to have noticed the Inspector; at least he didn't look up at him, not once during the whole conference: he kept his eyes fixed firmly on the floor and his arms folded; he didn't even indulge in the pantomime of note-taking. He gave the impression of one seeking to blend seamlessly into the background, an unfortunate impression to give in view of his all-round egregiousness. He looked awkward, to say the least.

"Without your friend today?" the Inspector asked him good-naturedly, by way of an aside, on his way out after the conference.

It was meant as a joke. Harry didn't have friends, but he knew whom the Inspector meant. He reddened, although the effect was academic: he was red already, complexion a mixture of carrot and beetroot, hair by shade and texture doormat ginger. His eyes, which he had lifted instinctively at the Inspector's address, returned their sullen gaze at once to the floor. He coughed, and thrust his unsullied pad into the pocket of his raincoat, withdrawing from therein a crumpled pack of cigarettes. This activity was meant to mask his discomfort, but the Inspector had passed on anyway, making redundant his efforts. Only the fat sergeant paid him any attention.

"No smoking in here please, gentlemen," he said pompously, dignifying Harry both by the style and plurality of his address: the others had already gone; Harry was the only hack left.

The only one, the last of his breed. He waved two fingers at the

Sergeant's back, then used them to straighten his cigarette. He lit up outside on the steps of the police station, then walked slowly to his car, idly kicking a paper bag with one scuffed toe.

Without your friend today? – Ha!

He climbed into his car. He tried to get the ashtray open, but it was jammed up with butts and wouldn't budge. That meant he had to open the window, which meant that he'd be getting the breeze in his face as he drove along. Harry hated fresh air. He loathed the feel of the sun even more, it made his skin crawl. Not a real reptile, you see, he would explain to colleagues at the bar. He looked at his watch. Half an hour till opening time. Not that the local watering holes were up to much, but at least they offered a refuge from the country air. God, how he hated the bloody country. Mud and cowshit, and dinky little cottages, hay fever, nasty smells, villages inhabited entirely by idiots. Why couldn't murderers just kill each other in Leicester Square? Bloody trees and fields and country lanes and meadows and all that crap. If he had his way he'd concrete over the bloody lot. With Dave "Dick" Turpin on the bottom.

"Dick" Turpin, his "friend".

Harry didn't have friends, but he had once bought Turpin a drink, which was a pretty bloody friendly gesture in his opinion. Turpin had been a kid then, wet as a wanker's sheets behind the ears, straight out of "journalism" school, whatever the hell that was when it was at home. The editor had said, give him a chance Harry, show him the ropes, I think the lad'll make out. . . . He'd been in the middle of covering the Stratford Strangler then, the occasion of one of his more memorable scoops: he'd got hold of the Strangler's wife, holed himself up with her in a hotel in Eastbourne, and filled the centre pages for a whole week with total crap: "I Married A Monster", "Secrets Of The Strangler", "More Sex Secrets Of The Strangler", "Kinky Sex Secrets of Savage Strangler", etc. Harry had employed Turpin as an errand boy, sending him on a series of triangular runs involving an off-licence, a bookmaker and a chippie. He had taught him everything he knew. Then he had sodded off and joined the opposition. The ungrateful git.

He gave the ashtray in the car a savage jerk. This time it budged, catapulting a few compressed butts into the already sordid gap between the front seats. He ignored them. He put his cigarette out in the ashtray, then tipped it out of the window and shook it empty. He shoved it half back into its hole and stared at it. It didn't look right empty. He lit another cigarette.

Of course, he hadn't actually sat him down like a classroom teacher and taught him, not as such. But Turpin had watched, and listened, and asked questions, some of which Harry had deigned to answer. He had been competent, and he had known his place. And he had treated Harry with due deference.

"Mr Craven, they say you're the most unscrupulous reporter in Fleet Stret."

He hadn't been able to resist smiling at that; he had swelled with pride.

"That's one of the politer things they'll say, Dick my lad. They call me the Hardest Hack. You've got to be hard in this business, lad. Namby-pamby blushing violets should sod off back to journalism school."

Turpin had taken his advice to heart. They didn't call Harry the Hardest Hack any more. They called him the Has-been Hardest Hack, or H.H.H. for short. Turpin had coined the name.

Harry started his car and reversed laboriously out of the station forecourt. Too early to get a drink, he thought, so he might as well try and do a bit of work. Not that there was a lot he could do. Turpin had seen to that.

Turpin had got Roddy Maclean. While all the other hacks had been stumbling round in the cowshit at the scene of the crime, Turpin had nabbed the star turn. It hadn't looked that way to Harry: he'd gone for the husband. It had been a piece of piss. He'd nabbed Mark Harvey as he came out of the police station, given him the soft sell, coaxed him along with a show of sympathy that was the product of priceless years of insincerity. He'd got a neat little angle on it too, under the headline "Hubby's Horror". It had bombed.

"I don't want to read this shit!" his editor had screamed at him. "Get me some shit like Turpin's got!"

The editor hadn't wanted to know about Mark Harvey.

"Look Harry," he had continued in a more reasonable tone. "I couldn't give a toss about that pillock. What you gonna get, a poor sod story? Like, poor sod didn't know who his wife was screwing, ah-bloody-ah bring on the violins? For Christ's sake get hold of who she was screwing!"

Like Turpin with Roddy Maclean. Grimly, Harry had forced himself to read it, although it had made him apoplectic: it was the most blatant rip-off of his own "Stratford Strangler" style he had ever read. He was indignant, but powerless. Thus has it ever been with trail-blazers: no one either to blame or to copy but themselves.

Harry hit the brakes and slammed on his horn. Two yabbering yokels in an antique Cortina had pulled out in front of him and were occupying the middle of the road. They carried on yabbering and paid him no attention. He flashed his lights and they ignored that too. He waved two fingers at them over his steering wheel, but they weren't looking in the mirror. They couldn't have been looking at the road much either, they were weaving all over it like drunken slalomists. Harry swore himself hoarse at them and waited impatiently for a chance to overtake. Unfortunately it was the only road into Fareham village.

He had been away when the Reg Talbot story broke. He had been in High Wycombe at the bed and breakfast where Eluned Watkins was staying, angling for the "My Brother The Mad Murderer" scoop. She had refused point-blank to talk to him, so he'd made it up anyway, quite a story too, all about how the looney loner's sister had always suspected that her brother was a sex-hungry misfit, but she was devastated to discover that he was a killer fiend into the bargain. Eluned Watkins was furious, she had reported him to the Press Council, which didn't bother Harry: if people wanted to spend their time pissing against the wind that was their business, not his. His editor had loved the story. Everyone had loved it. Until Reg Talbot broke.

A junior reporter was in Fareham covering for Harry. He got the story. He wasn't snappy enough to get Reg Talbot, but apparently no one had been: Talbot was his own man, untempted by cash inducements, refusing exclusives no matter the price and threatening to sue anyone who misquoted him, a threat which at least cut a sliver of a cube of ice on account of the fact that Talbot appeared to be loaded and had retained a libel lawyer at mention of whose name half the editors in Fleet Street scared themselves shitless. In the meantime the junior's story had relegated Harry's piece to a minor inside paragraph.

"Must be losing your touch, Harry," the editor had remarked sarcastically.

"Losing your touch, Harry?" asked Turpin, that same evening at the police press conference.

He was a laughing stock. It wasn't his fault, it was just bad luck. But they were all rubbing his nose in it now. He knew what Turpin was saying about him.

"Harry Craven? Over the hill, mate. Used to be the best, but who gives a toss about ancient history? Time the old git was put out to grass."

He could hear Turpin saying it. See him too, perched on his bar stool with some poncy cocktail in hand, holding forth. They all looked up to him, even the older ones, though there weren't many of them left. These days it was a young man's game, and the young men aped Turpin. They copied his designer suits, his gelled hair, the way he slung his Filofax carelessly on to the table. One day he set up a portable computer on the bar. Next day they all had one. He had more gimmicks than James Bond. What did Harry Craven have? A leaky biro and a packet of No.6.

He lit up another cigarette. He didn't count them any more, he'd given up the numbers game when he passed sixty a day. Turpin smoked slim panatellas now; they stank like smouldering armpits. Turpin'd say, you'll kill yourself if you carry on like that, Harry, and shake his head whenever he saw him light up. Nah, Harry thought, but I wouldn't mind killing you, you flash git.

The yabbering yokels continued along the main road. Harry gave them the benefit of one last blast on his horn, then turned into Fareham High Street. A grand sounding title, he thought, for a dozen or so tatty shops, a couple of banks and a two-pump garage. What the hell was Fareham Low Street like? There was a surprising amount of traffic about, though. It obviously qualified as some sort of yokels' shopping centre. There were quite a few new-looking offices dotted around among the shops. Most seemed to be estate agents. That meant commuter-belt house prices. The yokels must be pissed off. Death of the community, all that shit. Let 'em die, too many of the bastards already. Nowhere to park the bloody car. . . .

He left it on the garage forecourt, half-blocking the exit. The old git serving petrol didn't like that very much. Harry couldn't give a stuff.

"Mr Barker's expecting me," he said with a yawn. He waved at his car. "Give the windows a rub down, will you."

The old git's eyes popped indignantly. Harry didn't wait for him to recover the use of his voice. He went through the glass door into the offices. There was no one in reception.

"Billy about?" he shouted down the corridor, where he saw a couple of workmen pretending to be busy with a light fitting.

Billy was about. He stuck his head out of his office door in answer to his name and squinted suspiciously at Harry, like a scouting ferret. When he realised who it was a look of alarm transcended his cow-like features. He raised one hand to his lips and, with the other, beckoned Harry to join him.

Once they were both safely inside, Billy closed his office door and leant against it. Harry plonked himself casually in Billy's swivel chair. A girlie magazine was open on the desk. The unlikely pose that greeted his eye arrested his attention for a moment.

"The boss is about!" exclaimed Billy in a high decibel whisper. "Don't want to be seen talking to you!"

Harry turned the page through ninety degrees and examined the unlikely pose from another angle. It didn't seem either anatomically or gravitationally possible.

"You mean old Reg Talbot himself?"

"Yeah!" Billy nodded vigorously. "This garage is gonna be his showcase, right. He's keeping an eye on it."

Keeping an eye on you, more like, Harry thought, turning the page and keeping his eye on Melissa, 38-26-36.

"Nice tits!" Billy observed.

"The voice of the connoisseur," remarked Harry, who could be quite dry when he could be bothered.

"Bet you get an eyeful of good 'uns round your neck of the woods!" Billy snickered.

Like many of the dimmer members of the general public, i.e. Harry's readership, Billy fondly imagined that the offices of tabloid newspapers teemed with topless, pouting models, ready to go off and be snapped for Page 3 at the drop of a bra. Harry indulged him. He even gave him one of his rare half-smiles.

"No, I'm not the tits man. It's a bum job, they tell me." He waited for Billy to get the joke. He waited in vain. "I'm the crime man, remember?"

Billy nodded. He gave a glance towards the door. His eyes were pregnant with guilt. He dropped his voice still lower.

"He thinks she's still alive, you know."

"What, Maddie Harvey?"

"Yeah. 'Cos they didn't find no body. He says she said to him she was going to go away for a while, disappear like. Thinks she may have got hit on the head or something and is wandering round in a daze. Says she's got magnesia."

"Got what?"

"That's what he said. On the phone. To the telly people. I kept my ears to the wall, like you said."

For emphasis he tapped the wall which, being made of cardboard, shook. The partitions which divided the offices were temporary, pending renovation.

"What telly people?"

"They're sending a camera crew down. Tomorrow night. I heard Reg on the phone saying as he'd got important evidence and was going to expose Roddy Maclean for a fraud and prove that she'd loved him all along. Reg, I mean."

"I don't understand a word of this. What are you talking about?"

"He's got her shoe!"

"What?"

"Reg. He's got Mrs Harvey's shoe. It's evidence!"

Billy was leaning over the desk, his weight on his fingers, shoving his eager face into Harry's. His porcine eyes were bright with excitement. Harry stared at him blankly. What was Billy trying to say, that Reg Talbot was a foot fetishist? He couldn't make anything out of that; most of his readers wouldn't know what it was anyway. Harry put down the glossy magazine. He closed it. Melissa had been distracting him.

"I'm sorry, have I missed something? Say all that again, will you?"

He had Billy repeat himself, slowly. When he had finished he made him go back to the beginning and start all over again. Eventually he began to make some sort of sense of it.

"So what you're saying, Billy – and stop me if I'm wrong – is that our Reg is going to go on the box, and hold up this shoe like Cinderella's glass bleeding slipper, and say this proves that she was here that night canoodling with me and couldn't give a toss about that old git Maclean, and if the rozzers'll go through her wardrobe they'll find the other shoe and Bob's your uncle, right?"

"Yeh."

"Mm. Wacky."

Like everything else about this case, he added as a mental afterthought.

"And old Reg is going to speak to the nation tomorrow — Saturday?"

"S'right. One week after her disappearance. The anniversary like. He says he's gonna set it up just like it was, with candles and that, and tell his story."

"I see."

Even wackier, went the mental postscript.

Harry rose slowly, smoothing out and lighting a cigarette. It sounded as though old Reg had flipped. The telly people must have thought that Christmas had come early. He was willing to bet his bottom dollar that their version of what they'd promised Reg and his version of what they'd promised him had sod all in common.

That left an opening. He saw it glimmer in his mind's eye, like a luminous palm tree in the desert of missed opportunities.

"Thanks Billy, you've been a great help."

Harry produced his wallet. He counted out five tenners and pushed them across the table, together with his receipt pad. Billy took out his pen. He hadn't liked this bit at all, the first time Harry had given him money. Just a formality, Harry had explained, to keep the accountants happy: you can sign yourself as anything you like, Donald Duck for all I care. Billy pocketed the fifty pounds and passed back the receipt pad. Harry glanced at the signature. It read, D.Duck.

"That's great Billy. Give us a call if anything else crops up, and remember, mum's the word!"

Billy tapped the side of his nose to indicate that he understood. Harry winked back. He'd always been good at handling Billy's type, the Bad and the Ugly. The Good could sod off. Harry was pleased with Billy, he knew value for money when it came up and bit his arse: if old Reg really did have something on Roddy Maclean then it would kill two birds with one stone, give him a scoop and blow Turpin's gaffe all in one. And if Reg had just flipped, then that would be a good story too. Harry paused at the door and flared his upper lip at Billy. It was meant as a smile. Things were looking up.

When Harry had gone Billy tiptoed over to the window. He watched Harry come out of the office entrance, get into his car, stick two fingers up in response to something the pump attendant said, and drive away. Only when he had made quite sure with his own eyes that Harry had really gone did he return to his desk. He consulted a card in his wallet, then picked up the phone and dialled. It was answered almost at once. Billy cleared his throat.

"Is Mr Turpin there, please?"

17

He still hated the phone. The first ring was like an electric shock.
Actually picking up the receiver set off a chain reaction of Pavlovian
responses: increased heartbeat, sweating, a flicker of delirium
tremens. He knew it wasn't rational, but logic didn't help. If they
were going to get him they'd just come round, they wouldn't phone.
They knew where he was. There was nowhere left to hide.

So he listened, in the semi-darkness behind the thick curtains, until
the phone had played itself out. The last ring was cut off mid-way
through, like a strangled cry. It wasn't the first time it had rung
today. It wouldn't be the last. They knew where he was.

He was at Martin Bird's house. He had been there since Sunday,
since it had all happened. The police thought it was a good idea. They
had wanted the house to themselves for a few days, to look for
evidence. They wanted him out of the way. It would protect him
from the journalists too, they reckoned.

That had been the worst time, Monday, Tuesday . . . stuck in
Martin's house, waiting for the phone to ring, waiting for the knock
on the door. He had read things about forensic science. They could
find a hair, or a thread, and use it to deduce a whole history. There
was nothing that the microscopic eye couldn't see. They would get
him in the end, and the longer it took them the worse it would be. He
had better make the most of his freedom. If only he could put the
minutes in a cage.

Time dragged. Why should he have minded, when it was so
precious? But he did mind. Stretching time out, making it go further,
didn't much help when there was nowhere for it to go. He had never
known a sound as remorseless as the tick, tock of his watch. He
didn't sleep very well. The hours of consciousness rolled on. He
watched the television.

There was a big television in the living room, and a portable that
served for the kitchen and the bedroom. In the bedroom he had it set
up on Jean's dressing table, covering all angles, so that he could see it

even while lying in the bath. It was all done with mirrors. He liked to have it on loud, for company. In silence unpleasant thoughts could breed. Sometimes they cropped up in his dreams, but he learnt quickly to ignore them: the moment he opened his eyes in the morning he would leap out of bed to turn the switch and out would come the breakfast time sound, swamping the tendrils of his subconscious. He didn't really watch or listen, he didn't take much in, but it occupied part of his mind that could have been otherwise engaged. He watched a lot of Open University programmes, picking up snatches about engineering and astrophysics, and significant movements in the history of art. He watched news bulletins, and weather forecasts, and afternoon films that weren't good enough to be shown at any other time, and Australian soaps, and quizzes, quizzes, quizzes. The cumulative effect was hypnotic. His eyes ached from watching too much, but that was a small price to pay for plastering over so much time.

He felt detached from everything. Because he was never alone his awareness of self diminished. He became a creature of functions, and set his timetable by the most constant of functions, tele-watching. He never went out, and the curtains were always drawn. A policewoman had done some shopping for him in the middle of the week. The police had been very helpful. He wondered if they'd want something in return, like a confession.

He had almost confessed, in the small hours of last Sunday morning when they knocked on his door. There had been two of them, a fat Sergeant and a thin boy who looked much too young to be in uniform. The boy had been shocked, Mark felt sorry for him. He made him a cup of tea and sat him down in the kitchen, while the Sergeant plodded about upstairs, and they all waited for the ambulance and the big guns to arrive. It was gone four o'clock, way past anyone's bedtime. No time to inspect a body, hung by the neck until dead. Mark felt protective towards the young policeman. The arrangement in the kitchen was so cosily domestic, with the two of them sipping their tea and Mark munching the biscuits which had been offered and refused, that it was impossible for Mark to think that the young policeman could actually do him any harm. It was the perfect time to confess. Then they could all go off together and dig up Maddie's body, save the ambulance another trip. It would be a proper feather in the young policeman's cap, they'd probably make him an Inspector right away. He'd be very grateful, he might even come and visit Mark in prison, bring him flowers. He hoped they'd let him have a window box outside his cell. He would need to have a hobby. They probably wouldn't approve much of the old one, because of his dependence on his modelling knives. Which was silly really, because even with his best blade he wouldn't be able to saw through an iron bar in under twenty years. On the other hand, twenty years was about what he was going to have. Time was not really going to be a problem.

His thoughts meandered in this way while the Sergeant's heavy tread vibrated through the ceiling. He pictured him sniffing round the body, finding the suicide note and adding two and two together. No doubt the simple addition depressed him: when the footsteps ceased a weight of doom hung still in the air. How (the Sergeant was surely thinking) was he to break the news to the poor chap downstairs that the hanging man appeared to have murdered his wife? The young policeman, in blissful ignorance of the horrors about to break, blithely sipped his tea.

In the end, the Sergeant had done the sensible thing and left it to his superiors. More time had elapsed, and day had come. When the Inspector came and sat down with him, and asked him to prepare himself for a shock, the workmen were already laying the surface of the swimming pool next door.

The Inspector had asked him a lot of awkward questions: Where had he been? Martin Bird's. Why had he come back at 4 o'clock? He hadn't known it was so late; didn't time fly! Had anybody seen him? He didn't think so. What had he been doing at Martin's? Watching videos. Which videos? He named them. What had he been doing at Martin's in the first place? Avoiding Maddie.

That had been the clever answer. He hadn't tried to pretend that everything in the garden had been rosy. There wouldn't have been much point really: two minutes with anyone who knew them both would be enough to reveal the true state of the Harveys' marriage. Nonetheless, it was the sort of mistake an amateur murderer was likely to make. The Inspector had praised him for his frankness. There had been other clevernesses too.

Like his careful editing of their photograph albums. As Maddie so disliked having her photograph taken (the reality did not accord with her own self-image) there were very few of recent vintage, but those had had to go. Mark had kept only the oldest ones, and it had been these which he released to the police and press. The one they had all gone for was a fuzzy, long-distance shot of a slim youthful creature in tennis shorts. It hadn't looked at all like Maddie, but it might just conceivably have been a younger version of Madeleine. Reg Talbot had not denounced it.

That had been very clever. Thinking ahead, that had been. That had been what he had made himself do, sitting up in Roger's attic prior to calling the police. After typing the "P.S." to the suicide note he had methodically gone through Roger's papers, searching for references to Myfanwy Roberts. He had found several, in letters, in a diary, and a couple of extra suicide notes which had managed to work themselves free of the collected edition. He had gathered all the papers together, and burned them downstairs together with the photographs. He had wiped off all his fingerprints wherever it seemed appropriate, though not entirely, for he had often visited Roger's dirty den and evidence of dusting might arouse suspicion. That had been the way he had thought: he had tried to put himself in the shoes of the policemen, tried to lay a trail that would lead them where he wanted them to go. Oh, so clever he had been. And so utterly unprepared for what had come next.

He had not taken into account the press. It had not occurred to him that what he had so carefully concocted would turn out to be one of the major sensations of the year. He hardly ever read the papers, except at weekends, and then it was usually *The Sunday Telegraph*. He knew nothing at all about the tabloids, except that they were not the sort of thing he wanted to be spotted reading by W.W.Vernon. Now he knew why.

He was, quite simply, stunned. Everything he had read made him rub his eyes and question the state of his own consciousness. He had always assumed, for example, that if one were interviewed by the press, that if one were asked a question like, what was your opinion of Roger the lodger, Mr Harvey? and one replied that he seemed like a harmless enough chap, then "harmless enough chap" was what they would quote one as saying, not "he was a sex-crazed fiend and I hope he rots in hell!" But not one single word of anything he had said was reported with anything even remotely adjacent to accuracy. At the same time, it all made him terribly afraid.

The things he read about Roger made him feel guilty. None of them were fair. Roger had been a nice bloke, in his odd depressive way. He would have liked to say something to defend Roger's blasted reputation, but of course he couldn't, unless he was prepared to acknowledge the truth, in which case what they said about Roger they'd say about him, only ten times worse. That was the unbearable thought: he had seen what the tabloids were capable of. How much worse would it be if they got hold of the truth? What words would they put into his mouth then, and into the mouths of his myriad enemies? A fair trial would be out of the question. He'd get thirty years, with hard labour and triple sexual abuse.

Roger haunted him. The face hanging beneath the creaking rope hovered in his dreams. He tried to equivocate, to justify himself. Roger had accidentally committed suicide, it wasn't as if he had made him do it or anything. The timing had been fortuitous, that was all. He'd simply taken advantage of the situation as he found it, when Roger was past caring anyway. He tried to tell himself that he had done Roger a favour, listening to his drunken depressive ramblings all through the night, allowing Roger to use him as a sounding board and the echo of his conscience, so when all was said and done he was merely extracting a posthumous favour in return. It was a feeble argument that crumbled even as he framed it. Could he try it in respect of Maddie? he wondered bitterly to himself. Could he argue that he'd only been doing her a favour too, because no one who looked as bad as she did could possibly want to go on living? They'd brand him a Nazi if he came out with anything like that. He'd be bound to get a jury composed exclusively of Billy and Bessie Bunters. They'd give him a hundred years and chain him to the bottom of a bunk bed underneath the fattest prisoner in England. He dreamed of him sometimes – the fattest prisoner – leaning over the edge of the bed and leering at him with chocolate-covered fangs.

Gargoyles and griffins patrolled his dreams; consciousness was shared by the Open University and *Neighbours*. All of existence was marinated in morbidity. He wanted to run away. Instead he hid in Martin's and waited for the phone to ring. On Friday afternoon he made the mistake of answering it.

"Mr Harvey? I've been trying to get hold of you all day. It's Inspector Morris. I'd like a word with you, if you don't mind."

A word? It was more than Mark was capable of. Fortunately the Inspector did not require it then and there.

"I'll drop by and see you, if that's not inconvenient. I was just on my way home, I should be with you in about twenty minutes. That alright, is it?"

He must have taken Mark's grunt for a yes. The line went dead.

The waking dream that Mark now found himself in was even more surreal than usual. His body drifted aimlessly about the house on feet that must have had independent means of motor propulsion. So this was it, he thought. The policeman's casual manner hadn't deceived him, they were trained to put you off your guard. He felt resigned, but confused. He wondered why it was that he found himself in the bathroom. He supposed that the idea must have been to wash, to freshen up, at least to look one's best in adversity.

"A girl's got to look her best," he remarked to his reflection in the mirror.

He jumped. He even gave a little gasp as he staggered backwards. He stared dumbly at the face in the mirror.

A weird thing of a face, neither fish nor fowl: the unshaven chin, the short straight hair, the visible ears of plain Mark Harvey. But between them signs of something else altogether: Burgundy lips, light rioja cheeks, eyes like black velvet, lined with kohl. A hybrid hermaphrodite.

"Bloody hell!"

His head was spinning. Had he gone mad? What day was it? What time was it? When had he done this?

He threw cold water on his face, raised it again to the mirror and watched the droplets trickle down his chin. The cold water gave him a sense of being jolted. It jogged his memory.

He had done it in the morning, this Friday morning, first thing. He had wanted to for days, every day since he'd been there. The lingering urge reminded him of when he had given up smoking: that ache in the lungs, that insistent yearning, the voice in his head saying go on, just one, one won't do you any harm. . . .

Temptation was always within arm's reach. Whenever his eyes strayed from the television in the bedroom there it was: there, literally beside the telly on Jean Bird's dressing table, her neat cosmetic array. Some she had taken with her, of course, but there remained enough to ensnare the idle eye. How many times he had looked it over, how many times had he been tempted to examine, to sniff, to smear a finger tip! But no, he had told himself, he shouldn't, and what was the point anyway? Nothing in Jean's wardrobe would have fitted him. He didn't even have a wig, though he had looked in her cupboards when the craving had been at its most intense.

But he'd done it all the same. That morning, between *Breakfast Time* and *An Introduction To Advanced Calculus*. Just a dab of eyeliner and lipstick. For old times' sake, and to pass some time. Bit of a joke really, no harm intended. Sly old thing. Naughty Mark. Bloody silly Mark. He must have known it was wrong or he wouldn't have tried so hard to forget that he'd done it.

He ran out of the bathroom and grabbed Jean's cold cream jar off the dressing table. Soap and water did the rest. He scrubbed his face down to the bone.

The doorbell rang. His heart was beating so furiously already that there was no scope for further palpitations. He wondered if they'd arrest him on the doorstep. How many of them would there be? How many did it take to overpower a semi-transvestite wreck?

The Inspector was on his own. He nodded at Mark sympathetically.

"You're not looking a hundred per cent, Mr Harvey, I hope you don't mind me saying."

Mark eyed him cautiously. The Inspector's hands were hanging loosely at his sides. No handcuffs were visible.

"Mind if I come in? I won't keep you long."

Mark stood aside to let the Inspector in. They went into the dark, stuffy living room. Mark sat down in his accustomed armchair, in front of the telly.

"Mind if I open a window?" said the Inspector.

He drew the curtain, let in air and light. He sat down.

"I know this is very distressing for you, Mr Harvey," he began, with the air of one about to cause a great deal more distress, "but I need to talk to you some more about Mrs Harvey."

They talked, or rather the Inspector talked, while Mark half-listened and wondered what it was all leading to, where the twist would come. The Inspector hardly looked at him. Mark understood: it must have been difficult for him, talking about Maddie's various lovers, and the one who had murdered her.

"You know, I don't think Roger can have meant to murder her," Mark said, rather awkwardly, when the Inspector stopped to clear his throat. "Roger wasn't that sort, I'm sure it was only an accident."

Suddenly the Inspector looked at him. His eyes narrowed sharply, the gaze was concentrated and intense. Mark felt himself wilt. Trickles of sweat tickled his cheek. He wanted to look away but he didn't dare. He felt instinctively that anything he did would betray his guilt. He tried not to breathe. When at last the Inspector spoke, after an age, his voice was oddly soft.

"Had you noticed any peculiarities of behaviour in your wife during the weeks that led up to her disappearance?"

"Not really," Mark answered carefully, trying to recall what he had already divulged, and wondering at the same time why the Inspector had so carefully phrased the word "disappearance". "As I said, I hadn't seen much of her. We weren't on the best of terms."

"But you said that you weren't surprised to learn that she had been seeing Reg Talbot. Why not?"

A very good question, to which Mark did not know the answer. He shrugged.

"Perhaps she did seem to have changed a little," he said, making it up as he went along. "Perhaps I sensed that she was happier, I don't know. . . . " He was trying to think of Madeleine, putting himself back into her shoes, her brand-new patent leather stilettos. "Yes, I suppose that was it. She seemed to have become a new person in some way."

"And she hadn't seen so much of Roddy Maclean?"

"Oh yes, that's true. I think he came round a couple of times, I think he wanted to see her, but there was no . . . there wasn't any . . . if you see what I mean. . . . "

There hadn't been any bean-bagging, was what he meant. The Inspector nodded briskly to indicate that he understood. He reached into his inside pocket and pulled out a piece of paper. He handed it over.

"What do you make of this, Mr Harvey?"

Mark unfolded the paper. It was a photocopy of Madeleine's letter to Roddy. He reread his own handiwork with mounting embarrassment:

Dear Roddy

I do hope that nasty husband of mine didn't give you too much of a fright last night! I'm afraid he meant it, he's very violent. Besides the shotgun he has a whole arsenal of lethal firearms, not to mention a machete and a hatchet which he keeps at all times by his bedside. Incidentally, I have seen him practise with them on a pumpkin, and I'd advise keeping well out of his way when he's in a bad mood, which I'm afraid seems to be whenever he thinks of you. I know it's just jealousy, and who wouldn't be jealous of a real he-man like you, but for heaven's sake keep out of the way for a bit. I told you what my solicitor said about stirring him up. Your showing your face round here is like waving a red rag at a bull! I think it's a bad idea even to use the phone. Just hearing your voice puts him into a violent sulk. So write if you want to, but that's all! I ABSOLUTELY FORBID you to come round visiting again. I know it's hard for you, Roly-panda, and believe me, it's not easy at this end either. How your little gooey cream-cake misses your scrummy wobbly body! We'll be together again soon enough, my man-size slice of passion cake, but in the meantime you'll just have to be patient and keep away for the sake of our future together. Mum's the word!

I'm sorry to use a typewriter. It's not very intimate or romantic, I know, but I am trying to improve my wpm, just in case I need to go back to work to contribute a few feathers to our little love nest!

Love and hugs and kisses from your favourite sweet trolley,

Maddie (XXX)

Mark slowed down as he finished reading the letter. He didn't want to finish. He didn't want to have to hand the paper back and face the Inspector. His discomfort must have been plain to see. The Inspector reached over and gently took the paper from him.

"I'm sorry to have had to ask you to read it," he said sympathetically, "but I should like to have your opinion. Do you recognise the portrait of yourself in this letter?"

Mark shook his head.

"Do you possess a shotgun, or an arsenal, or even a machete or a hatchet?"

Mark shook his head again.

"The only weapons in your house are the reproductions on your study wall?"

Mark nodded.

"Would you say that hearing Mr Maclean's voice put you into a violent sulk?"

"No, I . . . I mean, I didn't like it, I don't like him, but I wouldn't go that far."

This time the Inspector did the nodding.

"You see, Mr Harvey, this letter just doesn't ring true to me. It's obviously meant to be a warning, and Mr Maclean says he took it as such, but it reads more like an excuse to me. I mean, an excuse for her not to have to see him. There is something rather exaggerated about the tone of this letter, wouldn't you agree?"

Mark would. He did. He nodded.

"Was your wife in the habit of using a typewriter for her personal correspondence?"

"I'm afraid I don't really know."

"Fair enough. Mr Maclean showed me a number of letters your wife had written to him over the past year. They are all handwritten. They don't read much like this one. Do you recognise the signature at the bottom?"

He held the paper up for Mark to see. He nodded. Of course he recognised the signature. He had done it himself.

"I don't think your wife wrote this letter, Mr Harvey."

Mark gaped at him. He didn't know what to say, apart from agreeing with him, and he didn't want to do that. He pointed instead at the signature.

"Oh yes, that's genuine enough," the Inspector continued. "I'm quite prepared to believe that she signed it alright. I just think that somebody else wrote it, somebody who wanted Mr Maclean out of the way. This solicitor business bothers me. As far as we can tell she didn't have a solicitor. But if she was acting in tandem with somebody, the same person, perhaps, who was responsible for this letter – I'm just, as it were, thinking aloud Mr Harvey, please excuse me – then that would explain a lot. We might be looking too locally. How well do you know Reg Talbot?"

The change of tack took Mark by surprise. There was no alteration of tone, not even a slight pause before the question. It took a moment for Mark actually to register that a question had been asked. He stuttered back his answer.

"Hardly at all."

"How long do you think your wife had been carrying on with him?"

"I can't say exactly, Inspector, I'm not even sure there's any evidence that — "

"You said that it couldn't have been much more than a week. Mr Talbot himself is very evasive on the subject. I get the impression that he wants me to think that it had been going on for a lot longer. His wife certainly thinks that, that is if you believe everything you read in the papers. Would you say your wife was an impulsive woman, Mr Harvey?"

"I don't really . . . sometimes."

Mark shrugged. The Inspector looked at him significantly.

"As you have pointed out, Mr Harvey, and as Mr Maclean himself has admitted, he had had no sexual relations with your wife for over a week prior to her disappearance. During exactly the period when, by your own testimony, she was most likely to have struck up her affair with Talbot. Suddenly she doesn't want to see Maclean any more. She writes him the letter I've just shown you, a letter in which, to say the least, she has been playful with the truth. I am almost inclined to believe that that letter may be a kind of joke at Mr Maclean's expense. I have a hunch that Reg Talbot himself may actually have written that letter. You see, all the evidence suggests that Talbot had suddenly superseded Maclean in your wife's affections. Neither seems to have known about the other, and I don't believe that they are lying. I have a quite different theory.

"You said when I first came in that you didn't believe Mr Jones was the murderous sort. I quite agree with you. I am now completely satisfied that the M— referred to in his suicide note was not your wife. There is not a shred of evidence, forensic or otherwise, to connect him with your wife. M— was a childhood sweetheart who had come to no good. Mr Jones may have been a manic depressive, but he was no murderer, and no rapist either.

"What I'm going to say will come as a shock to you, Mr Harvey.

"I am suggesting that your wife wasn't murdered at all. I think she is still alive, and in hiding."

The Inspector paused for effect. He sat forward on the edge of the seat, one ear slightly cocked towards Mark, as if waiting in case he should say something. Mark said nothing. What could he say? Besides that the Inspector was mistaken.

"I suspect that her disappearance is bound up with Reg Talbot, a man whom she had met only days before but with whom she had fallen passionately in love. She may not be responsible for her own actions, she may be entirely under Talbot's spell – "

"But – "

"I know it must be hard for you to accept, Mr Harvey, but look at the facts: there is no body; there is no evidence that a crime has been committed: Reg Talbot is behaving very oddly – he claims, and this is very significant, that he knows that Madeleine Harvey is still alive, and that she told him she was going to have to disappear for a while! There's been something very odd about this case from the beginning. At last I think I'm getting near the truth."

The Inspector gave Mark a little smile, as if inviting him to share his confidence. This was not something Mark felt able to do, but he smiled back nonetheless, warily.

"This puts a very different complexion on things, doesn't it, Inspector?"

The Inspector nodded vigorously.

"The important thing now is to find her, and that's where I need your help: can you think of anywhere your wife might have gone to, some favourite holiday resort perhaps, or even a friend somewhere who might have offered her shelter? Please try to think, Mr Harvey. Rack your brains."

His brains had been racked now for some minutes. They were in far too much of a scramble for him to be expected to come up with anything coherent. The Inspector looked at him with evident sympathy.

"I'm sorry, all this has probably been quite a shock, but I thought you'd better hear it from me first, before the papers get hold of it. Please have a think over what I said, and just try and remember if there was anywhere, anywhere at all, that your wife was particularly fond of, that she might have chosen as a hiding place. Like I say, have a think and give me a call if anything occurs to you. Here's my home number, look, I'll leave it by the phone."

He left it actually on the phone, stuck into the top of the dial. Mark got up to see him out, but he seemed in no hurry to go.

"I know this is a lot for you to swallow, Mr Harvey, but I've been a policeman for twenty-odd years now and, believe me, if you think this sounds peculiar it's nothing to some of the things I've come across in the course of a working life. You wouldn't credit what people get up to, Mr Harvey, you wouldn't credit it. Your wife's out there somewhere, I can sense it. Sooner or later Talbot will try to contact her, and I'll be waiting when he does. Meantime you'd better keep this under your hat. I know I can count on you."

"But why, Inspector?"

The Inspector had started to go out. He stopped at the door and met Mark's look of bafflement.

"Why?" Mark repeated. "What's the point of faking her own death? If she wanted to go off with Talbot, I couldn't have stopped her. It doesn't make sense!"

"Not yet, I agree. But does the other scenario make sense? No, there's more to this case than meets the eye. I'm working on the assumption that your wife's disappearance was unpremeditated. She and Talbot may have found Jones's body, may even have altered the suicide note – it wasn't signed, remember – and taken advantage of the opportunity that was presented to them. As for a motive, that's not hard to guess at. There's usually only one motive in cases of this sort. Life insurance."

"But my wife didn't have any life insurance!"

"Not that you know of. But Roddy Maclean insists that they had come to an arrangement that each would take out a policy in the other's favour. He showed me his own application form, which he had not yet sent off. He said that your wife was going to have a word with her solicitor when she saw him about instituting divorce proceedings. I am sure that this solicitor, whoever he is, must be working under Reg Talbot's instructions. And I am sure that the life insurance policy she took out is in Talbot's favour, not Maclean's. If your wife's death were to be confirmed in a court of law, then Talbot would be a very wealthy man."

"But he is a wealthy man!"

"Greed, Mr Harvey, knows no limits. I'm not saying I've got the definitive answer, but it bears thinking about, doesn't it? Oh, and one other thing, I'm afraid the photographs you let me have of your wife aren't much good, if you don't mind I'd like to send a police artist to see you. Good afternoon, sir, and thanks for your cooperation. Please don't hesitate to give me a call if you think of anything, anything at all."

Mark let the Inspector out, then returned to the living room. He shut the window again and drew the curtains. Automatically he turned on the television, but the chirpy voice of the continuity announcer irritated him. He flicked through the channels but found nothing soothing. In any case he felt too restless to sit down and watch. He went upstairs.

Without thinking he went towards the portable tv on the dressing table. His hand was actually on the switch, he was about to turn it on when he remembered that he didn't want to watch. His hand fell limply to his side. He felt enervated. He sat down on the dressing-table stool. He stared at himself in the mirror.

He couldn't cope. The crunch had come, or was coming. He was in for it now.

His hand brushed lightly over Jean Bird's face powder. He didn't like it, he didn't think much of her choice of cosmetics all round. Her lipstick was especially vulgar. He resisted the temptation to try it again. It just didn't suit him. He would be letting himself down. Letting Madeleine down.

The eyes he saw in the mirror shocked him. There was nothing behind them, they were empty, washed out. He felt the dull drug of hopelessness seep through his veins. Why should it be he who suffered? He pushed the containers of cosmetics away with an angry gesture. There was still a flicker of life in him, a flicker of defiance in those all but expressionless eyes. He stared grimly at his bland, uninteresting face. It hadn't always looked so nondescript. There was some comfort in remembrance of things past.

He tried to think of Maddie. They wanted an artist's impression. He could have laughed. He couldn't conjure up her face any more. When he tried, it was another's. That was in his mind's eye. In reality, in the mirror, there was only Mark. His lip curled up in scorn: what had Mark got to offer?

He continued to sit in silence, staring at himself in the mirror. Eventually it grew dark, and the features that oppressed him first became fuzzy, then disappeared altogether with the light.

18

There was a light breeze, wafting the scent of fresh manure into the night. The unkempt lawn was slippery with dew. A light glimmered through the trees but its source lay beyond the shadowy mass of the house. It came from chez Talbot. Willow Cottage itself was in darkness.

Mark had come over the fields, leaping ditches and fences and braving the stubborn clutching brambles like an ancient quester. The car was in a lay-by on the other side of the Trumans' farm. The entrance to his own drive was blocked by cars full of journalists on stake-out, awaiting oracular utterance from Reg. Thus he came stealthily the long way round, keeping the moat between them. He wore black and kept an old flat cap pulled down over his eyes.

He came through the gap in the hedge at the bottom of the garden, a gap enlarged by Roddy's frequent passages. Hugging the line of the trees he made his way towards the house. The floodlights on Reg's patio reached just across the fence to pick out the border of the lawn. The surface of the fishpond glistened. There was no water on the other side, in the pool wherein lay Maddie's body.

He flitted from the shadows under the trees to the shadows under the house. He was at the back, shielded from the drive by the whole density of masonry. He felt his keys with the tips of his fingers. The back-door key was the biggest. He located the lock by touch. He entered the kitchen softly and clicked the door shut behind him.

He felt his way along the wall, past the cooker and the sink to the flat work surface under the draining rack. He opened the drawer beneath and found his thick cylindrical torch. Holding it under his jacket he checked that it was on the "torch" setting; he didn't want to set off the flashing amber warning lens, or even the fluorescent striplight, the gravedigger's friend. Satisfied, he closed the drawer and took a step out towards the dining room.

"Agh!"

He yelped as something shot out from under his feet. The sound of his own voice was loud and terrifying, and for a moment he almost dissolved in blind panic. Then the cat miaowed and he understood.

He stood leaning against the sink, getting back his breath and regaining control of his trembling limbs, while the cat continued her rather plaintive mewling and came across the floor towards him. He felt her rub up against his leg; he could have almost sworn he'd heard her purr. Puzzled by this unusual overture he turned on the torch and pointed it at her.

Now the cause was obvious: she was starving. It wasn't that she looked especially haggard or down at heel, it was just that her eyes glistened with feline greed. It was one of only two expressions he associated with Maud Gonne, the other being feline contempt. He found tins in the cupboard, filled up her empty bowls with catmeat and some crunchy catty hard tack. He left her gorging herself as he crept out into the dining room.

He went through quickly into the hall, climbed the stairs, heard the familiar creaks; down the landing and into the bedroom . . . the door had been closed, the atmosphere was stuffy. He went to the window and opened it a few inches. Then he drew the curtains shut. All this time he took care to keep the torch pointed downwards, away from the window, adding precaution to precaution. He went first to the dressing table.

He took a carrier bag out of his pocket, opened it under the lip of the table and swept in all the jars and bottles and tubes. There was more in the drawer and he took that too. He put his booty on the bed. Underneath the bed there were some suitcases. He pulled one out, put it on top and opened it. He stashed his bag of goodies in a corner, and carefully laid next to it the two wigs on their blocks, the blonde and the unfavoured chestnut.

He opened the cupboard. Madeleine's suit was at the back, safe in its plastic cover. He folded it once and laid it neatly in the case, tucking the hook of the hanger under the carrier bag. In the chest of drawers he found clean underwear, suitable for all sexes. He searched in the bottom of the cupboard for Madeleine's shoes.

There was only one. He sat down on the edge of the bed, holding it in his hands, feeling in the darkness the delicate fine leather. The touch of it made him ache with longing. But where was the other shoe? It definitely wasn't in the cupboard, along with Maddie's collection of sandals, her ugly fleet of flat-bottomed boats. He felt the long slim heel with its point like a blunted dagger. He remembered now. The point had snapped off. But what had he done with the damaged shoe? His memories of that strange and awful night were confused. He'd have to have a good think later, make a thorough search downstairs. He tossed the good shoe into the suitcase. He turned back to the cupboard.

"Watch what you're doing with that thing!" said a voice in a very loud whisper.

In the rush of blood to the head which Mark now suffered he lost all sense of his bearings and banged his head hard against the top of the cupboard. Losing all control of his limbs he slid like a melting ice cream to the floor where he lay on his back staring into the darkness and licking his dry lips. About ten seconds passed.

Then the whispers returned and multiplied. Like all night-time whispers they sounded sinister, they floated ethereally out of the blackness. But not out of his head; no, he wasn't going mad. He sat up slowly, resting his weight on his palms, cocking his head to listen. He cocked it towards the window.

There were two voices and they came from outside. They must have been standing directly beneath the window. He couldn't make out the words any more, but the tone was heated. The argument went on for a little while and then there was a silence. Then came the sounds of something heavy being dragged across the gravel path. Then the something heavy was thumped against the windowsill.

It was a ladder.

They were coming up it, he could hear feet scraping the rungs, voices getting nearer. He got to his feet as quietly as he could and tiptoed out of the room. He stood on the landing quietly panicking to himself.

Burglars! They must have been watching the deserted cottage. He'd even opened the window for them, what a fool! He'd better get out the way, quick. Call the police. What would he tell them? They'd want to know what he'd been doing in the cottage. He'd have to lie.

He heard the sound of something breaking in the bedroom. One of Maddie's knicknacks, little pieces of glass and china with which she covered the windowsill. Burglars didn't care about things like that. They'd go through all his drawers and cupboards, throwing his possessions about, scattering and destroying what they didn't steal. It was a kind of desecration. He could hear them now, crossing the bedroom floor with exaggerated stealth. He had left it too late, he'd never get away now. The old creaky floorboards would give him away if he made a run for it. But he didn't feel like making a run for it. He felt angry.

He was standing outside his study, and the door was open. He reached out his hand and felt along the wall. His fingers closed around the butt of a pistol, which he lifted gently off its nails. It was a fake of course, but they weren't going to know that. He levelled the gun and advanced on the bedroom. There was a light switch out here, on the landing. He slammed it on with the flat of his hand and burst into the bedroom like a tv detective.

"Freeze or I shoot!"

Two men were rummaging in the wardrobe, torches in hand. They leapt up suddenly and their heads cracked. One of them screamed and flung himself on to the bed, covering his head with his hands. The other man looked at him disdainfully.

"Shut up, Roddy!"

Roddy did not shut up. Instead he made a continuous whimpering noise as he tried to scuttle across the bed towards the window. He didn't get very far. His feet were tangled up in the bedclothes and the suitcase.

"He's got a gun! He'll kill us! I told you he was a madman!"

Roddy grabbed for a pillow and held it in front of his face as a shield. His companion chuckled.

"Put your glasses on, luv. He's not going to kill anybody with that. . . . "

Mark glanced down at the pistol in his hand. Roddy's friend was right. It was his model of a seventeenth-century wheel-lock, the least lethal-looking fake in his collection.

Of course, Roddy couldn't see that. Unusually for him he had been wearing his glasses, but they had slipped off in all the confusion and were lying on the edge of the bed. His friend handed them to him. At the same moment he gave Mark a complicitous wink. He took a silver cigar-case out of his pocket.

Mark studied him warily. He was a relaxed and confident young man in his early thirties, sleek-looking and well-dressed in smart jeans and a leather jacket, the kind of clothes whose outsize labels seem to have been designed with aircraft recognition symbols in mind. He had glistening white teeth which he displayed a little too often in a smile that failed to find a corresponding echo in the dark little close-set eyes. All in all he looked about as trustworthy as a shark at a vegetarians' bathing party.

"Would you mind not smoking in the bedroom, please?"

But Mark was too late. Back went the silver case, out came the gold lighter and into the corner of the mouth went the now-glowing cigar. A strong smell pervaded the room.

"You must be Mark Harvey," said the shark-toothed man, exhaling slowly. "I'm Dick Turpin."

"Yeah and I'm the Wizard of Oz. What the hell do you think you're doing here?"

"Just paying a social call."

"Do you always climb in through a window?"

"Quite often. It's what investigative journalism's all about."

"Oh I see . . . " Mark nodded knowingly. He tried to appear calm, to match the journalist's cool stare, not to blink. "Give me one good reason why I shouldn't call the police."

Roddy gave a little whimper. Dick Turpin wasn't so easily disconcerted.

"Call who you want," he said with a shrug. "Only you're liable to find yourself landed with a suit for damages."

"You what!"

"Waving guns at people. It's not on, you know. Look at my friend here: you've turned him into a nervous wreck."

The wreck bit on the corner of his pillow. Through a mouthful of chewed linen he muttered something about his medical condition.

"I'll medical condition you!" exploded Mark, advancing on him aggressively. Dick Turpin stepped smartly between them, oozing conciliatory charm:

"Now now gents, no threatening behaviour with intent, please. Let's all try and behave like civilised adults."

"I thought civilised adults came in through the front door. When they were asked."

Turpin grinned. He took a long drag of his slim cigar and blew the smoke into Mark's face. Mark wrinkled up his nose and stepped back. Turpin continued to grin. He was only a little man, smaller even than Mark, but there was something creepily intimidating about him. Mark was beginning to feel twitchy.

"Why don't you just tell me what you're doing here!" he blurted out, making a last attempt to appear masterful.

Turpin sauntered over to the waste-paper basket and flicked the ashy tip of his cigar over the rim, an act of rare consideration on his part. He gave a nod towards the wreck on the bed.

"Tell him, Roddy."

Turpin sat down on the dressing-table stool, crossed his legs and continued to grin and smoke. Roddy looked at him uncertainly.

"Go on!" said Turpin. "Tell the man all about it."

Still unsure of himself, but taking the courageous first step of relinquishing his pillow, Roddy turned to face Mark. Mark felt uncomfortable. It was the first time Roddy had ever addressed him wearing his glasses. He wasn't used to his looking him in the eye.

"It's about Maddie. . . . "

Roddy's voice cracked. His lips and chins trembled. Liquid misted his eye. He coughed into his hand, sniffed like a pig and continued:

"Let's let bygones be bygones, Mark. I know we haven't always seen eye to eye – " (literally true, Mark thought) " – but now we are united in grief. We both loved the same woman – " (not literally true, Mark thought) " – it's not your fault she preferred me to you, anyway the time for recriminations is past. We must unite to uphold the truth, to honour the memory of our mutual object of adoration!"

Untangling himself from the bedspread he rose magnificently to his feet.

"An evil influence has sullied her reputation!"

A dramatic gesture accompanied this dramatic statement. It consisted of Roddy smiting his breast with one hand while waving the other vaguely out of the window. For good measure he raised his right foot and planted it squarely on the bed. Mark felt that he was expected to say something.

"Would you mind taking your feet off the bed, please."

"He means Reg Talbot," explained Turpin.

"Don't mention that name to me!" declared Roddy defiantly.

"Shut up and sit down," said Turpin.

Roddy did so. Turpin turned his oily grin back on Mark.

"It can't be very pleasant for you, Mr Harvey, having to sit here and listen to us rabbiting about your wife's infidelities. I said shut up, Roddy – " (no more than a murmur, strangled at birth) " – but you're a man of the world, I'd be prepared to say after a brief acquaintance of a minute or so, the sort who's quite prepared to call a spade a shovel, and the fact of the matter is that if your missus and our chum here were having a bonk, that's just life, isn't it?"

"Succinctly put, Mr Turpin," observed Mark wryly.

"Thank you," said Turpin, giving a nod of acknowledgement. "And please call me Dick."

"It wasn't just a bonk," murmured Roddy glumly. "It was music of the soul."

"As I was saying," Turpin continued, talking over him dismissively, for it is also the fact of the matter that bonks sell tabloid newspapers and soul music doesn't, "as I was saying, we shouldn't let past differences get in the way and muddy the old waters, so to speak, because we're both after the same thing, and that thing is – the truth!"

Mark wasn't sure how to react to this. Surely Turpin was being ironical . . . but no, he had actually stopped smiling. Surely he couldn't mean it? Or did he actually believe his own propaganda? Mark couldn't be sure. He tried to cover all possibilities by screwing his face up into an elaborate grimace that could have seemed like either a frown or a smile depending on which way you looked at it.

"The truth," he repeated neutrally.

"Yes, my son, the truth. The truth about Maddie Harvey. The truth about Reginald Randolph Talbot."

"Randolph?"

"Yup."

"I wondered what the other R stood for. How did you find that out?"

"Tricks of the trade. Anyway, our Reggie boy would have us believe that he and your missus were shacked up, an ongoing item, a two-piece suite so to speak. We know differently."

"Do we?"

"Of course we do, Mark my son. I mean, is it the sort of thing a wife could keep from her hubbie? You knew that our chum Roddy here was slipping her one, didn't you? But you and I and all of us know that she had sod all to do with our Reggie."

"Well I'm not so sure – "

"Not so sure is good enough for me. Cast-iron certainties are all I care about and if our chum Roddy here says he was the only boy that's good enough for me. The simple fact of the matter is, our

Reginald Randolph is a fraud. He's just cashing in on the tragic death of Maddie by basking in the limelight with a load of cock and bull, which in my opinion and moreover in the opinion of the great British public – or at least it will be their opinion when I tell them about it in a two-page colour-spread exclusive with generous mugshots of all key players, yourself included I have no doubts, there's one for your photo album – in the collective opinion of everyone that matters, my readership, the whole caboodle is utterly immoral and disgraceful and thoroughly reprehensible and it is therefore my duty and my responsibility without further ado to unmask the imposter!"

This declaration clearly inspired Roddy, who now interposed with a gnomic utterance of his own:

"We've got him on Maddie's feet!"

As casually as he could Mark walked over to the bed and sat down next to the open suitcase. Inside he could see the indeterminate material of Maddie's sensible suit. That didn't worry him. The single stiletto shoe that lay on top of the suit did. He ran a finger along the lid of the case and idly flipped it shut. He laid his wheel-lock pistol carefully on top.

"I'm sorry?" he said, when he was ready. He met Turpin's steady gaze without flinching.

"Going somewhere?" the journalist asked, indicating the suitcase.

"Maybe," answered Mark evenly.

"Sensible enough. The shit's really going to hit the proverbial when this all comes out. Much wailing and gnashing of teeth from over the fence. Did you know he's got a tv crew coming round tomorrow night?"

"No."

"Oh yes. Played it cool so far, he has, kept his cards to his chest. No exclusives, no interviews even, just the odd bland statement issued through his solicitor. Playing the tease, jacking his price up. Saving it all up to prove on tv that your missus was his lover in front of millions. Shrewd, you have to admit. Even a dummy could make a mint, and one thing our Reggie Randy is not is a dummy. Only we're going to put a spanner in his works: he's going to be up there, Mantovani playing his violins in the background, while he comes over all sensitive and lovestruck like a secondhand Romeo with a spare retread round the corset and spurting out *the* daft sob story of the decade: she's still alive! he'll say, I can feel it in my gizzard. God knows what he thinks happened to her, got knocked on the head and wandered off somewhere in a daze I suppose, and don't ask me why he thinks the old nutter in the attic went and topped himself, but there you go, ours not to reason why, that's his story and he's applying himself to it with super-glue. It's a fairy story actually, and it's called *Cinderella*. Only instead of a glass slipper he's got a black leather stiletto shoe with a broken heel. What do you make of that?"

Mark said nothing.

"You're quite right," Turpin continued. "Not a lot to make of it, I'd say. Bloody silliest story I've ever heard. Not sure exactly what's going through R.R.'s tiny head but intended scenario seems to be that there's old Maddie wandering around with a bandage wrapped round the dent in her head, probably sitting in some hotel in Bournemouth boring everyone sick with tales of amnesia, suddenly sees him holding up this shoe on the telly, screams 'that's mine!' and comes rushing round to claim it, marbles suddenly intact. How he managed to put this one over on the telly wallahs beats me, but then turn on the box any night of the week and it's pretty clear that the whole lot's run by a bunch of monkeys taking time off from typing up *Hamlet*. Old R.R. knows damned well that he's putting one over on them, that it's all off the top of his head and that Maddie Harvey is in no position to call his bluff because she's dead – sorry Roddy, shut up – so he's going to make his fortune selling his autobiography, the book of the film and his life as a mini-serial and whatever else he can get. But he has made a fatal miscalculation and we have rumbled him!

"A shoe can't talk, Mark my son. Pretty convenient that, I'd say. I mean, I bet you there are some cynics around who might say that what he's got is just any old shoe bought in some shop and with the heel lopped off to fit the loopy storyline. Perhaps he even nipped up here the same as us to check on her shoe size – very convenient of you to leave that ladder by the shed, thanks. Only there's one thing he doesn't know, and can't know, and why should he, because he never knew the real Maddie. But Roddy knows, and you know, and I know too, don't we?"

What in heaven's name is he talking about? Mark wondered. He looked at Turpin and at Roddy in turn, and didn't like the sharp-eyed way in which they were looking at him (the sharpness of Roddy's eye was relative). He tried his smile/frown grimace again but his expression came out as completely blank. Had he missed something? Was it staring him in the face, blinding him with its obviousness? He didn't have a clue. It occurred to him that he probably knew very little of the details of Maddie's life. It also must have occurred to Roddy.

"What are you doing?" demanded Mark suspiciously.

Roddy was on the move, lumbering round the foot of the bed, doing his best to get his feet tangled up in the linen again. His pink eyes were bright with excitement. He stumbled round to the open wardrobe and jabbed a finger at Mark.

"He doesn't know!" he shouted triumphantly over his shoulder at Turpin. "See, he doesn't know!"

"What don't I know?" demanded Mark through clenched teeth. The sight of Roddy was enough to set him on edge at the best of times; prolonged exposure in the privacy of his own bedroom was making him nauseous.

"About Maddie's feet," Roddy answered. He shuffled his own feet in an elephantine jig. "You don't know about Maddie's feet! She never wore shoes with heels!"

"Rubbish!"

"Don't you rubbish me, Mark. You never loved her, I did! You never cared about her feet, all the problems she had with her corns and bunions and swollen ankles. That's why she never wore shoes like Talbot's got, because of her medical condition."

"Rubbish!" Mark repeated faintly.

"See!" declared Roddy with a sweeping gesture that encompassed and dismissed Mark all in one. "He knows nothing at all about Maddie, he never gave a damn about her!"

"Why don't you get out of my house," Mark spluttered, rising.

"Not till I get what I came for. . . . "

Roddy stooped down and thrust his paw into the cupboard. When he withdrew it he was holding one of Maddie's sandals between thumb and forefinger, like a freshly caught fish.

"Wait till I stick this down Reg Talbot's gob!"

"Come on, Roddy," said Turpin quietly.

Roddy thrust the sandal into his jacket pocket. He took a step towards the window.

"I think we can go out the front door this time, my son. . . . "

"Give me back that shoe!" demanded Mark feebly.

"We're only borrowing it," said Turpin. "Come on, Roddy."

"This shoe is all I have left of her!" declared Roddy triumphantly, smiting his breast.

"You can't just come in here and take Maddie's things," Mark insisted. "Give it back at once."

"You can have it back afterwards," said Turpin.

"No he can't!" protested Roddy. "I want it for a keepsake."

"See?" said Mark.

"Shut up, Roddy!" snapped Turpin.

"You can't prove that's her shoe anyway," said Mark desperately. "Why should an impartial witness believe that's her shoe and the one Reg has isn't?"

"Come off it," said Turpin off-handedly. "We all know where it came from."

"You can leave me out of it!"

"That's just like you, Mark," said Roddy, turning purple, "abdicating responsibility. You've no right to thwart the course of justice."

Mark made one last desperate attempt:

"If there's justice involved I'd better call the police."

Turpin looked at him shrewdly.

"Roddy, wait outside a sec."

Roddy looked surprised but he had no time to utter a protest: Turpin grabbed him by the shoulders and gave him a smart shove out on to the landing. He closed the bedroom door.

"Here!" said Roddy weakly.

Turpin ignored him. Instead he came over to Mark, took him by the arm and led him to the window.

"Let's have a confidential word," he said quietly. "I can see there's no love lost between you two."

"That's an understatement."

"Yeah, I know he's a prat but he's all I've got. Dunno what your missus saw in him, by the by, but let's not get into that. The fact of the matter is that, unconventional as our means of entry were into your abode, and you have my full apologies — my paper will of course cover any damage done inadvertently to your estate, I don't think you'll find us ungenerous — the fact is, we had to go through all this palaver because Roddy needs that sandal."

"Why couldn't you have asked me?"

"Why not indeed? But the fact is we didn't and let's stick to the facts, which are complex enough without us getting into the old hypotheticals. Thing is, Mark my son, that I haven't told you quite all of what we're going to be up to tomorrow night, and if I do then perhaps you'll understand why it's so important. I've done a deal with the telly people. I've offered them the chance to interview Roddy as well as Reg. They love the idea. Want to put the two of them together, watch the sparks fly, it'll be great television. Only they know nothing about this shoe business. That is going to be our bombshell. Blow up the whole kaboodle in their faces, make Reg look a fraud – which he is, let's face it – make them look a bunch of dickheads and all the glory, exclusives, hallelujah chorus and a massive boost in circulation my humble but not entirely undeserved reward. Now. . . . "

He withdrew his wallet from his inside pocket. He opened it and displayed a thick wad of notes. He carried on talking.

"As for those expenses I was talking about. I know we broke something coming in, all that mess and inconvenience can be very tiresome don't I know . . . will this cover it?"

He showed Mark a fan of five fifty-pound notes. Mark said nothing. Turpin folded the notes and slipped them into Mark's breast pocket.

"Now . . . it strikes me that what you said about them maybe not believing that Roddy's sandal belonged to your missus is a fair point, so how's about if I then said to them – 'Alright loveys, if you don't believe us come with me over the garden fence and take a butchers at the real McCoy.' Now if they do that there might be camera crews and God knows what trampling over your geraniums so it's only fair to offer you what I believe they call in the trade a location fee, say. . . . "

He peeled off another five notes. Again he held them up for Mark's inspection. When he said nothing they too went into the breast pocket.

"I'm glad to see that we seem to be understanding each other, Mark my son. Now, would there be anything else. . . . ?"

"The police," said Mark.

Turpin smiled. Mark smiled back.

"You are a shrewd one, Mr Harvey, very shrewd. And quite right you are too. No, we do not want Mr Plod putting his truncheon in and arresting the evidence, certainly not till we've had our fun with Randy Reggie. I'd say that's a fairly major consideration. . . . "

He peeled off five more notes, but this time when he offered them Mark shook his head.

"You're asking me to pervert the course of justice, Mr Turpin. And then of course you're no doubt expecting me to keep my mouth shut in the presence of your colleagues, some of whom I couldn't help but noticing are out in the drive there now, even as we speak. . . . "

The smile spread slowly right across Turpin's face. The rows of small neat teeth had a predatorial gleam.

"You certainly are well shrewd . . . I'll tell you what I'll do. I'll up the two-fifty to five hundred, now, and as much again tomorrow night when it's in the bag. That's a grand and a half you'll have stung me for, can't say fairer than that, can you?"

Mark hesitated. Turpin gave a wry chuckle.

"Alright then, we'll make it seven-fifty tomorrow, after the shoot."

"Done!"

Turpin offered his hand and they shook on it. He put the other five hundred into Mark's breast pocket.

"Triffic, my son. We'll be off then. Roddy!"

Roddy must have been listening at the door, which swung open as if on automatic release. Turpin went towards him and beckoned him to follow, as to a dog.

"Er, Mr Turpin."

The journalist turned round at the door. Roddy hovered behind his shoulder. Mark tried to appear casual:

"I think I ought to have that other sandal back, you know. Keep it with the others, it'll be safer."

"You can try," said Turpin, indicating Roddy with his thumb. Roddy stiffened.

"Over my dead body!" he said with apparent conviction. He unbuttoned the top of his shirt and from inside it pulled out the sandal, which he had attached to a gold medallion he wore round his neck. "I shall wear this sandal about my person for ever. Till death do us part!"

Roddy's voice quivered. He sniffed. Turpin gave him a shove.

"Come on, let's get out of here. I'll give you a buzz here tomorrow night, Mark my son, I've got the number. . . . "

Turpin and Roddy went together out on to the landing. Mark

listened to them cursing in the darkness as they descended the creaky stairs. He sat down on the bed.

He was in trouble. The shoe on its own was bad enough – Prince Charming was going to be in for a shock when they compared sizes. But Maddie's "medical condition" . . . why had he never noticed that she only ever wore sandals? Why should he have noticed? Well, of course he had noticed, he'd just never thought anything of it. What Roddy had said was true – he hadn't cared about her feet. In fact, of all the things in the entire world that he didn't care about, the state of Maddie's feet was very near the top of the list. Nor was it the kind of subject that had ever tended to come up in any of their infrequent discussions. What could he do? Could he hide the evidence – the rest of the evidence, the other sandals? Roddy would still have the one round his neck, but did that matter? Could he bluff it out, deny the whole "medical condition" story, accuse Roddy of making it all up? No, he couldn't . . . Turpin and Roddy together were a dangerous combination. One he might have managed, not the two of them. With Turpin's help Roddy was going to wipe the floor with Reg. It was all going to end in tears. Behind bars.

The front door was slammed. He heard them talking on the path outside, their voices louder and more confident than before.

"I'll pick you up at four tomorrow," Turpin was saying.

"A bit later, please. I won't be able to get away from the muster before three."

"What do you want to go and ponce around like a wally for?" demanded Turpin with disgust.

"It's not like that!" protested Roddy indignantly. His voice wavered: "Maddie would have wanted me to go, she thought I looked handsome in my uniform. . . ."

"Alright, alright, don't start blubbing again, sorry I spoke. . . ."

Their voices faded away as they crossed the drawbridge. Mark listened to them go, and then to the silence, the thick profound silence of the country. For him the absence of sound was pregnant with sinister implications.

He got up and turned off the bedroom light, a pointless precaution now – such eyes as there had been to see would have supped their fill. But darkness was a mild comfort. There was solace in concealment.

He sat down again. He tried to clear his head and think. He was in trouble. He had to do something. He had to make an effort. He geed himself up: he had been decisive with Turpin, pushing up the money on offer. He had been surprised. It wasn't like him to be so insistent. See, he told himself, he could do it. He would need that money to get away. He was going to have to get away sooner or later, he'd better start making plans, accumulating funds. He'd made a good start but he was going to need a lot more. How on earth was he going to get it? He had to buy some time. He had to do something.

He retrieved the torch from the bed, turned on the striplight function and placed it carefully in the back of the wardrobe. Under the eerie blue light he rounded up Maddie's stray sandals, which he piled up in his arms and transferred to the suitcase. There was a municipal rubbish tip on the other side of Fareham. He would dispose of them there.

He proceeded carefully, double-checking the whole time. He gave the wardrobe, and then the whole bedroom, a thorough search. His diligence was rewarded: he found one odd sandal lying under the bed. His shoe search occupied his mind, it kept at bay the whispers of despair.

Kept them at bay only, they couldn't be dismissed: he was in trouble; he was going to be found out. He didn't dare ask himself what he hoped to achieve, hiding the sandals. It was a gesture, they'd get him anyway. And all because of a bloody shoe. Roddy was going to prove once and for all that Maddie had never even known Reg. The secret life of Madeleine would be uncovered. In the confrontation between the two men (recorded on film for posterity) how long would it be before anyone noticed that they were talking about two completely different women?

He was in trouble alright.

He had to sit on the bed again, his legs were trembling. If only there were some way of getting rid of Roddy. If only the earth would open and swallow him, him and the wretched sandal. If only he could be persuaded to tie a rope round his neck and jump out of the attic.

If only . . if it were only Turpin's word, what then? He didn't know. He could only think, and he had better think quick or else he would have all the time in the world in which to be wise after the event, staring at his little tent of blue.

He closed the suitcase and zipped it up. He shone the torch around to check that nothing had fallen out. There was nothing outside the case except for the wheel-lock pistol, the absurd burglar deterrent.

It was a fine model, carved from a single block of wood with metal working parts. He pulled back the cock, listening to the straining of the spring. He never did that, for fear of snapping the fragile spring. Guns weren't toys, not even imitation ones. He pressed the trigger, click! a noise like fingers snapping. He tried to cock it again but the mechanism had gone slack, the hammer fell back loosely. He muttered a little curse, directed at himself: the spring had broken. It was his own fault. He had broken a cardinal rule. He knew that it was wrong to play around with guns.

Wrong, what was wrong? He had done so much that was wrong already, one sin more or less wasn't going to make any difference. He was going to get life imprisonment anyway. How many lifetimes could they imprison him for?

He sat in the darkness, committing crimes in his head. His ingenuity surprised him; it seemed that he had missed his vocation.

He was going to get plenty of opportunity for making up lost ground.

19

It was raining hard. Between the heavy thumping wipes that traversed the windscreen the outside world was all but invisible. The rubber on one of the wipers was worn, metal grated the glass, faintly but enough to irritate. So many parts in the car needed replacing. Let's face it, Mark thought, the whole car needed replacing. The fingers of precipitation probed the rusty car for holes, and found them: water trickled under the door through a leaky seal, wetting the floor and the soles of his feet. The car interior smelt of dampness and decay.

The weather hadn't been this bad early on; the drive to Langley had been misty rather than wet. But now, while he sat waiting in the car park, the skies were emptying. It wasn't good news. If it carried on like this the public wouldn't come, and if the public didn't come the muster might be called off.

He turned on the radio and anaesthetised himself with Radio 2. He hummed along to a song that set his teeth on edge almost as much as the faulty wiper. The pips sounded and he heard the 1 o'clock news. He didn't take it in, but thinking of the time made him yawn. He hadn't slept much last night, and he had been up since six. At that hour the municipal rubbish tip had been pitch dark and deserted. To the garbage of Fareham he had consigned Maddie's footwear collection. He had spent most of the morning buying replacements.

Fareham had been the first stop. Nine o'clock sharp, opening time, the shop where Madeleine had been fitted for her big night out. He had bought something a little more utilitarian this time, and cheaper. In Madeleine's size, of course, which happened to be his own. He found another, casual pair, in the village charity shop, half a size larger but close enough, conceivably Madeleine's fit. Then it had been into the car and on to the next village, a tour of local shoe shops, the itinerary plotted before in the sleepless night with the help of Yellow Pages. One or two pairs in each, 'the wife's birthday' the pleasant answer to any query, a mix of styles, a range to suit the modern woman at work and leisure. By mid-day he had bought a dozen pairs and eaten through no less than six of Turpin's fifties. If it were the price of freedom, it would still be cheap.

The boot of the car was piled up with shoe boxes. He had driven straight from the last shop to Langley Park and had time on his hands: the muster wasn't due to begin till two, though the participants were already arriving in significant numbers. Clearly it took more than a spot of inclement weather to frighten off members of the Civil War Re-enactment Society.

He watched them arrive in their cars and vans, several groups by minibus and even a few impervious types by motorbike. The sensible ones waited in their vehicles but others banded together in the open crying hail fellow well met! or whatever a pikeman says to a musketeer on such an occasion. A few carried umbrellas but most disdained the elements: perhaps they revelled in the discomfort of dampness as part of the whole – the authentic – experience. The water dripped off wide collars and lacy sleeves and collected in floppy voluminous boots. The plumes in their felt hats sagged.

Mark had a felt hat of his own, with a white plume. He was wearing it now, as a disguise. It was not his only disguise, though it came down low enough to cast his nose and eyes into shadow. Under the hat he wore Maddie's second favourite wig: thick chestnut curls fell to his shoulder. He glanced at himself in the rear-view mirror. He was quite unrecognisable, and quite unremarkable too in the present company. He had leather breeches, and knee-length boots, and a black coat that covered his hips and a dark-blue cloak that looked as if it might even be waterproof. All items culled from Martin's wardrobe. And another item, borrowed from Martin too.

Nervously, and for the twentieth time, he reached a hand inside his black coat and touched the other item, which lay against his shirt, tucked into his belt. The long barrel was hard and cool. The trigger mechanism was solid and heavy, no fragile springs there. He knew, he had tested it the night before. He had passed some hours of the night with Martin's pride and joy.

He wanted to pull it out now, feel the weight of it, check it over, test his resolve. But no, he wouldn't let himself. He had checked and double-checked, in the night. And it wasn't a toy.

What of his resolve? He shouldn't think too much about that. Thoughts bred doubts. He must get out there and do, not think.

What alternative did he have? Confession? Out of the question. Flight? Where could he go? Criminals usually made a run for the Costa Brava if the papers were to be believed, but Mark wasn't that sort of criminal. That sort of criminal had villas and Swiss bank accounts and wallets stuffed with ill-gotten lucre. Mark had a two-man tent in the basement and about £400 in his deposit account. He did have the wallet, but that flattered only to deceive: his collection of fifty-pound notes was thinning out at an alarming rate already. He just couldn't afford to run away, not yet anyway. He had to slug it out, hold his ground, and more: he had to go on the counter-attack.

He switched from radio to cassette, put on one of Maddie's tapes which he'd never liked, but listened all the same, distracting himself. The car park steadily filled and the clusters of eager participants swarmed. The general public were there too, in surprisingly large numbers. It looked as though their faith might be rewarded: a little after half past one it stopped raining.

People were leaving the car park, filtering away down the several paths that led off through the trees. The general public merely ambled, but those in period dress hurried, for the time was getting on.

Mark got out of the car. His boots sunk to the ankles in squelchy mud. He pulled up the collar of his coat, turned down the brim of his hat and tramped off after the crowd. He kept his head down but no one paid him any attention: they all kept their heads down too, watching for puddles.

The path led through trees and between thick clumps of rhodo-dendron bushes, giving out at length on to a very large open space, thickly covered with unkept grass and dotted with the odd solitary tree. Mark had visited Langley Park before, and he remembered vaguely that the open space stretched for some distance, ending in fields and an old house that now contained offices. The trees were dense on either side of the open space, but to the right of where he stood now – as it were at the top of the park – he remembered that there was a landscaped garden and an odd little raised stone plinth at the rear arranged in someone's idea of classical style. He couldn't see the garden from where he was standing (it was obscured by the rhododendron bushes) but he did see a ditch in front of him, and that ditch led off to the right and enclosed the garden area like a moat. He recalled jumping across the moat when younger, but he didn't think he'd be able to manage any such feat of athleticism today: middle-aged torpor notwithstanding, the moat looked far too wide and much too deep; in fact it was overflowing with rain water.

Water spread in marshy pools over the whole open space. The long grasses drenched all comers up to the knee. Mark followed the crowd right along the edge of the moat and then on to a low "ridge" – a kind of fold in the ground – that ran down the middle of the open area. It was here that the public was congregating. On their right, where the ground was a little lower, and a great deal wetter, the forces of king and parliament were raising their standards.

One lot were at the moat end, the other a couple of hundred yards away, on the edge of the trees. They mustered round their flags by unit, mostly footmen, but with a little group from either side on horseback and specialist artillery teams to serve the two impressive-looking cannon. It was a colourful sight, and to the untrained eye there was little to distinguish the two sides. But Mark was able to spot the differences.

He saw what he was looking for in the group to his left, the one by the trees. Amongst the rich mix of colours a knot of men in scarlet coats stood out, clustered under a black and yellow banner; the colours of the Fareham Regiment of Foote. So this was the Royalist army. Mark tried to count the scarlet coats. There seemed to be about thirty of them, near full strength, though he was too far away to be able to pick out individuals. Nonetheless, the thought that Roddy must be somewhere amongst them made his heart go faster.

He turned his back on the Royalists and marched off towards the Parliamentarians. It was a good thing Martin Bird wasn't here today, to see him turn his coat.

The forces of Parliament numbered perhaps two hundred souls, slightly fewer than their opponents. Although grouped like the Royalists in regiments under their standards, there seemed to be little real distinction between the units, which coalesced and overlapped haphazardly and betrayed no evidence of superior organisation. Martin was famously disparaging about the opposition, who in his opinion were a disgrace and a shambles and an embodiment of the abuses of parliamentary power.

The parliamentary artillery, one enormous cannon mounted on a pair of surplus Ferris wheels, was in the van of the army, barrel pointed menacingly at the foe. Behind was a small group of horsemen, and behind them the not quite serried ranks of foot, or foote as they liked to be known. Individuals were still meandering over the open space on their way to join their units, so Mark didn't feel conspicuous. As he drew abreast of the cannon a single horseman came careering across the grass behind him, and the artillerymen scattered. Thinking that they probably knew something he didn't, Mark followed suit. The horseman raced over the spot where he had been standing and drew up abruptly in front of the small mounted group, almost slithering out of his saddle. He was not an accomplished rider.

"What the bloody hell's going on here then?" he demanded garrulously. He was a stout man kitted out in a buff coat with a red sash, breastplate and lobster-pot helmet. Mark recognised Martin's handiwork.

"And who the bloody hell do you think you are?" he screamed, jabbing a finger at another of the horsemen. His complexion had turned a shade complementary to his style of headgear.

The man so splenetically addressed put his heels to his horse and trotted it forward a few paces. He too had a bright red face and angry eyes and looked pretty garrulous himself. He was dressed identically to the first man.

"I'm bloody Oliver Cromwell, that's who I am!" he declared defiantly.

The first man looked as if he was about to burst a blood vessel.

"No you're bloody not! I'm Oliver Cromwell!"

"No you're not. This is my muster, I've done all the organising and it's my turn to be Oliver Cromwell."

"What do you mean it's your bloody turn, we don't have bloody turns!"

"We ought to have," murmured one of the other horsemen. The first Oliver Cromwell shot him a venomous look:

"And you can bloody well shut up, Henry Ireton."

Both the Cromwells' gallant steeds were twitching nervously, clearly alarmed by their riders' voices. By the same token much interest was apparent in the parliamentary ranks. The dispersed artillerymen reassembled around their cannon, riveted by this spectacle of internecine conflict.

"I'm Oliver Cromwell and I'm in command here and don't you forget it!" said Cromwell 1.

"I'm not saying that you can't be Cromwell most of the time," said Cromwell 2, adopting a conciliatory tone. "But this is my patch and I think I should be allowed a go, on a one-off basis."

"Bloody bollocks!" said Cromwell 1, who to one casual observer at least appeared to possess most of the necessary characteristics for a successful stab at dictatorship.

"Why can't you both be Cromwell?" suggested Henry Ireton half-heartedly.

Both Cromwells afforded him their most withering glances. He withered.

"Do you remember that muster in Milton Keynes?" one artillery-man murmured to the others. "Where the Royalists had two King Charleses and three Prince Ruperts? Sometimes they've got more members of the royal family than Balmoral at Christmas."

"That's nothing," said another. "When I was in the Waterloo Association I once counted six Napoleons in one afternoon. And you know a funny thing?" The others, Mark included, all looked at him. He indicated Cromwell 1, who was standing up in his stirrups and screaming at the top of his voice: "He was one of them."

At this juncture Cromwell 2, bowed if not yet quite beaten, was definitely on the wane, and a quick straw poll among the gunners rated his chances as slim to non-existent. However, the expected dénoue-ment did not materialise: before Cromwell 2 could be quite forced into a humiliating climbdown the attention of all parties was drawn to the enemy, at whom the massed ranks of parliamentary infantry had begun to jeer. Internal rivalries were temporarily suspended.

Two horsemen had ridden out from the Royalist ranks. They reined in some fifty yards away from the big gun. One of them carried a trumpet on which he attempted, somewhat unsuccessfully, to blow. The other read ostentatiously from a scroll of paper:

"In the name of His Majesty King Charles of Great Britain and Ireland, I demand that you forswear allegiance to the traitors' cause, throw down your arms and submit yourself to the mercy of our most gracious sovereign who – "

The rest of his little speech was drowned out in a crescendo of boos and cat-calls, amongst which Mark discerned such niceties of seven-teenth-century phraseology as "Piss off, you wally!" and "Up yours, you poncy git!" Unperturbed, the messenger finished his message and tucked his scroll back into his belt.

"Well?" he demanded, casting a scornful eye over the opposition. "Who answers for Parliament?"

Cromwell 1 and Cromwell 2 advanced simultaneously. At least Cromwell 2 did. Cromwell 1, who had never seemed comfortable on his horse, edged off sideways.

"I do!" they both answered together.

The violence of Cromwell 1's affirmation had an unfortunate effect on his horse. It bolted. Cromwell 2 rose to the occasion.

"Tell King Charles," he cried boldly, "that we shall dispute the sovereignty of this land on the field of arms!"

"I was going to say that!" Cromwell 1 protested faintly, but no one paid him any attention: his galloping horse was already half-way to the trees.

The Parliamentarian army gave a great cheer. They were behind Cromwell 2 to a man.

Drums were beaten, standards hoisted, matchlocks primed, pikes shouldered. The cannon belched flame and roared; moments later the Royalist gun spat its answer back. The detonations boomed across the huge open space and the crowd on the ridge, several hundred strong and growing, applauded and buzzed with excitement. A shaft of sunlight broke through the cloud cover, bringing a glitter to the pikeheads, guns and armour. The two armies advanced towards each other.

Mark skirted round the group of horsemen and found himself between two columns of pikemen. He darted through the gap and tagged on at the back. He felt a little conspicuous without a pike of his own, but no one paid him the slightest attention.

"For God and Parliament!" someone shouted from amongst the ranks. His cry found a ragged echo.

"Up the Hammers!" said another voice, less reverently.

The pikes were all pointed upwards, a hedgehog mass interspersed with heavily embroidered flapping flags. Now, through the metal-tipped forest, crossing the open ground like Birnam wood, there appeared the banners of the Royalists, growing larger with every pace. Stuck as he was at the back of the column Mark couldn't see the foe, but he could hear them: the ground shook with the trampling of feet, there was a roar from five hundred throats, and then the two armies clashed.

Mark had not been in a rugby scrum since schooldays but he could recognise one when he saw one: the funny costumes and the lack of an oval ball didn't fool him – this was ritualised warfare in game form; a struggle for territory with an inbuilt disregard for human life. It was merely an added bonus that it sounded so much like the real thing – that symphony of strained vocal chords, the sweated grunts, the constipative groans, the swelling chords of trampled pain and the undertone of barked obscenities. Pandemonium reigned. It was all beyond Mark's wildest hopes.

The middle of the scrum, he remembered, was, like the epicentre of an earthquake, the place to avoid. The tremor of violence shook through the front ranks and rippled to the rear. Those around Mark pushed on the backs of those in front, heaving them forward. Now a new sound was added to the shouts and curses and exaggerated war-cries, a sound like massive hail-stones falling, which was the clatter of the wooden pike hafts, kept aloft, striking against one another. Those who were bundled over or simply lost their footing were "dead". Already there was a heap of them at the front, lying hunched up and protecting themselves as best they could in their positions of prone helplessness. Their discarded pikes were more dangerous now than when upright, for they formed haphazard *chevaux de frise* as they fell and tripped up friend and foe alike. As the dead multiplied so they were more frequently trodden on. They swore and bore it, for it was all part of the game, a game in which anything went. Mark was counting on it.

He had worked himself along the rear face of the column until he found himself facing the black and yellow banner of the Fareham Foote. The Parliamentarians seemed to have the upper hand, despite their numerical inferiority: the Royalists were giving ground; Mark found himself stepping over some dead. A few were in scarlet coats. Roddy was not amongst them.

The ranks in front were thinning out. Now he could see the faces of the enemy, furious with the frenzy of combat. The din was tremendous, everyone shouting their heads off as they thumped each other. Officially offensive action was supposed to be limited to pushing and tripping, but there seemed to be a lot of illegal elbowing and kicking. Either way the dead were piling up. Now only a single ragged line stood between Mark and the men of Fareham. He unbuttoned his coat and reached inside; his trembling hand rested on cool metal.

Roddy was in front of him. His face was framed between the heads of two big Parliamentarians who were trying to knock him over; only the press of men behind was keeping him upright. Exertion had turned his normally pasty features livid; he shone with sweat; he gasped for air. His new green plume had been caught in the rain and lay squashed over his head like a pulped lettuce. His new floppy boots were covered in mud. The metal breastplate gleamed.

It was heavy that breastplate, made of thick metal, strong. Mark had watched Martin in his workshop beating them out. They could stop a sword or pike thrust easily. But they couldn't stop a bullet.

Mark's fingers, inside his coat, closed around the trigger of the pistol. Not his own pistol, not the lightweight wooden fake that he had waved at Roddy and Turpin last night, but something altogether different: Martin's working model, whose fire he had witnessed punching a hole through the bottom of a bucket.

He withdrew the pistol. It was loaded already, he had only to cock it. He did so. He heard the faint crackle of musketry on the flanks. There were no firearms in the middle of the mêlée, but would anyone notice a single discharge amidst so much noise? Why should they? With death all around a little extra wasn't going to make any difference.

He raised the pistol. He was ready. His hand shook a little, but not enough to affect his aim. He would do it alright. No time to stop and think, he'd been through all that, just do it and do it now . . . one of the two big Parliamentarians was down. Roddy and his friends were about to overwhelm the other one. He was about to murder Roddy.

And suddenly it was happening. Down went the last man, forward came the Royalists. Mark was not alone. Reinforcements came in behind and swept him forward. He was almost thrown against Roddy. He felt Roddy's breath on his cheeks, he even met his glazed unseeing eye. Roddy kicked him in the shin. It hurt. Now it was easy: he shoved Roddy back with his forearm, pointed the pistol at the middle of the breastplate and, at six inches, fired.

There was a puff of smoke and a noisy whoosh. And nothing else.

Mark stared at the gleaming smooth breastplate. Not a scratch. He gave the pistol a shake. As he finished the metal ball rolled gently out of the barrel and plopped on to the grass. For a moment he stood gawping at the useless weapon, then something like an elephant smashed into him.

The nearest thing to him at the time like an elephant happened to be Roddy. It was Roddy. There wasn't a lot he could do in the circumstances, except fall over. He fell over.

Unfortunately Roddy fell on top of him. Mark passed out.

When he came to the tide of battle had rolled on. The first sensation he felt was pain: he could still feel the impress of Roddy's armour on his chest; his ribs ached with each breath. He opened his eyes and found himself staring at a dull grey sky. He was bewildered and disorientated. It took him some little time to realise that the whispered voices which he heard were coming from all around him, not from inside his head.

"It's soaking wet this grass. How long have we got to lie here for?"

"Bloody ridiculous this is. No one even killed me properly. I just fell over, slipped."

"You can't be expected to keep your feet on this. It's like a bleeding ice rink."

"I hate being dead."

"Who do you think's winning?"

"Couldn't give a toss."

"If I catch pneumonia I'm going to bloody sue."

"Ah no, that's all we need – sodding rain!"

Mark had felt it already, cold drops of moisture that pricked his eyes. He closed them, and felt the rain intensify. A light shower became heavy in seconds. Then the monsoon resumed.

"Bugger this for a game of soldiers!"

All around him the dead were rising, the Lazarus legion. He too struggled to his feet. His back was sodden from lying in the grass. In a moment he was drenched all over.

A man on horseback galloped past.

"Where the bloody hell do you think you're going?" he demanded aggressively. "You're dead!"

"Don't talk to us like that, mate!" one shouted back with equal belligerence. "Who the bloody hell do you think you are?"

"I'm Oliver Cromwell!" declared Cromwell 1.

"Then you can sod off, wart-face!" answered the other, who was of the King's party. Both resurrected Parliamentarians and Royalists seconded him with jeers and gestures.

Cromwell 1 had attempted to rein in his horse in order to continue the conversation, but the horse had other ideas and continued galloping away. Neither were seen again that day and were last heard of heading in the direction of Windsor.

No one on either side had paid him any attention anyway. The living had already made a dash *en masse* for the trees, regardless of rivalries, and the dead were busy following suit. The watching public appeared to have vanished into thin air. In a few moments all that remained of the battle was a pile of abandoned weapons.

Hopelessly, Mark trailed along in the wake of the dead. He was tired, drenched through, bruised and utterly miserable. At the same time he found it hard to feel justifiably sorry for himself: his failure to murder Roddy really had been an inexcusable cock-up.

He couldn't believe how stupid he'd been. Why hadn't he test-fired the gun? He had been afraid of making a noise, that was why, but surely he could have made the effort to find some secluded spot first thing in the morning. He should have taken it with him to the rubbish tip, no one had been about there. Over-confidence had been his undoing, and over-reliance on Martin's gun. But he couldn't blame the gun. Of course it worked, he had seen Martin demonstrate it. No, the fault was his; he must have done something wrong in the loading.

All his plans had gone up in smoke, literally – gone up in one ineffectual pistol puff. His brilliant strategy was in shreds. And it had been brilliant: founded on coolness, boldness and a refusal to stop at anything, murder included. That way salvation might have lain. With Roddy disposed of what could Turpin have done? It would have been his word against Turpin's, and who was going to believe the journalist? And why should anyone have believed him? Mark would be more than happy to invite the camera crew round to his house, as Turpin planned, but when they looked in the cupboard what would they see? The shoes he'd bought this morning, of course!

Turpin would be discredited, Madeleine reprieved. Without Roddy as a witness the truth could be kept under. For how long was another matter, but any time was precious. And it was running out, fast.

It was raining so heavily now that he could hardly see more than a few feet in front of him. It had gone very dark; from what he could see of the sky it seemed to be an even shade of black. Obviously the muster was over, sabotaged by the weather. Those not sheltering under the trees streamed away towards the car park, hunched against the rain. Hopelessly Mark traipsed after them, stomping through the marshy grass in boots so sodden he strained his calf muscles lifting them. The rain poured off his hat and down his front and back in torrents, but he no longer cared. Doggedly he followed in Roddy's footsteps.

It took him a while to notice that Roddy was headed in an entirely different direction from everyone else. At first the deviation was very slight, but a strong and sustained gust of wind made him incline to the left, and when everybody else, once the wind had passed, resumed their rightwards trek, Roddy maintained his own unique bearing. When he reached the moat in front of the ornamental garden he had a simple choice: he had only to turn right and in half a minute he would regain the main procession. He turned left.

Mark followed him. A wild improbable thought flashed across his mind: what if he jumped on Roddy and clubbed him to death with the butt of his pistol? He was desperate enough. Of course, shooting Roddy was out of the question now. Even if he loaded the gun properly it would only misfire in the rain. But then, it would hardly look like an accident, would it? And that was what it had been meant to look like. It wouldn't have been the first fatality at one of these musters. They were always getting carried away, stabbing each other with their supposedly blunted weapons, pointing their supposedly unloaded guns in the wrong direction. Although of course it still wouldn't look much like an accident if he just went up to Roddy and started smashing his head in.

Roddy stopped suddenly. Mark reacted a little late and went on swishing his way through the long grasses for a pace or two. Roddy turned his head vaguely in Mark's direction and peered myopically through the sheeting rain.

"Am I on the right track for the car park?" he asked in a thoroughly miserable tone of voice.

"Mm . . ." said Mark, and coughed.

As usual Roddy's gaze was fixed on vacancy, and as usual he seemed surprised to be addressed from a spot some yards from the one on which he had been focusing.

"Thanks," he said, towards where Mark's voice had come from, and then, turning back to where he thought he had been standing, "to both of you".

Mark wondered if he should take a couple of steps to the side and make a suitable reply on behalf of his other self.

A sudden guest of wind lifted him almost off his feet. Rain whipped his face. He just managed to get his hands up to his head in time to hold down his sodden hat and wig. Roddy was not quick enough. The wind ripped his hat off, tossed it up wildly into the air, then dropped it twenty feet away. Mark watched it fall. It flopped dead into the centre of the moat and sat spinning slowly round on the surface of the water, collecting more in its brim.

Roddy staggered towards it with arms outstretched like a blind man, which to all intents he was. Why had he not brought his glasses? Mark wondered. Out of vanity or the quest for historical accuracy? He cut an absurd figure, floundering about with arms flapping. What a humiliating choice his wife had made for a lover. And what a deserving choice he would have made for a murder victim.

"Can you see my hat at all, you two?" Roddy called back over his shoulder. Mark answered for both.

"In front of you."

It was true. The hat was dead in front of him. What he hadn't mentioned was that it was on the water, but then he must have seen the water, or at least heard the rain splattering on its surface.

"I see it!"

Then why are you going the wrong way? Mark thought. He was heading off to the left again, approaching the bank of the moat from an angle while the hat drifted away gently in the other direction. His heavy boots clumped into the wet earth, then made a sucking noise as they were lifted from the mud. Mark watched the stubby little legs pump up and down. The action seemed exaggerated. It was like watching a slow-motion film.

The big boot came up very high, almost as if in parody of a goose step. Out swung the extended foot, pointing into the middle of the moat. The weight was transferred from the rear to the front foot. And the front foot came down on the water.

There was no splash. No sound from Roddy either. It happened too quickly. Mark blinked and almost missed it. One moment he was there, and the next he wasn't. He must have sunk like a stone, under the weight of his armour.

The rain continued to fall, slashing the surface with splashes and ripples, adding drop by drop to the already overflowing moat. It must have been deeper than it looked.

The only sound was of the rain. There was no one within sight or earshot. The park might have been deserted.

Mark walked away. He walked slowly at first, in a kind of daze, but quickened his pace as his surprise gave way to fear. Fear of what? He slowed down again. He stopped. He looked back towards the spot where Roddy had disappeared.

There was a moment of doubt, just a moment in which he almost asked himself if he'd really seen what he thought he'd seen. But he didn't ask it; he knew that he had. He remembered Roger hanging from the attic beam. He remembered Maddie dead in her armchair. He was getting used to the unexpected.

There was no trace of Roddy. Even the hat with the soggy green plume had sunk. Nothing at all remained of the short-sighted halberdier.

Mark continued walking. Not slowly, but not too fast either. There was nothing to fear. He hadn't done anything. He hadn't pushed him in. He hadn't tried to stop him either, but how could he have known what Roddy was going to do? If he was going to be so stupid as to try and walk on water he had no one to blame but himself if he sank.

Mark glanced at the stormy sky. It didn't look as if it was going to stop raining tonight. It might be days before the waters subsided, before the moat gave up its prize.

He was going to make the most of it.

20

Something was going on next door to Willow Cottage. The Talbots' driveway, habitually jammed with motor cars, was now completely blocked by a minibus and a transit van. The logo on the side of the van explained its provenance, but it was hardly necessary: the cables gave the game away; the great arc lights deployed on the patio; the cameras hooded against the unpredictable weather. Hacks wearied by a week of seemingly pointless reconnaissance duty stumbled from their Fords and engaged in bewildered conference, portable telephones at the ready. Reliefs and reinforcements poured in. Pretty soon they were all there, or nearly all.

"Where's Turpin?" screamed one in a voice hysterical with paranoia.

Shoulders froze in mid-shrug, jaws went slack.

"The bastard. . . . " somebody muttered, grinding his teeth. "The bastard's up to something, I can feel it. . . . "

"I haven't seen Harry Craven!" said another.

That drew a laugh.

"Probably pissed," one surmised.

"Try the pub," suggested another scornfully.

It was plain that they didn't much care where Harry was. The one who had mentioned his name blushed, insomuch as he was capable. His peers paid him no attention. They were already crowding round Reg Talbot's gate.

"That's far enough, thank you gentlemen," said the man in a blue uniform who barred their way. He had "Security" stamped in yellow letters on his hatband and carried a leash on the end of which a Rottweiler slavered uncongenially (at least they assumed it was a Rottweiler; none of them was actually up on dog identification). Impotent in their rage the hacks backed off, sullenly.

"He's done us again, the bastard," murmured the one with ground teeth, who had pursued a state of dental erosion so resolutely that he sounded like a lockjawed ventriloquist.

They stood at the gate forlornly, craning their necks in a vain attempt to see past the massive square shoulders of the security guard, but there was nothing to be seen. The cables led into the house; the lights on the patio were being directed through the french windows; the action was all going to be out of sight. One by one they drifted off, scoured their dull imaginations in vain for inspiration, then scuttled away into the sanctuary of their cars to beg for help down the telephone and make their preemptive excuses.

The telephone in the hall was a new model. Its ringing tone was electronic, a mechanical buzz. Not so the extension in the bedroom, an old black handset that rang irregularly like a tinny dinner bell. Reg glared at it. The noise was disturbing his concentration. Why didn't anyone answer it? Connie had asked him not to, and as that meant he would be screened from the journalists whose constant calls had driven him close to distraction he had been more than happy to accede to her request. But if they didn't pick it up soon. . . .

The ringing tone cut off suddenly and he heard the faint murmur of a voice downstairs. Then the voice was raised and Connie's name called. Reg turned back to his desk and picked up his pen again. He stared at the lines which he had just written, vainly attempting to regather his thoughts, but his concentration had been snapped. He pushed the pen away and stared dreamily out of the window. Somewhere in the gathering darkness an owl hooted, perhaps the same owl he had heard on the night when he'd first seen Madeleine's golden hair glowing in the frame of her bedroom window. All at once inspiration came flooding back to him. He seized up his pen again and began to write with dedicated fury.

"He says he wants to talk to the organ grinder, not the monkey," Ben explained quietly.

Connie sighed. Poor Ben, she thought, he was simply out of his depth. It wasn't his fault of course, it was hers. Her friends kept warning her about picking the pretty boys, they said it took more than good looks to make a director, and they were right. But she always did her own directing anyway, so did it really matter? And Ben had such a marvellous body. It was just a pity that the brain was missing. She smiled sympathetically at him and took the receiver.

"Organ grinder speaking. What are you playing at, Turpin?"

Dick Turpin laughed softly down the phone. The sound made Connie grit her teeth: he was using his "charming" tone: soft, insinuating, reptilian. It made her want to puke.

"Cut the crap, Turpin. What's your excuse this time?"

"I just need a couple more hours – "

"And then what? You kept us hanging round till 10 o'clock last night promising your guy was going to show, and at the end of it you couldn't even tell me where he was. Now you've had a whole extra day in which to find him and you still expect me and my crew to hang around like a bunch of spare pricks at a dike's tea party. Today's Sunday, Turpin. Have you got any idea what ACTT overtime rates run to?"

"You're not telling me you'd begrudge a few extra quid – "

"Yes I am. Six o'clock we're shooting, wrapping at 7, with or without you. Understood?"

She didn't wait for the acknowledgement. She wasn't putting on an act, she was angry enough already. She slammed down the phone.

"Yuck!" she said, passing over the receiver as if it were contaminated. Ben replaced it on the hook and gazed at her with admiration.

"You're incredible!"

She shrugged. There was nothing to it, really. She had got Turpin's number, that was all. The only problem was that she was bluffing. And she had an awful suspicion that Turpin knew it.

"Give me a ciggie, Ben."

He lit one for her and handed it over. She could see that he was nervous. She didn't like that. Tension had a way of conveying itself to the crew.

"Fetch me a drink, there's a love."

He went into the kitchen. She heard him pulling a bottle out of the fridge. What could she get him to do when he came back? Go out and mow the lawn? Clean the swimming pool, perhaps? The pool certainly needed cleaning. The bottom was covered with irregular strips of black plastic sheeting and it had a dusty, disused look. Normally she wouldn't have thought of devoting much attention to the swimming pool, but it was one of Reg Talbot's favourite topics of conversation. He spoke through clenched teeth of a man called Murphy, describing him variously as a botch artist, a two-bit con man and an Irish Nazi. He had confided that he had an ace up his sleeve and that he was going to cook Murphy's goose. To her it seemed an odd thing to make such a fuss about. Perhaps it was a way of taking his mind off things.

Ben came out of the kitchen carrying a glass of white wine. On second thoughts sending him outside didn't seem such a bright idea. Not only was it getting too dark for chores, but Ben might get waylaid by the press, in which case he would be bound to let something slip. And knowing him he'd get a limb ripped off by the guard dog.

"Pop upstairs will you, Ben. Check Mr Talbot's alright, ask if he needs anything."

She watched him run up the stairs three at a time, the thick powerful leg muscles straining the fabric of his jeans. Apparently he had got a rugby blue at Cambridge. That probably explained the missing brain.

She turned away with a rueful sigh and headed towards the living room. The crew were beginning to get noisy. They were obviously in need of a bollocking.

The phone was ringing downstairs. For a few seconds he let it ring, thinking — somebody else will answer it — until it occurred to him that there was nobody else. So, for a chill moment, an image of the dead of the house came to him and the fear awakened by the simple ringing of the phone was compounded with his elder terror. It was that which made him run with such abandon, along the darkening landing and down the still darker stairs, through the indeterminate gloom of the hall and dining room and into the black pit of the kitchen, where the blinds had not been drawn for a week. He fumbled his way to the phone and snatched it up.

"Everything alright there, Mark my son?"

It was Turpin, the journalist; tone of voice upbeat and cocky, as ever. It was a loathsome sound.

"Alright," murmured Mark, wondering what it was that he had to be so cocky about. After all. . . .

"Ready for the big one?"

Mark settled himself down on the kitchen stool and glanced out of the kitchen window. He could just see through the fence that the lights were on in Talbot's house. He had seen the preparations for the "big one".

"Oh, yes, I'm alright," he answered confidently.

"Great. Now look, there's been a change of plan. Seems like the telly types have been clunking around and making such an almighty that even my co-mates and brother scribblers have put two and two together and come up with about three and a half, which ain't bad for them if you know what I mean. Problem is, this makes the old coup I was planning of whipping them all over to your gizmo and saying let's compare what mummy bear left in this cupboard with the article of fancy footwear you have in your mit, Reg my old banana, well all that's gone out the window, fizz, stum, caput – it is an ex-parrot. So what I want you to do instead is grab an armful of her flip-flops and be ready to whip 'em over the road when I give the nod so as we get the old dénouement in brother Reg's establishment, tip the lot out over his carpet and say hey *voilà*! What do you say to that then, sunshine? Am I crystal clear and giving you the state of the art verbals? Of course we are talking a little cash adjustment here. What would you say to an extra monkey?"

"A monkey?"

"Alright, two, don't push your luck! Any questions?"

"What time – "

"Soon. Anything else? Good, then I'll – "

"Mr Turpin!"

He just got him. He sounded annoyed though: he muttered something about being in a hurry.

"Everything alright is it, Mr Turpin?"

He knew very well it wasn't. He wasn't even sure why he had asked, except out of annoyance at the cockiness in the voice, which was of course entirely misplaced. Or perhaps it was out of simple mischief. For twenty-four hours he had been listening to the same story, Turpin calling him to say look, it's all alright, everything's going to plan, just a minor postponement, nothing to worry about. And still the buoyancy in the voice was there. Still the belief that his missing star turn was going to materialise at any moment persisted.

"Yes, everything's alright," he said airily.

"Good. Roddy showed up yet?"

For the first time he hesitated. He answered brusquely, with real irritation in his voice:

"He will, he will!"

And saying he had to dash he put the phone down.

Mark retraced his steps through the darkened house up to the bedroom. He turned on his torch again and resumed his packing. He had almost finished. His biggest suitcase was open on the bed, crammed with clothes and portable possessions. There was a lot he had had to leave out, including all his modelling gear, a sacrifice he had particularly regretted: he doubted that replacements would be easy to come by in South America.

He emptied the shoes from the cupboard into his old blue laundry bag – the new shoes which he had scuffed up and planted so carefully earlier on. He tied up the laundry bag and left it by the door, ready to go. He sat down on the bed.

It had to be South America. Where else could a criminal go these days? Spain was no longer safe, even established villains faced deportation. But what was he going to live on? Turpin's money would take care of the plane fare, but no more. An extra monkey or two was nice but hardly sufficient; he would need a whole menagerie. And it wasn't as if he would be able to find employment easily. He needed cash, and he needed it in enormous quantities.

He sat in the thickening darkness, waiting, sweating, thinking of money.

Harry Craven didn't really notice the darkness fall. He had spent the whole day in Stygia.

He was trying not to breathe, and it wasn't easy: his lungs, fed for hours on stale air, craved oxygen. His body, too, hot and sticky under plastic, yearned for contact with the atmosphere. But he didn't dare free himself from his self-appointed prison until he was sure that the coast was clear, and how could he know that when the sound of his own breathing blocked out all other sounds, magnifying in the process his creeping terror?

He took a huge breath, held it, counted. He sat very still. He heard nothing, but what did that mean? Perhaps the dog had been muzzled, perhaps it was sitting just on the edge of the swimming pool waiting to ambush him. He shivered all over, despite the intolerable heat. The whole situation was intolerable. He couldn't stand this for much longer, he'd have to get out and risk it soon, and if he got ripped into bite-sized chunks of Chum then so much the – his held-in breath came whooshing out. He panted for more, but there wasn't enough. Stuff the sodding dog! his brain screamed at him, I'm going to DIE!

With flailing arms he tore at the black plastic that surrounded him. Suddenly cold air stung his hands. He thrust his head through the gap he'd made and gasped. Sweet cool oxygen flooded his lungs. It was all he could do to restrain himself from whooping with delight.

Suddenly he froze. He remembered the dog. He hadn't seen it, but he had heard it, and he knew it was a big ugly one. If it was around then surely it would have heard him. He cocked his ear and listened. He stared all about him suspiciously.

It was dark, much darker than he would have thought. It was therefore much later than he would have thought. He heard the breeze ruffling the strips of plastic all about him, but he could see nothing. It was pitch black at the bottom of the swimming pool.

He eased the top of his body out of the confines of his plastic prison. What was the time? It had to be getting on for 6 o'clock. Eleven hours he'd been in there! He ached all over. But what was a mere day of acute physical discomfort when set against a scoop?

What was a scoop when set against having your bum torn off by a rabid canine?

He hadn't reckoned on the dog. It had been a perfectly planned operation, executed with military style precision. Apart from the dog. Still, he couldn't have been expected to think of everything. He couldn't be blamed for not equipping himself with a doctored slab of rump steak just on the off-chance.

He reached back into his plastic hidey-hole and felt for the store of equipment he had brought: a now empty thermos, empty sandwich wrappings, two full cigarette packets (he'd have murdered for a drag), the camera with lens attachment, the cassette recorder, the pencil torch, the reserve chocolate bars (both eaten), the Ordnance Survey map, the walkie-talkie, the nicotine substitute chewing gum, the penknife, the tin of black boot polish, the black balaclava, the wad of ten-pound notes stuffed into his waistband, the big hip-flask, the small pocket flask (A sip still left in that), the forged letter from the Swimming Pools Inspectorate authorising him to conduct on-the-spot investigations, the binoculars, the spare jumper, the compass, the wire-clippers, the Sony Walkman with two double cassettes of Eazie Listening, the periscope.

He had bought the periscope in the Fareham toy shop. It was made of green plastic and had come in a cardboard box illustrated with pictures of ships blowing up and a bearded submarine captain with an I'm A Smug Bastard look written all over his face. Harry had worn exactly the same expression when he'd walked out of the shop with the box tucked under his arm.

He knelt up. He was against the angle of the shallow end wall, under the cover of which he had burrowed out his hideaway. He didn't have to push the periscope up very far.

The lawn was deserted. Through the french windows he could see the television crew, but there was no one outside. They were all probably terrified of the dog too. It looked as though something might be about to happen soon, but Harry wasn't worried about missing anything: his signal would be when they warmed up the big arc lights on the patio.

He lowered the periscope and settled himself down again, half in and half out of the plastic sheeting. If he should hear footsteps then he would just withdraw his head and then he would be invisible. Even if someone walked right up to the edge of the swimming pool and peered over they wouldn't see him now; the darkness around him was impenetrable. He began to feel cocky. He had a feeling that he was on top of things. Almost without thinking he opened the nearest cigarette packet and took one out. He lit up and took a lungful of bliss. No one would see it, he thought to himself dismissively, and stuff 'em anyway! He waved the glowing tip around playfully and flipped his other hand back over his head in a casual two-fingered gesture.

Then he remembered the dog and he put the cigarette out at once.

The crew were sitting around smoking and talking and eating and drinking, more or less simultaneously. Connie snapped her fingers and the younger ones jumped.

"Alright, let's get this show on the road. Better get the lights warmed up."

"I wouldn't go out there, Ted," the cameraman said to the lighting man, who was opening the french window. "Not with the Hound of the Baskervilles on the rampage."

"He's on a leash."

"Yeh, but Ted ain't!"

The others roared and hooted. Ted waved two fingers at them. Witty repartee abounded. Connie surveyed the scene with a practised eye: everything seemed in order: the dinner table centre-stage;

the positions of the lights and cameras; the cables tucked out of the way. There had been trouble with reflections in the window, but they had sorted that out. Jenny, the researcher, was polishing the two champagne glasses with a tea towel.

"It's like that Saki story, 'The Open Window'," she said with a nod outside. "A bit spooky really."

"Somehow I don't think anyone's going to come wandering through tonight," replied Connie softly. Then: "Jenny!"

The sudden sharpness in her voice made Jenny start. She looked at the table, thinking something was amiss there, but Connie's attention was fixed on the clapperboard, which lay on the sofa. She strode over, snatched it up, and pointed an accusing finger at the chalked-on programme title.

"This is bloody stupid!" she said angrily.

It read "English Eccentrics – prod. Connie Stevens."

"If he sees this he'll throw a fit!"

"Er, Connie – " Jenny began gently.

"This is worse than carelessness, Jenny, it jeopardises the whole shoot. What a – "

"Connie, it was Ben," said Jenny quickly.

A slight pause ensued.

"Oh," said Connie at the end of it, and then, almost swallowing the word, "sorry."

She wiped the clapperboard clean with her sleeve and sat down on the sofa, staring straight ahead and rather daring any of the crew to catch her eye. The crew worked studiously at their tasks. Connie lit a cigarette and fumed.

Bloody silly stupid bloody thick brainless bloody oafish moron, she thought, at the same time all too aware of the injustice of her accusations: after all, a man with no brain cannot really be blamed for acting brainlessly. The fault was hers. Still, he had excelled himself this time: she had been more than painstaking in stressing to all involved in the production the necessity of masking their true intentions from Reg. Not surprisingly, there had been unease in some quarters, but Connie justified herself on the grounds that a certain amount of deception was inevitable. After all, what she was trying to capture on film was eccentricity in action, and it should be as unforced as possible. Reg's appearances so far in front of camera had been quite unnatural enough without giving him any opportunity for playing up. If he was encouraged to "act" eccentric then the whole thing would degenerate into Pythonesque farce.

Meantime, the problem was to reconcile Reg's idea of what the programme should be about with her own. She had been necessarily vague about her intentions, but she had stressed that what she was engaged in was a character study. She had explained as much to the other five subjects in the series and they had been happy enough to be filmed pottering about performing whatever acts of mild lunacy qualified them for inclusion. Reg was different. For one thing he seemed not to have grasped that it was to be a documentary. Although she had explained to him countless times that she was an independent film-maker he had an unassailable fixed notion that she worked for *News at Ten*. He kept asking whether Sir Alastair Burnet was coming along. This may have had something to do with the fact that he had originally contacted television news and a kind editor friend had passed him on to her. But he couldn't get the idea out of his head that he was meant to be giving a kind of address to the nation. He seemed to think that he was being offered a platform from which he could defend the integrity of his missing lover, Madeleine Harvey, and declare his undying constancy. To this end he had some rather curious ideas about what would make compelling television.

Her big mistake had been to let him do one of his "poems" to camera. It had seemed like a harmless enough exercise at the time but in the event it had proved excruciating: even the crew, who were to poetry what Pam Ayres was to hang-gliding, had been embarrassed. The end-product was quite unusable. She had been racking her brains ever since to think of excuses to deter him, but he appeared to think that all she needed was a few more of his outpourings for her to be snowed under with Programme of the Year awards. Apparently he had never heard of E.J.Thribb.

Her best hope now was that Turpin would turn up with Reg's rival, the hated Roddy, but time was running out. The thought of being dependent on Turpin for anything turned her stomach, but unless Reg suddenly became co-operative and pulled out all the stops she was going to be stymied. What she had in the can so far wasn't worth a damn.

"And talk of the devil," she muttered to herself.

For here he was, the tabloid smoothie himself, his oily grin preceding him through the door like the Cheshire cat's:

"And how is England's answer to Leni Riefenstahl tonight?" he asked oozily.

Connie raised a disdainful eyebrow.

"Cut the crap, Turpin." The eyebrow went half-way to meet the other one. The frown was due to his garb, black slacks and scarf and an outsize combat jacket. "Why are you dressed like Michael Heseltine?"

He shrugged and made a little modest gesture, as if to say "what this old thing?"

"Just blending into the background. I couldn't simply come in through the front door now, could I? It's like Sodom and Gomorrah out there."

"You should know. Who's that?"

"That" was a thin-faced, sharp-eyed woman who had appeared at Turpin's shoulder. That she was of his party was evidenced by her appearance; the Heseltine look was clearly in this season.

"Just a friend of mine," Turpin replied, giving her a most unfriendly shove back out into the hallway.

"And where's the other friend of yours?"

"Give me a chance, give me a chance!"

"Oh God! What's your story this time?"

The grin spread all across Dick Turpin's face, from ear to shining ear. He took a cigar out of his silver case, lit it with his gold lighter and advanced on Connie like a clockwork steam engine on runners. Instinctively she shrank into the corner of the sofa.

"Lemme tell you a story . . ." he said, and sat down on the arm.

Reg Talbot had a dream.

He had dreamed these many years, but by rationed instalments, and his dreams had encompassed strictly the attainable: car, house, wife, car, new office, car, kids, record profits, Fareham showroom. Each of these dreams had borne fruit in time; reality making its takeover bid for fantasy and the merger going through on the nod. But now he had let slip the leash on his imagination and it was abroad in uncharted territory. Now he dreamt a new dream, more potent than any other.

His dream was of Madeleine of the rich gold hair. No love-tossed swain of tender years had ever conjured such vivid charged images as staid, middle-aged Reg Talbot. Romeo was just not on his level.

Tristan was a sot. True passion had found its berth in the moistening dry dock of his imagination. In the parlance of his trade, his big end had well and truly gone.

A knock on the door brought him abruptly out of his reverie. He checked himself quickly in the mirror, snatched up his pen and pored academically over the nearest of the many sheets of ink-filled paper that adorned his late wife's dressing table.

"Come in!" he boomed with headmasterly gravitas.

"Time to powder your nose," said Pam the make-up girl.

Reg smiled politely, trying to hide his disappointment. He had hoped that it might be Connie, wanting to discuss the shoot. The disquieting thought had already occurred to him that perhaps Connie was no lover of poetry.

He moved his papers to one side to make room for Pam's equipment. He made himself comfortable and waited nonchalantly for her to cover his shoulders with towel and bib.

"Still writing the old poetry, Mr T?" she asked, indicating the piles of paper.

"Mm. Perhaps you can help me. Can you think of a word that rhymes with Porsche?"

"I'm not much good with words I'm afraid. What's it for?"

"Just another little sonnet I'm tinkering with. The first line is 'Thou art more lovely than a brand new Porsche' but that's as far as I've got."

"I see," she said doubtfully. "Does it have to be a Porsche?"

"No, it was Ferrari originally but I couldn't think of anything to rhyme with that either."

She combed his hair back carefully, set it with a little gel, then powdered the gleam away from his forehead and cheeks. There was another knock on the door, it was opened a fraction and Jenny the assistant called through:

"Five minutes please!"

Reg looked at himself in the mirror with profound seriousness. Pam noticed the ponderous knitting together of the eyebrows.

"Anything bothering you, Mr T?"

He indulged her with a smile but a moment later the curl in the mouth was levelled and the expression of severe profundity resumed.

"No, no, my dear," he said quietly. "Something important is going to happen tonight, that's all. I have an appointment with fate."

Pam seemed surprised to hear it.

"Sounds a bit gloomy to me!" she said cheerfully.

"I don't mean to be gloomy at all," Reg insisted. "It's not every day that one has a tryst with destiny."

"A tryst with destiny," Pam repeated. "That sounds romantic...."

"Does it?" Reg perked up suddenly. "Good heavens! Destiny rhymes with Ferrari!"

He reached excitedly for pen and paper.

The logjam in the driveway hadn't eased; if anything it had got worse. Late arrivals now left their vehicles in the lane and proceeded on foot. But they had nothing new to offer their colleagues by way either of information or inspiration, and they merely added to the concentrated collective frustration. Tempers were worse than frayed; violence was potential. They circled Reg Talbot's fenced domain like ravenous piranhas, ready to snap at each other if nothing better presented itself.

"I'd keep back from there if I was you," one of the early arrivals said to a greenhorn who was attempting to stick his head through a gap in the hedge. "Got a whole pack of wild animals in there, he has: Alsatians, Rottweilers, you name it. ... "

"Killer chihuahuas," said a softly lilting voice behind.

The gentle mockery in the voice made the cataloguer of deadly breeds smart. He swung round aggressively, lips poised to explete, but one glance at the small neat man in a tan mac and his anger was stillborn. Instead he tried to smile, a not wholly successful experiment.

"Evening, Inspector."

Inspector Morris smiled back, to rather better effect.

"Well then, as we're supposed to say on the tv: what's all this going on here then?"

21

Mark came out of the back door. He skirted the fishpond and stepped over the flowerbeds to the garden fence. The big tv lights on the patio were turned up full. He could see the figure of Turpin silhouetted against the glow. The tip of his cigarette indicated where his mouth was.

"Got the gear?"

Mark shook the blue laundry bag in his hand.

"Come on then. Let's get you out the way before the opposition put in another appearance."

Mark had been upstairs at the window listening to the opposition padding about in his garden. Clearly the concept of trespass was alien to them. They had not had a very happy time: one had torn his jacket trying to climb a tree to get a better view over the fence; another had fallen into the fishpond. Then, just before Mark had been given the signal for his descent, the security man and the guard dog had appeared, setting off a frantic stampede to the rear in the course of which groans, screams and hideous cries had rent the air as the ineluctable Darwinian process was effected: not so much the survival of the fittest as the getting by of the least unfit.

Mark tucked the laundry bag under his arm and clambered over the fence. He hurried across the lawn in Turpin's shadowy wake.

"Watch out!" Turpin yelled suddenly.

Mark pulled himself up just in time – just before walking over the edge of the swimming pool.

"For Christ's sake, watch where you're going!"

Mark looked down into the black pit of the swimming pool. On the instant a terrible vision came to him: Turpin's warning had come too late and he had fallen in; and as he tried to scramble out again hands were grabbing at his legs and feet, hands that had burst out of the blue concrete crust and were pulling him down, down under the earth, where the dead had their roots and Maddie was awaiting her revenge. . . .

He ran madly across the lawn and caught up with Turpin on the edge of the patio. Turpin saw the wild look in his eyes and stared at him suspiciously.

"Have you been drinking?"

Mark glared at him indignantly. For the first time he was able to see Turpin properly, in the spillage of light from the tv lights.

"Why are you dressed like Michael Heseltine?"

"Shut up and follow me."

They went into the house through the french windows. As Mark's eyes adjusted to the bright lights he had a vivid sense of *déjà vu*: the room was exactly as he had last seen it: same table, glasses, cutlery; same ice bucket cooling a bottle of the same champagne; even the same naff prawn avocados on their personalised lettuce beds. The crowd of technicians and their expensive paraphernalia were the only unfamiliar features.

"Hey! Watch where you're going!" an impatient voice snapped.

Mark wasn't sure who was meant, but he got out of the way just in case. He ended up by the door that led to the hall. He watched the technicians at work with interest. He had never seen a tv programme being made and he found it all rather exciting. Everybody seemed engrossed in his or her own thing, and when they communicated it was in short rapid bursts of jargonised language, incomprehensible to the outside ear. As far as Mark was concerned this merely added to the mystique. But when the boss — a strong-jawed aggressive-looking woman with a severe haircut — when she snapped her fingers all the different functionaries seemed to come together, and the various human cogs could be seen to move in sync. He was eager to see what it was they were going to film. Where was Reg? Where was Roddy supposed to fit into it all? And what were they going to do when they realised that Roddy wasn't going to show? He felt a smirk coming on. He was confident that he could handle himself, and he was confident that he could handle Turpin. He took a longer and more critical look at the dinner table. There was something not quite right — what was it? He could see now: the single rose that had been laid at Madeleine's place was on the wrong side. Perhaps he should offer his services as historical consultant. . . .

Turpin walked into the room from the hall. As Mark hadn't even seen him go out he was quite surprised. Turpin was the nearest thing he'd ever met to a magician's white rabbit.

"There you are!" he said in a not altogether friendly tone. "Stay put where I can find you, will you. Want to keep all my eggs in the same basket. Come in, love!"

This last command he delivered over his shoulder. Mark was annoyed at his offhand tone. He was considering a suitably cold response when he had a terrible shock:

Lizzie Skinner walked through the door.

"Well, look who it isn't . . . " she said in her inimitable nasal way.

"Ha, ha! Hello Lizzie!"

"Don't you hello Lizzie me!"

"Ha, ha!"

"You two talk amongst yourselves," Turpin advised, giving them both a pat on the shoulder and propelling himself into the centre of the room, where Connie and her cameraman were in conference.

Mark began to shiver. It wasn't cold – on the contrary, it was hot under the lights. But he had the distinct impression of icicles forming in his bloodstream.

"And what brings you here, Mark Harvey?" Lizzie demanded contemptuously, in a voice that carried. One or two of the technicians looked round. Mark's ears burned even as his general body temperature took a further plummet.

"Oh you know!" he said idiotically, then, in a desperate bid to change the subject: "Like the jacket!"

The camouflage smock was a good fit; life in the marines would have probably suited her.

"Don't you try and sweet-talk me!" she growled (Mark raised an eyebrow – the thought!) "I know why you're here – money-grubbing, I'll bet. Typical!"

He felt stung. That wasn't fair! What made it worse was that he couldn't deny it. But it wasn't as if he'd been on the take all along, as Roddy had obviously been.

"Roddy – "

"How dare you mention his name! You're not half the man he is, and you know it!"

Not any more and that's for sure, he thought.

"I'm not going to waste my breath talking to you!" she declared roundly. "You make me sick!"

Sweat was running into his eyes. He blinked and washed it out.

Through a film of moisture he watched Lizzie step away from him, fold her arms deliberately and turn her back.

"Will someone shut the door!" a crewman ordered.

Mark was nearest. He stepped out smartly into the hall and closed the door after him.

There was no one about. He liked it that way. He wanted to keep it that way. Where could he go? He couldn't lock himself in the loo, there'd be a queue before long. His gaze rested a moment on the broom cupboard, but dark confined spaces made him nervous. He went into the kitchen.

The light was on but there was no one about. He pushed the door to and slithered on to a kitchen stool. He clutched the blue laundry bag to his bosom.

Things were going wrong. Nothing disastrous had happened—yet—but he had a palpable sense of imminent catastrophe. Premonition manifested itself physically: there was a tingling in his extremities, a sensation of enervation at the core. His body twitched like a divining rod over water.

Thirty seconds with Lizzie Skinner had been enough to reduce him to a jelly. What in heaven's name was she doing here? Whatever it was he knew he wasn't going to like it. Roddy would have been bad enough, but at least he might have stood a chance with Roddy. This was out of the frying-pan and into the thermonuclear reactor.

A door slamming out in the hall made him jump. Anything would have made him jump in his present state. He wanted to cry. He heard the voice of the tough lady producer, controlled but angry:

"Stop bullshitting me, Turpin!"

"Look Connie, it's just an unforeseen little difficulty – "

"You knew bloody well your man wasn't going to show, didn't you?"

"Of course not, I was just making contingency plans – "

"You can stop pissing me about, mate, and you can stop now. A confrontation between Talbot and Maclean I remain prepared to film under the conditions I laid out and to which you and they agreed. Use of substitutes is not permitted. Who are all these people you're cluttering up the house with? It's like Piccadilly Circus in there. Who are all these bloody people? Who's that bloody man there, just come in? There! You in the donkey jacket. Who are you, mister?"

"Er, is Mr Talbot about?"

"No he bloody isn't. What the bloody hell do you want?"

"Er, Murphy's the name, I've got to speak to Mr Talbot – "

"How did you get past security, matey?"

"Shut up Turpin, leave this to me. Talbot's not available, Murphy, so clear off, will you!"

"If you see him could you just – "

"GET OUT!"

"Okay, I'm going, I'm going. . . . "

"How the hell did he get past security? What am I paying them for? It's costing an arm and a leg."

"That's another thing, Turpin. You've got a bloody nerve trying to turn this place into Colditz. Half my crew have been scared shitless by that overinflated poodle – "

"A necessary precaution in the circumstances – "

" – only in the circumstances of your producing Roddy Maclean, which you have singularly failed to do. What the hell do you mean by bringing that Skinner woman in here?"

"She knows about Maddie Harvey's feet."

"She what?"

"All will be revealed in the fullness of time. I've got the husband here as well, you know."

"Maddie's husband?"

"The same."

"And does he think she's still alive?"

"Not as far as I know."

"I don't see what earthly use the husband is going to be. As I understand it he made no bones about the fact that he and his wife couldn't stand each other. What I wanted was an electric confrontation between two mad passionate rivals. I'm not going to – what the bloody hell do you want? I thought I told you to sod off!"

"Er, I wondered if Mr Talbot was about yet?"

"No, he bloody isn't. Ben! Ben! COME HERE!"

"What is it, Connie?"

"Get security and tell them to show Mr Murphy the door. He should know where it is. By the look of his jacket he can have only just finished painting it."

"Er, I'll be off then, sorry to bother you, miss. . . . "

"Jenny! Jenny, where are you?"

"Here, Connie."

"Has Pam finished?"

"I think so."

"Then get Talbot down here. We're going now."

"Look, love – "

"Without you, Turpin. We go without you, understood? I've got one hell of a salvage job to do and not much time. So clear your bloody circus out the way, will you. Some of us are trying to work."

The front door slammed. The hall door slammed. There was a pause, and then the sound of footsteps coming down the stairs: Mark heard Reg Talbot's voice, hard-edged with self-confidence:

"I knew he wouldn't have the guts to show up. To think that he even dared to think himself worthy of Madeleine!"

"Don't do that please, Mr T. You'll smudge your make-up."

The door into the living room was opened and closed again. Through the thicknesses of walls and doors Mark could just hear the muffled voices of the crew. A minute or so passed. Then the most furious row erupted and the living-room door was flung open again.

"For Christ's sake get out, Turpin! You and your stupid bitch are wrecking my shoot!"

"Don't call me a stupid bitch, you stupid cow!" Lizzie Skinner screamed.

"Madeleine hated you anyway, she told me!" Reg butted in from somewhere off.

Lizzie screamed again. There was a high-pitched exchange of insults and then a scuffling noise.

"Calm down, ladies!" said Turpin.

Mark slipped off his stool and tiptoed over to the door. He knelt and peered through the keyhole. Unfortunately he could only get a partial view of what was going on, but it appeared that the two women were trying to throttle each other. Then they broke apart and Lizzie aimed a kick, which must have registered because Connie yelped. Next there was a blur of flesh and the unmistakable smack of knuckles striking home. Lizzie went sprawling.

"She's knocked my teeth out, the cow!" she wailed.

"BEN! Show these two the door!"

An almighty slam, greater than all preceding, made the walls shake. A human shape blocked Mark's line of sight and he moved away, just in case anyone came in and caught him peeping. He could still hear Lizzie's wild sobs:

"I'm bleeding to death! She could have killed me!"

An unlucky escape, thought Mark.

"Come on then love, let's get you cleaned up," said Dick Turpin. Their voices receded. Mark heard them go into the downstairs loo. He heard the sounds of water running and the toilet flushing.

"Would you mind hurrying up in there and going, please . . . " said an ineffectual male voice.

For answer Mark heard the door being kicked shut and the bolt slammed across. He held his breath and listened out eagerly for further developments. To his great disappointment none came. He returned to the keyhole, but saw nothing. He turned away and punched the air with both fists. It was all he could do to stop himself whooping for joy.

He forced himself to calm down. Now was no time to get carried away, he had to think. What were his options? They didn't amount to a hill of beans: lie low or make a run for it shared equal billing on the bottom line. Although superficially attractive the first option had drawbacks, i.e. by no stretch of the imagination could Reg's kitchen qualify as the most brilliant hiding place in the world. If Turpin and Lizzie found him there might still be trouble. That left option two. And if he was going to get out, there was no point in hanging around for a moment longer.

He tucked the blue laundry bag under his arm and dashed over to the window. He lifted the catch, pushed it open, and clambered on to the sink. Poking his nose out of the window he was surprised to discover that he could see into the living room, whose nearest wall stuck out at a ninety-degree angle from the kitchen. There was a small square window at the side through which he could see the back of a man's head and, beyond, the edge of the dinner table. It looked as though something was going on. Succumbing to natural curiosity, the old cat-killer, he craned his neck to get a better view.

Dick Turpin's face materialised out of the darkness, inches from his own.

Mark gasped. He recoiled instinctively and lost his balance. He fell over backwards and ended up with his bottom in the sink and his feet sticking out of the window.

"Don't make such a bloody racket!" Turpin hissed. "It's only me."

"Where did you come from?" asked Mark in a whisper, not because he meant to whisper but rather because he was pretty much incapable of speech.

"Nicked out the bog window. Where's the shoes?"

The blue laundry bag was on Mark's stomach. Turpin made a grab for it. Mark held on.

"Give it here!"

"It's mine!"

"Give it to me!"

"What are you going to do with it?"

"I don't know, I'm busking!"

Mark heard a tearing sound as the blue plastic bag began to come apart. Terrified of being deluged with the fake shoes he relinquished his grip.

"What the hell are you playing at?" Turpin muttered angrily. Mark didn't answer. "I said you'd get your dosh. Here." He stuffed a wad of notes into Mark's top pocket. "You stay here while I go and get Lizzie. She's still sobbing her eyes out in the bog. . . . "

Turpin disappeared. Mark struggled to lift his bottom out of the sink. If there was one place where he had no intention of staying it was where he was now.

He squeezed himself feet first out of the window and landed on the patio. In front of him lay the lawn and just to the right the flowerbeds and an archipelago of comforting shadows that led all the way up to safety. To the left, through the little window in the living-room wall, he caught a glimpse of Reg Talbot standing by the dinner table. He hesitated. What was going on in there? He took a step towards the window. Are you mad? the other half of his brain screamed at him. Get out of here! Still he hesitated. He could see the candles on the table. He could see Madeleine in his mind's eye. The cat-killer caught him. He pushed his face up to the glass.

The camera and lights were in an arc around the table, at which Reg was now sitting. He was talking. Mark's ear touched the glass. He heard Connie's voice:

"I've told you, Reg, we'll do the poem later."

She sounded exasperated. Reg looked unhappy.

"I don't know what's the point of my sitting here like a lemon. . . ."

"Look . . . think of it as a mood shot, creating an atmosphere. We'll have a voice-over setting the scene, explaining everything. You just have to get up and do what I told you when I give you the wink. It's very simple."

"Not to me, it isn't. I'm sorry. I realise you know a great deal more about all this than I do, and I'm sure you're very clever, but I don't see how you can expect me to just sit here and act natural if I don't even know what it is you're saying about me."

"Okay, okay. I'll tell you what: we don't have a finished script, but I'll improvise something. Just for you, to give you a flavour. Okay?"

Reg nodded reluctantly. The crew resumed their places. Connie took up station beside the camera.

"Speed," said the cameraman.

"Action!" said Connie. "Reg!"

Reg, not altogether happy, sat very still and fixed his gaze on the empty place opposite. Connie cleared her throat.

"It was on such a night as this that Reg Talbot and Madeleine Harvey sat down to their last romantic supper. Champagne flowed; love was in the air; they held hands and murmured sweet nothings by candlelight. But then cruel fate intervened: out through the open window she went, out into the darkness that swallowed her and out of Reg's life for ever. She has not been seen since, but is there more to her disappearance than the police would have us believe? A rich vein of mystery runs through the seam of this affair, and – "

"Excuse me," said Reg turning to face the camera, "but this is a load of crap."

"I'm just giving you a bloody idea!" yelled Connie. "I'm not expecting Oscar for best screenplay!"

Mark heard footsteps behind him. He wheeled round, heart in mouth, and saw three shadowy figures in flak jackets coming round the side of the house. Turpin was in the lead, followed by Lizzie and a man weighed down with cameras.

"What are they doing?" Turpin demanded.

"They're filming him sitting at the table."

"Shit! It's the shoes next!"

So saying, and clutching the blue laundry bag to his chest, he tiptoed past Mark, dropped to his knees and crawled round the corner on to the patio where, hugging the wall, he slithered along towards the open french windows.

"Excuse me, please!" muttered Lizzie through clenched teeth as she brushed past Mark and followed in Turpin's wake. The cameraman brought up the rear.

Mark stood rooted to the spot. He thought about running away: thought about it in purely an abstract way, for the sense of impending doom that gripped him had rendered contact with his own nervous system incidental — the possibility of locomotion may have been theoretical only. He stared goggle-eyed through the window:

"Everything crystal-clear now, Reg?" he heard Connie demanding in an acid tone. Reg nodded. "Good. Action!"

Reg sat at the table again and faced the empty place. He stared grimly ahead while Connie directed him:

"Alright Reg, just sit there, imagine you're facing Madeleine, and maybe we'll use a bit of your poetry as a voice-over to set the scene, alright? Good. Now, when I give you the word you get up and walk round the table . . . hold that pose, that's lovely, and . . . go!"

Reg got up ponderously and walked round the table. He put his hands under the back of Madeleine's chair and pulled it out.

"So this is where we're saying that Madeleine disappeared and left no trace, except for . . . now Reg!"

Reg bent down and picked something off the seat of the chair. He held it up to camera.

"Hold it up, Reg, I can't see what it is."

Mark could. He knew it at once, poor memento of Madeleine, with its broken heel, oddly angled.

"That's great, Reg. So now the voice-over will be saying something about Cinder — "

"It's a fake!" screamed Lizzie Skinner, bursting in through the french windows.

Earlier, Turpin had advised Mark that all hell was going to break loose. Now he understood that the expression had been meant literally rather than figuratively. Through his little window screen he watched spellbound an electric succession of *petits tableaux*:

Lizzie snatching the shoe from Reg and slamming it down into the avocado set for Madeleine;

Turpin popping up between them like a jack in the box, tipping up the blue laundry bag and spewing shoes over the entire table;

(The above accompanied by profanities and insults hurled from Connie's sandpaper-textured throat);

Connie springing into the action with a right hook aimed at Lizzie's jaw which, had it connected, would have kept her dentist in clover for a year;

Reg snatching up a knife (after mistakenly first selecting a fork) and chasing Turpin round the table;

The photographer in the flak jacket dancing around between them flashing like a demented ambulance;

Connie and Lizzie rolling to the floor, biting and scratching and tearing, and remaining locked together in unholy combat despite the efforts of the crew to prise them apart;

The props girl, an island of calm in a sea of seething passion, deftly lifting Madeleine's shoe from the squashed avocado and flicking off a few prawns before wiping it down with a tissue;

Mr Murphy, at the french window, trying to attract Reg's attention by waving a scrap of paper at him;

Mr Murphy?

"What the bloody hell are you doing here?" Connie screamed, disengaging herself from Lizzie's throat and struggling to her feet.

"Er, I was just wondering if Mr Talbot could spare a moment. . . ."

"I'll spare you a moment alright," muttered Reg, bearing down on him with knife *en tierce*.

"It's about this cheque you gave me," Murphy continued, showing Reg the scrap of paper. "Is it meant to be a joke or something?"

"A joke?" thundered Reg magnificently.

"Couldn't you discuss this later?" butted in Dick Turpin. "We're about to make a revelation."

"Keep out of my personal affairs!" snarled Reg. He jabbed a finger into Murphy's breast-bone. "I just moved the decimal point a few places, that's all."

"Er, that's hardly fair, Mr Talbot. There's not a lot I can do with a cheque for £2.50."

"Well that's about £2.45 more than you're worth, Murphy. That pool's a disgrace!"

"I don't believe this!" Turpin exclaimed. Reg ignored him.

"You've got one last chance, Murphy: either you're here first thing tomorrow with your excavating machine and as many of your useless boyos as it takes to work it, either you dig up the entire swimming pool and start again, or this cheque's your lot!"

"Stuff the bleeding pool!" yelled Turpin. "We're exposing you for a fraud. Look!"

Lizzie staggered to the table and snatched Madeleine's shoe. She looked somewhat ruffled after her all-in tussle, but triumphant conviction ran through her speech and gesture:

"This isn't Maddie's shoe, it's a fake. Maddie had problems with her feet, everyone knows that. She found it physically impossible to wear any kind of shoe at all, certainly not one with heels. She only wore sandals."

She threw Madeleine's shoe into the pile from the blue laundry bag. She held her pose, daring anyone to challenge her.

Reg snorted. Connie walked casually over to the table, and picked out a shoe at random.

"And what's this then?" she drawled.

Lizzie didn't answer.

"I'd say it's a shoe."

She shoved it under Lizzie's nose. It was stout, made of canvas, with a rather flat heel. It was casual, but it was a shoe. It certainly wasn't a sandal.

"And this?" said Connie, indicating another. "And these?"

Turpin pushed his way past her. He thrust his hand into the pile of shoes and turned it over. He failed to find what he was looking for. In exasperation he swept half the shoes on to the floor.

"I've been conned!"

"Good evening, ladies and gentlemen," said Inspector Morris affably, stepping in through the french windows like a *deus ex* Christie. Connie made to intercept him. "CID, ma'am," he said flashing his identity card, and then, turning to Reg, "I've got one or two questions I'd like to ask you please, Mr Talbot."

"Inspector, there's been an attempt to pervert the course of justice!" declared Lizzie dramatically, waving Madeleine's shoe at him. "Maddie Harvey had bad feet!"

The Inspector smiled at her politely.

"Er, I'll be off then," murmured Murphy.

"I'd rather you didn't if it's all the same to you sir," said the Inspector firmly. "Easier to get everything sorted out if everyone stays exactly where they are. Good evening, Mr Turpin, I thought I'd find you here."

Dick Turpin was staring open-mouthed at the pile of shoes. Comprehension flickered in his eyes.

"Where's Mark Harvey?"

Not at his little square window looking in on them, that was for sure.

He was running, running for all he was worth, stretching and tearing every fibre and muscle. He ran on wings of terror, his feet barely touching the ground, blind, though his ping-pong eyes were almost bursting from their sockets: he tripped, he fell, he picked himself up again, he crashed heavily against the wall and felt an agony of bruising erupt all down his side. He struggled on and felt something clawing at his leg. He thrust out a hand to free himself and yelped as rose-thorns stung his palm.

"Who's that?" demanded a thick menacing voice from somewhere among the shadows under the house.

And at the same moment Mark heard the rattle of a chain and a deep deadly canine growl.

He spun round on his feet and ran back the way he had come, faster even than before, faster than he had ever run even in his dreams. He ran, strangely, out of darkness into light, and a kind of luminance must have dispelled the fog in his brain, for on the instant he understood that before he had been running in the wrong direction, whereas now he could see before him, across the floodlit patio and glimmering lawn, the sanctuary of Willow Cottage.

Behind him the bluff and burly challenge was repeated. The hound bayed and was let slip.

He skirted the edge of the lawn and ran where the arc of light was at its extremity and barely touched his fleeting soles. He heard the hideous beast behind, bounding free of its world of shadows, and he cut across the lawn towards the nearest part of the fence.

The abyss yawned in front of him. At the same moment his toe caught on something and he went sprawling. He slithered along the ground and came to a halt with his chin jutting over the edge of the swimming pool.

Something stirred beneath. The wind? He heard the rustle of plastic, and then he heard something else — a voice, a disembodied murmur from below. Something was stirring in the depths: and now he saw it, rising out of the earth, the white oval blur of a human face.

His scream merged into the general din: into voices filled with mortal terror, anger, mere curiosity, and the dog's savage bark. They lingered in his head long after he had left them all behind, when he was running, running, running across the fields. Running to Brazil.

22

W.W.Vernon arrived at the bank at a quarter to nine, a little earlier than usual. He ordered a coffee from Miss Temple and then, as it was a Monday, checked through his engagements for the week with Mrs Stephenson. They were pleasantly few. He considered regretfully that in normal times he might have been able to allocate provisionally no fewer than three afternoons for golf, whereas now he could not in all conscience commit himself to more than one. Unfortunately, in Mark Harvey's continued absence, times were not normal. In fact, Vernon had been rather surprised to discover just how much the smooth day-to-day running of the bank had owed to Harvey. Fortunately Miss Price had proved an able deputy, but rather more work than he was accustomed to was still coming his way. Hence his early arrival at the bank.

Having delegated some rather tiresome chores, and having been seen to do his duty, Vernon relaxed with a second cup of coffee and today's *Times*. This was one of the times of day he liked best, a fact well known to the entire staff. He presumed, therefore, that the phone call routed through to him at ten past nine must be urgent. His presumption proved to be well-founded.

"Lady de Burgh is on the phone, Mr Vernon," Mrs Stephenson explained. "She wishes to speak to you personally."

"Yes of course. Put her through."

He cleared his throat. Rather unnecessarily, he adjusted his tie.

"Lady de Burgh? Walter Vernon, at your service, ma'am."

"Ah yes, Mr Vernon. I've heard a great deal about you."

It was a light pleasant voice. Highly refined, as one would expect. Certainly as W.W. Vernon would expect. It was also slightly familiar; slightly.

"Nothing too bad, I hope. Ha! ha!"

She laughed too. She shared the joke, though in a very restrained, very refined way. As one would expect. It was so pleasant for one to be able to strike up an instant rapport with a lady clearly of no little breeding.

"No, no, Mr Vernon, you may rest assured your good name has not been traduced. On the contrary, my late husband, God rest his soul, spoke of you with cordiality and no little condescension. I believe you played golf with Sir Henry on a number of occasions?"

"Of course, ma'am, how could I forget? I am deeply honoured that he should have conveyed so favourable an impression of me, particularly after witnessing at first hand my feeble attempts on the old links!"

"No false modesty please, Mr Vernon. I understand that you are the very devil of a fellow over eighteen holes, and the soul of conviviality itself at the nineteenth."

Compliments and good humour flowed. He could quite happily have continued in the same vein all morning. It was Lady de Burgh who got down to business.

"There are some matters concerning my investment portfolio on which I am anxious to seek advice. I find that I shall be in Fareham on other business this morning. Perhaps you could do me the great kindness of consenting to a meeting. Please accept my apologies for the short notice, most inconsiderate I know."

"No, no, not at all, Lady de Burgh. I am entirely at your service. Please name a time and I will give you my full and undivided attention."

"Would 10 o'clock be too soon?"

He looked at his watch. Ten o'clock would be very soon indeed. He was a little surprised, but only too delighted to agree the time. All in all, the entire conversation so far had afforded him nothing but delight.

"Thank you so much, Mr Vernon. I look forward to making your acquaintance at ten."

"Not as much as I look forward to making yours, Lady de Burgh."

He felt a positive thrill as he replaced the handset. He was reminded – as he had cause to be reminded so often – of the superiority of his present position to his former. The vulgar question of remuneration apart, one was simply so much better off amidst the charms of the home counties than racing with the city ratpack. And of course one met a better class of person. Lady de Burgh . . . she had sounded familiar, perhaps he had met her. Sir Henry, now who was he . . . ? "My late husband" she had said. He remembered: he must have been that fellow with the gold Rolls Royce convertible. He had died, about a year ago. Funny though, he could have sworn he'd been called George. Perhaps he'd been George Henry, or Henry George. They loved their little pet names, the upper classes. Perhaps he'd been called George at Eton. Not much shakes as a golfer, as he recalled, but a splendid fellow, good sort. Jolly decent of him to have mentioned a humble bank manager chappie to his wife.

Feeling very happy with life Vernon got up and began to pace about the room, pausing every now and again to address an imaginary golf ball. He stopped at the window and gazed over his parking lot. It looked like rather a gloomy day. Not jolly boating weather; not golfing neither. Just as well he had to stay in and work. Of course, his putter was behind the door, he could always put in a little practice with the waste bin. He glanced at his watch. He had time for a quick session before Lady de Burgh arrived.

He was about to go and get his putter when a movement caught his eye: one of the windows at the back of Reg Talbot's showroom had just been thrown open. This in itself was not an event guaranteed to hold his attention for overlong, but a moment later he saw something distinctly odd – a trousered leg was swung over the windowsill. Another moment and a hand and an arm appeared and then, by degrees, the rest of a man's body. The man eased himself out through the window backwards and glanced to left and right before turning round. It was only then that Vernon recognised Reg Talbot.

Vernon stepped back from the window. He had no wish to be seen by Talbot, the complexities of whose private life, which he could only deplore, put him, Vernon, in a delicate position (he was after all Mark Harvey's superior). Additionally, he had a rather more pressing reason for avoiding Talbot's eye, namely that he had been responsible for blackballing Talbot's application to join the golf club. As it had been he who suggested that Talbot apply in the first place, he couldn't help but feel embarrassed.

So he stepped well back from the window and tucked himself away behind the curtain, from where he was able to observe Talbot without making it appear too obvious. He need not have worried: although Talbot did give another surreptitious glance to left and right, he did not look in Vernon's direction. Instead he climbed over a low fence that ran along the back of the village ironmongers' and disappeared from view.

Vernon had not had time even to begin reflecting on this odd behaviour when he became aware that a second person had entered the parking lot. He too ran over to the fence and had a good look to left and right. Letting curiosity get the better of him Vernon pressed himself up close to the window to get a decent view, but at that moment the man at the fence turned round and their eyes met. Vernon tried to appear unconcerned, to make it appear, indeed, as if he had just perchance happened idly to glance out of the window at that precise moment, but the man at the fence wasn't fooled. He leered at him. Vernon was shocked. He was a most vulgar-looking fellow, greasy-haired and unshaven and dressed in a torn and filthy mackintosh. He wore a heavy plaster on his left cheek and carried his left arm in a sling. A more ruffianly individual Vernon had never seen. And not content with leering at him, the fellow had the effrontery to raise his good hand to his lips in a gesture of silence, and then to wink at him in a lewd and complicitous manner.

"I say! . . . " Vernon spluttered indignantly, but to no good effect: the fellow had already climbed over the fence and disappeared in the same direction as Talbot.

Vernon returned to his desk in a state of near-apoplexy. When at last he succeeded in calming down, some five minutes later, it was to reflect that at least he was left with no illusions as to the state of depravity into which Talbot had sunk. The sort of man who was followed around by the sort of scoundrel whom Talbot was being followed around by was clearly not the right sort of material for membership of the golf club. With this thought to console him Vernon reached for his putter and relaxed himself with a quick round of his very own patent version of one-hole crazy golf.

At about the same time as Vernon was rediscovering his karma, Reg Talbot was entering Fareham Park. The park lay at the bottom of the High Street whereto his circuitous journey through backyards and odd passageways had eventually led him. The community centre and the village green lay just over the road, and beyond these the park proper, whose entrance was marked by rather grand wrought-iron gates. Just inside and to the left was a long single-storey building. This was the village library and it was Reg's destination. He paused on the steps a moment and had a good look over his shoulder. Satisfied that no one was watching he went on in. He did not see the man in the sling.

The man in the sling saw him. At the moment that Reg turned round he was hiding behind one of the two brick pillars that stood on either side of the park entrance. He had already ascertained that there was only one door into the library and so he felt able to afford himself the luxury of a brief pause before proceeding. He pulled cigarettes from his pocket and tried to light one. The attempt proved unsuccessful: he couldn't grasp the matchbox properly in his bandaged fingers.

"I'll light it for you if you give us a fag," said a twelve-year-old on a bicycle who happened to be passing.

"I'll give you a boot up the arse if you don't sod off, you little git!"

"Sod off yourself you filthy bastard!" shouted back the twelve-year-old, riding off and waving two fingers over his shoulder.

Harry Craven waved back, though he was only going through the motions. He had more important fish to fry than snot-nosed kids. He had a brainwave: he stuffed his box of matches into one of the curly bits on the wrought-iron gate. It worked a treat. He took a long, deep satisfying drag and wandered over to the library.

"No smoking in here!" said the librarian crossly. Harry groaned and clutched at his wounded hand:

"That's bloody typical! Get shot to pieces fighting for your country and this is all the thanks you get. Let me tell you something, young lady, I didn't risk having my balls shot off in the Falklands just so as people like you could work in the comfort of libraries and feel safe to walk the streets at night. You risk life and limb for freedom and democracy and you don't even get the freedom to light a fag in peace. I ask you!"

"I'm a pacifist," said the librarian. "And anyway, if you were in the Falklands, I'm a King Edward's potato."

Harry gave her his hardest, most pitiless look. She didn't flinch. And she was only a slip of a thing, thin and spotty and probably not much older than the kid outside on the bike. Harry sighed. His inability to handle even pre-pubescents was yet another worrying sign of onrushing senility.

Harry wandered over to the nearest bookcase and pretended to browse. Reg was right at the other end of the room, leafing through a book. He was a slippery fellow was this Reg Talbot, the sort of fellow it paid to keep an eye on. Harry wasn't so senile that he hadn't managed to do just that.

He sat down, took the weight off his feet. He was worried about his left leg. Underneath his trouser a big bandage swathed him from knee to mid-thigh. That bloody dog had ripped him up a treat. He'd been bloody lucky to get away with a mild crippling. Thank God the security guard had called the dog off in time, allowing him to scramble more or less intact over the fence. He still didn't have a clue what had been going on in Talbot's house or why that bloody idiot had come tearing across the lawn jabbering and screaming at him. Unfortunately none of the photographs he'd taken had come out. The bloke who developed them said he'd used a slow film, he was a stupid git. Harry told him he was a stupid git himself, he hated wankers who tried to lord it over you with spouting technical crap. The pain was that the cassette tapes hadn't come out either. He'd crawled over the lawn as near to the house as he dared and set up a microphone on a long lead facing the french windows. But all he'd got was a lot of background fuzz, so he was going to be in for another round of technical crap when that came out. All in all it had been a pretty miserable bloody day, not to mention a complete waste of time. Hardly worth getting your bum ripped off for. The only consolation was that Turpin seemed to have come out of it with bugger all too: the silence on the front page of his rag this morning had been deafening.

Harry slapped himself lightly on the face. Sitting down was all very well, but he couldn't let himself doze off. However much he needed a kip, his need for a miracle was greater. He forced himself to keep one eye open, and he kept it on Reg. Reg had to be his best bet. If he didn't get something soon he'd be out on his ear with a Georgian silver travelling clock.

The clock would have been useful. He had lost his watch the night before, left it somewhere in the swimming pool. He kept having to twist around in his seat to be able to see the library clock. The hands had crept round to ten o'clock by the time Reg had made his selection and gone to get his books stamped.

The hour sounded on the Fareham church clock. Mrs Stephenson knocked on Mr Vernon's door and entered.

"Lady Madeleine de Burgh," she announced.

"Walter Vernon at your service, Lady de Burgh. Charmed to meet you."

She offered him her hand. He wasn't sure whether he should shake it or kiss it. He opted for the latter.

"How gallant, Mr Vernon!" said Madeleine graciously.

Vernon bowed his head in an obsequious cringe. He indicated a chair.

"Pray be seated. And kindly bring in some coffee, Mrs Stephenson."

Mrs Stephenson went out. Vernon resumed his seat and waited for Lady de Burgh to settle. She was looking in her handbag and seemed to be having trouble finding something. Vernon took the opportunity of appraising her: she was a slim, attractive blonde, fortyish, neat, well dressed. There was something slightly familiar about her, as there was about the voice. Unfortunately she was wearing dark glasses, which rather obscured her features, but he felt sure that they must have met somewhere. A golf club dance, perhaps? At last she finished looking in her handbag.

"How delighted I was to receive your phonecall this morning, Lady de Burgh. It set in train many happy memories of shared sporting encounters with your late and, if I may say so, much lamented husband."

"Indeed, Mr Vernon. I believe it was your appreciation of the noble game of golf that first brought you to the attention of Sir Henry."

"I am flattered and supremely grateful, Lady de Burgh, that my poor attempts should have merited such fulsome consideration."

"No, no, Mr Vernon. It is I who should be grateful to you for affording such delightful recreation to my poor husband in his last years."

Vernon commiserated with a smile. In truth he was beginning to feel a little uneasy. He wished he could be sure if Sir Henry really had been George. Unfortunately his files revealed that neither de Burgh had ever held an account with the bank, so there were no records to consult. The possibility of committing a *faux pas* weighed heavily on him.

Mrs Stephenson returned with the coffee tray.

"That will be all thank you," Vernon said to her. "Kindly see that I am not disturbed."

Mrs Stephenson went out and closed the door. Vernon poured the coffee. Lady de Burgh asked for it black.

"Although your little pot of cream looks very tempting, Mr Vernon, one simply must watch one's figure."

"If I may say so without appearing presumptuous, Lady de Burgh, one would never guess from looking at you that such precautions were necessary."

She took his compliment with good grace, but then, as he reflected to himself with enormous satisfaction, everything about her betokened grace. It was such a joy to deal with a lady of exquisite refinement and perfect manners. It made one's job so worthwhile.

"In what way may I be of assistance, Lady de Burgh?"

"I am in need of advice. My poor husband died leaving his financial affairs in a frightful tangle, and my lawyers have recommended that I seek expert counsel. I do wish Sir Henry had been a little better organised, but then, one never knows when the hour will strike, does one?"

She sniffed. She opened her handbag. She reached inside, no doubt looking for a handkerchief. Vernon offered her his own, but she declined.

"Was it . . . very sudden?" he asked delicately.

"About as sudden as you can get, I'm afraid. He was eaten by a great white shark."

"Good God!"

"Yes, terrible isn't it? He was windsurfing off the Great Barrier Reef. Ridiculous for a man of seventy-three, but he always was stubborn. Poor Harry. Would you like to see a photograph?"

"Of your husband?"

"No, of the shark."

She withdrew her hand from her bag. She was holding an automatic pistol. She was pointing it at his face.

"Move a hair and you're history, Vernon."

For a few moments her warning appeared superfluous: he sat utterly frozen; not a single follicle stirred. Then he blinked, not once, but many times, madly flickering his eyelids like a rapid-fire camera. At the same time he began to tremble. His legs and feet twitched. His hands shook and objects on the table – pen, ink, paperclips – began to vibrate.

"What d-d-d-y – "

"One more word and I'll redistribute your brains over the wall."

She was rising, walking round the desk towards him, keeping the gun trained on his head. Sweat stung his eyes. He felt her presence behind him, and then something hard was pressed against his temple.

"Open the safe. Don't even think of using the alarm, or you're a dead man."

Her voice was deadly and cool as the gun barrel against his skin. With her other hand she grabbed him by the shirt collar and hoisted him to his feet. She was very strong. She pushed him over to the safe, now with the gun pressing against the base of his skull.

"Open it."

Somehow he managed to find the right combination. The safe gave a loud click and he pulled it open. The piles of bank notes were in front of him, seated on their little trays. He was rather alarmed to see them moving backwards and forwards, swimming in and out of focus before his eyes. The gun was pressed to his ribs.

"Face the wall and put your hands on your head."

His legs were so weak he could hardly support his weight. He leant against the wall, biting his lip, trying not to cry. He could hear her scooping the bank notes out of the safe.

"Lie face down on the floor."

He all but fell over. She was standing over him, the gun in her right hand, a bulging green carrier bag in her left.

"W-what are you going to do with me?" he stammered weakly.

"I haven't decided. But I think I'll probably shoot you anyway."

He swooned.

He was not aware of the hands that dragged him into the corner of the room, that secured him by the wrists and ankles and gagged his mouth. He was not aware of anything at all for some considerable time. Madeleine did a thorough job. She carefully wiped off her fingerprints from the arm of the chair and packed her handbag into the large green carrier bag. Then she put away her replica Walther automatic and calmly walked out of the office, dropping the latch behind her.

She left the bank, with a polite good morning to Mrs Stephenson, at a quarter past ten.

Reg Talbot, clutching copies of *From Dryden to Keats* and *A Choice of Kipling's Verse*, returned to the village by an even more circuitous route than the one which he had earlier taken to the library. Just as the church clock rested on the quarter hour he appeared beneath it, hurrying along the path that led through the churchyard. It was on the other side, in Church Road, that he had left instructions for a car to be parked. Not his own Jag — that was performing decoy duty back at the showroom — but one of the Mercedes saloons from his forecourt. Church Road was a quiet street at the best of times, and at this hour of the morning it was completely deserted. The car was parked exactly where he had requested it, just outside the churchyard gate. He slowed down as he approached it, reaching into his trouser pocket for the keys.

"Mr Talbot?" said a voice behind him.

He knew at once the occupation of the voice's owner. He knew it by its timbre, the combination of cockiness and brazen effrontery. He could recognise the inflections of journalese by now.

"Go away!" he said to the shabby individual who sidled up to him wearing a greasy smile. Nor was that the only objectionable thing he was wearing. Reg turned up his nose: the man's clothes were filthy. Reg had seen him in the library arguing with the assistant and had assumed that he was just a crippled vagrant causing trouble. Of course it was too much to expect decency from the journalistic profession, but frankly this was beyond the pale. . . .

"Mr Talbot, if you could just spare me one moment, I – "

"I don't have a moment, excuse me!"

"Mr Talbot, I'm on your side – "

"In that case I'm defecting!"

Reg jumped smartly into the Mercedes and locked the door after him. As he put the key into the ignition he was surprised to see the filthy journalist run round to the front of the car. He was even more surprised when he lay down across the bonnet.

"What the hell do you think you're doing?" Reg demanded furiously, lowering the window.

"I just want a quick word, Reggie, that's all! I'm nothing to do with that git Turpin, if that's what you're worried about."

"Get off my bloody car! It's only just been cleaned."

"Just a word, mate. I'd just like to talk about last night, no more than a minute, then I swear – "

"You asked for it!"

Reg turned on the ignition and put his foot down on the accelerator. The car pulled away jerkily from the kerb.

"Here! What you doing?"

276

Reg noticed with satisfaction the look of terror on the face pressed to his windscreen. He braked suddenly and the journalist slithered off over the bumper into the road.

"Let that teach you a lesson!" Reg snarled vindictively.

Harry rolled over three or four times and ended on his bad left side. He wasn't sure which part of his damaged body to clutch at first — most of him seemed to be in agony. He staggered slowly to his feet, gritting his teeth and fighting back the tears. He hoped that his right arm was still in reasonable shape. He was going to need something with which to slug Talbot.

Talbot got out of his car. Suddenly Harry was alarmed. Was Talbot coming to finish him off? He looked mad enough. There was a real crazy glint in his eye. He was bearing down on him like a man possessed, arms outstretched as in one of those Boris Karloff movies. Harry flung up his good arm to defend himself, but Reg walked straight on past. Harry was bewildered. Slowly, he lowered his arm and turned round. Talbot had continued on down the street. He was heading towards where a blonde woman in sunglasses with her shopping in hand was standing next to a silver car. The woman began to back off. She cried out suddenly:

"Keep away from me!"

Harry limped off down the street towards them. The woman needed help and there was no one else about. Talbot must be a nutter. It was his duty to help a lady in distress, and besides, there might be a story in it, especially if he started to molest her. And that was precisely what he did start doing: he actually knelt down in the road and tried to grab the woman's hands. She pushed him off, but he kept coming back like a yo-yo. Hope glimmered in Harry's breast: could he be about to witness some act of brazen sexual perversity? He wouldn't even have to make anything up for a change.

"Oh Madeleine, Madeleine! I knew you'd come back to me!"

Harry stopped dead. He gasped. The penny dropped and the Hallelujah chorus erupted in the heavens.

"You're . . . you're Maddie Harvey!" he declared, raising his good arm and pointing his trembling finger at her. He felt so elated that he almost added "and I claim my five pounds!"

Her response took him by surprise.

"Keep your voice down or I'll blow your head off."

Yes, she was pointing a gun at him. He took a deep breath and tried to consider the situation rationally. The effort defeated him. He hadn't the slightest comprehension of why it should be that he found himself under threat of execution from a woman missing presumed dead in a cul-de-sac in a dead end dump in Buckinghamshire.

"Oh Madeleine, what – "

"Shut up. You – put your hands up!"

Harry presumed she was talking to him. There wasn't anyone else around, though for how long that would be the case was another matter. Perhaps the same thought had occurred to her: at any rate she didn't look entirely in control of the situation.

"I can put one hand up," said Harry trying to sound helpful. He put his right hand on his head. The left continued to hang in its sling.

Reg Talbot was still kneeling in the middle of the road, gibbering and clawing at Madeleine and paying no attention to the gun which she kept poking him with. Harry bit his lip. Headlines were beginning to ferment in his brain: the word "Exclusive!" flashed on and off in his mind's eye. He tried to get a grip on himself, to quell the flood of near hysterical excitement that surged up in his breast.

"Why don't we go somewhere quiet and talk all this over, Mrs Harvey," he suggested calmly.

She just about heard him over Reg's fretful outpourings. He couldn't see the eyes behind the shades but he sensed desperation. He gave her a sympathetic smile. She glared at Reg.

"If you don't shut up and take your hands off me I swear I'll never speak to you again for as long as I live."

Reg turned white. But he shut up. Madeleine looked up and down the street. Two mothers pushing prams had appeared at the churchyard gate and were coming towards them. She had to act quickly.

"Get into your car," she instructed Reg, and then, waving her gun at Harry: "You in the front."

Joyfully, although for different reasons, Reg and Harry leapt into the car. Keeping her green carrier bag close to her breast, and the gun pointed mid-way between the two of them, Madeleine climbed into the back seat.

"Drive out of Fareham. Take the London road."

"Anything you say, my sweet!" Reg whooped.

The big car turned out of Church Road and accelerated down the

High Street. At the bottom Reg turned left and headed out past the park and library towards the main road. He could scarcely contain himself.

"Oh Madeleine, I knew you'd come back to me! I never believed you were dead, not for a moment. It was like you said it was going to be, I had faith, I remembered! The police knew you were alive too, they were round last night asking questions, trying to bully me, but I didn't tell them anything and nor would I have done even if I'd had anything to tell. My poor love, I don't know what you've been through. I don't know what this is all about, I don't care what you've done or what your reasons are, but I shall be true to you whatever!"

She was sitting in the corner of the back seat pressed against the window behind Reg's head. Harry could just see her in the edge of the rear-view mirror.

"What exactly have you done, Mrs Harvey?" he asked.

"You keep your mouth shut!" she said angrily, waving her gun at the back of his head.

"Yes you, shut up!" said Reg.

"Shut up yourself!" said Maddie, turning the gun on him.

"There's no need to point that at me!" said Reg in a wounded tone. "I'm on your side!"

"So am I," insisted Harry.

"Shut up the pair of you or you'll be on the side of the angels."

They headed out east along the old London road. Harry continued to keep his eye on the rear-view mirror. Reg continued to moan.

"Please don't talk to me like that, Madeleine. After all I've been through it's not fair. I realise you must have been under stress, but so have I! I think it's only fair that you should tell me what you've been up to and what you're planning to do. I think I have a right to know. You know how I feel about you, Madeleine. And I'm pretty sure you feel the same way about me too."

"I'm going to tell you one last time – shut up!"

"But you at least ought to tell me where we're going. Do you want to go to London? In that case we have to decide on the M4 or the M40."

"Alright, that's enough! Pull over. Here, in this lay-by."

Reg pulled the car over, as instructed. Madeleine pointed the gun at Harry.

"You stay put!" Harry nodded tamely. Madeleine tapped Reg on the shoulder. "Turn off the engine, give me the keys and get out of the car."

Reg did as he was told. Madeleine also got out and walked round to the rear of the car. She opened the boot with the keys that Reg had just given her. She summoned him to her.

"Get in!"

For a moment he didn't understand.

"You mean . . . get into the boot!"

She nodded. She meant exactly that. He started to protest but she slapped a hand over his mouth.

"One more word and I swear that I will never speak to you again as long as I live. I mean it this time. If you really love me as you keep saying you do then you will get into the boot and not utter another sound. The alternative is that you walk out of my life altogether."

A terrible internal struggle manifested itself in Reg's watery eyes. For a good ten seconds his inner demons seethed and then, quite meekly, he climbed in with the spare tyre and the toolkit. Her last sight of him before closing the boot was a poignant picture of wounded trust.

She got back into the rear of the car and dangled the keys over the front seat.

"You drive."

Reluctantly Harry tapped his injured hand. Madeleine frowned.

"Alright," she said, training her gun on him. "Get out!"

"Now hang on, you're not going to dump me here – "

"Just do as you're told!"

"You're making a big mistake – "

"Not as big as you'll be making if you don't – "

"I can make you rich beyond your wildest dreams!"

The gun barrel was pressing into the back of his neck. He was sweating and breathing fast. He wasn't a brave man. Another few moments and he would have cracked.

"How rich?" she said quietly.

He breathed deeper. He tried to catch her eye in the mirror, but the angle was wrong. He said:

"Would you mind pointing that thing somewhere else, please."

The cold pressure against his neck was withdrawn. Some of his old jauntiness returned.

"In all this excitement I don't think we've been properly introduced, Maddie. Harry Craven's the name, front-page exclusives the game. You may even have heard of me. I'm talking big money here, my life story by Maddie Harvey. It'll be the scoop of the year and no mistake. I'm talking fifty g's."

"Ha!" she exclaimed derisively. She tossed on to the driver's seat her green carrier bag.

"Take a look in there!"

He had a look. What he saw impressed him.

"Don't talk peanuts to me, Craven. And don't call me Maddie."

"Alright," answered Harry respectfully. He didn't have to put it on: anyone who carried around about twenty thousand quid in spare cash deserved a bit of respect. "What are your terms?"

"Your fifty plus another hundred. One hundred and fifty grand plus an airline ticket to the destination of my choice and a new passport."

"Passport could be tricky."

"Not to a man like you. The offer's not negotiable, Craven. Take it or leave it."

"Done!"

She got out of the back and came round to the driving seat. She put her gun away in the carrier bag and the carrier bag between her feet. She started the car and pulled out onto the main road. She drove very fast.

"Where to?" she asked.

"London. We'll go to a hotel I know from there."

"I could get you Mark's story too," she offered. "At a cut price."

"Your husband?" Harry shrugged. "Not worth a damn, I'm afraid."

She smiled thinly.

"No, he never did amount to much. . . . "

Harry watched the speedometer needle climb. It touched a hundred. He gazed at Madeleine Harvey attentively. Her features were set determinedly, she knew what she was about alright. More than that, she was distinctly fanciable. He began to understand what all the fuss was about.

"You're quite a lady, Mrs Harvey."

She smiled again, that thin smile.

"If you say so, Mr Craven. If you say so. . . . "

23

One cold November Tuesday morning, head hunched against the wind and fine drizzle, Detective Inspector Morris watched grimly as police frogmen raised the bloated armoured body to the surface.

MACLEAN MYSTERY — ROMEO RODDY IN DROWNING DRAMA

The autopsy revealed no signs of foul play. The whole case in a nutshell: no evidence, no witnesses.

MISSING MARK — MYSTERY OF HUSBAND HARVEY

For a time it seemed as if everyone connected with the case was either dead or missing. No sign of either Harvey or Reg Talbot, until

RANDY REGGIE IN CAR BOOT BOTHER

Some kids joyriding had been pulled over on the A40 at Denham. The police had heard strange whimperings from the boot and out had popped Reg Talbot, raving and gibbering, to the coequal surprise of constabulary and adolescent delinquents. The kids claimed to have stolen the car from some wasteland in Acton. Reg Talbot had been in the back for two days and was in no fit state to answer questions.

EXCLUSIVE! THE MADELEINE HARVEY STORY
AS TOLD TO HARRY CRAVEN
FLEET ST'S NO. I

There were a lot of questions the Inspector wanted to ask Harry Craven, but he too had disappeared, away on leave according to his editor, flagrantly obstructing the police and perverting the course of justice as far as the Inspector was concerned. He found himself caught in the crossfire while the tabloid war raged:

MADDIE HARVEY STORY A FAKE! EXCLUSIVE
BY DICK TURPIN. FLEET ST'S REAL NO. 1

Who was conning whom? And where did the most recent episode in the Fareham crime-wave fit in?

BONNIE BLONDE BANKROBBER BAGS BUNDLE

Had it really been Maddie Harvey? Vernon the manager claimed not, but he was under sedation at the time and his testimony was frankly incoherent. The bank robbery had been the latest "confession" in Harry Craven's story and it all sounded plausible enough to the Inspector, until Friday morning.

Friday was cold and drizzly, like every other day this late November. Again the Inspector watched while a body was brought to the surface, the shocked workmen rubbing shoulders with the routine-dulled police. It was the workmen's picks and shovels that had broken the concrete and found the concealed corpse. The Inspector watched as his officers finished the job, hoisting the body with its trail of bandages out of Reg Talbot's swimming pool.

The autopsy confirmed that the search for Maddie Harvey was over.

The trial of Reg Talbot for the murder of Maddie Harvey attracted worldwide attention. Camera crews and journalists flocked to Fareham; Willow Cottage became as famous as 10 Rillington Place. The Prime Minister, on a Far Eastern tour to promote British trade, was deluged with questions concerning the case. Reg Talbot's photo made the front cover of *Paris Match* and *Time*. Coachloads of Japanese tourists began appearing in Fareham High Street where an enterprising landlord made a quick killing with raw fish in a basket.

And all over the world the expatriate English scanned eagerly their week-old newspapers for coverage in depth of the murder sensation of the century.

*

Once a fortnight Miguel would stand in front of the grand white house with green shutters waiting for the newspapers to be brought from the town. Often the truck was late, sometimes by a day or more, and then his employer would grow anxious. Miguel would explain patiently that the roads were bad and that it was a miracle the truck ever came at all. But it always got through in the end. Up to the house he would come, the gringo truck driver with the load of newspapers balanced on his shoulder, and ask in his bad Spanish:

"And how is the fine English lady this week?"

They would sit on the verandah and drink beer and Miguel would tell him about the fine English lady. The truck driver wanted very much to see her but she never showed her face to strangers. If he wanted to talk to another gringo there was always the gardener, Miguel suggested, but no, he was not interested in the gardener. He only wanted to know about the lady. Miguel happily told him all he knew, without letting on why he thought she never showed her face.

For Miguel was no provincial. He had seen the big world; the English he had learned in Florida and London was the reason for his employment at the house with green shutters. He had been to Hamburg and Paris and Rio. And he could tell a transvestite when he saw one.

It didn't bother him if a man wanted to dress up as a woman, so long as he was left alone and paid his wages. His wages were more than sufficient to purchase his discretion.

So he called his employer "*señora*" and played his part in the fiction. If any of the local villagers guessed the truth they were far too polite to let on. In any case it was tacitly understood that the presence of a wealthy foreigner added tone to the locality.

His employer would cut up the newspapers and paste pieces into a scrapbook. Miguel had glanced through it on occasion, but though he considered his English pretty good he could make little sense of what he read. He had concluded that the quality of these newspapers was not of the best, which surprised him, for there was nothing vulgar about the "*señora*". It seemed odd to send such a long way, and at such great expense, for mere rubbish.

Odd, but none of his business. He liked his job too much to ask questions. Each day he would take his place on the verandah, and drink his beer, and in the afternoon he would lie back in his chair, put

284

his feet up on the table, pull his hat down over his eyes and sleep peacefully.

"Oi! Shift yourself!"

Miguel woke with a start as his feet were yanked off the table. He sat bolt upright blinking at the sun-drenched afternoon.

"Got a fag?"

It was the gardener, resting his backside on the spot where Miguel's heels had been moments before and riffling eagerly through the pile of newspapers with his yellow-stained pudgy fingers. Miguel smelt his sweat and wrinkled up his nose. The sight of the red puffy face and the damp clumps of gingery hair was enough to make him want to wrinkle up his eyes too.

Miguel shook his head.

"You mean old git!"

Miguel realised that his packet of Kent was sticking out of his top pocket. The gardener simply reached over and took it. Miguel caught another whiff of his armpits.

"Aw, that's better. . . . "

The gardener took a long deep drag and resumed his perusal of the papers. The smell of tobacco cleared the air. Miguel lit one for himself and took a sip of his now rather flattened beer.

"Those papers no for you," he said, thinking that they were in fact exactly up his street.

The gardener waved two fingers at him.

"Señor Crane —"

"It's Craven, you daft dago, Harry Craven."

"Señor . . . why you never work in the garden? Is terrible mess."

"'Cos I'm not a sodding gardener. Do I look like a sodding gardener?"

"Why you called gardener then?"

Harry waved a thumb at the house.

"Ask her inside. Her idea of a bleeding joke. Ha bloody ha! Screwed me sideways she did. Bloody conwoman!"

More of a conwoman than you know, Miguel thought, watching him suck in his cheeks and inhale. Not only did this gardener not know the difference between fertilizer and weed-killer (he had wiped out all the tomato plants with an overdose of the latter), it appeared that he was unable to spot a practising transvestite even after prolonged exposure.

"Got to hand it to her though . . . " Harry continued to mumble, sitting on the edge of the table and reading. "She stitched me up a treat alright. . . . "

That was one of his favourite expressions. Miguel had first heard it on the night when Harry had appeared baying and hollering at the front door.

"Why don't you go back to England?" his employer had suggested, rather uneasily, through the firmly bolted door.

"I can't show my face there after what you did to me!" Harry had yelled back. "You've made me the laughing-stock of Fleet Street! I'll need the scoop of the bloody century before they let me back in. Stitched me up a treat and no mistake, you have!"

He had begged and implored to be let in. He said he had no money and nowhere to go. Eventually Miguel had been instructed to let him in. And in the morning he had been offered the post of gardener.

"Well bugger me backwards!"

This invitation, which held no appeal for Miguel, nonetheless attracted his attention.

"I don't believe it!"

As if to assuage his incredulity Harry tossed his stub over his shoulder and lit a fresh cigarette from the packet on the table.

"Why you no buy your own, please?" Miguel asked, wearily.

"On what she pays me? Leave it out, you mean git. Get a butchers of this though!"

Harry held out the front page of one of the papers. Miguel saw a photo of a rather serious-looking man with thick eyebrows under a huge banner headline which he tried to spell out:

"Reg Talbot ac-, acq-, acqui?"

"Acquitted. Reg Talbot acquitted! Old Bill must be kicking himself!"

Miguel squinted in an effort to read the story under the headline. He could find no reference to anyone called Bill.

"Well sod me sideways . . . " Harry chuckled, then sighed: "Trust my bleeding luck though. Marooned with a conwoman in the middle of nowhere while that bastard Turpin has a clear run at Talbot. I wonder what her indoors'll think of it all. Talbot'll make what she screwed out of me look like third prize in a Christmas raffle. I think I'll take these on in and savour the expression on her face. . . ."

Harry scooped the pile of newspapers up in his arms and took a step towards the house.

"What's that?" he demanded, stopping abruptly.

Miguel had heard it too, the straining engine noise of the truck as it laboured up the hill in low gear.

"Is only the truck. He go to the village after here, see. Now he return to town."

As he spoke the truck came into view. The driver leaned out of the window as he passed the house, and Miguel caught a glimpse of a thick moustache over strong white teeth set in a tanned handsome face. He smiled and waved back.

"Who is that geezer?"

"The driver? Is another gringo. I think he is Ingles too. You know him?"

"He looks familiar . . . what's his name?"

"He is called Lucky. Is a nickname, I think."

"Lucky?"

Harry dropped the pile of newspapers back on to the table. His eyebrows knotted together in a frown. He mopped his forehead with a stiff dirty handkerchief.

"Lucky?"

"Si."

"Oh my God. . . . "

Harry's voice became a whisper. His mouth fell open and hung loosely, displaying a lifetime's dental neglect. A look of awe mixed with stupefaction entered his normally opaque eyes.

"I don't believe it. Christ!" – the voice was coming back now, the vocal chords beginning to hum with excitement – "I knew that face was familiar!"

He stumbled off the verandah and on to the gravel drive. He took a last drag of his cigarette, threw it down, and began jogging towards the road. This incongruous sight startled Miguel.

"Where you going?"

"To book my passage home!" Harry called back over his shoulder, beginning to puff already. "I may be gone some time!"

"What I tell Mrs Harvey?"

"Tell her this!"

Harry stopped running, turned and waved two fingers at the house. He gave a vulgar laugh, coughed and laughed again.

"Tell her she can keep Reg Talbot and Roddy Maclean and all the small fry. I'm after the big one, scoop of the decade and journalist of the year award rolled into one. Tell her I'll send her a copy of the front page, with my name in six-inch-high block capitals:

HARRY CRAVEN — THE MAN WHO FOUND LORD LUCAN!"

Miguel stared blankly at the peculiar gardener running up the road in the full heat of the afternoon after the dust-wake of the departing truck. He thought for a moment about what he was going to tell his employer and decided that it was probably best to say nothing. It would be easy to find another gardener. He reached out for his cigarettes, then realised that the packet was no longer on the table. He chuckled:

"Stitched me up a treat, huh?"

He stretched in his chair, put his feet up on the table, pulled his hat down over his eyes, and went back to sleep.